THE DEVIL YOU KNOW

A CHILDREN OF THE MOUNTAIN NOVEL

R. A. HAKOK

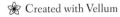

———

Cody Doyle

Viable

If you'd like to be notified of new releases, sign up to my reader list at www.rahakok.com. You'll also receive a free copy of *The Shoebox* and *The Map*, the companion ebooks to the *Children of the Mountain* series.

———

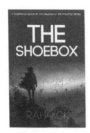 

———

Alternatively, simply email contact@rahakok.com with 'Reader List' in the subject heading. Feel free to say hi while you're at it. I love getting emails from readers!

RECAP?

If it's been a while since you read *Among Wolves* there's a
recap at the end of this book.

CHAPTER ONE

LIGHTNING SPLITS THE DARKNESS, and for a second I can see.

I grab the last piece of rebar and haul myself over the edge. Beneath me the river has already disappeared; there's just a black chasm into which the snow twists and tumbles. Ahead the storm drives the drifts in long, shifting ridges that snake across the road, clearing everything in their path. I tell myself that's a good thing; soon my tracks will be covered too. But the truth is this is bad, far worse than I had counted on.

I'd like to rest after the climb, but there's no time for that. I untie the snowshoes from my pack and step into them. It hurts as I ratchet the straps tight. I can no longer tell if it's from the cold or the bindings.

I should never have let them take my boots.

I look down. The plastic I've used to wrap my feet still seems to be holding, but I can see the duct tape starting to fray where the straps have worked against it. That's not good, but there's not much I can do about it. I lift my head and set off into the blizzard.

The wind blows hard, making me fight it for every step. My hood's zipped all the way up but still it finds its way in, squeezing tears from my eyes that freeze on my cheeks, biting at the exposed skin there. I curse it for a bitch, but it pays me no mind. It just snatches the breath from my lungs and gusts even harder.

I hug the parka tighter around me. The cold is raw now, relentless. Normally pounding the snow like this would keep it at bay, but somewhere down on the river it's managed to slip inside; I can already feel the chill from my sweat-soaked thermals seeping into my core. My teeth are chattering and I don't seem to be able to stop them. I try to focus on the sound of my breathing behind the thin cotton mask, anything to shut it out. But I can't. Marv used to say the cold was a vicious bitch, that it could mess with your thinking. I need to remember that. I don't reckon it'll be hard. Because the cold is an onslaught. It refuses to be ignored.

Bitch. Bitch. Bitch.

Bitch.

I lift a snowshoe up, place it down again. One foot in front of the other, that's the trick. If I just keep doing that I can make it. But the drifts are getting deeper. The crash barriers I was following earlier have already disappeared; all I have left are the mile markers. I use the flashes to search for them, but they're getting harder to find. I need to hurry, before they get covered over too. I can't afford to get lost out here.

I pick up the pace. The snow senses it; it swirls around me, faster now, all I can see in the flashlight's faltering beam. I wind the stubby plastic handle anyway, until I imagine that's somehow what's working my legs and as long as I keep turning it they'll keep rising and falling, like it's the key stuck in the back of some clever clockwork toy. I keep that up for what seems like a long time, but might be less. Then I catch an edge and stumble, landing awkwardly in a drift.

Bitch.

I lay there for a while, getting my breath back. At last I push myself up and kneel in the snow. I'm trembling quite badly, long shuddering spasms that run up and down my spine and rattle my teeth together. I don't think I was down for that long, but when I set off again my legs no longer seem to want to do my bidding. The muscles there have stiffened; they don't want to work, no matter how much I twist the handle. I give up on the flashlight and jam my hands up into my armpits. Maybe it'll warm them a little. But it doesn't seem to make any difference. Inside my mittens my fingers have tightened into claws.

The sky flares again, followed by a deafening crash as the heavens are rent asunder. The storm's on me, the gap between lightning and thunder no more than a heartbeat. In the instant before darkness returns a gap opens, revealing a shotgun shack, set back from the road. I stop, stare at it. The shelter it offers is a gift; Marv would curse me for not taking it. But I can't. I have to get back; Mags can't be another night in there. An image returns, the only one I can summon, one I would burn from my eyes if I could. Forced onto her toes, her feet scrabbling for purchase on the smooth tiles as the noose tightens around her neck. The muscles along Truck's arms bunch as he hoists her up. I hear him grunt with the effort of it, but he holds her there and I would kill him if I could but there's nothing I can do to stop it. I turn my head from the shack and face back to the road. The wind howls and the gray curtain closes around me again and it is gone.

How could I have been so stupid? I had been sure that

the world that waited for us outside was empty; that once we escaped all we would need to concern ourselves with was staying out of Kane's way. It hadn't occurred to me that there might be others out here.

Others worse than he was.

I try and put that thought from my mind. It won't help me, and I have other things to concern myself with. I don't even know where they're keeping her; I'll need to figure that out once I get inside. First I have to find the blast door. I try and work out where it might be from what I know of the hallways and corridors above, anything to take my mind off the bone-piercing cold. It should be easy enough, but after a few minutes I give up and return to the simpler business of placing one foot in front of the other. Anything more complicated seems beyond me.

I trudge on, stumbling through the deepening drifts like some lock-limbed Frankenstein's monster. I search the darkness ahead for the next sign. I think it's been a while since I found one, although when I try and remember I'm not entirely sure. I'm beginning to worry I've strayed from the road, but then the sky strobes again, revealing a tractor-trailer that's jack-knifed, its cargo strewn across both lanes. Did I pass it on the way out? I think so, but I can't be sure. I stagger up to it, feeling for its outline so I can make my way around.

I leave the truck behind. I'm moving much more slowly now. My limbs feel like they're seizing. Lifting each snowshoe has become a gargantuan effort, requiring all my powers of concentration. At least my feet no longer hurt. Actually I can't feel them at all. I realize I've stopped shivering. I wonder how long ago that was, but I can't remember. I don't know if it's a good or a bad thing.

Bitch?

Lightning strikes again, somewhere nearby, followed immediately by a crack of thunder, and for a second the world around me is bathed in stark white light. And in that instant I see something ahead, a small corner of metal almost buried under the snow. I stare at it absently. I know what it is, but for some reason it won't come to me.

A mile marker.

That's it.

The markers are important, I know that. I'm just not sure why. Maybe if I make my way over towards it it'll come to me. My frozen fingers reach for the flashlight's handle, getting ready to wind me forward, but there's nothing there. That thought is troubling, but eventually I let it be and focus on lifting one foot, setting it down again. But the sign seems to be further away than I first thought. I'm beginning to wonder if I've missed it when the front of my snowshoe catches something hard, just under the surface. I trip and fall into a thick quilt of gray snow. I lay there for an unknowable amount of time, just listening to the pounding of my heart as it slows. My blood feels like it's thickening in my veins, like when you tap the sump of an engine for oil to mix with gas for the fire.

Fire.

A fire would be nice.

For a while that thought occupies me, but there's another that hovers annoyingly at the edge of my consciousness, refusing to let me be. I can't stay here. There's something I have to do. Something important. I try to push myself up, but my mittens just sink into the powder and it seems like far too much of an effort to extract them. I let my head fall forward again. The snow crunches softly against the hood of my parka and I lay still. Whatever I was worrying about recedes, washed away by a wave of cold exhaustion. If I can just rest here for a little while everything will be okay. The wind howls, pushing the swirling snow over me, slowly covering me up. I feel the last of my body's heat leaching out into the thick, enveloping flakes.

It occurs to me that maybe I should be scared now. But fear is a concept that floats somewhere just beyond my reach, just like the numb hands that lie buried beneath me in the snow. Somebody I once knew called Martin (Marlin? *Marv*in) once told me something important. He said I had to mind the cold because it was vicious.

But Marvin was wrong.

The cold's not really anything at all. It's an emptiness; an absence of things. An absence of heat, of warmth.

An absence of caring.

Bitch.

Ten days earlier

CHAPTER TWO

DAWN'S little more than a faint gray smear on the horizon as I step out of the tunnel. I look through the bars of the half-raised guillotine gate, my eyes searching for the tattered windsock that hangs beside the control tower. It was gusting yesterday, but the wind's eased overnight and now it shifts only occasionally. Heavy thunderheads lumber along the spiny mountain ridge beyond, carrying what I hope will be the last of the big winter storms east. I know what Marv would say: it'd be safer to hold off another week. But I figure anything we get this late in the season should blow itself out in a day or two, and we've already waited long enough.

I look back over my shoulder. The Juvies have gathered to see us off, but I can tell they're already anxious to get back inside. They wait inside the shadow of the tunnel, reluctant to step into the grainy pre-dawn light. Most of them haven't been outside since we arrived.

I've tried to warn them. We're not safe here. As soon as the weather clears Kane will send Peck for us, I know it. They used to listen; when we first arrived it was all any of us could think about. But back then the memories of our escape were still fresh. As the days slipped into weeks and those became months things began to change. Nobody wants to talk about Kane now. I've heard more than one of them say that maybe Peck won't even come.

I should have seen it. Outside the storms might have raged, but inside the mountain life was good. No morning buzzer to jar them from sleep; no endless hours in the chapel; no curfew forcing them back to a cramped cell at night. There isn't even much in the way of chores anymore, least not for those who don't care to do them. Jake had his growing benches up and running within weeks of our arrival, and the truth is we don't need those; anything any of us might want is right there in the stores for the taking. Now I want to bring them away from all that, and all I can offer in return is Marv's map; an uncertain destination and until we find it, the promise of cold and hunger.

So I figure if I'm to have any chance of convincing them to move, first I'll need to find somewhere for us to go. I've already made the hike out to Culpeper, the nearest facility in the Federal Relocation Arc, a network of underground shelters stretching all the way through Pennsylvania, Maryland, Virginia and down into the Carolinas. It was less than sixty miles so I was there and back inside a week, even allowing for a day holed up against the storms on the way out.

The bunker was just where the map said it would be, carved right into the side of the mountain, its squat bulk waiting patiently for me behind a rusting razor wire fence. Silent guard towers watched down as I cut a hole in the chain-link and pushed my way through. Lead-lined shutters covered the narrow, recessed windows, sealing them tight, but Benjamin's code worked just fine on the blast door, just like it had at Mount Weather.

Culpeper was no use to us however; I don't think it had even been designed for people. The ground floor housed nothing but banks of long-dead servers, here and there the occasional computer terminal, all covered in a thick layer of dust. A wide metal ramp led down to a huge subterranean vault. Row after row of pallets, each stacked four or five deep, stretching all the way back into darkness.

I dug out my flashlight and cranked the handle as I made my way between them. Each was packed with shrink-wrapped bales. The blade on the leatherman sliced through the plastic easily, releasing a pristine wedge of green bills, bound tight and stamped with a seal that said Federal Reserve Bank of Richmond. I wandered the aisles, freeing a bundle from each of the bales until I had a collection of presidents and founding fathers from Washington to Franklin that put me in mind of Miss Kimble's civics and government class all those years ago. I saved one of each to show Mags and piled the rest in the middle of the floor. I figured they might do for kindling, but it turns out money doesn't burn so well after all. I left early the following morning, the best part of a week gone and nothing for my efforts but a first grade show and tell.

Most of the Juvies had already been against leaving Mount Weather, but even those that might still have been worried enough about Kane to consider it lost their enthusiasm when they heard what I'd found at Culpeper. Jake asked me what I thought Marv would do and I had to admit I didn't think he'd have led us out without a destination either, so that settled it. Mags and I will head south for Sulfur Springs, the location of The Greenbrier, the next facility on the map. It's all the way down in West Virginia, I reckon a seven-day hike each way, but if it checks out we'll be that much further from Kane, so maybe it's for the best. It means we'll be gone at least a couple of weeks, though; more than enough time for Peck to get here from Eden if Kane has a mind to send him early.

I've told them they need to post sentries while we're gone. I wanted them all the way out on the Blue Ridge Mountain Road, where Marv's buried. That's how we got here from Eden, and it's the route I reckon Peck will choose too, when he comes. It's a good spot; from up there you can see for miles along the highway in either direction. But no one wanted to hike out that far so we finally settled on two-hour shifts in the control tower on top of the ridge. They'll have next to no warning when he shows, but I guess it's better than nothing. Jake's worked out a roster. He says he'll make sure it gets done.

I've already applied UV block back in the apartment so I pull my hood up and slide a pair of ski goggles down over my eyes. As soon as Mags has said the last of her goodbyes we snap on our snowshoes and walk out underneath the gate. Marv's gun weighs down the side pocket of my parka. I almost wasn't going to bring it. It's heavy and besides, the magazine's empty. Mount Weather has an armory just like Eden's, but the door's locked and the only code Marv gave me was for the blast door. I considered heading back up to Fort Narrows to look for some more bullets; I reckon that's where Marv had been getting the stuff he'd been stashing under the floorboards in the farmhouse. But it's the best part of a two-day hike each way, and right now I figure that's time better spent looking for somewhere to move us. Besides, I can't see how I'll need them. Mount Weather and Culpeper were both abandoned, and in all the years I was scavenging I never saw so much as a single print in the snow to suggest there's anyone else waiting for us out there.

I look back over my shoulder one last time, but most of the Juvies are already heading back into the tunnel. Soon only Jake remains, just standing there in the shadow of the portal, watching as we leave. I raise my hand but it takes him a moment to wave back, like it wasn't ever my departure he'd come to see.

We make our way out of the compound. Dotted here and there around the perimeter are the concrete cowls of the airshaft vents that lead deep into the mountain. Mags has figured out how to seal them from the inside, so at least when Peck comes he won't be getting in that way. I guess that should be a comfort, although I can't see why he'd go to that trouble. Kane will send him out with the same code for the blast door that Marv gave me.

The first of the morning light's finally seeping into the sky, like water into an old rag, as we trudge up to the entrance. The gate towers over us, on either side a high chain-link fence stretching off into the distance, its rusting diamonds topped by a half-dozen strands of razor wire. It all looks formidable, but I know it won't hold them long. I find the section I opened with bolt cutters the day I first arrived and pull the wire back for Mags to step through.

CHAPTER THREE

FOR THE FIRST six miles we follow the road south along the ridge. There hasn't been a fresh fall in a few days and the snow's settled. Good tracking skiff, Marv would have called it. Our path descends gently then flattens, snaking along the spine of the mountain. At some point we cross over and drop down onto the western rim of the valley. There's little to tell where the road is now, but I've hiked this way several times over the winter and I have to stop only occasionally to make sure we're still on the right path.

I break trail while Mags follows in my footsteps, her breath rolling from her in short frosted puffs. She seems excited; she kept asking me whether I thought we'd have time to go looking for books. She's read everything we have in Mount Weather and the few trips I've made out over the winter have yielded little new, just a single weary copy of *A Prayer For Owen Meany* I lucked into on the way back from Culpeper. She finished it the same day I returned. I've told her to keep her pack light, but I'm pretty sure it's found its way in among the supplies I laid out for her.

I watch as she stops to takes a swig from her canteen. I'm glad to have her with me, but the truth is I'm more nervous about this than she is. For the first time I think I understand why Marv was reluctant to take me out with him after Benjamin died. I've spent the last few weeks trying to remember everything I learnt from him. I even dug out the first aid book I used to keep under my bed in the farmhouse and read it through again, cover to cover. But what if I forget something? What if I screw up and get us lost, or worse? Mags says I should stop worrying, and maybe she's right. The worst of the storms have passed and we're both carrying enough MREs for several weeks, more than enough to get us to The Greenbrier and back without having to worry about finding food along the way.

We've been tracking steadily downhill for maybe an hour when we come to a road sign. I scrape off the ice; the rusting metal underneath says we're approaching the highway. I tell Mags it's time for frostbite checks. She unsnaps the respirator, lifts her goggles onto her forehead and closes her eyes. I study the faint smattering of freckles that run along her cheekbones underneath those long, dark eyelashes. There's little wind but the cold still bites at every inch of exposed skin and I know I should hurry. Nevertheless I can't help but pull down the surgical mask I still prefer so that I can kiss her.

'Hey! Pay attention. I thought you said we had to take this seriously.'

I offer her a sheepish grin and lift my goggles onto my forehead so she can check me. A moment later I feel her arms slip around my waist and she leans in to me and I feel her lips, soft and warm, back on mine. We've barely left and already I find myself wishing we could just forget about

Kane and turn around and go back to the warmth of our small apartment.

———

The mountain road ends quarter of a mile later and a long, straight section of highway, two, maybe three lanes in each direction, stretches off in both directions. The wind's stayed low and it's eerily quiet. I look up. The storms might be moving on, but the skies are still heavy with snow. When I hiked out to Culpeper a week ago I took the road east from here. I haven't ventured west yet, but I doubt there'll be much in the way of shelter, least not along the highway.

We make our way down. The snow's heavier now and we're trudging through drifts, Indian file, from the get-go. The road inclines for a mile or so and for the next hour it's a long steady climb uphill. I listen to the sound of Mags' breathing as she follows in my tracks. She's been in Mount Weather's gym over the winter preparing for this, but my legs are longer than hers and I can already feel them burning with the effort.

Eventually the road crests and levels and we come to a faded sign that says *Ashby Gap* and beneath it *Welcome to Clarke County*. We sit next to it in the snow, our breath escaping in white plumes as we sip water from our canteens. A wide, open valley stretches out, gray and cold and lifeless, beneath us. I search the shrouded landscape for anything of color but there's nothing.

———

We stop for lunch where US340 crosses the highway. The

wind's picking up again, blowing the gray snow across the road, already starting to cover the tracks we've made behind us. Up ahead the traffic light gantry's collapsed, the virus-weakened metal no longer able to bear the weight of the gantry arm, which now lies buried in the middle of the intersection. It's deep enough to step over, but I take us out wide around it anyway. What Kane did to the skies means it shouldn't be a threat, but you can never be too careful.

I ask Mags where she wants to eat and she takes a moment to weigh the options. There's a McDonalds right there, a faded red flag with the arches fluttering next to a tattered stars and stripes, but she chooses a Dunkin' Donuts that sits kitty corner opposite. It's been turned over like everywhere else, but overall it looks in better shape than the other places currently competing for our business. We trudge up to the entrance and step out of our snowshoes. The door's definitely seen better days; all that's left is a mostly empty frame, the last of the glass gripped in fragments around the edges and in the corners. Broken shards crunch under our boots as we walk in.

I get our MREs heating while Mags stares out the busted window at a panel van that's settled on to its tires under the snow. I can tell she's taking it in, processing it, so I don't say anything. It used to happen to me sometimes, even after I'd been scavenging for a while. Sometimes something simple like an abandoned car or a faded road sign will cause the enormity of it all to suddenly hit you, and you realize the way the world once was is nothing more than an idea now, a place to be visited in memories but never again found.

CHAPTER FOUR

AFTER LUNCH MAGS fixes herself a coffee and I use it as an excuse to bag our trash. I've never cared much for it; sometimes, if I haven't eaten, the bitter aroma's almost enough to turn my stomach. Tell the truth I'm not sure Mags started out with much of a taste for it either. I think it's something she taught herself to like because we weren't allowed to have it while Kane was in charge.

When she's done we strap our snowshoes back on and take 340 south. The road narrows to two lanes but stays mostly flat. After we've been on it for an hour it swings west and then we hit another junction. The road switches back and forth for a while, then it straightens and starts a gentle incline. As we make our way slowly up it I see a sharp corner of something that looks metal, way too tall to be a vehicle, just beyond the next crest.

I used to be good at working out what was buried under the drifts just from the shapes they made in the snow; when I was scavenging with Marv there wasn't a car or truck on the turnpike I couldn't name just from a glimpse of its roofline. But whatever this is has me stumped. I stare at it as we approach, trying to figure it out, but it's not till the road levels and I can see the extent of it laid out before me that I realize what I've been staring at.

It's a plane, or at least what's left of one. It was the tail I spotted first, but now I see the whole rear section's detached itself; it lies across the road, blocking our way. I stop and gaze at the impossible sweep of it, jutting up into the gray sky. As I look around I see another piece of the fuselage has reached its final resting place a few hundred yards beyond, but it, too, ends abruptly, incomplete. I scan the fields on either side. There's wreckage from the crash scattered all around, but no sign of the missing cockpit.

I start down towards it. Mags makes to follow, but I tell her to wait until I've checked it out. The drifts probably conceal a multitude of twisted, charred metal; there's no sense both of us venturing in amongst it till I've found a path through.

As I get closer the debris is everywhere and I slow down, picking my way around whatever's lying under the snow. I pass something that might be an engine, sitting at a haphazard angle on the hard shoulder, a length of wing still attached. A little further along on the other side of the road there's a giant set of wheels, the strut broken off and poking skyward. Finally I draw level with the section of fuselage I first saw. It tilts forward at an improbable angle, like it has crumpled on impact. This close it's huge; it towers over me. I step around its jagged-edged side and look up into the darkened interior, realizing, too late, my mistake.

There used to be an amusement park in Baton Rouge. I don't remember now how I'd gotten wind of its existence –

TV probably – but I'd pestered Mom for weeks to take me, and in the end she'd relented. Jack had driven us. Mom said I was too young for any of the really interesting rides, so I'd spent the morning sitting in little plastic teacups or astride smiling elephants with huge ears and tiny hats, all the while loading up on soda and cotton candy and dreaming of the ride I really wanted: *The Intimidator*. You could hear the screams from that all the way across the park. I figured there was little point even putting in a request for something like that, but I guess Jack must have worked it out because as soon as she went looking for the rest room he grabbed me by the arm and we doubled back. The person handing out the tickets looked at me funny, and I figured then we were sunk. But I've always been one-part daddy long-legger and when I stood against the board there was no denying I was tall enough to ride the ride.

The Intimidator was a monster: there had to be a dozen cars, each wide enough to accommodate six abreast. I remember the restraining bar coming down onto my lap and locking in place, and the never-ending *clunk-clunk-clunk* as it slowly climbed all the way up to the top and started to roll. I can still hear the shrieks from the cars ahead as one by one they disappeared until it was our turn and then the first sickening moment of free-fall and somewhere before the loop-the-loop I threw up pink cotton candy all over my shoes.

Now as I stare up into what remains of the cabin it's like I'm back there, in that amusement park. It's not the oxygen masks, dangling like plastic fronds, twisting this way and that in the wind, or the luggage bins that hang open above, their contents disgorged into the snow. It's the passengers, or at least what remains of them. They're still strapped to their seats, and now they just hang there, like they've come to an abrupt halt on the world's most gruesome roller coaster ride.

I tear my eyes from it and look back up the road to where Mags is waiting. I've seen my share of dead bodies; I can't say I care much for it, but it doesn't bother me anything like it used to. I'll never forget my first, though, the guy clutching the jar of Maraschino cherries in the frozen foods aisle of the Walmart back in Providence. I'll spare her that for as long as I can.

I turn my snowshoes around and retrace my steps through the wreckage. I tell her it's not safe, we have to go around. She glances over my shoulder, at the tracks I've already plotted, and then looks at me. I know what she's thinking. She's desperate for something new to read, and the luggage scattered in the snow will be a treasure trove. But in the end she just says okay and we make our way out into the fields, giving the plane a wider berth than I can possibly justify.

———

We spend the first night in a Waffle House that sits next to the long concrete sweep of the on-ramp at the interchange with I-81. We passed a Comfort Inn on the way up, a strip of rooms two stories tall horseshoed around a long-emptied swimming pool. The walls were brick, and the roof looked like it had mostly held, which meant that some of the beds might even have been dry. I could see Mags looking at it as we walked by, the sky slowly darkening around us. I knew what we'd find in there, though. When the weather changed and people finally figured out they had to get themselves south the motels got busy. But by then it was cold and few of those that had taken to the roads had prepared for it. Most that checked into places like that never checked out again.

We cut some firewood from a stand of thin black trees perched on the edge of the highway and head inside. The wood's damp so I head out to find fuel and something that'll work as kindling while Mags checks the kitchen for anything that might have been missed. When I come back in she's already built the fire. I go to light it but she says she wants to, so I hand her a stack of flyers I found in the Comfort Inn's lobby and a small soda bottle of gas I siphoned from a Honda in the parking lot that had been overlooked. She examines the flyers for a moment and then scrunches them up. She pours the gas into one of the plastic spoons we saved from the MREs we had at lunch and places it underneath the kindling, just like Marv showed me. Then she takes a lighter from her pocket and strikes the wheel. The lighter's new, fresh from the stores, but still it takes a dozen tries before it sparks, which makes me think I should have checked it before we left. But finally it catches and she cups her fingers around it and offers it to the spoon. The flames slowly climb up into the crumpled flyers and then start to lick at the wicker of blackened limbs above.

She steps back, proud of her work. But the wood's damp and it hisses and steams, sending slow coils of white smoke rising into the air. It throws off little light and even less warmth, and we eat our MREs wrapped up in our parkas and then quickly transfer to the sleeping bag I've unfurled next to the fire. It's cold, and my muscles ache from the day's hike, but I have been looking forward to this moment all day. After a winter together in Mount Weather I know exactly how we fit together. As I slip my arm around her shoulder she seems tense, however. I figure she's still working through all the things she's seen so I don't say anything. It's a long time before she speaks.

'Is it the same everywhere?'

'Everywhere I've been.'

She nods, like this is the answer she was expecting, but doesn't say anything more. I try and inject a cheery tone into my voice.

'But then Marv and I never really went that far. It could be different somewhere else. Maybe further south.'

It's full dark outside now and what remains of the diner's scattered furniture sits like so many humped gray shadows around us. The fire's already dying down; only a handful of scattered flames survive among the embers. She reaches for one of the branches and stirs what's left of the damp wood. Red sparks rise in a shudder and then disappear in the blackness overhead.

'You can't protect me from all of it, Gabe. Sooner or later I'm going to see something.'

'I know but...'

She turns around and props herself up on one elbow so that she can look at me.

'But nothing. Marv didn't stop you from seeing things, did he? I think it'll be better if I get it over with.'

I don't know what to say, so instead I slip out of the sleeping bag and bank the fire. Sometimes my feelings for her ambush me, threatening to crush my chest with the whole weight of them. When I climb back in beside her again she slips one arm around me and closes her eyes.

I lay awake for a long time staring up into the darkness after she's drifted off to sleep, just thinking about what she's said. The fear that I may have done something foolish and selfish and dangerous by bringing her out here with me settles cold and heavy inside my ribcage.

Mags is smart, and brave, braver than any of us, but she can't understand yet what she's asking for. There's a whole world out there, filled with things that are too terrible to contemplate. And no good will ever come now of seeing them.

CHAPTER FIVE

I-81 WINDS its way through the middle of a wide, flat valley. For the next four days we hike south, slowly cresting low rises, trudging into the shallows between, the gray foothills of the Appalachians always to our right in the distance, the Blue Ridge Mountains on our left. There's little on either side of the highway but dead fields, only the occasional bare and blackened tree poking up through the shroud, the remains of recent falls lying in skiffs in the crooks of the branches and along its stunted limbs. Most of the interchanges we come to have collapsed. The crumbling concrete has been softened by the snow, but I know its sharper edges, its bent and twisted rebar, lies waiting for us underneath. We pick our way slowly through the rubble, taking our snowshoes off to clamber over girders, testing for metal buried in the snow that might break an ankle or shatter a kneecap.

Most days we take our lunches huddled under an overpass rather than wasting time searching for anything better off the highway. We eat our MREs cowled up in our parkas, our backs to the cold concrete. Each evening as the banished sun tracks westward towards the horizon we leave the road in search of shelter, gathering what little wood might hold a fire and then curling up inside our shared sleeping bag next to it.

And then finally, just as we're about to lose the light on the fourth day we spot the junction where I-64 splits from I-81 and turns west for Lexington and Charleston, the road that will take us to Sulfur Springs and The Greenbrier.

———

That night we sleep in the Rockbridge County High School, a concrete two-story that sits, bleak and grim, atop a low embankment. The parking lot opposite is filled with school buses like the one that brought us to the White House on the Last Day. They line up in neat rows, sunken onto their perished tires under a blanket of gray snow.

It's already growing dark outside as we climb the steps to the entrance. The door's not locked and we snap off our snowshoes and make our way in. It sighs closed behind us, sending a soft stir of echoes down the empty hallway. We head up the staircase and make camp in what used to be the library. I noticed a couple of withered trees still clinging to the embankment when we came in so I dig the handsaw from my backpack and head back outside to cut a few limbs while she checks the shelves to see if anything's been left behind.

On my way back in I stop at the noticeboard in the hall-way, looking for something that might serve for kindling. A faded flyer announces try-outs for the Wildcats. Next to it a sign reads: *Lexington County Fire and Rescue* and under-neath it *Volunteers Needed!!!* In the space underneath where you're supposed to put your name somebody's written *It won't help.* I pull both notices down and stuff them in the pocket of my parka.

When I get back upstairs Mags has a small fire going. I hand her the branches I've collected and one by one she feeds them to the flames. Afterwards we eat our MREs and then climb into the sleeping bag. She pulls *Owen Meany* from her pack, but before she has a chance to open it she's fast asleep.

———

I half wake from a dream I don't remember. Dawn's not far off, but the fire's died down and it's cold. I reach for Mags, but she's no longer lying next to me. I sit up and slowly scan the room, rubbing sleep from my eyes while I chart gray shapes and darkness against memory to try and place where I am. I find her at the window, wrapped in her parka, staring out.

I climb out of the sleeping bag, picking my way between the scattered chairs to stand behind her. For some reason I'm suddenly feeling uneasy, and there's that scratchy feeling I sometimes get inside my head when something's not right. Spidey's been dormant all winter, but now he's back and telling me I need to pay attention.

Without saying a word she points to a spot between two of the school buses. At first I don't see anything, and I'm beginning to wonder what it is she's looking at. But then I catch it. Little more than a shifting of shadows at first, so slight that at first I think I might have imagined it.

Until I see it again.

CHAPTER SIX

WHEN I first started going outside, all those years ago now, I had been sure I'd find someone. Or at least evidence that people were still out here. A smudge of smoke on the horizon; fresh tracks in the snow; the faintest glimmer of a fire through a silted window. But in all my time with Marv I never saw so much as a single footprint to suggest there was anyone else out here. Kane used to say that if we were to happen upon others while we were scavenging we were to give them a wide berth; that if there was anyone still left after all this time they'd most likely be desperate, dangerous men, lawless and Godless. Of course a lot of what Kane told us wasn't true, I know that now. But still it's those words that go through my head as I watch the three men step from the shadows between the school buses.

Now that they're out in the open I can see that at least two of them have rifles. They hold them across their chests, the barrels pointed down, just like I remember Marv and Benjamin carrying their guns on the day we arrived at Eden. They cross the parking lot and then the one in the middle, the one who doesn't seem to be armed, stops and looks up. The fire died down hours ago, and the glass is coated with a decade of grime, so I know he won't be able to see us here, but nevertheless I find myself shrinking back under the weight of that gaze. He turns his head, as if saying something to his companions, and then looks over his shoulder, back in the direction of the highway. For a brief moment I allow myself the hope that they'll pass us by. But when they set off again it's towards the embankment, and the steps that will lead them to the entrance.

I whisper to Mags that we need to go. She nods once, then starts gathering her things. While she's wriggling into her pants I pull on my boots, not bothering with the laces. I stuff our sleeping bag into my backpack and hoist it onto my shoulder. We're already at the stairs when she stops and says she's forgotten her book. But it's too late to go back for it now so I grab her hand and moments later we're running down a wide hallway past row after row of metal lockers. At the end I turn right and follow the signs marked Fire Exit. Somewhere in the darkness behind us I hear the sound of a door being opened. I think they're coming in the way we did last night, but I don't stop to make sure.

We take a left and a right and then there's another long corridor. We run down it, a set of double doors with a push handle slowly separating itself from the gloom at the end. A sign says the door's alarmed, but that's not what's worrying me now. I reach for the bar, convinced it won't move and that we'll be trapped. But it sticks for just an instant then gives with a loud clunk, announcing our presence to whoever's behind us. I push against it, no longer worried about being quiet, but the door only opens a fraction. I look down and see why: snow's drifted up against the bottom on the other side. I lean my shoulder into it and shove, feeling my boots scrabble for purchase on the tiled floor. It opens a little further, enough now for Mags to squeeze through. I step back and she disappears into the gap just as a dark shape appears at the end of the hallway behind us and shouts something. I shuck off my backpack and push it through then force myself after it.

I stagger out into the snow. As I close the door behind me I see a hasp that was designed to take a padlock. I don't have one of those, but the pry bar's sitting right on top of my backpack; it'll do to hold it shut while we get clear of whoever's chasing us. But as I'm bending down to reach inside I hear Mags cry out and I stop and look up. For the first time I notice there's a huge shape standing in front of me, silhouetted against the first of the morning light. It takes me a moment to work out that it's a man. His size and the bushy blond beard covering the bottom half of his face makes him look like the world's largest Viking. He's got Mags pinned to his side under one gigantic arm. She's struggling to break free, but it's like he doesn't even notice.

I drop the pack and fumble inside the pocket of my parka for the gun. There's no bullets of course, so right now I'm hoping that Marv was right when he said most people would just turn tail at the sight of it. But the man-mountain that's holding Mags doesn't show any sign of doing that. I take a step closer and point the gun at his head, but he just blinks once and continues to stare back at me.

I hear something slam into the door behind me. There's a pause and another crash and the sound of wood splintering and when I look back over my shoulder the three men we saw in the parking lot are standing there. The hoods on their parkas are up and the throats are fastened so I can't make out their faces. I see enough in the second before I return my gaze to the Viking to realize that exactly none of their weapons are pointed at the ground any more though. I flick the safety on Marv's gun, trying to stop my hand from shaking.

'Whoa now, son. Steady with that before someone gets hurt.'

The voice is deep, slow and calm. I risk another glance behind me. It's the man in the middle who's spoken. His parka's unzipped, and I catch a glimpse of something silver hanging low on one hip as he steps forward, but his hands are empty. His hood's up, and even though it's barely light out he's wearing sunglasses. He raises his hands and holds them out, palms up.

'Tell him to let her go first.'

'Sure thing. Hey Jax, why don't you do like the kid here says and put the girl down?'

The Viking waits for a moment, like he's processing that instruction, then he releases Mags. She takes a quick step away from him and stops, fists balled at her sides inside her mittens, like she's considering what punishment the giant deserves for having had the temerity to pick her up. I catch her eye and shake my head. She pauses for a moment and then backs over towards me.

'Okay kid, now how about lowering that sidearm? I know Jax there must look like a pretty tempting target, but trust me now, that's an opportunity you'd do well to pass on. If you shoot him with anything less than a fifty cal you're just going to piss him off.'

I look back over my shoulder again. The man who seems to be in charge unsnaps the throat of his parka and slowly lowers his hood. The shades he's wearing are old, the kind with dark, round lenses and leather side blinkers, so I can't make out his eyes. His hair's short, and silver as Kane's. In place of a respirator he's got a simple black bandana, and now he pulls it down revealing a lean face that looks like it might have been cut straight from the same granite as Eden's tunnels. A thick mustache covers his upper lip and then angles down almost to his jawline.

The lines that bracket his mouth deepen as he smiles. He reaches up, slowly removes the sunglasses. One eye is covered with a patch, but the other squints back at me from underneath an eyebrow that's surprisingly dark given the color of his hair. He motions to the other two men to lower their rifles.

I glance over at Mags, but her expression's hard to read. I'm sensing we'll be having a conversation about why I suddenly have a pistol I hadn't previously disclosed, but that's for later; right now I need to work out what to do about our immediate situation. The men might have lowered their weapons, but seeing as my gun's the one without bullets I doubt we'll be shooting our way out of this.

I look at the men surrounding us. They're all wearing the same parka, what appears in the scant light to be a mix of greens and grays in a pixelated camouflage pattern. The zip pulls and the snappers have all been replaced and when I glance down at their boots I see it's the same with the eyelets; they've been swapped out for plastic too. Spidey grumbles a little at that but it's vague, non-directional, and right then I think he's just fussing; my parka and boots are rigged the same after all. I look over at the man with the silver hair who seems to be their leader. His hands are still raised and for the first time I spot the patch velcro'd high on his arm. I look around at the others and see they're each wearing the same familiar flag. I allow my hopes to lift a little. These men are soldiers, just like Marv and Benjamin were.

I take one last look around and then flick the pistol back to safe and slide it back into the pocket of my parka. The man who seems to be in charge whistles softly through his teeth, then lets his hands drop to his sides. As he does so his parka slides forward, once again covering the pistol on his hip. He smiles at me like he's relieved, but something in the way he does it makes me think the Viking may not ever have been in danger, even if Marv's gun had been loaded.

He gestures to the door we've all just come through.

'Alright, then. Now what say we make our introductions inside?'

CHAPTER SEVEN

WE HEAD BACK into the school. The three soldiers we first saw coming up to the entrance lead the way. Mags slips through the busted door after them and I follow. There's a groan and the sound of wood parting company from hinges as behind me the giant they called Jax ducks his head and squeezes his bulk into the inadequate gap. I can't help but look back at him. Benjamin always seemed huge, but then I guess we were small when we knew him. There's no doubt that this man is bigger. He doesn't say anything, just meets my gaze and stares back at me with these flat blue eyes.

When we get to the staircase the soldier with the eye patch turns to me as if looking for direction. I point up the stairs towards the library.

'Alright. I'm guessing you didn't have a fire goin'?'

The fire we had burned down overnight. I shake my head no.

'Do you have the makings of another?'

'We used the last of the wood we cut last night.'

'Fair enough. Jax, run outside and gather us up some, will you? Go on now. You're making the kid here nervous.'

The Viking looks at me for a long moment, then lumbers off towards the entrance. I keep my eye on his back until he's out the door, then start up the stairs. The soldier with the eye patch and the silver hair walks beside me.

'Don't mind Jax none; he's just interested in you is all. We ain't seen anyone new in years so I expect he'll stare some until he gets used to you. Boy's not right in the head.' He taps one temple as if to emphasize his point. 'His understanding never got much beyond what the movie people would have called soft focus.'

I nod like I get it, but in spite of his words I still find the Viking's size unsettling. We return to the library where Mags and I spent the night. One of the soldiers takes up station by the door and the other heads over to the window. The one who so far has done all the talking drags a couple of plastic chairs into the middle of the room and motions for us to sit. I hesitate a moment and then take a seat. Mags looks at the chair like she's considering it but remains standing. If the soldier cares whether she sits or not he doesn't show it, he just grabs another chair for himself and straddles it backwards, facing us. The parka falls open again, this time offering me a longer look at the pistol on his hip. It seems old, like it might be an antique. The metal's dull, and the grip that sticks out of the holster's inlaid with something cut from the tusk or bone of some long-dead animal, something that might once have been white but which years of use have stained a deep yellow. As I look closer I can see there's something scrimshawed there: a vulture or a buzzard or some other carrion bird.

The soldier reaches into his parka, pulls out a crumpled

pack of Camels and holds it forward, like he's offering me one. I shake my head.

'I know, filthy habit, right? Still, I guess you gotta die of something.'

He shakes a cigarette out of the packet, places it in his mouth, and goes digging in his pocket for something to light it. He has a habit of squinting, which together with the mustache, the bandana and the piece of hardware on his hip puts me in mind of a gunslinger from the old west.

His hand reappears holding a book of matches. He tears one off and strikes it, and for a second before he cups the flame to the end of the cigarette it shows me a long, puckered burn scar that runs down one side of his neck and disappears under his collar. The creases in his narrow face deepen as he takes a drag, then exhales a jet of smoke through the side of his mouth. The tang of stale tobacco drifts over and for a moment the smell reminds me of Marv.

'Alright then, introductions. I'm Hicks. That there Mexican-lookin' fella with a face like the north end of a south-bound mule is Ortiz.' He nods in the direction of a shorter, stockier man with caramel skin and dark, hooded eyes who's taken up station by the door. Ortiz flips Hicks the finger but manages a smile back in our direction.

'You've probably figured out the big fella's name's Jax. And the runt of the litter over there's Kavanagh. Everyone calls him Boots, though.'

The last soldier he points to has greasy brown hair and a scrub of beard that barely covers his chin. He hardly looks old enough to be wearing a uniform; back in Eden I reckon he might have edged out Alice as my main market for zit cream. He blinks continuously behind thick glasses with heavily taped rims that look like they haven't been cleaned more recently than the window he's standing in front of. He offers me a distracted smile and then goes back to staring at Mags.

'So what're your names?'

'I'm Gabriel but everyone calls me Gabe. And that's Mags.'

'Nice to meet you Gabe. And Mags. What's that short for, darlin'?'

I wince. Hicks doesn't seem to mean any offense by it but I could have told him Mags won't like being called darling.

'Just Mags.'

'Alright then Gabe short for Gabriel and Mags short for Mags, are you hungry? We have food. Can't say it's great, but we're happy to share it.'

I'm about to answer, but Mags just says: 'No thanks. We have our own.'

Hicks looks over at her and then down at the floor. The MRE cartons from last night's meal are still lying there, next to the remains of the fire. I didn't have time to bag them before we high-tailed it out of here.

'So I can see.' The cigarette held loosely between his fingers continues to burn; he hasn't taken another drag since he first lit it. He looks at Mags for a while, then at me, then back to Mags again. 'You pair look well fed. Where you been hiding out?'

I open my mouth to answer, but Mags beats me to it again.

'How did you find us?'

'Just lucky I guess. We picked up your tracks out by the highway, followed them in here. Almost missed you, though. I reckon another hour and the wind would have covered them over. Which way you headed?'

'Some place called The Greenbrier.'

Hicks exchanges a look with the soldier he called Ortiz and smiles.

'Well then it is your lucky day; that's where we've come from. Matter of fact we're headed back there now. We'll be happy to bring you with us. Are there any more of you?'

Mags says no, but Hicks looks at me for a long moment, like he's trying to work out what the real answer to that question might be. I shake my head. Eventually he says, *Alright then*, but keeps studying me through the smoke that drifts languidly up from the cigarette, like maybe he's expecting something else. I figure I need to get us onto another topic so I ask him how many of them there are.

'Hmm? Oh, in The Greenbrier.' He flicks the cigarette, sending gray flakes floating slowly to the dusty floor. 'We're down to eight, all told. Mostly regular army, a couple of Rangers like me and Ortiz over there. We have a scientist though. She's working on a cure for the virus.'

'A cure?' I look over at Mags. Before he died Marv told me what Kane had done to the skies hadn't killed the virus, just set it back. That's why the furies weren't decaying; it was regrouping, he said, slowly building itself back up inside them. Marv hadn't known how long it would take but at some point he reckoned they'd be able to move again, just like the one I ran into when I first went into Mount Weather's tunnel. That would be a real problem. It's been on my list of things to worry about, right after finding a place for us that'll be safe from Kane, that is.

Hicks nods.

'Yep. She reckons she's pretty close too.'

'And how're your supplies holding out?'

Hicks looks over at Mags' question. 'The Greenbrier was

stocked pretty good when we arrived and we've been managing it for the long haul, so there's enough to go around, at least for now. We've been working the surrounding towns, too. Not much left out there anymore, though.'

Ortiz touches one of our empty MRE cartons from last night with the toe of his boot. 'Sure would be good to find some more of these. If you kids have come across a stash of them anywhere on your travels we'd love to hear about it.'

Hicks holds up his hand as if to hush him. The cuff of his parka drops and for the first time I notice he's wearing something inside his liners. It looks like latex; I have a box of disposables just like them in my pack. I thought Marv was pretty careful about the virus, but even he didn't make me put those on unless I was actually fixing to touch metal.

'Ortiz are you ever not hungry? I swear you have worms. Y'ate my breakfast this morning as well as your own. There'll be plenty of time for questions when we get back to The Greenbrier. I'm sure these kids'll help us if they can.'

We hear Jax stomping up the stairs and a few moments later the door swings open. It looks like the Viking's found the small stand clinging to the embankment I took from the night before. He hasn't bothered to cut the limbs though, he's just pulled the trees up, roots and all, and dragged them back. The trunks are slender enough, little more than saplings, but the ground's been frozen solid for the best part of a decade and won't have given them up easily. Hicks drops the cigarette to the floor and crushes it under his boot.

'Goddammit Jax, now what in the hell are we supposed to do with those? We need smaller stuff for the fire, remember?'

The Viking just looks at the pile of wood tucked under his arm and then at Hicks, and then back at the wood again, taking a moment to stare at Mags and me for good measure. He drops what he's gathered on the ground and picks up one of the trees and tries to snap it with his hands. The wood's been dead for years but it's wet with snow; it bends and twists, occasionally splintering but mostly just holding, not matter how hard the blond giant tries to break it.

I dig into my backpack and set to work with the handsaw while Mags strips some of the smaller branches and starts building a fire. The soldier Hicks had called Boots watches her from his spot by the window. When it looks like there's enough he pulls a squeeze bottle from the pocket of his parka and walks over. He kneels down next to her and starts squirting the contents liberally over the branches and for a second the rich, sweet smell of gasoline hangs heavy in the air. Gas is pretty hard to come by - Marv only allowed me to use it in emergencies - but Boots doesn't seem to be rationing himself. When he's done he pulls a cheap plastic lighter from his pocket and strikes the wheel with the base of his thumb. He holds it to his face and for a moment the small blue-tinged flame reflects back off the lenses in his grubby glasses. When he presents it to the wood the gas catches with a *whumpf!* that makes me wonder how many times Private Kavanagh has had to wait for his eyebrows to grow back. I have to admit though, whatever mix he's using seems to do the trick; it's not long till the flames are licking up through the damp wood. The smoke makes me cough and I have to step back from it, but he doesn't seem to be able to tear himself away. He watches the fire as though transfixed, occasionally reaching for another branch from the pile to feed it. I guess I should be grateful for small mercies; for a few minutes at least he's not staring at Mags.

The soldiers wait while we fix breakfast. Hicks says

they've already eaten but I offer Ortiz some of the sausage patty from my MRE just because he's staring so hard. Hicks shakes his head and says I oughtn't do that; I'll only teach him bad habits by feeding him from the table. Ortiz's mouth's full so he just flips him the finger again and holds out his hand for a hash brown.

As we're finishing up Hicks bends down and retrieves Mags' copy of *Owen Meany* from where she left it. Her eyes dart over to the fire. The flames are already dying down. She sets her MRE aside and stands up.

'That's not for burning.'

He looks up at her.

'Don't worry darlin', that wasn't my intention. This yours?'

She nods.

'Have you read it?'

Mags hesitates, like maybe it's a trick question. Back in Eden Kane didn't allow us to read.

'Yes.'

'It's good, isn't it? I liked the little guy; he knew what had to be done. Can't say I cared much for his friend, though. Not sure what use a man is without a trigger finger.'

He examines the tatty paperback a moment longer then hands it over. She takes it and returns it to her backpack. I scoop the last of my breakfast from its pouch, bag our trash and we set off.

CHAPTER EIGHT

ROCKBRIDGE COUNTY HIGH'S right off I-64, the road that Marv's map says will take us all the way to The Greenbrier.

There hasn't been a fresh fall in a few days and the snow's settled, so the going's not so bad. Hicks sets a steady pace and soon I settle into an easy rhythm. But after a while I notice Mags falling behind. I'm beginning to wonder if everything's okay; maybe she hurt herself as we were running through the school earlier. I hang back and soon the soldiers are a stretch ahead of us. I'm about to ask what's wrong when she rests a hand on my arm. Jax has taken to stopping every few minutes to gawp in our direction, but he's just finishing up a stare-break. As soon as he's eyes-forward again she unsnaps one side of her respirator. The wind's picked up a little, enough to prevent anyone ahead from hearing. Nevertheless she keeps her voice low.

'What should we tell them?'

'About what?'

'About where we've come from. Sooner or later they're going to ask again.'

Hicks and Ortiz both appear friendly, and it does seem like Jax's staring is simply curiosity. I really don't care for the way Boots has been looking at her, but these certainly don't seem like the desperate, lawless men Kane had warned of. Maybe Mags is right, though; we have only just met them.

'Well, it's either Eden or Mount Weather; we won't be able to make up a story about anywhere else that'd sound even halfway believable. I think we should just say we've come from Eden. That way at least they won't know where the rest of the Juvies are.'

She considers this for a moment. 'But if they figure out where that is and go there they'll find Kane. They're soldiers; wouldn't he still be their commanding officer? And he knows where we've gone.'

I think about this for a moment. She's right, of course, but I'm not sure it widens our options any.

'After all this time I'm not so sure they'd still take orders from him. He was the one that caused all this after all. We can prove it if we have to; we still have the virus. Besides we don't have to use Eden's real name. I don't think anyone other than Kane called it that. Even if they work out where it is by the time they get there we could be gone from Mount Weather.'

She considers this for a while. In the end she nods like maybe it's not the best plan she's ever heard, but right now she can't think of another that might be better. She snaps the respirator back over her mouth and we pick up the pace.

Up ahead the soldiers have stopped next to an RV that's come to a sideways halt in the middle of the road. Jax is using his break time to get some more staring in and now Hicks turns around as well. The Viking's gaze is blank, vacant, but with Hicks it's different; I feel like behind those blinkered shades our progress is being measured. When we catch up to them he pulls down his bandana.

'How're you two doin'?'

Mags stops and unsnaps her respirator again.

'I was finding the snow a little heavy back there. I'm fine now.'

Hicks just nods and leads us on.

———

We stick to the interstate as it winds its way west into the Appalachians.

The first morning we pass a succession of exit signs – Shank's Creek, Longhorn Furnace, Forge – but we don't take any of them, stopping only to warm our MREs by the side of the road. Hicks sits off to one side and sips from a thermos he pulls from his pack.

As soon as we're done eating he stands, like he's keen to get back now. I bag our trash and we set off again. For a while the road opens out and billboards compete for our attention on both sides. A decade of weather has left them faded and tattered, but it's still a riot of color compared with what we've been seeing. Then the mountains close in on us again and they're gone.

The last of the light's leaving the sky when Hicks finally leads us towards an off-ramp. We make our way into a small town called Covington in almost darkness. I'm not used to hiking at night; Marv always had us off the road before dusk. We may not have seen the sun since the Last Day but I guess it's still up there doing something because once it dips below the horizon it turns real cold real quick, and without a moon or even stars to light your way it'd be easy to get lost. Hicks seems to know where he's going, though. He brings us to a small brick and shingle building just off the highway. The weather-beaten sign outside says *New Hope Baptist Church*, and underneath in smaller letters, *Praying For A Miracle*.

Hicks sends Jax off in search of firewood and then heads out himself shortly after. All the Viking comes back with are a handful of blackened limbs that do little more than smoke up the place, no matter how much gasoline Boots pours on them. We huddle around the reluctant fire scooping our rapidly cooling MREs from their plastic pouches while Ortiz, Boots and Jax eat a supper of cold franks and beans. I tear the wrapper off a HOOAH! for dessert and Jax stares at me like the world's largest, dumbest wolfhound. I break it in two and toss one half over. It disappears into his beard and I have to hold my hands up so he'll believe I'm not holding out on him.

Hicks returns a little while after. He doesn't bother with dinner or the fire, just walks past us and up into the shadows by the altar. He eases himself to the ground and sits with his back to the pulpit. A quart bottle of bourbon appears from the pocket of his parka and he unscrews the cap. Boots is staring into the dwindling flames, absent-mindedly picking at a scab on the inside of his arm. He looks up at the sound but Hicks makes no move to offer it around.

The church has a small organ balcony, so I figure that's where Mags and I will sleep. As we get up Boots tears his eyes from the fire; I can feel his gaze following us as we climb the stairs. I unfurl the sleeping bag and lay it on the dusty floor. Mags has been quiet over dinner and she still hasn't said anything as we climb inside. She lays still for a while, her back to my chest, but I know she's still awake. Eventually she whispers:

'We should hide the map. It has the code for Mount Weather on it.'

I nod. She closes her eyes and rests her head against my shoulder, like having decided this is a comfort. But it's a long time before she finally drifts off.

———

I wake from an uneasy sleep sometime in the middle of the night. The fire's gone out so there's little to see, but something's stirring down below. I hear footsteps as someone makes their way down the aisle, then the door at the back of the church opens and from outside there's the sound of retching. After a while it stops and then for a long time silence returns to the darkness.

I'm beginning to think whoever it was has snuck back inside without me noticing when I hear the door opening again. I ease my arm out from under Mags' head. She mumbles something and then shifts in her sleep, like whatever's troubling her has found its way into her dreams, but she doesn't wake. I slip out of the sleeping bag and creep over to the balustrade. My eyes have adjusted as much as they will, but without a fire there's nothing but inky blackness. I strain to hear. Whoever's moving around down there seems to be retracing their steps up the aisle. There's a pause and some shuffling sounds as they settle themselves, then the dry rasp of a lighter wheel being struck and Hicks' face suddenly appears out of the darkness as he holds the flame to the end of a cigarette and draws on it. He's about to extinguish the lighter, but then something causes him to stop. He turns and looks up in my direction. I suddenly feel the need to announce my presence; like I've been caught spying on him. I raise my hand to wave down, but then I stop myself. I'm hidden behind the balustrade, in total darkness; there's no way he can see me up here. After a moment he lets the lighter go out so that all that remains is the glowing red tip.

I creep back to the sleeping bag and climb inside.

CHAPTER NINE

HE'S the last one now.

Still they keep the lights off. He's told them they don't bother him, that he's not like the others, that he'd rather have them on. He's told them more than once; he mentions it every time one of them comes down. He wants them to believe it, even though it's not really true anymore. When they put the flashlight on him it hurts now.

He doesn't have a name, or if he does he doesn't remember it. He's heard the doctor refer to him as Subject 99 and sometimes the mean soldier sings snatches of a tune that has the words Johnny 99 in it. He wonders if his name might be Johnny. The mean soldier doesn't have a nice voice, but the boy who might be Johnny likes the song anyway. Sometimes after they've gone he hums it to himself in the darkness, even though he doesn't know what an auto plant is or if Mahwah's even a real place or for that matter what Ralph was thinking mixing Tanqueray and wine if it can get you in that kind of trouble. He asked the doctor once whether his name might be Johnny, but when she wanted to know why he couldn't think of a reason other than the song and so he said he wasn't sure. The doctor never answered him. But after that the mean soldier didn't sing anymore. And the next time he came down he glared into his cage like he was mad at him for something, and then he put his food tray on the ground and spat in it. He had to eat the food anyway, even though he wasn't really hungry. Because not eating your food is a sign, like not looking at the doctor's flashlight, and he doesn't want to go to the other room.

He's been here a very long time. He doesn't know how long exactly, because days don't mean much with the lights off. But definitely a long time. He wasn't always here. He's sure of that, even though he doesn't know where he might have been before. He doesn't remember anything about it. The doctor says he needs to try and he wants to, he really does, and not just to please her. But it's no use. It's like whatever was before is behind some thick gray curtain in his mind and there's just no way to pull it back, no matter how hard he tries.

He thinks the room he's in now is underground. There are no windows, although of course he knows that doesn't prove anything. It's definitely at the bottom of a long flight of stairs though, because he can hear the soldiers' boots ringing off the metal each time they descend. Sometimes he counts the steps. The highest he's ever got before the door opens is eighty-nine, but the first ones are always really faint and it's possible there are more he's not hearing.

He can always tell who's coming. The mean soldier's boots are the loudest. He can hear their lumbering *thunk-clang* echoing down the stairwell for ages before he reaches the bottom. It's the mean soldier he sees the most, because he's the one who brings his food. He always carries the stick and he looks at him like he's some sort of dangerous animal in a poorly built cage. He doesn't need to be afraid, though. Johnny 99 would never hurt him, ever, he's told him that. But still he makes sure to keep all the way to the back of the cage while the tray gets pushed through the slot at the front. They don't bother to heat the food, but that's okay; they're still bringing it, which is the main thing. He always eats everything they give him, even if he's not hungry, or if he suspects the mean soldier has done something to it. That way they'll know he's still fine and doesn't need to go in the next room, like the others.

The other soldier comes down, too, although it's been a while now since he visited. His footsteps are much quieter; sometimes he makes it all the way down the stairs without Johnny even hearing and the first thing he knows the door at the end's opening and he has to scurry to the back of his cage. The other soldier doesn't bother with a stick or even a flashlight. He just sits there in the darkness, studying him through the bars. When he's done he gets up and leaves without saying a word.

The doctor doesn't come as often as she used to either, now there's only him left. And sometimes when she does she just shines the light into his eyes and then leaves without saying anything and he is disappointed. But other times there are questions. He has to answer them as truthfully as he can, which he does, he always does, even though most of the time he just can't remember. He's not allowed to ask any questions of his own, even though he has so many and sometimes it feels like he might burst with the not knowing. That would ruin the experiment the doctor says. He must try and remember himself. It's really important.

He knows he is sick, like the others were. That's why he

can't remember. But the doctor says the medicine she gives him will make him better. He has to drink it all, every last drop, even though it makes him feel like he's going to throw up. The medicine didn't help the others, though. He watched each of them take it and one by one they all changed.

98 was the last, and she turned a long time ago now. Her cage had been directly opposite; she'd been there when he'd first woken up. He doesn't remember much about before he got sick, but he remembers that. He had been very frightened then. He can see quite well now; his eyes have grown used to the darkness. But back then he hadn't been able to see anything. He hadn't known where he was, or what he was doing, here, in this tiny plastic enclosure.

98 had calmed him down. She'd whispered that it would be okay, but for now it was important that he be quiet. That was one of the rules, she'd said. If the mean soldier caught you making noise he'd come down and put the lights on and even though Johnny 99 hadn't minded the lights back then it would drive some of the others, the ones who were already turning, crazy.

Well, crazier.

Later 98 had taught him the other rules as well, like going to the back of your cage whenever the soldiers came down and never, ever putting your hand through the bars. There were more rules than that, but those were the main ones. You couldn't forget them, even for a second. If you did the mean soldier was apt to pay you a visit with the stick.

He misses 98. She had been nice to him. It had frightened him when the doctor had come down and shone a light into her cage and he had seen her for the first time. How could anyone's eyes be like that? But after a while he had gotten used to it and then it hadn't bothered him so much. He wonders if he looks now like 98 did then. There aren't any mirrors in his cage, no surfaces that might give back even the faintest reflection, so he doesn't know. His arms and legs seem very thin and pale, but then he is small, and it is always dark down here, so maybe that is normal.

98 lasted a long time, longer than any of the others. But then one day the mean soldier started taking her food away untouched, and a little while after that she had started acting up whenever the doctor had shone a light into her cage. Johnny 99 had tried to calm her down, just like she had done when he had first arrived. That had seemed to help a little, at first. But then the doctor would come down with the flashlight and that would set her off again. After that Johnny 99 knew it wouldn't be long. There's never much time left after you change.

It was the mean soldier who came to get her, with the catchpole and the stick. Johnny 99 hadn't been able to look. He'd pushed himself to the back of his cage and covered his head with his hands when it happened. He is ashamed of that because 98 was his friend, although in the end he doesn't think she knew who he was anymore.

Johnny 99's decided that won't happen to him. He'll keep taking the medicine and eating the regular food, even if he doesn't feel like it, and he won't flinch or look away when the doctor shines a light into his eyes, even if it hurts.

That way they'll know.

He's not like the others.

CHAPTER TEN

WE'RE on the road again at first light. If Hicks' head is hurting from the bourbon he's not showing any sign of it; the pace he's setting doesn't slacken. The morning passes much as the day before did: a succession of frozen landscapes, like a series of old black and white photos. We hike through each, aiming for the bend or the crest that will show us the next. When the time comes we eat by the side of the road, huddled up in our parkas. Hicks' stomach must still be feeling delicate from the whisky; he just sips from his thermos and lets another cigarette burn down between his fingers. I'm beginning to wonder if Hicks is actually a smoker or if he's just worried what the world's lacking right now is a steady supply of ash.

When we're done eating I bag our trash and bury it in the snow and we set off again. The road inclines for a couple of miles and when it finally crests we come to a small green sign, almost buried under a drift, that reads *Greenbrier County*. A little further on a high gantry that's somehow survived rust and storm and virus spans the highway. A large sign mounted to it says *Welcome to West Virginia* and underneath *Wild and Wonderful.*

A mile or so after the sign the road fishhooks and then passes over what looks like train tracks. Beneath us, maybe a hundred yards back in the direction we've come, I can just make out the entrance to a tunnel. Ashen drifts reach almost all the way up the curved walls, almost hiding it completely. Hicks knocks snow off the guardrail then throws a leg over and drops down a steep embankment on the other side, sliding his way to the floor of a narrow ravine. Ortiz goes next and then I shuck off my backpack and follow him. A second later Mags gets to her feet beside me and dusts herself off, followed a little too closely by Jax, who arrives in an avalanche of snow. Boots spends a while looking down at us until Hicks loses patience and barks at him to hurry it up. He slips as he's clambering over the guardrail and tumbles down the slope, shedding his goggles and respirator on the way down. The drifts are deep at the bottom and Hicks has to send Jax to dig him out. He finally gets to his feet, furiously wiping snow off his glasses. It might be the first time they've been cleaned since he got fitted for them.

The track curves around for a half mile or so and then straightens. The ravine widens out and we pass a short siding, a corroded railcar sitting idle against the buffers. In the distance I can see what looks like a long shelter, the roof timbers swaybacked under the weight of snow, running the length of what I'm guessing was once a platform. As we get closer a faded Amtrak sign says *Sulfur Springs.*

We leave the railway tracks behind us and make our way through a parking lot to the road. There's a station house, almost buried under a blanket of gray snow, its small porch supported by two red and white pillars. The paint's faded and peeling but they look like candy cane and for a moment it puts me in mind of a story Miss Kimble used to read to us about these kids who get abandoned in a forest by their ne'er-do-well father and then stumble on a witch. Miss Kimble said it was a classic, but it always seemed kinda lame to me. I mean, really, we're supposed to believe the witch wants to eat these two kids, even though she lives in a house made of nothing but Hershey's kisses and Reese's peanut butter cups? Mags said she liked it though, because in the end the witch gets her ass thrown in an oven.

On the other side of the road two matching sections of wall curve inward to a pair of large stone gateposts, marking an entrance. The gatepost on the left has started to crumble, but the other's mostly intact. The once-white paintwork's flaking badly, but the sign there's still legible. The dark green cursive announces that we have arrived at *The Greenbrier*. Underneath, in neat capitals, it says *America's Resort*.

Hicks leads us between the gateposts and we start up a long driveway. I'm beginning to think there's been a mistake. I look over at Mags and I can see she's thinking the same thing. The facility listed on Marv's map definitely shared the name on the post, but it was supposed to be a bunker. And then as the road curves around I finally get my first glimpse of The Greenbrier and I'm sure of it.

I stop, pushing my goggles up onto my forehead. Beside me Mags does the same. It's like we're back at the White House on the Last Day. But it's clear even from this distance that The Greenbrier is much, much bigger; almost too big to take in in a single glance. The front is dominated by a huge portico, four massive columns supporting a low triangular gable that slopes down to a flat roof. I count five, no, six stories, rows of tall, dark windows marching off in each direction. They continue around on both sides, the wings forming a giant squared-off horseshoe that surrounds what must once have been the gardens. A line of tattered, weather-faded flags hang from poles that jut from the first floor balustrade.

We set off again, hurrying to catch up to the soldiers. As we get closer I see a dark shape squatting on the lawn, covered under a thick mantle of snow. I keep looking at it as we hike up to the entrance. The outline is unfamiliar, and it takes me a while to figure out that it's a helicopter. It's way bigger than the one that brought us to Eden, though, and it has two sets of rotors, not one. The first are mounted on a tall hump above the cockpit; the second rest on top of a tail section at the back and sit even higher above the long, riveted fuselage. The thick blades hang down under their own weight, the tips almost touching the gray powder. As we walk past I can see that the loading ramp at the back is down; snow drifts up into the darkened interior.

On the other side of the helicopter a path has been cleared. We step into the shadow of the portico; the colossal columns tower over us as we bend down to undo our snow-shoes. I notice a camera mounted high on the wall above the entrance. As I watch its red light blinks once, then goes dark again. There's something about that that doesn't seem right, but Hicks is already making his way inside so I kick the snow off my boots and follow him through a set of double doors into a huge lobby.

And for a moment all I can do is stare.

CHAPTER ELEVEN

KANE'S HOUSE in Eden always seemed luxurious. The sofas and armchairs where we would sit for confession were so much more comfortable than the plastic chairs in the mess or the chapel's wooden pews; the soft glow from the reading lamps so much kinder than the glare from the cavern's arc lights. But underneath the rugs the floor was the same riveted metal my feet would touch first thing in the morning; behind the pictures that hung on his walls were the same welded panels I'd stare up at from my cot before the curfew buzzer each night.

This place couldn't be more different. I look around, slowly taking it all in. Large black and white marble tiles stretch off in all directions, like I'm standing on a giant checkerboard. Above me a massive chandelier hangs from an ornate ceiling. The crystals are covered in dust, but they still manage to catch the last of the day's light coming through the lobby's tall windows. A wide, carpeted staircase leads down to a lower level; next to it another spirals upwards. And scattered everywhere, items of furniture. Dustsheets shroud much of it, but here and there something has gone uncovered. A pair of armchairs, the pattern on the upholstery like the feathers of a giant, exotic bird. A tall wooden clock, its golden face intricately carved, the pendulum beneath now still.

But what strikes me even more than these extravagances are the colors. Eden was steel and rock; a handful of small, windowless metal boxes huddled together inside a cavern dug deep into a mountain. It had no need for cheery tones; no part of it had been designed with joyful times in mind. What little there was got washed out by the arc lights, or faded to grainy shadow once the curfew buzzer sounded and those were cut. Mount Weather might be bigger, and more modern, but ultimately its purpose was no different. It existed solely to get whatever remained of humanity through its darkest hours.

It's not like that here. As I look around I see large colorful paintings hanging from wallpapered walls; thick red carpets climb the staircases and from underneath the dust cloths the once-vivid fabrics of sofas and armchairs peek out. The patterns may have faded with time, and here and there the paper on the walls is starting to peel. But even in the failing evening light this place is a riot of blues and greens and pinks and reds.

The thought I had as I caught my first glimpse of The Greenbrier from outside returns: Hicks has brought us to the wrong place. The facility marked on Marv's map was supposed to be a bunker. After ten years I know what those look like, and whatever this place might be, it isn't one. I'm about to ask him about it when he looks over and points at my boots.

'You'll need to take those off. Doc doesn't like us tracking dirt in from the outside.' Spidey pings a warning at this. But as I look over at Ortiz I see he's already removed his and is stacking them on a nearby bellhop cart next to his rifle. Beside him Jax is hard at work on his laces, a task that seems to be consuming all of his powers of concentration.

I hesitate for a second then undo my boots and hand them over. Hicks flips one over to check the size and then adds them to the cart. Mags frowns like she's not happy about this either, but in the end she does the same. He disappears down the stairs and comes back a moment later with a pair of trainers for her and some slippers with *The Greenbrier* embroidered on the front for me.

'Sorry kid, nothing in your size. You'll have to give me that sidearm now too. All weapons get locked away here. Doc don't allow guns inside the house. No exceptions.'

Marv's gun's not loaded anyway, so unless I'm planning to hit someone with it it's not going to be much use. I reach into the pocket of my parka and hand it over.

He takes it out of the Ziploc bag and ejects the magazine. Then he pulls the slide back and checks the chamber for a round. When he doesn't find one he looks up at me and raises an eyebrow in what I think might be an expression of amusement, but maybe not. Behind him Jax has finally worked out how many times the bunny has to hop around the tree before his footwear comes off. He stands up and lumbers off through the lobby like he's suddenly remembered somewhere important he has to be. Ortiz grabs his backpack and hauls it into the corner with the others. He collects the giant's outsized boots from where they've been discarded and adds them to the others on the bellhop cart, then he sets off down the corridor with it. Hicks follows him into the gloom.

Boots blinks at Mags behind his glasses and asks if she

wants dinner. She looks at me. I'm not sure I care much for more of Private Kavanagh's company, but we've hiked a long way since lunch and my stomach's already betrayed me by growling loudly at the mention of food, so I shrug my shoulders and nod. He digs into his pack and pulls out a packet of boil-in-the-bag frankfurters and a tin of beans.

We follow him across the lobby and down a long, wide hallway. Tall windows look out onto what I'm guessing would once have been the gardens, where now the gray outline of the helicopter squats in the dying light. The muffled sounds of conversation drift up from somewhere ahead of us on the right.

Boots stops in front of a set of double doors and holds one open for Mags to go through. I follow her into a huge dining room. Two rows of sculpted columns support a high ceiling, at least a dozen chandeliers like the one in the lobby hanging between them. Large, ornate mirrors that would once have reflected the light back line the walls, their surfaces spackled black with years of neglect.

Most of the furniture's been stacked neatly in one corner, but in the center a single table remains. I see Jax already seated at it, his broad back to us. Three other men sit with him, all in uniform, the remains of a meal spread out in front of them. The soldier at the head of the table seems to be giving forth on something, but he stops mid-sentence as we step in, a smile splitting his face.

'Well, look what we got here.'

CHAPTER TWELVE

THE OTHER TWO men turn around in their seats, and for a long moment no one speaks. Boots is over at a sideboard fiddling with the knobs on a camping stove, trying to get the burners to light. He doesn't seem to be having much success and without gasoline I wonder how much longer it's going to take him.

One of the men inclines his head to the soldier at the head of the table, the one who first spotted us.

'Damn but that boy looks tall enough to hunt geese with a rake, don't he Truck?'

I'm not sure what to say to that, but Boots has finally managed to get the stove going and now he scurries across the room and darts in front of us, anxious not to relinquish control of his prize. He pulls out a chair for Mags and motions for her to sit. I slide myself into the next one along before he has the chance to claim it for himself. Across the table Jax is loading a rubbery-looking frankfurter into his mouth whole. He stares back at me as he chews on it. It's unclear from those flat blue eyes whether he recognizes us from before or not.

Boots makes the introductions. The soldier at the end of the table who looked like he was holding court when we came in is a big man, thickset, although the way his sweat-stained fatigues hang on his frame suggests he was once even larger. His sleeves are rolled up and he rests a pair of meaty forearms on the table. A pair of dark eyes examine us from underneath thick eyebrows that almost meet in the middle. The lower half of his face is dominated by a large jaw and heavy jowls that are darkened with stubble. Taken together his features lend him the appearance of a big old bulldog, perhaps fallen on hard times. His fatigues say his name is Truckle, but Boots introduces him as Truck. His bottom lip bumps out and he pokes at something there with his tongue for a second. Then he spits a long stream of something brown into a cut-off plastic soda bottle at his elbow, offering us a yellow gap-toothed smile.

The soldier to his left who commented on my height is thin, wiry. He smiles as it's his turn to be introduced, but his eyes keep darting back to Truck, like he's less interested in us than in the larger man's reaction to our presence. The name patch on his breast reads Wiesmann but Boots calls him Weasel. The smile flickers a little at that, like it's not a name he cares much for. I have to admit it's pretty apt though. The sharp, inquisitive eyes and overbite don't call to mind someone you'd leave in charge of the henhouse.

The third man's name is Rudd. He looks older than the others seated around him. What little hair he has left is gray, and cut to a brisk military stubble. Deep horizontal lines have grooved themselves across his forehead; more bracket his mouth, which seems naturally inclined to pull down at the corners. He seems dour, stern; hard-eyed and humorless. He looks up briefly at the mention of his name, his puffy eyes narrowing to slits, and then returns to the more serious business of digging a plastic fork into his plate of beans. His fatigues are frayed and patched, and like the other soldiers they seem to hang on him, like they once belonged to a bigger man. But at least they seem like they've been washed recently.

With the introductions over Boots heads back to the sideboard to check on our food. The heavyset man he introduced as Truck reaches into his breast pocket and extracts a small metal tin with the words *Grizzly Wide Cut* stamped across the lid, a picture of a bear above. He raps it on the table a couple of times and then pops the lid and works three fingers deep into the tobacco, pulling out a thick wad. As he holds it up to his nose I notice a small, grubby bandage taped to the inside of his arm, in the same spot Boots was picking at last night. He inhales deeply, then places the tobacco between bottom lip and gum. He works his lip in and out a few times to get the juices flowing, smacking them together in satisfaction. When he's done he replaces the lid on the tin and leans backs in his chair.

'So Huckleberry, where y'all from?'

The accent's southern, but not polished or polite like Kane's was. Maybe it's the tobacco he's just placed in his mouth, but he slurs over his consonants, omitting some altogether, instead choosing to linger lazily on the vowels. The nickname I seem to have acquired comes out *Huck-a-beh-ree*.

I tell him we're from a place called Eden. His eyebrows knit together as if he's thinking hard about where that might be. It looks like he might be building up to ask some more questions, so I decide to head him off with one of my own first. Boots has just set a plate with an anemic looking frank-furter and a spoonful of watery beans in front of me. I pick up a plastic fork and point at it.

'So, is this all you have left?'

Truck's face hardens and he spits another stream of brown tobacco juice into the container at his elbow.

'Franks and beans not good enough for you, boy? Some might say you're lucky we're sharing with you at all.'

I open my mouth to explain that I didn't mean to cause offense; I was just asking a question. The food actually smells okay; I've certainly had worse. But Mags beats me to it. She pushes her plate out in front of her, the contents untouched. I see what's coming and put my fork down with a sigh.

'You needn't worry. We have our own food; we won't need to trouble you for any of yours.'

Boots pipes up behind me.

'It's true Truck. They've got a bunch of army rations on them. All sorts of flavors.'

'Is that so?' Truck's gaze shift from Boots back to Mags. 'And just where are y'all headed, miss?'

'South.'

'South, is it?'

'Yes. We'll be moving on soon.'

The soldier Boots introduced as Weasel turns to the big man I've just managed to rile with my unfortunate question.

'Just like all the others, right Truck?'

'Right, Weez, just like all the others.'

But he stares at me as he says it, his tongue still working the tobacco he's got tucked behind his lip. Beside him the older man whose fatigues say his name is Rudd looks up long enough to cut me some stink-eye and then goes back to rounding up stray beans with his fork. The atmosphere around the table's definitely turned a little frosty after my attempt to divert Truck from questions about Eden. I'm trying to figure out how to get us back on track when from somewhere else in the building there's a sound like a lawnmower being started. It catches, revs for a couple of seconds then settles into a languid idle. Around the room emergency lights flicker to life. I see Mags looking up as well. The chandeliers' dusty crystals reflect the soft glow, but that's not what's caught my attention, and now I realize what was bugging me about the camera above the entrance, when we came in. We're above ground, and this place can't have been shielded. I look across the table.

'How do you still have lights?'

Truck's busy getting the wad of tobacco situated and for a while the question goes unanswered. I wait while he pokes at it with his tongue, until it finally looks like he's got it in a good place.

'Lights is it, Huckleberry?'

I nod.

'Well, that was the Doc. Dare say you'll meet her later.'

He looks at me and smiles, but somehow it's not an expression that makes me feel like he's warming to me again.

'Yep, the Doc she's a smart lady, alright. Right after we got here she had us go room to room and strip the bulbs, along with anything else she thought we might need that would have been affected by the burst. Afterwards we had to replace fuses, some of the wiring, but once we got it all hooked up again most things came back. 'Course we only run the genny on the emergency circuit now, to save fuel.'

There's something troubling me about his answer, but before I can get on to that I hear Mags ask another question.

'You said we were headed south like the others. You've had survivors come through here before?'

Rudd shoots a sour glance in her direction, but then just goes back to spearing the last of the beans on his plate. Truck eyes him for a moment and then looks down the table at her.

'Oh, sure. Whole bunch of 'em. When we first got here Doc had us hike out to the interstate, put signs up, the whole works. For a while that brought us a steady stream. Nothing for a long time now, though. Until you, that is.'

He looks back at me as he says this, and it seems like the twinkle's returned to his dark eyes. A half-smile bends his lips and he pokes the wad of tobacco around some more with his tongue.

'What happened to them?'

Rudd looks up from his plate again and this time he looks like he might be about to say something. But just as he opens his mouth Truck spits a thick wad of tobacco into the container at his elbow. The plastic bottle tips over and dark juice splashes the sleeve of the older man's fatigues. He stands up as though he's just been scalded.

'Dammit Truck.'

'Aw, sorry, Pops. And all over your good Class A's as well. Guess you'll need to tend to that. Lickety-split now. Could be an inspection any minute.'

Rudd pushes back his chair and makes for the door, rubbing his sleeve and muttering under his breath. Truck's gaze follows him across the room. It stays there until the door's closed behind him. Then he looks back at me and winks.

'That old coot's been in the service since Jesus was a corporal and he's still wound tighter than a duck's asshole.'

The smile's still playing across Truck's lips but it's gone again from his eyes.

'And what happened to the survivors?'

'Oh, they just moved on. I guess they never took to the place.'

Boots has been staring at Mags, but as Truck says this he finds something interesting to study on the table. Weasel just grins. I'm about to ask Truck if he knows where they went when behind me the door opens. I look over my shoulder and Hicks is standing there.

He says Doctor Gilbey will see us now.

CHAPTER THIRTEEN

WE GET up from the table. I can see Jax already eyeing the franks and beans we're leaving behind. I'm halfway to the door when from behind me I hear Truck's lazy drawl.

'Be seein' ya, Huckleberry.'

I turn around and he winks at me. Next to him Weasel's still grinning. Boots is picking at the spot on his arm he was working over last night, like he's making a point of not looking up.

Hicks heads back towards the entrance. Outside night has fallen and the temperature's dropping; I can see our breath as we follow him down the hallway. But if the cold's bothering him he isn't showing it. He's wearing his glove liners but he's shed his parka and without its bulk he looks painfully thin. I guess Dr. Gilbey's 'no firearms' policy doesn't apply to the sergeant, either; his gun belt's still strapped around his waist, the old silver pistol slung low on his hip.

When we get to the lobby the bellhop cart has returned, but our boots are nowhere in sight. Hicks leads us past a bank of elevators and down a long, dark corridor. Most of the emergency lights are out here and those few that remain flicker and buzz, like the bulbs inside are close to failing. We pass a succession of double doors. Some are closed, but others hang ajar. I look in as we walk by. The banquet halls and ballrooms behind sit in darkness, the furniture under the drop cloths so many gray shapes in the gloom.

Ahead of us a thick red rope hangs from a pair of brass stanchions, blocking the way. Hicks stops before we get to it and turns to a door on the right. A varnished wooden sign above reads *The Colonial Lounge*. He knocks once and from somewhere inside I hear a muffled 'Come'. He opens the door and we step into a large semicircular room. Tall, arched windows stare back at us from between heavy silk drapes, the night-darkened glass reflecting the quivering light from the handful of emergency lamps that remain on. Large pink flowers with bright green leaves adorn the walls and as I look up I see another chandelier hanging from a high, domed ceiling. Beneath its dusty crystals more items of furniture, scattered across the checkerboard marble just like in the lobby. Most hide themselves under gray dustsheets, but the shapes are easy to make out. Chairs, sofas, occasional tables, lamps; in the corner what looks like a piano. In the middle of the room three high-backed chairs have been arranged around a low table.

I look around, confused; I thought I heard somebody telling Hicks to come in, but there doesn't seem to be anyone here. I walk over to one of the windows. The snow's drifted up, obscuring the panes near the bottom, but higher up it's only found purchase in the corners. I cup my hand to the glass and peer out. Tables and chairs have arranged themselves haphazardly around something that might once have been a fountain; large plant pots sit empty under a blanket of gray snow. It all seems cheerless and vacant now, but I can imagine how it must once have been to stand here and look out onto that terrace, with sunlight streaming in through the windows.

'It has lost some of its former glory, hasn't it?'

I turn around to face the voice behind me. A slender woman sits in one of the chairs, her back to the door we just came through. Her head doesn't come close to clearing the top of the chair, but that's not why I've missed her. The white lab coat she's wearing has been washed so often it's hard to distinguish from the dustsheet that covers the chair she's sitting in. Above it her skin is wan, pale, and the hair that frames her narrow face is the color of ash. Even the eyes that regard me over the top of her narrow, metal-rimmed glasses are gray. It's like she's an almost perfect absence of color.

'Dorothy Draper, wasn't she just a genius?'

She speaks in clipped, precise tones, each syllable enunciated perfectly. The accent is foreign, but immediately familiar. It's the same one Mom was going for when she'd read to me from the book about the English rabbits.

The expression on my face must tell her I have no idea who Dorothy Draper is however. She smiles, a barely perceptible lift of her thin lips, and raises one hand from the arm of the chair to gesture around the room.

'Romance and Rhododendrons. It was her theme for The Greenbrier.'

This doesn't get me much further; I've no idea what a rhododendron is either. I look over at Mags for help. She shrugs and says 'The big pink flowers on the wall, Gabe.'

The woman looks over at Mags, as if noticing her for the first time.

'Yes dear, very clever. A big flower. The state flower of West Virginia in fact. So delightfully pretty.' She sits forward in her chair, as if sharing a secret. 'They'd burn it all if I let them, you know. Wouldn't you Sergeant?'

Hicks' voice drifts out from somewhere in the shadows behind her.

'Yes ma'am, I believe I would.'

'Every stick of furniture, each beautiful painting, traded for an instant of light, a few moments' warmth. The world is so full of old and broken things now. I just can't bear to let a treasure like this place go.'

Outside the wind gusts, rattling the windows behind me in their frames. It's cold in here, and even though I like that there are colors, some of the furniture actually looks kinda ugly, so maybe I'm inclined to side with Hicks on this one. After my unfortunate comment in the dining room I figure that's an opinion best kept to myself however.

'Please, do have a seat.' She points to the chairs opposite. On the table in front of her a porcelain teapot and three matching teacups wait on a tray. The rims of the saucers are trimmed with gold and what looks like the same pink flower adorns the teapot and each of the cups.

'My name is Doctor Myra Gilbey.' As she lifts the teapot and starts to pour the light catches something silver circling her neck. But the pendant that hangs from the delicate chain that shows itself just above her lab coat spells out the word Amanda, not Myra. 'And you must be Gabriel and Magdalene.'

I catch Mags rolling her eyes at that, but she doesn't say anything. Dr. Gilbey's busy serving us tea so I don't think she notices. I take a seat while Mags looks around the room one more time.

She passes me one of the cups. It shifts in the saucer as I take it and for a moment I'm afraid I'll drop it. I'm not used to drinking out of anything so delicate.

'I'm afraid I can't offer you milk or sugar. Sergeant Hicks does what he can, but unfortunately there are limits to even his considerable talents. We must accept our lot and live as barbarians.' She looks at me and smiles again, but this effort's not much more convincing than the last. It's an expression that just doesn't come naturally to her, like she's had to teach herself to do it, and maybe somewhere along the way she's lost enthusiasm for the practicing.

Mags finally sits down. Dr. Gilbey holds up one of the cups, but she just shakes her head.

'We thought this place was a bunker. But it's just a big hotel.'

Dr. Gilbey finishes pouring her own tea while she answers.

'Oh, The Greenbrier has its secrets, my dear, she just hasn't revealed them to you yet. This is indeed a hotel, once perhaps America's finest. But for thirty years this is also where your politicians would have come in the event of a nuclear war.' She sets the pot down. 'That was the genius of it, you see. Everything hidden right where you could see it, all in plain sight. The entire wing you're in now actually sits on top of a huge bunker. It was decommissioned decades ago of course, and then for a quarter of a century it simply sat idle. It was only re-activated when it became clear that places like this would soon once again be needed. I'm not sure any of your leaders ever made it here, however. There was only one poor soul waiting for us when we arrived.' She looks up. 'I believe you've met Private Kavanagh.'

There's a noise from behind her as Hicks opens the door to let himself out. Dr. Gilbey leans forward in her chair.

'Excuse me for a moment, will you?' She turns her head, even though she's not tall enough to see over the back of the chair. 'Sergeant Hicks?'

There's a pause and Hicks steps out of the shadows.

'Yes, ma'am.'

'Could you wait outside? I'll need to speak with you when I'm done here.'

'Ma'am.'

The door closes behind him. Dr. Gilbey raises the cup to her lips, takes a sip and returns it to its saucer. She looks at me again but for a long moment she says nothing and for some reason I feel uncomfortable, like I'm being sized up, examined. It's Mags who breaks the silence.

'You're not American?'

Dr. Gilbey turns her head to answer and I'm released from her gaze.

'Oh good Lord, no.'

'But Hicks obeys your orders.'

'Yes.'

'So how's that?'

Dr. Gilbey gives Mags a look like she's not used to being the one who answers questions.

'Well, my dear, as it turns out I hold the rank of colonel in what remains of your armed forces. Does that surprise you?'

I'm not sure Dr. Gilbey's expecting an answer to that. Mags takes a moment to consider what she's just heard and then says 'Yeah, sort of.'

'And why might that be, dear? Is it my diminutive size? Or the lack of uniform? Or because I'm British?'

Mags just looks back at her and shrugs inside her parka. *Take your pick.*

I sense this conversation might soon be headed the way of the franks-and-beans misunderstanding with Truck earlier. I put on my sweetest smile and try to steer us back to safer waters.

'That sounds like an interesting story Dr. Gilbey, you becoming a colonel I mean. How exactly did it come about?'

Dr. Gilbey looks at Mags a second longer, then turns her attention back to me.

'Well Gabriel that's kind of you to say, but it was all rather mundane, actually. I was a virologist. A rather good one, if I do say so myself.' She smiles again. I kind of wish she'd stop; she's not getting any better at it. 'I used to carry out research for your government, at a place called Fort Detrick. I don't suppose you've heard of it?'

I have, as it turns out, but I reckon owning up to that might give Dr. Gilbey a clue as to where we've come from so I just shake my head. Fort Detrick's one of the places marked on the map Marv gave me. It's right off the Catoctin Mountain Highway, the route we took when he brought me to Mount Weather. But there's no code written next to it so I figured it wasn't a bunker. It always puzzled me why he'd gone to the trouble of circling it, though.

'Well, no matter. When it became clear how serious the situation was becoming the powers that be moved me to Atlanta, to the Centers for Disease Control, and put me in charge of the efforts to find a cure. Shortly afterwards that facility was brought under the control of the military and they made me a colonel. I'm not sure it was entirely legal, but then when you're the President I suppose you can pretty much do as you please.'

I exchange a look with Mags.

'So you took your orders from President Kane?'

The tea cup's on its way to Dr. Gilbey's lips but at the mention of Kane's name it stops, and a look of cold, glassy anger crosses her face. In spite of her size I feel a shiver run through me that has little to do with the cold.

'I did, once. If he were still alive I doubt there's an order that man could give that I might follow now. I only hope he met the end he deserved.'

CHAPTER FOURTEEN

DR. GILBEY RETURNS the cup to its saucer and places it on the table beside her. When she looks up again the anger has gone.

'Well, enough about me. So where have you two come from?'

I'm glad now that Mags made us get our story straight before we arrived. I tell her we're from Eden.

'Eden? I'm not sure I'm familiar with it.' She looks at me, and again I get the feeling that I'm being assessed, evaluated. 'Well, wherever it is it looks like they were feeding you there. Whatever made you want to leave?'

'We didn't care for the way the place was being run.'

Dr. Gilbey looks over at Mags as she says this and then simply says *I see*, although I don't know how she can.

'And who's in charge there?'

I glance over at Mags again. I wasn't going to mention Kane, but Dr. Gilbey's reaction to his name earlier seemed genuine. I guess Mags must think the same because she nods.

'President Kane is the person in charge of Eden.'

Dr. Gilbey's eyes widen and she stares at us for a long moment. The wind suddenly picks up, howling around the terrace outside. Then just as quick it dies down and the shrouded silence of the Colonial Lounge settles around us again, the only sound the occasional flicker and buzz of the emergency lights. Dr. Gilbey seems to regain her composure. She reaches for the teapot and starts to pour herself another cup of tea. But as she does so I can see the hand that lifts the pot is shaking.

'So Kane is still alive. You must tell me everything.'

I start at the beginning, explaining how we came to be at the White House on the Last Day, and how we fled in helicopters with Kane when the bombs started to fall. I notice her leaning forward in her seat at the mention of Miss Kimble and our class of first graders, but mostly she just listens while I tell her about Eden and our time there, every now and then raising the cup from its saucer to take a sip. I finish by recounting Kane's plans for us. I confine the details of our escape to just Mags and me, so she won't wonder where the rest of the Juvies might be hiding out. When I'm done she stares at me for a long moment.

'Why, what an adventure you've both had.' She pauses a moment. 'And you say there are more of you, in this place you call Eden? How many?'

'There were thirty of us in Miss Kimble's class. Kane exiled Lena and she died outside in the cold.'

'And you two managed to escape. How brave. But twenty-seven others remain. Twenty-seven children.' She shakes her head. 'Why how awful.'

Her interest seems genuine, but somehow the last sentence seems like an afterthought, as though something else is preoccupying her.

'And tell me dear, how did you know to come here?'

I explain how Marv told me about it. I don't mention that he gave me a map to other places like The Greenbrier, and Benjamin's codes to get us into each of them.

'I see. And this Marvin, did he tell anyone else about The Greenbrier? Is there any chance others will know to come here too?'

I shake my head. 'Marv's dead. He only told me about it.'

'What a pity.' She takes another sip from her tea. 'And what do you plan to do now?'

I hesitate. The truth is I don't know. I can't see there's much for us here; the soldiers barely seem to have enough supplies for themselves. But we need to do something about Peck; if we just return to Mount Weather we'll be no better off than when we left. An idea's coming to me, but I'll need to discuss it with Mags first. She seems to have already made up her mind, however.

'We'll be moving on. It seems like you've already got enough mouths to feed here.'

Dr. Gilbey glances over as she says this, and for an instant I think the eyes behind the thin metal glasses narrow, but it's so brief that later I convince myself I've imagined it. When she looks back at me she's doing her version of smiling again.

'Well you must do as you see fit, of course. Surely there's no need to rush to a decision, though. Supplies are certainly tight, but it's been years since we've had visitors; it would be a shame to see you leave so soon.' She raises the cup to her lips again. 'And tell me, where will you go?'

'I guess we'll keep heading south, see if we can find any other places like this, where there might be more survivors.'

She pauses, as if considering something, and then turns to me.

'Gabriel, maybe you could speak with the Sergeant. I believe he's scouted most of the area around here. You might be able to ask him what he's found.'

'Do you know if he ever made it to a place called Fear-rington?'

Fearrington's the next facility marked on Marv's map. It's all the way down in North Carolina, more than two hundred and fifty miles from where we are now. We don't have supplies to make it there and back on this trip, but if I can find out something about it maybe our visit to The Green-brier won't have been wasted.

'Is that one of the places your friend Marvin told you about?'

I nod. She pauses, as if she's considering it.

'I'm not sure. It certainly rings a bell, but then the Sergeant has been to a lot of places. I'm sure if he can help you he will.' She brings her hands together, like she's reached a decision. 'Well, it's getting late and you've had a long jour-ney. You must both be simply exhausted. Rooms have been prepared for you in the hotel.'

'You don't all live in the bunker?'

Dr. Gilbey looks over at Mags again.

'No, dear, the bunker is strictly off limits; I need it for my work. Besides, the rooms up here are so much nicer than the dormitories down there.'

'Hicks said you were working on a cure for the virus.'

'Yes, dear, I have been since before we arrived here. But I really think that's enough questions for now. Magdalene, you'll be sleeping over by the North Entrance. And Gabriel, we've got a room for you with the other men near the front of the house.'

My disappointment at these arrangements must show. Dr. Gilbey looks at me over the top of her glasses.

'Now, Gabriel, whatever relationship you and Magdalene might be having I'd suggest you take care not to flaunt it while you're here. The men haven't seen a woman other than me in a very long time. I will speak to them of course, but I think it's wise that we put Magdalene in a part of the hotel that is uninhabited. I hope it's an unnecessary precaution, but...'

She spreads her hands, leaving the sentence unfinished. Maybe she has a point. I've sort of gotten used to Jax's staring, but I remember how Boots had looked at us as we climbed the steps to the balcony in the church in Covington.

She turns her head again and calls for Hicks. A second later the door opens and he steps in.

'Ah, yes, Sergeant, would you be so good as to show Gabriel and Magdalene to their rooms? And have Corporal Truckle assemble the men.'

CHAPTER FIFTEEN

WE FOLLOW Hicks down the corridor back towards the entrance. It's colder now than it was earlier, but he still isn't feeling the need for a parka. When we get to the lobby he tells us to wait. Outside the wind occasionally gusts against the doors and from somewhere below us I can hear the drone of the generator, but otherwise The Greenbrier's quiet. Mags hugs her arms to her side and stomps her feet on the marble. I take a step closer, meaning to wrap my arms around her, but then stop myself. Hicks will be back in a minute and I'm mindful now of what Dr. Gilbey said about how we should act around the soldiers.

Hicks returns a few minutes later carrying a flashlight and we set off across the checkerboard marble, this time in the opposite direction to the dining room Boots brought us to earlier. We climb a wide staircase, the thick carpet muffling the sound of our footsteps. None of the emergency lamps are on up here, but there's just enough light from the lobby below to make out a landing. Long hallways stretch off into darkness in both directions. Hicks chooses one and we follow him down it past rows of numbered doors. The inky blackness quickly wraps itself around us; we've barely gone a dozen paces and already I'm no longer able to see a thing. The flashlight was still in his hand coming up the stairs but it's like he's forgotten he has it, and the wind-up I normally carry's downstairs in my backpack. I feel Mags slip her hand into mine.

'How many rooms are there, Sergeant?'

There's a pause then Hicks' response comes back from somewhere in front of me.

'More than seven hundred, all told.'

There's no more to his answer, and we go back to walking in silence. I resist the urge to reach out with my free hand for the wall I know must be there. Instead I strain for the sound of his footfalls ahead.

We continue on for what seems like a long time. We're mostly heading in the same direction but occasionally we round a corner, or climb or descend a flight of stairs. Hicks must know where he's going but this place is like a labyrinth; it'd be easy to lose your way in the darkness. After the first turn I start to count our steps, just like I used to do in the tunnel in Eden.

At last I see something that might be the faintest sliver of light, and in front of me Hicks' outline once again separates itself from the darkness. As we get closer I can see it's coming from underneath a door. Hicks stops when he gets to it and reaches for the handle. We follow him into a large room. A fire burns in the fireplace and someone's pulled the dustsheets off the furniture. A large four-poster bed sits against one wall.

Hicks turns to face us.

'I expect you two'll have things to talk about.' He hands

me the flashlight. 'Your room's on the first floor above the lobby, at the top of the stairs. Reckon you can find your way back?'

I nod.

'Good. Don't be long now; I'll be listening for you.'

He turns to leave.

'Sergeant Hicks?'

He stops, one hand resting on the door handle.

'Dr. Gilbey said you had been south of here.'

I think I see his jaw shift from side to side, but he makes to move to turn around. The light from the fire catches the ridges on the puckered scar tissue that runs down one side of his neck.

'That's right.'

'She said you might be able to tell us whether there's anything there. You know, anywhere like this, where there might be other survivors.'

He turns around and squints back at me for a long moment. There's an expression on his face I can't read.

'She did, did she?'

I nod.

'It's getting late. You can ask me your questions in the morning.'

He leaves, closing the door behind him.

Mags looks over at me.

'Well that was helpful.'

She shucks off her parka and slides down to sit on the carpet, her back to the bed. I sit down next to her and slip my arm around her shoulders. She leans in to me and I feel a warm happiness that has little to do with the fire easing itself through my whole body. It's been a while since we've had to obey a curfew and I don't care much for it. But I'm grateful to Hicks for giving us some time alone.

We stay like that for a while, just staring at the flames. It's actually a pretty good fire. The soldiers must be cutting timber; the logs are big, and they've had time to dry. They crack and spit in the flames, sending flurries of red sparks swirling up into the chimney. Eventually Mags speaks.

'What did you think of Doctor Gilbey?'

'She certainly doesn't seem to care much for Kane.'

'Yeah, but didn't she seem creepy to you?'

I shrug. Dr. Gilbey was a little odd, but then the whole world's messed up. I'm not sure what even counts as normal anymore.

'She's been living in this place with a bunch of soldiers for ten years. It'd be strange if it hadn't affected her a little.'

Mags considers this for a while, but I don't get the impression she's buying it.

'I'm not sure this place is any better than Mount Weather, Gabe.'

'Yeah, I think you might be right. But we're not safe there; it's way too close to Eden.' The idea that was coming to me downstairs resurfaces. 'Maybe we could do a deal with Dr. Gilbey; have her send some of the soldiers back with us to Mount Weather to scare Peck off. They seem to be running low on supplies and we have plenty to share.'

Her brow creases, like this isn't something she'd be happy with.

'I'm not sure. What about that guy Truck? He just seems like an asshole.'

'Truck's probably okay. I just got off on the wrong foot with him with that comment I made about their food. Anyway, it wouldn't have to be him. One or two of the others would be enough. I mean, look at the size of Jax. And I bet Hicks is pretty handy with that gun.'

She doesn't say anything. I know she's not convinced, but I don't want to return to Mount Weather with nothing, and Fearrington's simply too far for us to check out on this trip. I've been running through our provisions in my head and we can't stretch the supplies we have left for a hike of that distance, even if we ration them. That means we'd have to scavenge as we went. I might risk it if it was just me, but this is Mags' first time out and I don't mean to bring her anywhere without food enough to get us home.

For a long while neither of us speak. There's a sound from the fire as one of the logs shifts in the grate. Outside the wind picks up; it gusts against the window, rattling the glass in its frame. She shivers against me and I pull her tighter.

'I guess you'd better get back to your room.'

But she makes no move to stand so instead I slip my hand under her chin and bend down to kiss her. Her parted lips meet mine and even though their taste is familiar to me now I experience that same moment of fascinating breathlessness I always get when they first touch. It's as though I'm suddenly aware of everything at once, the pressure of her lips and the taste of her mouth and the warmth from the fire on my cheek and its light through my closed eyelids and the breath we share as we pull away before it starts again.

She twists around and slides underneath me. Her fingers slide up into my hair and curl into it, drawing my face down to hers. I kiss her on her mouth, under her jaw, above her collarbone, lingering there for a few seconds. Her skin is soft and tastes of salt from the day's hike. I trace a line with my lips from the hollow of her throat to that spot on her neck that always makes her sigh.

I feel her hands tighten around my waist and suddenly something has changed. Her kisses are deeper, no longer gentle. After what happened with Lena we know to only go so far, but it's always Mags that has to stop us. But now it's like she wants me to go on and it's suddenly scary because I don't think I can be trusted. All I ever want is more.

I feel her hands twist into my thermals and pull them up. Cold air slips across my skin in spite of the fire but her fingers are warm. I shiver as they brush over my skin just above my belt and then slide around and up my sides. Her fingertips trace a line over my ribs; I feel them rising and falling with the bones there.

I breathe her name against the side of her neck, gently at first and then more urgently as I feel the last of what little self-control I began with evaporating. At last she stops and I bury my face in her neck and hold her tight, just breathing in her smell. I'm aware of every inch where our bodies are touching, the angle of her hips, the rise of her ribcage. Eventually she slides a hand up into my hair and tugs gently and I lift my head a fraction. Her eyelashes flutter against my cheek as she opens her eyes.

'You becoming immune to my charms Gabe?'

If only she knew. If you asked me what I know of hunger I would tell you, *All there is*. But not like this. There is no satisfaction here; each taste of her just leaves me wanting more.

Across the room the fire's slowly burning down, the flames that remain scattered among a nest of quaking embers.

'You'd better get going.'

'You going to be okay here by yourself?'

'Yeah, 'course. I'd prefer it if you were staying though.'

I bend my head down to kiss her, but this time before I get too far she tugs my hair again.

'Go on, get out of here. Hicks'll be waiting up for you.'

I stand and make my way to the door. I check for a lock on the way out but there's only one of those keycard readers, its circuits long since fried by what Kane did to the skies to stop the furies.

CHAPTER SIXTEEN

I MAKE my way back towards the lobby, following the cone of light cast by the flashlight as it meanders down the never-ending hallway ahead of me. Tell the truth I'm dragging my feet a little; all I really want to do right now is turn around and go back to Mags' room so we can pick up where we just left off. But Dr. Gilbey's in charge so I guess we have to do as she says while we're here. Whatever, it'll not be for long. Mags is right; there's nothing to keep us. Tomorrow morning I'll find out from Hicks what he knows about Fearrington, and then we can be gone.

I'm more than a little distracted replaying what just happened with Mags over in my head, so I'm not really paying attention. I don't realize there's someone standing a little further down the corridor, just out reach of the beam, until he speaks.

'Well how y'all doin' there Huckleberry?'

The voice makes me start. I jerk the flashlight up. It casts ugly shadows, distorting Truck's already lumpen features. I hear a tapping sound and when I look in that direction I see something flashing in his hand. It's the tin of chewing tobacco. He spins it then grabs the edge between his thumb and finger, rapping the lid once with his pinkie. *Spin. Tap. Spin. Tap.* For the first time I notice a small bird tattooed in the crook of his thumb. As he flips the tin the muscles there flex, making it seem like it's moving.

'Fine, Truck.'

The tin stops mid-spin.

'*Corporal* Truckle.'

Yeah, I guess Mags called it; Truck is just an asshole. I'm tired, and hungry, and pissed at not being able to stay with Mags and generally not in the mood for whatever back-of-the-school-bus entertainment he has in store for me.

'Sure. Well, good night Corporal Truckle.'

I take a step towards him but he makes no move to get out of my way. I'm close enough now to smell his breath. It reeks of frankfurter and chewing tobacco, and underneath it something else: the smoky, sweet smell of whisky.

He goes back to flipping the tin over in his fingers.

'Weez here said I was rude to you earlier, at dinner.'

At the mention of his name Weasel steps out of the darkness behind him and grins at me. Great. Somehow I doubt he's here to witness Truck deliver a heartfelt apology.

'Didn't offer you any of my dip.' He holds up the tin.

'Yeah, well, thanks, but I don't think I'd like it.'

'But you've never tried it. It's Wide Cut, see? Only the best.' His hand flips the tin again. *Spin. Tap. Spin. Tap.* 'You sure?'

'Positive, thanks.'

'Well then, suit yourself. Whaddya say, Weez? Do you think that girlfriend of his'll want some? Perhaps she'll be more friendly to us?'

I glance behind me in the direction I've come. There's no way Truck or Weasel would actually do anything, would they? But Dr. Gilbey was already worried about the effect Mags might have on the soldiers; that's why she's sleeping all the way out here by herself. In a room without a lock. And they've been drinking. I back up a step.

'Okay, maybe I will try some.'

Weasel looks disappointed, but Truck just flashes me that gap-toothed smile. He spins the tin one more time and then pops the lid and holds it out. The pungent aroma fills my nostrils. I reach over and tentatively stick my thumb and index finger into the tobacco. It's moist, spongy; I feel it slide up under my nails. I'm trying to extract the smallest amount I can when without warning Truck's other hand darts out and closes around my wrist.

'Grab yourself a decent pinch there, boy.'

I work a lump of the tobacco free and pull it out as quickly as I can. It smells pretty gross, but how bad can it be? I hesitate for a moment then place it in my mouth against my gum, like I saw him do earlier at dinner.

At first there's not much, just a little warmth on the inside of my lip. But then I feel the juices start to build, and it's like a faucet's been turned on in my mouth. I look around, but I have nowhere to spit. Saliva wells up over my lip and runs down my jaw. Loose bits of tobacco have started to break off. They float around my tongue; I can feel them start to slide down my throat.

Beads of sweat break out on my forehead and my stomach does a slow forward roll. My head feels light and my heart starts to race and suddenly I'm on my hands and knees, still clutching the flashlight, as what little's left of the MRE I had for lunch comes flying out of my mouth onto the carpet along with a dark brown wad of tobacco. I continue to retch long after my stomach's expelled the last trace of it. Above me Truck's still chuckling, but somewhere along the way Weasel's stopped. Now I hear him whisper:

'Whaddya say, Truck; shall we go pay the girl a visit?'

I feel something inside me harden, and my head empties of all thoughts but one. I spit the last of the tobacco and wipe my chin with the back of my hand. The corridor's narrow here; it's as good a place as any. I glance up. Weasel's still standing behind Truck, so he'll have to wait his turn. I slide my hand into the parka's side pocket, my fingers slipping around the metal they find there. The blade opens easily under my thumb; I feel it lock into place. It's already halfway out when from somewhere further along the corridor I hear a familiar drawl.

'What're you fellas doing over this side of the house?'

Truck turns around.

'Aw, now nuthin' for you to concern yourself with, Sarge. We was just funnin' with young Huckleberry here is all.'

'Time for you boys to be in bed I reckon.'

I hear a *Yes, Sarge* from Weasel as he turns and scurries down the hallway. Truck makes no move to follow him.

'You might want to think on now, Hicks. Those stripes on your shoulder don't mean what they used to.'

'Maybe not, but this pistol here stands for the same as it always did. Any time you'd like a closer look at it, Corporal, you be sure to say.'

Truck casts one last look in my direction, then he hitches up his pants and makes his way off into the darkness.

I fold the blade back into the leatherman and let it slip from my fingers. My hand reaches for the flashlight and I get to my feet. I'm not really paying attention to where the beam goes and it slides off the wall and catches Hicks standing in the middle of the corridor. He squints and raises one hand as if to deflect it.

'Get that damn thing out of my face.'

'Sorry.'

I point the flashlight back at the floor. The beam circles the mess of mostly-digested MRE and ground tobacco that's already starting to seep into the thick red pile. Hicks looks at it and then back up at me.

'You'll need to get that squared away before Doc sees it; she'll have a shit-fit if she finds you've puked on her carpet.' He glances behind him along the hallway, then looks back at me again. 'But first let's go check on that girl of yours.'

CHAPTER SEVENTEEN

MAGS IS STILL up when we get back to her room. Her brow creases as I tell her about Truck and Weasel. She looks over at Hicks.

'It was lucky you showed up when you did.'

He shrugs.

'Luck had little to do with it. I was watching to see what that pair would do. I doubt they'll be back, but all the same I'd rest easier if you slept in the bunker tonight.'

Mags looks over at me and I nod. Dr. Gilbey might be a little creepy, but she'll be safer down there with her than out here by herself. It only takes a moment to gather up her things. I sling her pack over my shoulder and we follow Hicks down the corridor.

When we get back to the Colonial Lounge Dr. Gilbey's gone. The rope hanging from the brass stanchions blocks our way, but Hicks just steps over it and continues on. A little further along the corridor ends in a wide staircase. A sign says *The Exhibition Hall* with an arrow pointing straight on. We make our way down a long flight of steps. At the bottom a short passageway opens abruptly into a huge room, bigger than the dining hall we were in earlier. Garish wallpaper covers the windowless walls for most of their considerable height, but otherwise everything's plain, without any ornamentation other than the flickering emergency lights.

Hicks crosses the floor. He stops on the other side under a bulkhead lamp and feels along the wall with his fingertips. When he finds what he's looking for he pushes and a panel pops out. Dr. Gilbey said The Greenbrier had its secrets, and now I see what she meant. The busy pattern does a good job of hiding the seam; you'd need to be right up against it to see it.

He slides his fingers behind and pulls, and a whole section of fake wall concertinas out, revealing a deep alcove behind. Set back in the shadows there's a steel vault door. It's no taller than a regular door, and maybe only half again as wide. A large latch handle sits in the center. Above it the words 'Mosler Safe Co.' have been impressed on the metal.

There's a small intercom mounted flush to the wall on one side. Hicks pushes the button. There's a burst of static and then Dr. Gilbey's voice, rendered tinny by the small speaker, drifts out.

'Yes, Sergeant?'

'There's been an incident, ma'am. I need you to open up.'

There's a long pause and then from somewhere inside the buzz of an electric motor and the sound of bolts being recessed. Hicks grabs the handle and pushes it down. There's a heavy clunk and he pulls the door out towards us.

The doorway's not that wide, but behind it I can see a long, low-ceilinged corridor. A single fluorescent tube halfway along its length flickers, casting just enough light to see to the end. From this point all pretense of luxury or grandeur has been dropped, and in its place familiar concrete and steel.

A door at the end of the corridor creaks open and Dr. Gilbey steps through.

'What's the reason for this disturbance, Sergeant?'

'Just a little trouble with the men, ma'am. Nothing for you to concern yourself with. All the same I reckon it'd be safer if the girl spent the night in the bunker.'

Dr. Gilbey looks at Mags and simply says, *I see.*

'Can I stay with her?'

She switches her gaze to me.

'Is the boy in any danger, Sergeant?'

'I don't believe so ma'am. It was the girl they were interested in.'

She looks at me for a long moment and I get the feeling I had earlier, in the Colonial Lounge, like I'm being sized up, examined.

'I'm afraid not, Gabriel. As I explained earlier the bunker is strictly off limits; one of you down here will be quite enough.' She turns to Mags. 'Now Magdalene, you'll need to confine yourself to one of the dormitories. No exploring. Is that clear?'

Mags nods.

'Alright. Well, come along then.'

I hand Mags her backpack. She takes it from me and leans in to kiss my cheek.

'Take care, okay?'

'I'll be fine. Sergeant Hicks is right next door.'

I watch as she follows Dr. Gilbey down the cheerless corridor. She pauses for a moment at the end and gives me one more backward glance. Then she steps through into shadow and is gone.

CHAPTER EIGHTEEN

IT'S STILL EARLY when I wake the following morning. I climb out of bed, rubbing the sleep from my eyes. Mags was right; there's nothing for us here, and after what happened with Truck and Weasel last night I don't care to linger. I'll find out from Hicks what he knows about Fearrington and then we can be on our way.

His room's next to mine but there's no answer when I knock, so I make my way down to the lobby. There's no one there either. The bellhop cart's returned, but our boots are nowhere in sight. I head for the dining hall but the only person there is Jax, just sitting by himself at the table. He looks up as I enter but doesn't say anything, just stares back at me with these flat blue eyes and then goes back to shoving frankfurters into his bushy Viking beard. I return to the lobby and take the long corridor down to the Colonial Lounge. The door's open. Outside the first of the day's light's already settling over the terrace, but it doesn't look any more appealing than it did in darkness. Beyond the frozen fountain there's a low, crumbling wall and then the ground slopes upwards into hillside. Blackened trees poke through the gray snow. The ones nearest the house have been felled, but it looks too neat to be the work of storms. I guess that's where the soldiers must be collecting their firewood.

There's still no sign of Hicks, but Mags will be up by now; I might as well go get her. I step over the rope and head for the stairs to the Exhibition Hall. The emergency lights are off; it grows darker as I descend. I'm halfway across the floor when I hear the voice.

'Lookin' for something Huckleberry? Some more dip maybe?'

I start; I hadn't realized there was anyone down here. As my eyes adjust to the gloom I see Truck, sitting at a table in the far corner. He holds up the tin of Grizzly and smiles.

I glance behind me, half expecting to see Weasel, but the stairs are clear. I turn back to face him.

'I want to go into the bunker.'

'The bunker is it?'

He pokes the wad of tobacco behind his lip with his tongue and squirts a stream of tobacco juice into a cut-off plastic soda bottle on the table.

'Yeah, the bunker.'

'Well, Huckleberry, if that's what y'all are after look no further. You're already in it.'

I'm beginning to think Truck might have been left on the Tilt-A-Whirl too long as a baby. But then I remember what Dr. Gilbey told us about The Greenbrier, how everything here was hidden in plain sight. The Exhibition Hall has no windows. And you have to come down a long flight of stairs to get to it. I look back at the entrance. The wallpaper distracts your attention from it, but you can see how thick the walls are.

'That's right, Huckleberry; maybe you ain't as dumb as you look after all.'

He stands and hitches up his pants.

'Can't let you in, though. Doc's a regular night owl; she won't be up for hours yet. And she don't like being disturbed.'

It's clear I'm not going to get anywhere with Truck so I leave the Exhibition Hall and continue my search for Hicks. I find him in the lobby, kneeling on the marble floor in front of the gold-faced clock, fastening the snaps on his backpack. He looks up when he sees me. The shadow of the portico darkens The Greenbrier's entrance but he's already wearing those funny sunglasses with the leather side-blinkers.

'Sergeant Hicks, can I talk to you?'

'Now's not a good time, Gabriel. Got some things to pick up for the Doc. Maybe when I get back.'

I look over towards the entrance. I need to find out what he knows, but I wasn't planning on hanging around; I was hoping for us to be gone as soon as Mags gets out of the bunker. He finishes with his pack and looks up.

'You can join ne if you want. I'll answer your questions on the way.'

'Where are you going?'

'Just to Lynch.'

'Is it far?'

He shakes his head.

'Next town over.'

I look back in the direction of the Exhibition Hall.

'The girl will be fine, if that's what you're worried about. I'll leave word you've come with me.'

I've nothing to do until Dr. Gilbey opens the bunker, so I guess I might as well use the time to find out all I can about

Fearrington. I run up to my room and grab my backpack. I take the stairs back down two at a time, smearing UV block across my face as I go. When I get back to the lobby my boots are on the bellhop cart. Hicks is already making his way outside.

Our snowshoes are where we left them when we came in yesterday evening; the Greenbrier's massive columns tower over us as we snap them on. The day's already as bright as it means to get, but it's little more than a grudging half-light that spreads itself over the ashen landscape beyond. Hicks takes some time fussing with his sunglasses, making sure the blinkers sit flush. When he's done he adjusts his bandana and draws the hood up over his head; his face disappears into the shadow of the cowl.

We make our way past the helicopter. There hasn't been a fresh fall, but the temperature must have dropped overnight because the snow's covered with a skin of ice. Our snowshoes crunch through it, sinking deep into the soft powder underneath. Hicks sets a quicker pace than I was expecting and soon I'm sweating inside my parka. In snow like this Marv and I would have taken it in turns to break trail, but Hicks seems happy enough on point and if he means to keep this up I don't plan to argue with him over it. There's not much scope for conversation, but I figure that's okay; there'll be time later on to ask him what I need.

At the gates we turn right. We've not gone more than a couple of hundred yards when the road curves around and a large gray structure rises up on our left, a bell tower marking it out as a church. The long roof's swaybacked with the weight of snow and in places it's been breached, what remains of the rafters poking through around the edges. A large, arched doorway stares vacantly back at us as we pass;

THE DEVIL YOU KNOW 99

one of the doors there is gone and the other hangs inward on its last hinge. A weather-rotten sign says *St. Charles Borromeo* and lists times for service underneath.

We follow the road as it winds its way westward through the mountains. After a mile we pick up water. It's little more than a stream, for the most part frozen solid and covered over by snow. It meanders beside us, switching back and forth as we trudge on. We cross it three times, but on each occasion the bridge has held. Shortly after the road dips under the interstate but Hicks shows no sign of switching trails and we continue on.

I'm beginning to wonder just how far Lynch is when we hit water for the fourth time. The road inclines gently up to the bank, but even from a distance it's clear this is no stream; beyond a narrow rim of shelving ice a wide, gray river flows sluggishly south, the dark waters thick and oily with the cold. As we get closer I can see that the bridge is out; it's collapsed into the water no more than a quarter of the way into its span on either side. Hicks doesn't alter course. He marches right up to where the concrete ends, slides off his backpack and bends down to unsnap his snowshoes. As soon as he's tethered them to his pack he shoulders it again and disappears over. I inch forward and look down. There's a fifty-foot drop to the river and I get that weird sensation in the pit of my stomach, like when I'd go up on the roof in Eden with Mags and she'd perch herself right on the edge. Beneath me Hicks is making short work of the climb; he's already most of the way down.

I step out of my snowshoes, tie them to my pack and follow him, wishing I'd paid more attention to the route he was taking. Once I start I realize it's actually not that bad, however. A rust-pitted guardrail follows what once must have been the road almost the whole way to the water, and for the most part it seems to have held. The twisted metal jutting here and there from the concrete offers a choice of hand- and toeholds.

Hicks is waiting for me at the bottom. From down here the river looks even wider than it did up on the bridge. A small wooden skiff bobs lazily in the water, moored to a section of rebar that protrudes from the rubble just above the waterline. He rolls back an old tarpaulin that's covering it and stands to one side so I can get in. It pitches alarmingly as I throw my leg over the side. I quickly find a spot and sit down, gripping the sides tight with my mittens. He casts us off and jumps in after me. As soon as he's got himself settled he lifts a pair of oars and dips them into the gray water. The wind's picked up a little since we set off and the waves lap steadily against the shallow sides. By the time we reach the middle I've got my breath back, but Hicks looks like he's having to fight the current and I figure this isn't the time to start asking questions, so I just sit there, holding the sides, watching as he works the oars. Before long what remains of the bridge on the other side looms over us. I feel the prow crunch into ice and a second later nudge bottom. I climb out and wait while he ties the mooring line off to another piece of rebar.

I'm thinking he might want to rest for a few minutes but he doesn't. I follow him up the other side and we continue on.

CHAPTER NINETEEN

HICKS' pace doesn't slacken after the river but even so it's already well past noon by the time we hike into Lynch. There's not much to it, jus a little one-stoplight town, the shop windows we pass darkened, broken, those that remain silted with a decade of grime. He finally stops in front of a small wooden building with a sign outside that reads *The Livery Tavern*. He says we'll be spending the night here.

I guess I don't look too happy about that.

'Took us longer than I expected to get here.' He says it like if it wasn't for me he might have been here sooner, although I don't see how that's possible; we got here pretty quick, given how far it is. He holds up a hand. 'Don't worry about the girl; she'll be safe enough in the bunker with the Doc till we get back.'

He digs in his pocket and hands me a slip of paper with a dozen items written on it. He doesn't ask whether I can read, he just says to get what I can; he'll answer my questions when I return. He steps inside, leaving me alone on the street.

I look at the scrap of paper again. I hadn't planned on having to trade for the information I need but there's nothing difficult there, and the faster I get done the more time I'll have to ask him about Fearrington.

I adjust the straps on my pack and set off.

———

I get back to the Livery Tavern a few hours later.

I unsnap my snowshoes, kick the powder from my boots and make my way inside. The curtains are drawn and it takes a few seconds for my eyes to adjust to the gloom. Hicks is sitting at a long wooden table in the center of the room. He nods in my direction as I set the backpack down, but makes no move to get up. The thermos he had on the way back from Covington's open in front of him, but otherwise the table's bare.

My eyes shift to a large stone hearth in the corner, still banked with ash from the last time it was used. I'm tired but outside dusk's already settling; I should really get a fire going. I'm a little surprised Hicks hasn't bothered to light one; it's freezing in here. I guess he just doesn't feel the cold like a regular person. His parka's unzipped and as he reaches for the flask I can see he's taken his gloves off too; all he's wearing are his liners.

I shuck off my backpack and get to work. It doesn't take long; everything you might need is stacked neatly to one side. I guess the soldiers must scavenge here regularly enough to keep places like this provisioned.

My stomach's reminding me I haven't had breakfast or lunch so as soon the flames are licking up through the wood I dig in my backpack for a can of roast beef and gravy I found while I was out. I hold it up to Hicks but he just shakes his head and says he's already eaten. Even if I'd had a bellyful of cold franks there'd be no way I'd turn down a meal like this. But hey, his loss. I take the top off the can and pop it in the fire. The label chars as the flames lick up the sides and soon the gravy's bubbling away, filling the room with its thick, rich aroma. My mouth's already watering; I can barely wait. As soon as it's ready I fish it out with the leatherman's pliers and take it back to the table. I grab a plastic spoon from my pack and start slurping the pieces of meat straight from the can. Within seconds I've burned the roof of my mouth in at least two places.

Hicks picks up the thermos, lifts it to his lips and takes a sip. He grimaces like he doesn't like the taste much, then nods in the direction of my pack.

'Looks like you did good.'

I've just taken a spoonful of hot gravy so it takes me a moment to answer.

'Yep, got everything on your list.' And something that wasn't: a pint bottle of bourbon with the tamper ring still in place. I don't think it's the brand he was drinking the other night, but the Sergeant strikes me as more of a pragmatist than Quartermaster. I reckon it'll do to get him in the right frame of mind for the discussion I mean us to have.

'Who taught you how to find stuff?'

Between mouthfuls of roast beef I tell him about Marv and how we used to go out and get things for the others in Eden.

'Eden. You mentioned that when we picked you up yesterday. Where'd you say it was again? Somewhere north of here?'

I don't want to get on to the topic of where Eden might

be so I just nod and turn my attention back to the can. But he doesn't seem satisfied with that answer.

'Do you remember any of the names of the towns you and Marv used to scavenge? Trapp? Briggs? Linden?'

Those are all places near Mount Weather. I shake my head.

'I don't think so. I'm not sure. I don't read so well.' I catch him glancing over at my backpack, now full of items from the list he gave me, so I add: 'I mostly go by the word shapes.'

He squints across the table at me for a while, like he's trying to figure out where the truth in that statement might be. I go back to digging in the can. In the end he must decide it's not worth pushing me on it.

'So what happened to him, this Marv fella?'

'He died.'

'How'd that come about?'

'He caught the virus while we were out scavenging. He killed himself before he could do me any harm.'

'He get it from a fury?'

'No, Marv was too careful for that. It was President Kane. He put it in his respirator the last time we went out.'

If Hicks is surprised by this he doesn't show it. He just takes another sip from the thermos.

'Doc says you and the girl plan to move on.'

I shrug. Probably.

'That's a pity; we could use you. Where'll you go next?'

'South, I guess.'

'You don't have provisions enough to get very far.'

I tilt the almost empty can of roast beef in his direction.

'We'll get by.'

He takes another swig from the thermos and works his jaw from side to side as if to say *Maybe. Maybe Not.* I think he's about to say something else, but he doesn't. I reckon this is as good a time as any to start getting the information I need. I fish the bourbon from my pocket and slide it across the table. He looks at it for a long while, and I think I catch a look like the one Quartermaster used to get when I'd bring him back something like that. But in the end he just shakes his head.

'Thanks kid, but me and bourbon don't get on like we used to.'

Well, worth a try. For a few moments I go back to scraping bits of burned beef from the bottom of the can.

'I heard there was another bunker, just outside Pittsboro, in North Carolina. Some place called Fearrington. Dr. Gilbey said you might have been there.'

The thermos is halfway to his lips again, but it stops at the mention of Fearrington.

'How'd you come to know about that, anyway?'

I tell him Marv told me about it, which is close enough to the truth.

'Remarkably well informed fella, this Marv.'

The thermos continues its journey to his lips. He takes another sip, winces, then sets it down again.

'So, do you know anything about it?'

He nods.

'It was our first stop, after Atlanta.'

CHAPTER TWENTY

I SET the can of roast beef I've been working on aside.

I remember a scrap of newspaper I dug out of a fireplace, not long after I started going outside with Marv. It was little more than a headline and a date, a corner of grainy black and white photo and a couple of column inches that had somehow escaped the flames. I don't know why but I kept it anyway, put it with the other clippings I'd collected. I'd go through them, when I was in my room in the farmhouse, sitting out quarantine, trying to figure out how our world got to be the way it is. Mags brought them with us to Mount Weather, but they've sat in a shoebox under the bed all winter. I guess I've had other things on my mind, and besides, that mystery's been solved: it was Kane, all of it.

I'll never forget that charred headline though. It was about Atlanta.

It simply read Our Last Stand.

———

'Were you there?'

Hicks just nods but doesn't say anything further. I remind myself I came here to find out what he knows about Fearrington, but now we're here for the night I have time and I figure it'll be easy enough to bring us back to that topic when I need to.

'What was it like?'

He doesn't say anything, just reaches into his parka and pulls out a crumpled pack of Camels. He lights one and exhales a plume of smoke that disappears into the gloom.

'How old're you, kid?'

'Seventeen. Almost.'

'Close enough.' He pushes the bourbon across the table towards me. 'Don't care much for drinking by myself.' He raises the thermos.

I want him to keep talking so I pick up the bottle and unscrew the cap. It smells like wood and smoke and leather sofas and the cigars I used to get for Kane. I take a small sip. It's smoother than the Fireball I shared with Mags on the roof of the mess back in Eden, but it makes my eyes water, nonetheless.

Across the table Hicks is staring into the hearth, like maybe he's trying to figure out the right place to start. There's a soft crack as a branch shifts in the fire. A handful of sparks rise in a swirl and then disappear up into the chimney.

'It was a bad business. We'd already lost New York, Philly and DC to the strikes. Detroit fell to the virus a few weeks later, then Chicago. After that it was like dominoes. Pittsburgh, Columbus and Indianapolis went dark within days of each other, then Charlotte and Nashville. Each city that fell pushed a new wave of them south towards us; they flooded in through the Carolinas along 85 and through

Tennessee down 75.' He stops and looks over at me. 'You came down 81, right? Probably all the way from up near Reliance?'

Reliance is a small town just a little ways west of the Blue Ridge Mountain Road, not far from Mount Weather. I saw signs for it on our way down.

'I'm not sure. We came through a lot of places.'

He waves the question away, like it doesn't matter. He picks up the thermos again and gestures at the bottle with the cigarette. I take another sip. The bourbon hits the back of my throat and burns its way down. It's all I can do to keep from coughing.

'Well, whatever. Where you started's not important. Point is you were on the road a while, right? Maybe a week, give or take a day?'

Mags and I made much better time than that; we were only on I-81 for four days. But I nod anyway.

'Right. Well, imagine what that road would have looked like with a million other people on it, all of them towing carts, pushing barrows, shopping trolleys, whatever they could find. That's enough people to stretch back along 81 almost as far as you travelled it. Helluva lot of people.'

I nod again, like I understand, but in truth there's been so few of us for so long I have trouble imagining what a hundred people all together might look like, let alone a million.

He raises the thermos and looks over at the bourbon.

'Am I drinking by myself here kid?'

I take another sip and he continues.

'It was the rumor that brought them, of course. I don't know where it started, but pretty soon that didn't matter anymore. We heard it from each new batch that arrived. The scientists were close to finding a cure, they said; they were working on it right here in Atlanta. The government would never let the city fall. This would be where we'd turn it around. Hell, I'd heard it so often I think some days I even believed it myself.'

He looks over at the fire again and shakes his head.

'Back then we still had power of course, and a little heat, a few lights, it goes a long way. The army patrolled the streets at night and during the day the grunts went house to house clearing out any furies that were holed up inside. Infantry trains for urban combat so they were good at that, and south of Home Park and east of Decatur was pretty much fury-free. It felt like we were winning, or at least holding our own. Who knows, maybe if we'd had a little longer to prepare.'

Outside the wind gusts under the eaves and then settles. The cigarette continues to burn between his fingers, but it's like he's forgotten he has it now.

'But that was time we never had. Those that had survived had taken to the freeways, and they were leading the furies right to us. There wasn't nothing we could do about that, so the brass figured we might as well use it to our advantage. 75 and 85 come together just north of the city and I guess when they looked at their maps it seemed like a good spot, so that's where we picked to make our stand. The sappers stretched concertina wire right across the highway, just north of the 17th Street Bridge. Behind that they lined up the tanks, the Bradleys, Strykers, the Humvees with the roof-mounted fifty cals. They basically emptied out Fort Benning; it was everything we had. All the other roads into and out of the city were blocked off. Jersey barriers, shipping containers, school buses, you name it; we used anything we could lay our hands on. After that it was just a matter of waiting. The survivors would bring them to us, and we'd end it.'

He gives a short, humorless laugh. 'Sure wasn't how that worked out.'

He takes another sip from the thermos and nods at the bourbon.

'How're you getting on with that?'

I hold up the bottle, surprised to see there's already a couple of fingers missing. I take another hit. It's definitely getting easier. I feel it warming my insides as it slides down.

'Ortiz and I had picked ourselves out a spot on the roof of the Wells Fargo building, right by the interstate. We had orders to take out the first ones to show themselves. Brass thought it'd be good for morale. The grunts had always liked having us watching over them when they were on door-kickin' duty.'

'We'd walked both highways that morning, placing our rangefinders. It was a shade over twelve hundred yards to the Peachtree overpass where the interstates came together. Not an easy distance to make, especially with the light. But Ortiz and I were the best sniper team in the 75th; on a good day with him spotting for me I could shoot the ticks off a hound at a thousand yards. The Win Mag was waiting on a tarp at my side. I'd always favored the SR-25; you don't have to work a bolt so it's faster. But at that sort of distance the 'Mag shoots tighter groups.'

He flicks the cigarette, sending ash see-sawing down to the floor.

'So we're sitting up there, waiting, our comms dialed in to the AC-130 that's patrolling above. They haven't seen anything yet, but it's early and besides the infrared they're using never worked well on the furies; they're just too damn cold. Soon as it turns dark and they start making their way down the highway I figure we'll hear about it, though.'

'The last of the stragglers make their way through the gaps in the razor wire and I can see the engineers getting ready to close it up. Down on the line the grunts are waiting behind sandbags, just smoking or cleaning their weapons. Ortiz and I had stopped to chat to a few of them when we'd been down there earlier. The mood was pretty good. The general consensus was that brother fury didn't have a prayer. Once we opened up with all that firepower he wouldn't know whether to shit or go blind.'

He lifts the thermos and I take another hit from the bourbon. I run my tongue across the roof of my mouth; I can no longer tell where I burned it.

'The sun starts to set and the arc lights the engineers have rigged all along the highway come on, lighting up the kill zone. A cheer drifts up, for a few moments drowning the drone of cicadas that's been building since dusk.' He lifts the hand that's holding the cigarette and points it at me. 'Something's bothering me about that, mind, but right then I can't put my finger on what it is.'

'Well, we don't have long to wait after that. Ortiz taps me on the shoulder and points in the direction of the overpass. When I look through the scope there's a single fury, crouched on all fours, right in the middle of the road. It's moving its head, shifting it from side to side like a dog scenting the air, you know how they do.'

I nod. That's exactly what the one I ran into in Mount Weather's tunnel had been doing. A shiver runs down my spine and I take another sip of bourbon. Hicks squints at me for a moment, then he continues.

'I know what's troubling it, of course. Ortiz and I had scrounged a half-dozen blood bags from a casualty clearing station they'd set up on 14th. We'd sprayed the area under the overpass when we'd been up there placing our markers; I figured it might give me a few extra seconds to make the first shot. Ortiz is already calling it in so I take the 'Mag off safe. The scope's dialed out for the range so I just line the sights square on its forehead and squeeze, and a second later the top of its head comes off, like I'm shooting melon at the fair. We'd been ordered to ditch the suppressors so everyone down on the line could hear and my ears are ringing, but right away I can tell something's not right. Only minutes before they'd been whoopin' and hollerin' like Rapture just because somebody'd turned the lights on, but now there's not a sound other than the damn cicadas. I look up over the top of my scope, but I can't see a thing. I never cared much for the night vision the army gives you; at that sort of distance it's more hindrance than help. But the light's fading fast now and I can't make out whatever it is has the grunts spooked, so I reach up and switch it on. The arc lights lined up all along the highway cause it to flare out at first, but after a second it calms down. And then I see it.'

He reaches for the thermos again.

'You ever been to Atlanta, kid?'

I shake my head.

'Well, for a city, it's got a lot of trees. They start immediately north of the point where 75 and 85 come together.'

He trails off, as if remembering.

'Infrared may not work so good on the furies, but let me tell you: night vision works like a treat. All along the tree line it lights up their silver eyes like it's Christmas.'

CHAPTER TWENTY-ONE

HICKS TAKES another sip from the thermos and leans back in his chair. Outside the tavern darkness has drawn down over the world, but I've barely noticed. I look over at the hearth. The fire's burned low; there's little more than a handful of scattered flames among the embers. I should go build it up, but whether it's the roast beef and gravy or the liquor my insides feel pretty warm, and I really want to hear what happens next.

Hicks sets the thermos back on the table.

'Where was I?'

'The furies. They were in the trees.'

'Right. Well that's when it hits me. That noise I'm hearing, drifting up to us from the tree line. I'd mistaken it for cicadas. We were coming into summer, but of course it had already turned cold by then, so it couldn't have been that; we hadn't heard insects in weeks. It was the furies. Have you heard the sound they make?'

I take another sip of bourbon.

'It's like a clicking, from back in their throat.'

He squints across the table at me.

'You must have gotten pretty close to one, to tell that.'

I nod.

'Yeah, just last year.'

He looks at me again, and then at the bourbon, like he's trying to work something out. After a moment he raises the thermos to his lips and continues.

'Well anyway, I guess me shooting the first one must have set the rest of them off because they're breaking cover now, just swarming out of the trees and onto the highway. I get to work with the rifle. I've got my eye in and they're dropping, but there's just too damn many of them; I can't crank the bolt fast enough. I grab the SR-25 and start squeezing off rounds. Down on the line it's gone deathly quiet, and when I stop to reload I see why. They're knocking out the arc lights as they come; it's like they're bringing the darkness with them.'

An image floats into my head, unbidden. A black and white snapshot of Mount Weather's tunnel, the fury lit by the muzzle flash as it bounded towards me, and for a second the terror I had felt in that moment returns. I take another swig of bourbon to banish it.

'There's a few pops from the grunts now, but they're just wasting ammo. Even if their hands were steady they couldn't be expected to make shots count, not at that distance, not on things that move that quick.'

'As I'm jamming another magazine into the rifle I hear a noise and look up. A Warthog's banking around from the east. It opens up with that massive gun in its nose and for a few seconds it's like God Himself has taken a weed whacker to the tree line. The Comanches come whining in, right on its heels, sending their Hellfires streaking down towards the overpass. But the things coming down the highway don't even seem to notice what's going on behind them.'

'The AC-130 that'd been spotting for us earlier drops altitude and now tracer rounds from its mini guns are lighting up the sky, too. Down on the line the tanks and the Bradleys have finally gotten in the game. A few moments later the Humvees and the Strykers join in with their chain guns and their fifty cals. The noise is deafening. Down on the highway it's just carnage. I lay the rifle up. There's no point; nothing could get through that. And for a second I think, *They were right; this* is *where we'll stop them.* But then Ortiz taps me on the shoulder and points.'

He stops to take another hit from the thermos and I realize I'm leaning forward.

'What did he see?'

He glances at the bottle of bourbon. I raise it to my lips and take another swig so he'll get back to the story.

'Remember what I told you about Atlanta, kid?'

I nod. 'The trees.'

'Right. Well, those trees weren't just in front of us, they were all around. Sure, for a couple of blocks on either side of the highway it was mostly concrete. But pretty quickly the skyscrapers and the offices give way to regular neighborhoods and then the trees are back, spreading right out into the suburbs.' He looks across the table. 'We assumed because the furies were following the survivors that they'd stick to the interstate. But nobody thought to check with brother fury whether that was his plan. Turns out it wasn't, because now they're breaking cover on both sides.'

'The Comanches pull back and head out to the sides and begin laying down fire. A few seconds later the AC-130 hauls off to join them. Down on the line they're trying to move whatever of the armor they can around to face the flanks, but it's chaos, and now there's less fire going forward and the furies are getting through again. I jam another clip into the SR-25 and get back to work. It's no good, though. The first of them hits the razor wire without even slowing. The ones behind immediately start climbing over, struggling and thrashing and tangling themselves up in the barbs. But the weight's compressing the coils, and now others are clambering over the top. The first few make it through and crash headlong into the last of the arc lights and there's that moment, where you know it's all going to get decided.'

He lifts the thermos to his lips, like he's about to take another sip, then decides against it and puts it back down.

'Some of the Humvees have got their headlights pointed up the highway, so I can still make out a little of what's going on. That virus may be contagious, but let me tell you son, nothing spreads faster than panic. The grunts had been trained to fire in short, controlled bursts but there's little of that now. I see one kid, can't have been much older'n you, step out from behind his sandbags, switch his M4 to auto and just open up into the wire. He's empty in no more than a couple of seconds. They're on him before he's fumbled a fresh clip out of his flak vest.'

'The line collapses pretty quick after that. There's just too many of them. The Warthog's still circling, but the fire from the AC-130's more sporadic now, like it's trying to conserve ammo. Then I see the Comanches banking around, heading back to base to reload. By the time they return it'll be over. The furies are spilling out over the freeway guardrails, jumping down onto the streets below. I mean, you've seen how quick they move, right?'

I nod. He holds the thermos up, looks at me.

'Where'd you run into yours? A hospital?'

I take another sip of the bourbon and shake my head.

'Marv said we had to stay clear of the hospitals.'

'Smart fella.'

'So what happened?'

'Well, I crank the scope till it bottoms out and then step up onto the ledge so I can fire directly down into them. But before I can get a shot off I hear a roar and when I look up there's an F-16 coming in on afterburners. It drops down low as it approaches the highway and I know even before I see the bomb detach that it's over. Somebody's called it. The pilot's already banking away and I don't wait to see where it'll hit, I just shout at Ortiz to take cover. I guess it must have been a bunker buster because a second later it's like the ground's turned to jello and the next thing I know the air's sucked from my lungs and I feel the rifle ripped from my hands. The windows on the north side of the building blow out and a great plume of dust and dirt rises up into the sky like a geyser. The last thing I see before I'm hurled back from the edge is one of the Humvees being tossed through the air like a child's toy.'

He reaches for the thermos and I raise the bourbon to my lips again.

'I'm not sure how long I lay there, after, just staring up into the sky. I can't hear a thing. Now and then a chopper passes overhead, but I guess Ortiz and me don't look like a good bet, because none of them are stopping. By the time I finally manage to haul myself up the blinking landing lights are almost all the way to the horizon and I don't reckon any of them'll be coming back. Ortiz is still out of it. I look over the edge; the streets below are swarming. I figure we're not going anywhere till dawn, so I sit down to wait.'

'My ears are still shot so it's a good thing I'm facing east or I might not have seen the Chinook lifting off from CDC. I dig in my pack for a flare and then jump up on the ledge and start waving it above my head for all I'm worth. At first I don't think it's coming, but then finally it swings around and dips its nose in our direction.'

'Only takes it a couple of minutes to reach us. The Chinook's too big to land on the roof, so the pilot holds it in a hover and drops the ramp at the back. I hoist Ortiz onto my shoulder. There's a bunch of grunts inside waving at me to pass him up. I still can't hear worth a damn so I've no idea what they're saying, but then I see the look on this young red-haired kid's face change. I turn around and there's a couple of furies on the roof behind me. I guess I've attracted them, waving the flare around and hollering like an idiot. They're already running at me so I heave Ortiz up. The SR-25 I was using earlier's long gone, but the 'Mag's at my feet so I reach down for it. The elevation's still set for a distance shot and there's no time to dial it back, so I just hold it low and squeeze. The gun rises up and when it drops again one of them's disappeared, but the other's still coming. I figure I don't have time to reload so I ditch the rifle and reach for my sidearm.'

'And?'

The cigarette between his fingers has burned down to a butt. He drops it to the floor and crushes it under his boot.

'Turns out I just wasn't fast enough.'

CHAPTER TWENTY-TWO

'WHAT HAPPENED?'

He pulls the throat of his parka back and turns his head so I can see the long, ugly scar that runs down one side of his neck.

'Doc's what happened. The Chinook had been sent to fetch her and whatever equipment they could salvage from her lab, bring her someplace where she could continue working on a cure. Truck and his boys were her escort. They were all for shooting me then and there, but she said there was a chance, if we were quick. She burned the skin off where it had touched me. Then they stuck me in one of the plastic cages they'd taken from her lab, to see whether I'd turn. My lucky day I guess.'

He reaches for the thermos, glancing over at the bottle of bourbon I'm holding as he does it.

'So where'd you run into yours, then, if it wasn't in a hospital?'

'A tunnel.'

He pauses, like he's thinking about this.

'Probably had to have been shielded, for it to have survived the burst. Was it at that Eden place you and the other kids were holed up with Kane?' But before I have a chance to agree he waves that possibility away. 'Nope, can't have been, not if it was just last year. You and Marv, coming and going all that time, you'd have run into it long before then.'

I'm not ready for the turn the conversation's taken. I take another swig from the bottle while I work out what to say. Hicks seems okay, and he did save me from Truck and Weasel, but I hadn't planned on telling him about Mount Weather. I rack my brains for another answer but my head's fuggy from the liquor and for a long moment there's nothing. At last something pops into my head and it doesn't seem like anything better's following on its heels so I seize it.

'It was at a place called Culpeper.'

He takes a sip from his thermos, then works his jaw from side to side, like he's figured there's something not quite right with my story.

'How'd you say you came down here again? On 81?'

Even as I'm nodding I realize Culpeper's nowhere near I-81. It takes me a couple of seconds to stumble onto an excuse.

'Yeah, but I took us off the highway looking for food and then we got lost in a snowstorm and ended up wandering around a bit.'

He squints at me a while, like he knows I'm not telling him the truth and he's trying to work out whether to call me on it. In the end he must decide to let it go.

'Well, it can happen. So how'd you get away from it?'

'It chased me out into the light and I shot it.' I'm anxious to move on from my lie so I stick to the short version. I figure he doesn't need to know that I must have missed it a dozen or more times in the tunnel, and once more outside, when it was just lying there in the snow. Or that I was so afraid I peed myself in the process.

He raises the thermos again and looks at me, but I realize I can't have any more bourbon. I hold the bottle up and take a false swig, just enough to wet my lips.

'And the helicopter brought you to The Greenbrier?'

He shakes his head.

'The Greenbrier wasn't the plan, at least not at first. Doc was supposed to be headed for North Carolina.'

That was what I was supposed to be finding out from Hicks all along. With everything that had been going on in Atlanta I'd almost forgotten.

'The bunker at Fearrington?'

He nods.

'If you were thinking of checking it out I can save you the bother. Nothing for you there, kid.'

'You've been inside?'

He shakes his head and reaches for the thermos again.

'We landed but the place was locked down. None of the codes Doc had worked.'

'Yeah, Kane changed them all, the day he brought us from the White House to Eden.'

As soon as it's out I realize my mistake. Hicks' flask is almost at his lips but when I mention the codes it stops in midair.

'Your friend Marv tell you that too?'

I nod.

'He didn't happen to give you the new ones did he?'

I shake my head, perhaps a little too quickly. *Crap.* I

really can't be trusted with liquor. I ask him another question, to keep him from dwelling on the subject.

'What'd it look like, from the outside?'

He stares at me for a moment before answering.

'Can't rightly say. I was lying at the bottom of a cage designed for something no bigger than a chimpanzee, pretty much out of it on the painkillers the Doc had given me. Ortiz saw it though; he'd come around by then. He told me later it was nothing special; just a guard hut and a couple of concrete buildings. But then Doc said most of it was underground anyway. The silo was supposed to go down thirteen stories.'

'And you never went back there, after?'

'Why would we do that? We had no way in.'

I was expecting it, but I'm a little disheartened nonetheless.

'Doc's fallback was The Greenbrier. It was touch and go whether we'd even make it; we'd used a lot of our fuel getting out to Fearrington. Later when we checked the tanks for anything that might burn there was nothing. I reckon we must have landed on fumes.'

'How'd you get in? Wasn't it locked down too?'

'That was our one piece of good fortune that night. Turns out someone was still inside. Young Private Kavanagh had been part of the guard detail that got posted there when they reactivated it. They got the evacuation order, but somehow he got himself trapped inside. As soon as his squad stepped outside they got overrun. He said he saw it all on the monitors. Shook him up pretty bad, so bad he wouldn't let us in at first. It was only when Doc explained she was working on a cure for the virus that he changed his mind.'

'Is she close, to a cure I mean?'

'She says she is. Not sure there's anyone left who can call her on it, though.'

He takes another sip from the thermos and goes quiet for a long while, just staring into the hearth. The fire's almost burned down and the tavern's turning cold. I pull my parka around me.

'Alright kid, time to hit the sack. Early start tomorrow.'

I get up, a little unsteadily, and make my way over to my backpack to get my sleeping bag. This hasn't worked out how I'd hoped. I've wasted a whole day coming out with Hicks; Dr. Gilbey already knew as much about Fearrington as he did. That bit's bothering me, too. I mean, how could she not remember it? It might have been ten years ago, but it was supposed to be where she was going to continue her research. She must have expected to spend months, maybe even years there.

Surely you wouldn't just forget something like that?

CHAPTER TWENTY-THREE

SHE'S WAKING UP!

He's so excited he can barely contain himself. He's been watching her since the mean soldier brought her down earlier. For a long time she just lay there, a dark shape curled up on the floor of the cage, and at first he wasn't even sure she was breathing. But he just saw her move, he's sure of it.

He creeps forward until his face is only inches from the bars, even though he knows this is against the rules. They put her in the cage next to 98's, so she's almost directly opposite. It looks like she's wearing the same dark overalls he is, which must mean...

There! She just moved again! Without thinking he presses closer to the bars. He would jump with excitement if he could, but the cage is too low and all he can manage is a small shuffling dance. He takes a deep breath and forces himself to be still. He must be calm now. If she's like he was when he first arrived she'll be frightened. She won't know where she is or what she's doing down here in the darkness.

She props herself up on one elbow and shakes her head,

as if she's trying to clear it. They've shaved her hair. He runs his hands over his own shorn scalp, remembering how that had felt when he had first woken up.

She opens her eyes and slowly looks around. He knows she won't be able to see much, not yet, but nevertheless he shrinks back a little further as her eyes glide over his cage. He doesn't want to scare her, the way 98 had frightened him when he had first seen what she looked like. But then she looks right at him and his heart leaps with joy. Her eyes are still normal. She will probably be here for a long time.

Her hands reach forward and grasp the bars of the cage, and for a moment she explores them, testing the thickness of the plastic, its strength. Her fingers move to the edges and she finds the hinges and then she searches on the opposite side for the release. She's wasting her time of course. He knows where the catch is, but there's no way it can be reached from the inside.

She must figure that out because after a while she gives up and instead grips the bars with both hands and pulls. When that doesn't work she braces herself against the sides and starts kicking. That won't do any good either; the plastic's strong. He saw everything that 98 did to the cage in the end, and still it held. But she's making a lot of noise and now he's worried; if she keeps this up the mean soldier will come down, and then there'll be trouble. He creeps to the front of the cage and tries to hush her, just like 98 did with him when he first arrived. It takes her a moment to notice, but then she stops and looks right at him. He knows she probably can't see him but he retreats from the bars anyway.

'Who's there?'

That's a difficult question when you're not sure of your

own name. He thinks about it for a moment and then figures Johnny 99 will do for now.

She repeats the name, like she's testing the sound of it.

'Well Johnny, hello. I'm Mags. Do you know where I am?'

That question is difficult too, so instead of answering he tells her she needs to be quiet. But she doesn't seem to get it, because she just asks more questions. As quickly as he can he explains that making noise isn't allowed; even talking like this is bad. She must go to the back of her cage and be still, or the soldier will come. That finally seems to work, because for a moment she says nothing.

'So the soldier comes if I make noise?'

He nods. Yes, yes. At last she's getting it. But then she just starts kicking the bars again and shouting, and she won't stop no matter how much he pleads with her. Soon he hears footsteps on the stairs outside and he knows it's too late now. He scurries to the back of his cage, presses himself into the corner and starts counting. He must have missed the first few steps because of the racket the girl's making; he only gets as far as eighty when they stop, and then the door at the end of the room opens with a soft groan.

He tells himself it might be okay. Maybe the mean soldier won't do anything to her this time. She's new; she couldn't be expected to know about the rules yet. He hears the sound of his boots on the concrete, growing louder as he marches towards them between the cages. The beam from his flashlight bounces ahead of him, getting stronger with each step. Moments later grubby fatigues appear in front of his cage, the bottoms tucked into a pair of large boots. He's got the stick; he's holding it behind his back; Johnny 99 can see the two metal prongs that protrude from the end of the black plastic. The girl mustn't have noticed it yet because she doesn't move away. She just looks up at him.

'Corporal Truckle. What am I doing in here?'

The mean soldier doesn't say anything. He just pushes the stick through the bars. There's a flash of blue light and the girl cries out once but doesn't let go. Her hands grip the plastic tighter as the muscles in her arms spasm. Johnny 99 covers his head with his hands so he won't have to see. Surely the soldier will stop soon. But he keeps jamming the stick through the bars. Soon the air smells like it's burning.

Before Johnny 99 knows what he's doing he's shuffled forward to the front of the cage. He shouts at the mean soldier to stop.

The soldier hits the girl one more time with the stick and then uses it to push her way from the bars. She slumps to the floor of the cage, twitches once and then lies still.

The last thing Johnny 99 remembers is the blue light arcing between the metal prongs as the soldier turns around to face him.

CHAPTER TWENTY-FOUR

I WAKE some time just before dawn. When I look over at the table I see Hicks is already up, sitting in the same spot where I left him last night. I banked the fire before I went to bed but it's died anyway and now it's bitterly cold. He doesn't seem to care, though. He's just staring into the dead hearth, occasionally sipping from his thermos.

My head hurts a little from the bourbon, but in spite of it I'm feeling better than when I went to bed last night. I still don't understand how Dr. Gilbey could have forgotten about Fearrington, but maybe it doesn't matter; Hicks has already told me as much as I need to know. It might not be the underground city Mount Weather is, but thirteen stories should be plenty big enough for the twenty-three of us that are left. And if Dr. Gilbey had planned to go there to continue her work on a cure it must have been stocked. It'd put us far from Eden too, with The Greenbrier between us, and that could be to our advantage. There's clearly no love lost between Dr. Gilbey and Kane.

I climb out of my sleeping bag, already starting to feel

excited. It'll be a long hike for the Juvies, but now that winter's almost over they can manage it. I'd really like to go there first to check it out, but the shortest route I can figure puts it seven days away, which means three weeks at the earliest before we could be back in Mount Weather. Even if we had supplies for the trip that's too long; Peck might already be on his way. Besides, Benjamin's codes have worked everywhere else I've been; there's no reason they shouldn't work there.

I get a fire going and open a can of devilled ham I picked up yesterday for breakfast. I offer some to Hicks, but he says he's already eaten. Must have been hours ago, because I can't smell any of it. He must be a night-grazer, like Marv used to be. Whatever, more for me. I scoop the last of the ground meat from the tin, bag our trash and start packing up my kit.

———

It can't be much after noon as we pass through The Green-brier's crumbling gateposts, but already it seems like the day's darkening. Hicks cups one glove to his forehead and squints up at the thunderheads gathering along the horizon to the south.

'Weather's comin'.'

I follow his gaze. The sky there's got a mean look to it. I wonder what this is going to do to our plans. Storms like this right at the end of winter rarely last long, but now that I know what we have to do I don't want to lose any more time at The Greenbrier.

The breeze is quickening, sending flurries of gray snow dancing up the loading ramp into the helicopter's cargo bay as we pass. Up at the house the tattered flags snap and flutter on their flagpoles. We stop under the portico to remove our snowshoes and head inside. I shuck off my backpack, swap my boots for The Greenbrier slippers that are waiting for me on the bellhop cart and head straight for the corridor that leads to the bunker without waiting for Hicks. I'm hungry from the hike back, but I can eat later; right now I just want to let Mags know I'm back and that I've found us somewhere to go.

When I get to the Exhibition Hall it's empty. I see Truck's makeshift spittoon sitting on the table, brimming with dark tobacco juice, but thankfully there's no sign of him. I walk over to the corner and search for the panel he opened. It's not easy to find, even now I know where to look, but eventually I locate the join in the gaudy wallpaper.

I push the panel and it pops out, allowing me to fold it back. In the recess behind the vault door waits. Flecks of paint still cling to the underside of the handle, but on top the metal's burnished smooth from years of wear. I hesitate for a moment and then press down. The mechanism's stiff and the handle reaches the end of its travel with a heavy clunk, but the door doesn't budge.

I look at the intercom. Truck said Dr. Gilbey didn't like to be disturbed, but I don't care; soon we'll be gone, and then we'll never see these people again. My finger's already on the button when I hear a voice behind me.

'Whaddya up to there, Huckleberry? Want to see if your little friend can come out to play?'

I turn around like I've been caught doing something I shouldn't. Truck's standing at the bottom of the stairs.

'I want to see Mags.'

He hitches up his pants and crosses the Exhibition Hall towards me.

'You'll see her soon enough I expect.' He says it with a smile that sends a chill through me. 'Right now Doc ain't in there, though, so I can't let you through.'

I sigh. Why couldn't Kane just have released a virus that infected assholes? I tell myself it'll be fine. Hicks will sort this out. I just need to get him.

I leave Truck in the Exhibition Hall and make my way back up the steps to the long corridor, taking them two at a time. There's something about the way he smiled at me when he said I'd see Mags soon that's got me worried now. As I'm passing the Colonial Lounge I hear voices coming from within. They're muffled by the heavy door, but there's no mistaking Dr. Gilbey's clipped, precise tones. I stop outside.

'But you haven't brought me one in months.'

I hesitate for a moment. There's clearly somebody else in there with her, and Dr. Gilbey's not the sort of person you just barge in on. My hand's hovering over the door when I hear Hicks' drawl.

'I know, ma'am, but...'

I don't wait for him to finish. I knock once, harder than I intended to. There's a long pause and then I hear Dr. Gilbey say 'Come'.

I open the door and step in. The same three high-backed chairs wait in the center of the room but now they're empty. I scan the room and find her standing by one of the tall windows, looking out at the terrace. She turns to face me. In the scant light that filters through the silted panes she seems older. Her skin looks thin, fragile, almost translucent; like if it were to get much brighter you might be able to see clear through to the bones there. The hair that frames her face is so fine that when she turns her head the contours of her skull show.

'How long were you standing out there?'

'Not long at all. I mean, I was just walking past.' I turn to Hicks. 'Can I see Mags now?'

There's a moment of silence that draws out for longer than it should. Off in the distance lightning flashes across the darkening sky and for a second the light from it plays across the lenses of Dr. Gilbey's narrow glasses. She exchanges a look with Hicks and it's as if a large, dark void has suddenly opened up under my breastbone.

'Gabriel, son, you'd best sit down. There's something the Doc needs to tell you.'

I feel my throat tighten and for a moment I think I may not actually be able to breathe, but somehow I manage to stammer out a question.

'What is it?'

Dr. Gilbey purses her lips.

'You must prepare yourself, Gabriel. There's been a terrible accident.' But the voice that delivers this news is brusque, matter-of-fact. 'I told Magdalene she had to stay in the dormitory, but it seems she didn't listen. For some reason she took it upon herself to break into the laboratory last night. I found her this morning.'

'Gabriel, son, she's been infected.'

CHAPTER TWENTY-FIVE

THE ROOM SEEMS to spin around me and it's like I've been delivered straight into one of those nightmares where nothing's right and you know it and all you want is to wake up but you can't.

'You need to bring me to her.'

Dr. Gilbey shakes her head.

'I'm afraid that won't be possible, Gabriel. Magdalene was quite distraught. I've had to give her something to help her rest. I don't expect her to regain consciousness for a day or two.'

'As soon as she comes round you can see her, son.'

Dr. Gilbey's eyes narrow and she gives Hicks a sharp look, like this is not something she had approved. She tucks her lower lip, like she's about to deliver a rebuke, but Hicks cuts her off and in spite of what I've just heard gratitude wells up in me for him.

'Ma'am, with all due respect the kid needs to see the girl. Until we know how this happened I don't think you want to risk another accident in the lab, do you? When she comes to we'll bring her out here.'

He turns back to me.

'Son, I know this looks bad, but there's hope. Doc's close to a cure. And in the meantime she has medicine that can suppress the virus. Slow it way down.'

I look at Dr. Gilbey.

'How long does she have?'

'Unfortunately it's very difficult to say, Gabriel. Right now her body is attempting to come to terms with the virus, but very soon it will try and reject it. When that happens Magdalene is going to become quite unwell.'

'But she's young, and healthy. That's in her favor, right?'

'Yes, Sergeant, that is indeed fortunate. The chances are that she will pull through.'

'And then what?'

Dr. Gilbey folds her arms across her chest. She stares at me for a long moment before answering.

'Well assuming she does indeed survive the initial infection the physical symptoms – the changes to hair color, the silvering of the retina – will manifest themselves. Given the pathology of the virus acute degradation in long-term memory then unfortunately becomes inevitable, even with the drugs I'll be giving her. But I've had some success in staving off the more extreme personality changes.'

She stops, like she's done answering the question. I see Hicks' jaw tighten, but when he speaks his tone is calm, patient, as though he's grown used to drawing blood from this particular stone.

'Ma'am, the kid needs a timeframe.'

Dr. Gilbey purses her lips, like she's already provided all the information that could possibly be expected of her.

But Hicks keeps squinting at her and in the end she just sighs.

'Well, as long as she keeps taking the medication I dare say I can prevent her ultimate transformation for quite some time.' She pauses, like this time she might not go on, but finally she continues. 'For someone of Magdalene's age, months, possibly even longer.'

I nod, like I'm taking all of this in, but in reality my mind's reeling, still refusing to believe what I've just heard. I realize Hicks and Dr. Gilbey are both looking at me, like they're expecting me to say something.

'What can I do?'

Dr. Gilbey folds her arms across her chest and studies me. For a moment it's like I can almost see the calculations being performed behind those gray eyes.

'Well, Gabriel, I have been working on a prototype for an antivirus. But before I can risk giving it to Magdalene it has to be tested.'

'You need to help me find more furies, son. They have to be live ones though, functioning, like the one you ran into in that tunnel. The ones that had their circuits fried by what Kane did are no good to us.'

'Is that what you were out looking for, when we ran into you?'

He nods.

'We were on our way back from a hospital over in Catawba. Those are our best bet for finding what Doc needs. There's places in them that would have been shielded, just like in the bunkers.'

Marv said we had to give the hospitals a wide berth. I always assumed it was on account of the bodies, but I guess he must have figured out what Hicks has.

'How many do you need?'

She walks over towards me, her heels clicking on the checkerboard floor.

'As many as you can get me, dear. The more I can test the antivirus the lower the risk to Magdalene when I give it to her.'

I look over at Hicks.

'How many have you found so far?'

He pauses, like this isn't an answer he much wants to give.

'Not near enough.'

'How many?'

'Seven. Four that we've managed to bring back.'

'And how many hospitals have you been to?'

'Pretty much everything within a two-day hike of here.' When he sees I need a number he adds: 'Twenty-five.'

He scratches his jaw.

'Yeah, it ain't good. I'll be honest with you son, the odds are long that a fury would have been hanging out in one of the shielded areas when the burst went off. Kane detonated the missiles at night, when most of them would have been out hunting. And there's another thing, just so you know what you'd be signing up for.'

He looks up, fixing me with a stare from his one good eye, like this is something I need to pay attention to.

'First few we caught we just walked up to them, zapped them with the baton then slipped a plastic gunny sack over their heads; it was all over long before they came out of whatever hibernation they put themselves in when they run out of food. Last couple of times they've come to much quicker. They're getting to be a real handful.'

I think of the fury that chased me out of Mount Weather's tunnel. Even the thought of going into whatever dark place we have to to find one of those things makes my blood run cold. But then I remember the last time I saw Marv. The sunken shadows around his eyes, his pupils impossibly dilated, flashing silver where the light caught them. The way his jaw worked, clenching and unclenching as he fought to control the madness that would soon be upon him.

I can't let that happen to Mags.

'How soon can we start?'

CHAPTER TWENTY-SIX

HE COMES TO SLOWLY.

Somebody's calling to him. It sounds like the girl but he lies still, keeping his eyes closed, trying to decide if it's a trick. There's something poking into his side. It takes him a second to work out it's the food tray; he can feel the ridges and hollows of the compartments through his overalls, the soft squelch as the congealed beans press into the thin material. The tray is uncomfortable but if he moves it hurts more, so he stays where he is.

He's had the stick before, but not for a long time now, and never this much. He lets his mind go to all the places where he thinks the prongs may have found him. His ribs definitely got the worst of it, but there's something wrong with his insides too; it feels like somebody's scrambled them all up. He wonders how many times the soldier hit him. He doesn't remember anything after the first one. The stick makes his mind go blank, like someone's found the switch that turns him off and flicked it. The soldier normally loses interest soon after that happens. He doesn't remember that from his own beatings, of course. By then he's gone; he's nothing; just a rag doll lying on the floor of the cage, with no more sense of what's happening to him than a stuffed toy set upon by an agitated dog. But he's seen the soldier use the stick on the others, and afterwards he can feel all the places he's been hit. Right now there's too many to count. The soldier must have been really mad to keep working him like that.

The girl's still calling to him. He opens his eyes a fraction. She's sitting by the bars, clutching her side like that's where it hurts too. And now he hears another sound: footsteps on the stairs outside, still faint, but getting closer. He starts the count, even though he doesn't know how many he's already missed. He suddenly realizes how close he is to the front of his own cage; he'll get in trouble if the soldier finds him here. He picks himself up, keeping his movements as small as possible to avoid fresh flares of pain. The tray that's stuck itself to his overalls detaches and clatters to the floor.

The girl must hear the sound because she shifts her head in his direction and asks if he's okay. When he replies his voice is little more than a croaked whisper.

'Yes, but we have to be quiet now. He's coming back.'

He sees her nod in the darkness, like she finally understands. She moves away from the bars. Good; she's learning. He shuffles to the back of his cage and presses himself into the corner to wait.

The soldier's boots echo off the metal, growing louder as he descends. When he reaches the bottom there's a pause and a click as the locks disengage and then a distant groan as the door opens. Somewhere at the end of the row of cages there's the faintest glimmer of light and then the sound of the soldier's boots scuffing the concrete, accompanied by something else: the hollow *clack-clack-clack* of plastic hitting plastic as he drags the stick along the bars. The beam's getting brighter; it bounces along the aisle as he approaches. Johnny 99 pushes himself as far as he can into the shadows and tries not to cover his eyes. The cone of light stops outside his cage and then stretches out as the soldier places the flashlight on the ground. A plastic tray gets pushed through the slot in the front of his cage. The soldier uses the end of the stick to slide it forward, but he doesn't withdraw it afterwards.

Johnny 99 eyes the prongs nervously. He doesn't even want the food; he'd have no interest in it even if he hadn't seen the remains of a wad of tobacco floating among the congealed beans. But in one of the tray's compartments, next to his water, there's the container with his medicine. The soldier rattles the stick impatiently against the sides of the slot but makes no move to pull it back.

'C'mon 99. Don't keep me waiting.'

The soldier will get annoyed if he doesn't take his medicine but the metal prongs are only inches from the tray and he doesn't want to go near them. He hesitates another moment and then reaches out as quickly as he can and snatches the container back into the darkness.

The soldier chuckles and then draws the stick back out. Johnny 99 unscrews the cap and drinks the contents. He gags as the bitter, metallic liquid hits the back of his throat and that causes a fresh burst of pain from his ribs, but he presses his lips tight together and forces it down. The soldier will get really mad if he throws up the medicine and he has to go back up the stairs and get him another. He reaches for the plastic cup of water and washes the taste from his mouth. He'll try and eat some of the food later, because that's what you have to do so they'll know you're still okay and don't need to go to the other room. But he doesn't think he can manage any of it now.

He screws the cap back on the container and places it near the front of his cage so the soldier can collect it. But the soldier has already lost interest in him. He bends down in front of the girl's cage and slides another food tray through the slot there. Johnny 99 stays back, keeping himself hidden in the shadows so the girl doesn't see him. He really hopes she doesn't do anything to provoke the soldier. But she seems to have learned her lesson. She's crouched all the way at the back, just like he told her.

The soldier squats in front of the bars.

'How you doin' in there, darlin'?'

Johnny 99 can hear the smile in the soldier's voice. He pushes the girl's food forward with the stick. The girl backs up, like she's frightened of the prongs too, but then without warning she launches herself forward.

The soldier's taken by surprise; he manages to yank the stick back through the slot, but as he staggers backwards he trips over his own feet and lands heavily on his elbows. His boots scrabble for purchase on the concrete as he tries to push himself out of the way. The girl's hands shoot through the bars, but he's just done enough to get himself out of her reach. Her fingers miss him by inches.

For a long moment the soldier just sits in front of Johnny 99's cage, his chest rising and falling inside his sweat-stained fatigues. Strands of his hair have fallen across his forehead and his cheeks are flushed, but there's something else that's bothering Johnny 99 now, a smell so heavy, so pungent that it makes him feel dizzy.

The soldier slowly picks himself up. He squats down in

front of the girl's cage again, only this time he keeps his distance. The girl makes no move to step back from the bars.

'So, Corporal, you're scared of me.'

The soldier reaches for the flashlight, and that's when Johnny sees it. The arm of his fatigues is ripped. He must have done it scrambling backwards to put himself beyond the girl's grasp. His elbow pokes through the tear in the fabric.

Something flickers inside him, a feeling he has not had for so long that at first he does not recognize it. The pain from his ribs is forgotten. He crawls to the front of the cage, even though some rapidly receding part of him knows this is not allowed. His hands slip between the bars (*definitely* against the rules, *definitely*), reaching out to the pale flesh that shows through the torn fabric. The baton's right there. The boy knows he will be in trouble if he is caught now, but he is unable to stop himself. He is mesmerized by the heavy beads of bright red blood that have welled up all along the skin where the soldier has scraped his elbow on the concrete.

The soldier smoothes back the strands of hair that have fallen across his face, oblivious to the small hands that reach out through the bars of the cage behind him.

'And have you figured out why yet, Miss Smartybritches? I guess you must have to pull a stunt like that. But just in case you haven't, you've got the same thing he has.'

The boy's fingers stretch out, but just as they're about to touch the soldier's arm the soldier reaches for the flashlight. He swings it around and shines it into his cage. Johnny 99 scrabbles back as far as he can, but there's nowhere to hide from the cruel beam. He pulls his hands up to block the light, but in the moment before he squeezes his eyes shut he catches a glimpse of the girl's face as she sees him for the first time. Her eyes widen and in that instant something passes behind them, a recognition of the horror the soldier has just described. The soldier holds the beam on him a few seconds longer then points it along the aisle and sets it down. When Johnny dares to open his eyes again the soldier's reaching into his pocket. He pulls out a plastic vial just like the one he's just given him.

'See this here?' He holds it up so the girl can see. 'This is Doc's medicine. Take it every day like you're supposed to and the thing you've got inside you slows right down. Could take it months before it gets a good hold on you, years even. Look at 99 over there. He's been with us a long while, haven't you, boy?'

Johnny 99 thinks the soldier means to shine the light on him again. He raises his arms and tries to push himself further into the corner. But the soldier makes no move for the flashlight. He's preoccupied with the plastic container. He turns it over in his fingers, watching as the pale liquid shifts sluggishly against the sides.

'But see, without it, with the dose you've had, you'll turn in three days, four tops. And Doc hasn't figured out how to make people change back yet, so when that happens I have to come back down here with the baton and the catchpole and take you next door. Want to know what happens in there?'

The soldier waits for a response. When he doesn't get one he continues anyway.

'Well, first Doc takes a bone saw to the top of that pretty little head of yours and scoops out all the bits that interest her. After that, if you're still ticking, of course, there's another cage waiting for you, on the far side. You think it's nice in here? Just wait till you see what we got for you in there.'

He pauses to let this sink in, then he holds up the plastic container again.

'Now Doc says I have to watch you take this. I even have to fill out a little report, give her the exact time I saw you swallow it.'

'That's a lot of responsibility for a man with your abilities, Corporal. Let me know if you need any help.'

Johnny 99 thinks he hears her voice waver as she says it, but even so he's never heard anybody talk back to the mean soldier before. He covers his face with his hands, afraid of what will happen next. The soldier's fingers reach for the stick and this time they close around it. For a moment he hefts it like he means to use it, but then he stops.

'Well that's very kind of you, sugar, but I think I can manage. Now, today my report's going to say you had yourself a hissy fit and refused to take your medicine. We'll see how you feel tomorrow. Maybe if your attitude improves I'll let you have one of these.'

He holds the container up a moment longer then slips it back in his pocket.

'Or then again maybe I won't.'

CHAPTER TWENTY-SEVEN

THE NIGHT CRAWLS PAST.

I'm tired but sleep won't come and so I just sit on the floor in my parka, staring out at the gathering storm. Outside the weather's worsening. Along the horizon the sky's restless with lightning; it shudders inside the clouds, occasionally breaking free to stab down at the ground below.

When I got back to my room I threw up the ham I ate for breakfast. I went back to the bathroom twice more until there was nothing left. There was a knock on my door soon after and when I opened it Hicks was standing there with a rifle. He said there were things I needed to learn. I followed him down to the dining room and he sat me down at the table and laid the rifle in front of me. It was called an M4, he said. He showed me how to check it was safe and then he taught me how to strip it. He made it look easy; it's like his fingers knew what to do without him even watching then. It took me a while to get the hang of it, but soon I could break it down until it wasn't more than a collection of receivers, assemblies, pins and springs. He made me memorize the names of each, and where they fit in relation to each other, so I'd be able to put it back together again afterwards.

When he was happy I could do that he handed me a dozen cotton swabs and a small plastic container of something that said *Weapons Oil Arctic* on the front. Every component had to be inspected, wiped down and oiled, he said. The gun already looked pretty clean to me but he said pretty clean wouldn't cut it: the tiniest grain of dirt could screw up the mechanism or prevent the firing pin striking the tail of the bullet. I thought of Marv's pistol, buried for weeks in the snow outside Mount Weather where I dropped it after I shot the fury. I doubt it would have worked even if I'd had bullets for it.

I set to with the swabs. He watched me for a while and then he reached down to his hip and slid the pistol he carries out of its holster. He laid it on the table and started emptying the bullets from the chamber. We worked in silence. When I finished with the last piece he had me reassemble the rifle and then he inspected it. He said I hadn't wiped the bolt carrier down properly. He told me to strip it and start again.

The bolt carrier was fine; it was the last thing I checked before I put the rifle back together. I reckon Hicks was trying to give me something to do, something to keep my mind from turning to what I had just learned, and I guess I should be grateful to him for that. But all I could think of as I sat there surrounded by slides and springs and receivers, the smell of the oiled metal heavy in the air, was Eden's armory. The assault rifles standing to attention in their racks, the blue-gray steel gleaming dully in the glare from the overhead lights. The bank of refrigerator cabinets against the back wall that for a decade housed the virus that ended our world.

The same virus that now works its way through Mags' veins.

Outside the wind howls, rattling the silted panes in their frames. The fire in the grate slowly burns down and one by one the quaking embers die. I don't bother to stoke it, I just wait in the darkness, letting the room turn cold around me.

Hicks says it'll be okay. The medicine Dr. Gilbey's giving Mags will keep her from turning until she can find a cure. But all I can think of is Marv. Marv had been strong, but he didn't last the three days it took us to hike the Catoctin Mountain Highway to the Blue Ridge Mountain Road.

I go back to watching the storm. As long as it stays to the south of us we'll leave in the morning. There's a big hospital out in Blacksburg. It'll be a hard hike through the mountains, but Hicks reckons we can be there in a little over a day if we push. It has a radiology department. There's a good chance we'll find what Dr. Gilbey needs there.

The thought of going looking for one of those things that attacked me in Mount Weather's tunnel scares me almost more than I can bear. But that's what I must do now, for as long as it takes Dr. Gilbey to find a cure for Mags.

CHAPTER TWENTY-EIGHT

WE SET off at first light. Ortiz and Jax are already waiting in the lobby when I get down. Ortiz asks if I want breakfast but I don't think I can eat so I just shake my head and hoist my pack onto my back. Hicks hands me a rifle and I sling it over my shoulder.

We leave The Greenbrier and head for the interstate. The storm continues to pound the horizon but it's keeping its distance, so we press on into Virginia and pick up a road the sign says is the Kanawha Trail. From there it's a steep climb. Hicks doesn't let the pace drop and soon my legs are burning, but I'm glad for it. No one speaks. That suits me fine, too.

We stop for lunch by the side of the road at a place called Crows. Ortiz and Jax share a pack of cold frankfurters between them while Hicks just sips from his thermos. I'm not feeling hungry but he says I have to eat, so I dig an MRE out of my pack and set it to warm. When it's done I pick at it for a while and then hand the pouch to Ortiz. While he's scooping out the remains Hicks picks up the cardboard carton my meal came in. He packs it with snow and then hands it to Jax.

'Take that down the road and place it on the guardrail, just in front of that first tree.'

He looks at me.

'Alright, on your feet. Time for your first lesson with the rifle.'

I stand.

'Show me your trigger finger.'

I slide off my mitten and hold up my right hand. The cold bites immediately, even through the liners I'm wearing. He reaches over and grabs my index finger. A short knife with a serrated edge appears in his other hand. Before I have a chance to protest he tucks the tip of the blade into the liner at the crook of the first joint and slides it forward. The knife must be sharp; the material puts up no resistance as it slices through. He withdraws the blade, folds it back into its handle, and just as quickly it disappears back into his parka.

'You always need to be able to feel the trigger. Now you can poke your finger out when you need to take the shot and slide it back in again when you're done.

I hold my hand up and examine the liner, still a little shocked by the speed with which it happened. There's a slit that reaches almost up to the tip of the glove.

He reaches for my backpack and sets it down in the snow in front of me.

'Alright now, lay down.'

I snap off my snowshoes and lie behind the pack. He squats next to me and sets the rifle down so the barrel rests across it. He tells me to take hold of it. It feels a little weird at first; the thick down of the parka makes it hard for the stock to sit snug into my shoulder.

'Push it a little bit forward and away from you, then tuck it back in to get it at the right spot. That's it.'

Down the road Jax is placing the MRE carton on top of the guardrail, packing snow around it. When he's done he turns around and starts lumbering back towards us.

Hicks pulls a clip from his pocket, thumbs in three bullets and hands it to me. I slide it up into the housing and feel it lock into place. He points to the charging handle and tells me to pull it back to load the first round into the chamber.

'It's a shade under a hundred yards to that carton. The scope's zeroed to that range. Take a look.'

The rifle feels cold against my cheek, even through the thin cotton of the mask. I squint through the sights, adjusting my aim until the center of the crosshairs settles on the cardboard container. Jax is already safely out of the way so I poke my finger through the slit Hicks made in my glove liner and start to slide it onto the trigger.

'Did I tell you to do that yet?'

I slide my finger back out of the trigger guard.

'Alright, first take a long deep breath and let it out. Now remember to keep looking through the scope after you take the shot. You'll want to see where the bullet lands.'

I nod.

'Take the weapon off safe, but only one click, mind. You want it on semi, not auto.'

I find the switch with my thumb and slide it forward one notch.

'Good. Now you're set.'

The metal feels cold as I curl my finger around it. I realize my heart's pounding. I slowly start to squeeze, feeling the slack come out of the mechanism. All of a sudden there's a loud crack and the rifle thumps back into my shoulder before I'm ready for it. The parka absorbs most of the recoil but nevertheless it startles me and I allow the muzzle to jump. By the time it settles back down again it's all over. I have no idea where the bullet's gone. All I know is the MRE carton remains exactly where Jax placed it on the guardrail, unmolested.

'Alright, shift your shoulder forward for me. That's it; make sure your body's leaning into the stock. Now remember you need to hold the gun on target long enough to see where the bullet hits.'

I put my cheek back to the metal, once again finding the carton through the scope. I breathe out slowly, squeezing the trigger as the air slips from my lungs, and this time when the gun jumps I'm ready for it. The muzzle rises up a little but not much and I catch a puff of snow behind and to the right of the carton where the bullet lands.

Hicks unsnaps the throat of his parka and pulls down his bandana. He just stands there for a moment, like he's checking something. When he's done he holds his hand out for the rifle.

'That'll do for now. Wind's picking up and I haven't shown you how to compensate for it. No point in wasting bullets.'

I remember the thing that chased me out of Mount Weather's tunnel. I kept firing Marv's pistol at it, but not a single bullet found its target. This gun might be the only thing standing between me and whatever we find in Blacksburg tomorrow. I need to know I can do it.

'There's a round left. Let me try one more time.'

Hicks squints down at me. For a moment he looks like he's going to say no, but then he just shrugs.

'Alright.'

This time I pull my mask down so I can feel the wind on my face. I imagine it blowing across the tracks we made, slowly filling in the prints left by our snowshoes. I put my cheek back to the rifle. Without the thin cotton the freezing metal bites the flesh there, but I ignore it. I look through the scope, finding the carton again. I see how the wind picks up the snow, swirling the flakes in little eddies over the guardrail, dancing them around the cardboard. I shift the barrel a fraction so the crosshairs hover in the air no more than a hand's breadth to the left then I exhale slowly and squeeze. I feel the recoil, but this time I'm on it and the muzzle barely moves. For an instant I smell burnt gas; it mixes with the sweet scent of the gun oil and then just as quickly the wind carries it away. Down the road the carton disappears from the guardrail in a puff of snow.

]Behind me Ortiz whistles.

'Damn, Sarge. The kid might just have a talent for this.'

CHAPTER TWENTY-NINE

IT'S the footsteps he hears first, just like always. He looks across at the girl. She still hasn't moved from the back of her cage. She went there after the mean soldier left and she hasn't stirred since.

He shuffles himself away from the bars and starts the count. There's something different, now: not one set of footsteps but two. He closes his eyes and concentrates on separating them. The first is definitely the lumbering *thunk-clang* of the boots the mean soldier wears. But the second are lighter, quieter; the footsteps of a much smaller person. He knows immediately who they belong to.

It's been a while since the doctor visited. He casts a guilty glance in the direction of the food tray that sits, untouched, near the front of his cage. He had meant to eat some of it, but he thought he would have more time. He wonders if he should try now. He scurries forward and lifts the plastic spoon from the congealed mess of beans and tobacco, but then thinks better of it. He only has moments; he'll be able to manage a mouthful at best. And recently the food has started to make him feel like he might throw up, even when the mean soldier hasn't done anything to it. It will be worse if the doctor thinks that the food is making him sick.

The count reaches eighty-nine and somewhere off in the darkness he hears the click as the locks disengage and a soft groan as the door is opened. Across from him the girl has moved to the front of her cage and is looking out through the bars. He shuffles back into the corner and listens. The doctor is coming first; the heels she wears click hollowly on the hard floor. He can hear the soldier's boots scuffing the concrete in her wake, the beam from the flashlight he carries dancing between the rows of cages. He keeps his eyes open, making an effort not to squint. He does not want the doctor to know the light bothers him.

She stops in front of his cage. Her face appears in front of the bars as she bends down to look in, but it's a perfunctory examination and for once he is grateful. She turns around to face the girl. The soldier catches up and stands beside her, the stick held loosely by his side. Johnny 99 wishes the girl would go to the back of her cage like she's supposed to, but she doesn't. She just sits there holding the bars.

'Do I need to have the Corporal place you in restraints?'

The girl considers this for a moment and then shakes her head.

'Good. He told me you refused to take your medicine yesterday.'

The girl looks up at the soldier.

'That's not how I would have described it. We had a misunderstanding over his use of the cattle prod.'

The doctor *tsks* her disapproval.

'Yes, he is something of a blunt instrument, aren't you Corporal?'

'Ma'am.'

She turns to the soldier and holds out her hand. He passes her the stick. Her fingers slide along the shaft, all the way to the metal prongs that protrude from the end. The girl doesn't move, but she watches the doctor closely.

'They are such ugly things, aren't they? Do you know we found them here? I suppose the powers that be – the powers that *were* I should say – anticipated a certain amount of unrest, even among their appointed representatives. They have proved useful, though. Those infected with the ferrovirus are quite susceptible to the effects of electricity, far more so than the rest of us.'

'Was it you, who gave it to me?'

'Yes, dear, and no doubt you feel aggrieved. What you need to understand is that I really had no alternative. We are running very short on time. The electromagnetic pulse Kane thought would destroy the virus did not have that effect. I could have told him of course, had he thought to consult me. It is so much more resilient than he ever gave it credit for. But then the man was always such a buffoon. The only real surprise is that he was capable of conceiving a plan of such scope in the first place.'

The doctor regards the baton a moment longer and then hands it back to the soldier.

'But I digress. The net result of course is that the infected were not permanently disabled; they have merely been temporarily incapacitated. At some point, I suspect not very long from now, they will begin to wake from their slumber. And when that happens there will be nowhere for you or Gabriel or anyone else who might still be alive out there to hide. So you see my dear, in a sense your fate was already sealed. I just speeded the process up a little in the interest of finding a cure for all of us.'

The girl's brow furrows as the doctor explains this.

'You didn't come down here to give me that speech so you could feel better about what you've done.'

'Quite right dear, well said. Let's cut to the chase, shall we? The reason I am here is Gabriel.'

'Does he know?'

'That you have become infected? Yes. He thinks you accidentally contracted the virus while trespassing in my laboratory. I know dear, another awful deception; no doubt you are horrified. But if I could just have your attention for a few more minutes; this is really rather important. I have developed several prototypes of an antivirus, but unfortunately I am lacking subjects on which to test them. If it were not for Sergeant Hicks' intervention Gabriel would already be down here with you. But the Sergeant has convinced me that your young man can be more valuable to us on the outside. I have therefore agreed to give him a short trial. He has left this morning with the other men to try and find a suitable subject for my experiments.'

'What do you mean, "a suitable subject for your experiments"?'

'Why, a live infected, of course.'

The expression on the girl's face doesn't change, but Johnny 99 thinks he sees her grip on the bars tighten. If the doctor notices she shows no sign of caring.

'As long as Gabriel proves himself useful he won't have to join you down here. He has however insisted on seeing you, and against my better judgment I'm considering having you brought out to him, assuming of course that he returns. Would you like that, Magdalene?'

This seems to take the girl by surprise. She looks up at the doctor.

'Yes.'

'Good. You will need to maintain the fiction of how you came to be here, of course. Do you understand?'

The girl nods.

'Very well. Corporal Truckle will come down to prepare you. You will do exactly as he says or the next time you see Gabriel he will be in the cage next to you. Is that clear?'

The girl nods her head again, but doesn't say anything. The doctor is about to turn away when she speaks.

'Can you do it?'

'Do what, dear?'

'Find a cure for Kane's virus.'

The doctor pauses for a long moment, and when she finally answers it seems to Johnny 99 that she is speaking to herself as much as to the girl.

'It is a truly remarkable piece of engineering; so incredibly tenacious. You only have to look at how little time it took to supplant us as the dominant organism on this planet.' She looks down at the girl. 'But yes, given enough time and an adequate supply of subjects on which to test my work, I can find a cure.'

'What makes you so sure?'

'Because the virus isn't Kane's, my dear. It's mine.'

CHAPTER THIRTY

WE REACH Blacksburg the morning after. We pick up signs for the hospital on the outskirts of town, following them up a winding access road. Cars mount the sidewalk at haphazard angles; others sit abandoned where they came to rest, their trunks agape like startled mouths.

Stonewall Hospital waits for us atop a low promontory. What must once have been an imposing structure now lies in ruin. One entire wing seems to have crumbled under its own weight; to the west it ends abruptly in a mound of broken concrete and twisted rebar. On the other side things seem to have fared only slightly better; the roofline dips alarmingly at various points as whatever was bracing it there has succumbed. Rows of dark windows march off towards the last remaining corner, staring down at us as we approach.

Marv always said we had to stay clear of places like this, so I've never set foot inside one. I've read enough from the newspaper articles I used to collect to imagine what they must have been like, though. The hospitals were where the virus cases were taken, at least at first, before anyone knew what we were dealing with. Later they would work it out, but by then of course it was too late. There were reports the military took to targeting them in the end, in a last desperate attempt to halt the spread. I can't say if that was true. I only know that if it was it didn't work.

Hicks leads us towards a tall atrium that juts from the center. The steel uprights have buckled and now they list drunkenly, the large glass panes that would have once completed that part of the structure long since released from their frames. The parking lot's full, a sea of humped gray shapes resting silent under a blanket of snow; we have to pick our way through. As we get closer I can see an ambulance has crashed into the entrance, coming to rest half-in, half-out of the lobby. The rear doors hang open. A gurney that looks like it might have been ejected from the back pokes out of the snow nearby.

We unsnap our snowshoes and make our way in. Hicks goes first. The Viking follows, pressing himself up against the ambulance's paneled flank as he squeezes past. I'm beginning to wonder whether Jax even realizes there's been a virus; maybe to him the world seems just like how it's always been. Ortiz goes next, but at least he shows the good sense to give the once-contaminated vehicle a wider berth.

I hang back. I've been preparing myself for this, but now I hesitate. The fear of what we will find in here rises up, coiling around my insides, settling in my stomach like ice water.

I take a deep breath and step through. Inside it's darker; I lift my goggles onto my forehead and look around. A sign on the wall says to use the hand sanitizer provided, but the dispenser's been ripped from beneath it and is nowhere in sight. Over in the far corner a soft drinks machine lies on its side, its front smashed, the contents long since plundered.

The soldiers have already taken off their backpacks and set them on the ground. I shuck mine off too. Hicks removes his gloves and unzips his parka. He draws the pistol from the holster on his hip and starts rotating the cylinder, checking each of the chambers in turn. When he's done he steps over to a directory that's hanging from the wall behind reception.

Ortiz draws a long black stick from his pack, like one of the billy clubs the Guardians used to carry in Eden, except for the two metal prongs protruding from the end. Hicks told me the furies don't care much for electricity; a single jolt should be enough to knock one out long enough for Jax to bag it. As I watch Ortiz holds the baton up and thumbs a switch on the handle. An arc of blue light jumps between the prongs. He looks at me and then over to Hicks.

'Remind me again why this ain't the kid's job?'

Hicks doesn't take his eyes off the wall.

'Gabe'll get his turn. But first he's going to watch how you do it.'

He turns to me.

'You ready?'

I nod, mostly because right now I don't trust myself to speak. I sling the rifle off my shoulder and pull the handle back to load a round into the chamber, like he showed me.

'Alright. Just keep your eyes peeled and try not to shoot anything you don't mean to.'

I tell myself I can do that.

'Jax, you got the bag?' The Viking's huge fist finally emerges from his backpack gripping a large sack made of thick black plastic.

'Okay then. Let's get this done.'

We follow Ortiz down a long hallway into darkness, our footfalls the only sound in the cold silence. I can hear my heart hammering, beating wild inside my ribcage. I check each doorway and alcove we pass, my eyes darting into the shadows, searching for whatever might be waiting for us there.

At last the corridor ends, and another runs off at right angles. Ortiz stops to get his bearings. There's a map stuck to the wall next to me, above a drinking fountain. I shoulder the rifle and dig in my pocket for the flashlight. The little dynamo whirs as I turn the stubby plastic handle, but before the bulb has the chance to warm Hicks growls at me to turn it off.

Up ahead Ortiz must have figured it out because he holds the stick up and signals left. We follow him around the corner. I see him reach inside his parka and a second later a cone of red light appears in front of him, casting the corridor in shades of crimson and black.

A bank of elevators appears out of the gloom. As we approach I can see that the doors of the last one are open. I'm not in control of the flashlight so it takes me a moment to figure out why. The body of what once was a man is holding them open. He's lying there inside his rotting clothes, all shriveled and drawn, what little remains of his flesh cloven along the bones. His ligaments have dried taut as wires, curling him up into a tight ball. We step around him and continue on.

The beam from the flashlight settles on an abandoned gurney ahead of us. It's sitting at an angle across the corridor in front of what looks like a nurse's station. Something that might once have been a woman lies slumped over it, little more than the trellis of a person, the hide stretched over the bones all dried and shrunken inside what's left of her uniform. The wheels of the gurney are locked. Their screeched complaint echoes down the corridor as Ortiz pushes it out of the way.

We make our way further into the darkness. There are more bodies now, strewn about like so much flotsam and jetsam. Sometimes they lie by themselves, other times they huddle together, a frieze of heads and limbs and torsos, so many that we have to pick our way between them. I try not to look down as I step over them, but I can't help it. All their faces are alike, the same rictus grins and gray, rotting teeth and hollow eyes.

I thought I was used to seeing stuff like this, from the years I spent scavenging with Marv.

It turns out I'm not.

CHAPTER THIRTY-ONE

THE HALLWAY ENDS at a door with a sign for a staircase above. Ortiz opens it with the toe of his boot and points the flashlight into the crack. He peers after it for a long while, then pushes it open and disappears through. Hicks follows him.

We make our way down the concrete stairwell, the sound of our boots echoing and rebounding around us. It gets colder as we descend; every time Ortiz exhales now I see his breath hanging red in the air in front of him. Hicks pulls off his liners and starts slowly opening and closing his hands, flexing his fingers.

Eventually we reach the bottom. Ortiz opens another door and steps through. We follow him into another corridor, this one mostly free of bodies. More doors lead off to the left and right. We come to a section where the wall's blown out. Jagged fragments of metal, what looks like the remains of an oxygen tank, have embedded themselves in the concrete. More lie scattered across the floor. They clink against each other as Ortiz moves them out of the way with his boot.

Up ahead the corridor opens into what seems to have been a makeshift ward. On both sides cots stretch off into darkness. Ortiz stops and raises the stick in the air and we wait while he slowly scans from left to right with the flashlight. It looks like there was a fire here. The paint on the walls has blistered and the floor and ceiling are covered in a thick layer of soot. As the beam slides over the beds I can see that the bodies that lie there are just so much charred meat, their blackened skin stretched over their bones, their faces split and shrunken on their skulls. The air down here is stale, spent, and for once I'm thankful; the smells that remain are mercifully faint.

We move forward again. To the right another row of cots, this time untouched by flame. But the bodies that lie strapped to the beds are different from the ones we saw in the corridor upstairs. Scraps of clothing hang in rotten tatters from their cadaverous frames, but as the beam from Ortiz's flashlight slides over them I can see that underneath the skin is the color of the snow outside, and unblemished by decay. They look just like they're sleeping. I close my eyes and take a deep breath, gathering what remains of my courage around me. When I open them again Hicks has already moved on ahead.

———

The corridor ends at a set of large double doors underneath a sign that says *Radiology*. A glass panel, reinforced with crisscrossed safety wire, sits in the center of each. Ortiz holds his flashlight up and peers through for a long time before he finally goes in.

The first door we come to is ajar. A small plaque in the

center says *Darkroom*. Ortiz pushes it with his boot and it creaks back. He points the flashlight inside. The beam slips over a series of shallow stainless-steel tanks. Racks hanging haphazardly from the ceiling cast strange shadows against the walls. When he's satisfied there's nothing hiding among them Ortiz motions with the baton and we continue on.

We make our way slowly down the corridor, checking each room as we go. As we get to the end a large sliding door stretches across one wall, from floor to ceiling. Ortiz shines the flashlight across the metal. Leprous patches spread across it, almost obscuring a yellow and black radiation warning sign. A panel to one side that looks like it would once have lit up reads *X-Ray In Use*. Ortiz tries to slide the door out of the way, but it's slipped off its track on one side and won't budge.

Hicks turns to Jax.

'Well don't just stand there. Go on and help him.'

The blond giant steps forward and bends down, slipping his fingers under the door. It groans in protest as he takes its weight and then there's a loud metallic clang that echoes along the hallway as he lets it fall back onto its track. He grips one edge with a huge glove and pulls. The runners screech in protest, but inch by inch the door slides back until there's a gap large enough for a person to fit through.

Hicks' fingers move closer to the pistol on his hip. He tells me to be ready, so I press the rifle to my cheek. I take a deep breath to try and steady the barrel, but my hands are shaking too much for that to work.

Ortiz picks up the flashlight and shines it into a large, tiled room. Some of the tiles have peeled away, revealing a dark surface that shines dully as the light slides over it. A table where people would have had their X-rays taken waits in the center; even from here I can see how badly corroded the metal is. There's a cubicle in the far corner from where the machine would have been controlled. The glass is broken; it gives back fractured carmine images as Ortiz points the beam at it. After a moment he steps inside, continuing to sweep the room. I wait, holding my breath. My insides feel like they've been scooped out and replaced with *Reddi-wip*. But there's nothing. He turns around and motions to Hicks that we can move on.

As I step back to let him out I catch a glimpse of something, slipping from behind the operator booth. Ortiz has his back to it; he hasn't noticed yet. My eyes widen but for a second I just stand, paralyzed with fear, the gun heavy and useless in my hands.

Hicks must see it now too, or maybe he just reads what's written on my face. If he's shocked he doesn't show it: his expression doesn't alter. But then I reckon Hicks is the kind of person who does his freaking and starting mostly on the inside. By the time I open my mouth to stammer a warning he's already shoving me out of the way. The hands that were empty a moment ago now hold a pistol.

Ortiz finally realizes something's wrong an instant before Hicks starts firing. I'm expecting it, but the noise the old gun makes is loud in such a confined space and I jump. The inside of the room reveals itself in a series of flashbulb images. The fury suddenly on top of the X-ray table, lit for an instant by the flare from the muzzle. Dark circles surrounding silvered eyes, thin lips pulled back wide. Sparks fly and a bullet shrieks and whines off the metal where an instant before it was perched. The next time Hicks fires the flash catches it in midair as it launches itself. I think I see the bullet graze its shoulder, but it barely seems to notice.

Ortiz has dropped the flashlight and is desperately trying

to bring the baton up to ward off the attack, but he's left it way too late. Long, thin fingers are already clawing at his neck; its teeth snap furiously.

Hicks adjusts his aim and fires one last time, and this time the bullet finds its mark. The fury releases its grip and drops to the floor. The burnt stench of gunpowder hangs heavy in the air. Hicks steps into the room.

'Did it get you?'

Ortiz doesn't respond. He just stares at the thing lying there on the floor, the beam from the discarded flashlight casting ugly red shadows across its contorted features. Hicks grabs him by the shoulder and repeats the question. When he still gets no answer he unsnaps the throat of Ortiz's parka and pulls the collar back. A second later his hand falls away. Ortiz finally seems to come back from wherever he's been. He tears his eyes off the fury and looks up at Hicks.

'How bad is it, man? Can you fix it?'

Hicks looks for a moment longer and then just shakes his head. Ortiz just nods, once, like he understands.

'You know I can't go back, Sarge, not like this.'

I see Hicks raise a finger to his lips. Without turning around he tells Jax to get me out. But I just stand there, rooted to the spot with fear. The Viking steps in front of me and extends one huge arm. At last I tear my gaze from the fury and allow myself to be shepherded back in the direction of the stairwell. I've barely made it a half-dozen paces when a single final shot rings out and then it goes quiet again.

CHAPTER THIRTY-TWO

THE STORM that's been keeping its distance for the last couple of days looks like it's finally coming our way. It's still too far off to hear the thunder, but the sky behind us crackles with lightning.

Hicks picks up the pace. There's no talking and the hike back passes in cold silence. When we finally stop to eat he sits apart and sips from his thermos. I break out an MRE but I'm not hungry and after a few mouthfuls I hand it to Jax.

I wonder if he blames me for what happened to Ortiz. Maybe if I hadn't frozen when I first saw that thing crawl out from behind the booth he could have been saved. Well even if that's true there's nothing I can do about it now. The fact is Ortiz is dead and we have nothing to show for it. It's already been days since Mags was infected. The best I can hope for is that the storm will shift course and Hicks will want to take us out again soon.

Only next time it'll be my turn to step into a darkened room with a baton and wait for one of those things to come at me.

———

It's long after dark when we make it back to The Greenbrier. The storm hasn't switched direction. All afternoon it's followed us, growing steadily closer, and now the lightning is accompanied by the low rumble of thunder. It'll be with us tonight, tomorrow morning at the latest.

The flags snap and flutter on their flagpoles as we make our way up to the entrance. We pass under the massive portico and remove our snowshoes. The camera above me blinks as I open the door and step through. A flurry of snowflakes follows me inside.

I take my mittens off and rub my hands together to get some feeling back into my frozen fingers. The emergency lights are on and from somewhere down below I hear the low thrum of a generator. Hicks has already shucked off his backpack and is unzipping his parka. He still hasn't said a word to me. Whether or not he holds me responsible for Ortiz I need something from him now. I undo my boots and bring them over to the bellhop cart.

'You promised you'd let me see Mags.'

He looks at me for a long moment.

'Yes, I did.'

He hands me Ortiz's rifle.

'Get that cleaned, yours too. I'll come find you when we're ready.'

I sling the rifles over my shoulder and head for the dining room. The Viking is already sitting at the table when I walk in. He looks up from his plate of franks, his flat blue stare following me as I cross the room.

When we first met Hicks said Jax was harmless, but after what happened in the hospital I'm not so sure. Marv warned me when Peck came for us there'd be no reasoning or pleading with him, and I wonder if it'd be any different with the Viking. I saw the look on his face when Hicks told him to get me out of there, after the fury got Ortiz. It was the same vacant expression I'd pretty much gotten used to. But I think I know how it would have gone if I hadn't complied.

I go to work, trying not to look over at him. At some point he finishes eating. He stares at me a while longer then gets up and lumbers off in the direction of the door without saying a word. When I'm done with Ortiz's rifle I start stripping down mine. When they're both clean I reassemble them and then just sit there and wait.

Hicks shows up not long after. He says they're ready for me. I follow him back through the lobby and then down the long corridor that leads to the Colonial Lounge. When we get to the Exhibition Hall Dr. Gilbey's already there. She turns around and gives me a tight-lipped smile. Behind her the screen's been pulled back. The emergency lamp bolted to the wall above it flickers, casting the alcove behind in intermittent shadow. I can see the vault door's open, but little beyond. I start to cross the hall to join her, but she holds up a hand.

'That's far enough, Gabriel.'

She turns back towards the entrance to the bunker.

'You can bring her out now, Corporal.'

Hicks puts a gloved hand on my arm.

'Prepare yourself, son. They've had to bind her.'

At first there's nothing and then I hear a shuffling coming from the darkness and for an instant all I can think is that it's the same sound the fury that was stalking me in Mount Weather's tunnel made. The footsteps grow steadily louder until eventually something steps out of the shadows.

Her head's been shaved, her almost-black hair a stubbled furze. A strip of duct tape covers her mouth and there's a thin plastic noose around her neck. She's wearing dark overalls that seem several sizes too big for her. The cuffs are rolled up and her hands are held together at her waist, like they've been cable-tied there. There are more plastic restraints binding her ankles.

Her eyes scan the room for a second before they find me. There are worrying shadows there, but when she turns her head I can see the pupils are dark, just like they've always been.

She continues to shuffle forward until she clears the door and then she stops and Truck steps out from behind her. The noose around her neck's attached to a long pole, the kind of device you might see being used to round up strays for the pound. Truck's gripping the other end with both hands, his tongue working the wad of tobacco that's tucked behind his lip. He glances over at me and I think I catch a trace of a smile, like maybe this is a show he's glad he got tickets for.

I look back at Mags.

'Are you okay?'

She nods, once, a terse gesture.

I turn to Hicks.

'Take the tape off. I want to talk to her.'

Hicks' eyes never leave her. His voice remains calm, but the tips of his fingers don't stray far from the pistol on his hip.

'Can't do that son.'

Mags' eyes flick over to Hicks then back to me, like she's trying to work something out.

'How... how did it happen?'

It seems like a stupid question, but it's the only one I can think of right now.

Dr. Gilbey slips her hands into the pockets of her lab coat and turns to face me.

'Well, I blame myself, of course, Gabriel. It was an unforgivable error.' She shakes her head, but it's a brusque gesture, sterile and unconvincing. 'I asked Magdalene to remain in the dormitory, but I didn't think to lock her in there. I thought she could be trusted not to wander off. After I had gone to sleep she must have taken it upon herself to explore.'

I look back at Mags. The expression on her face hasn't changed, but I recognize that look in her eyes. She's furious. She glances over at Hicks, like she's checking whether he's still watching. Her eyes switch back to me one last time and for a second she holds my gaze, like she's trying to tell me something. Then without warning she throws herself forward towards Dr. Gilbey. It happens so fast she catches Truck by surprise.

For all his size he recovers quickly. He yanks the pole back towards him and then lifts it up. I see the noose tighten around her neck; her head jerks backwards and she's forced onto her toes, her feet scrabbling for purchase on the tiles. The muscles along Truck's arms bunch as he hoists her up and I hear him grunt with the effort of it, but he holds her there and in that moment I know I would kill him if I had the means. I take a step forward but I make no more than that. Something grabs my arm and in the same instant I feel a pressure against my thigh and then the room's spinning around me; the next thing I know I'm lying on my back staring up at the Exhibition Hall's ceiling. I try to get up but Hicks has a knee on my chest, pinning me there; for someone so thin he's surprisingly strong. He fixes me with a stare from his one good eye while he barks an order at Truck to set Mags down.

Truck hesitates for a second and then lowers the pole. She drops to her knees, gasping for breath.

If Dr. Gilbey is shaken by this she doesn't show it. She slowly removes her hands from the pockets of her lab coat and folds them across her chest. She nods at Truck.

'Take her back inside Corporal.'

Hicks looks up for a second.

'Gently, Truck.'

He lifts the pole and Mags gets unsteadily to her feet. She manages one last glance in my direction before she's herded back through the door and in that second our eyes meet and I nod.

The emergency lights flicker, like they might go out, then steady. Hicks watches the door for a second more, then looks back down at me.

'If I let you up will you be calm?'

I nod and a moment later I feel a weight lifted from my chest as he stands. He holds out a gloved hand to help me up.

'Now I know today was rough. That was to be expected, your first time and all. But you can't give up. She needs you now, son. And trust me, it'll get easier.'

I nod again, so he'll think I'm listening, but the truth is I'm not. I know what I have to do now, and it doesn't involve following him into another hospital to look for one of those things that attacked Ortiz. I need to be by myself to work this through, though. I glance over at Dr. Gilbey and then back at him.

'How soon can we go out again?'

CHAPTER THIRTY-THREE

THE GIRL HAS BEEN GONE for some time now, but still the scent lingers.

It was worse before.

After the doctor left she sat quietly for a while. Then without warning she leaned back and kicked the bars. He had been worried she was going to bring the mean soldier down again, but she only did it once, and afterwards she went to the back of her cage and sat there for a long time without moving. When she finally stirred it was only to reach for the food tray and he had been happy then because he thought maybe she was going to eat something. But all she took was the plastic spoon. He saw her wipe it on her overalls and a little while later he thought he heard a sound like plastic splintering.

It was shortly after that he smelled it. Faint at first, fainter than when the soldier had hurt his elbow right in front of his cage, but growing stronger with every passing minute. He felt the now-familiar knot in his stomach, felt it begin to twist, to gnaw at his insides. He pushed himself all the way to the back of his cage and covered his face with his hands to try and shut it out. It was no use, though. The scent was still there; it slipped between his fingers, filling his nostrils, sliding down the back of his throat until he could almost taste it. There was no way to escape it.

It had been a relief when the soldier had come to take her away.

He had watched as she had put on the restraints. She had glared at the soldier when he had slid the catchpole into the cage, but in the end she had let him slip the noose over her head and bring her out. She had been a little unsteady on her feet at first, and at one point as the soldier had led her towards the door he had heard her stumble and the soldier had cursed. It had taken her a long time to climb the stairs.

Now he hears footsteps again and he knows she is returning. She descends very slowly, but then finally he hears the click as the locks disengage and then the door opens and moments later there's the soft shuffle of her feet on the concrete as she approaches. The beam from the soldier's flashlight bounces ahead of them down the aisle. It seems brighter than it was earlier; he screws his eyes shut against it. The footsteps stop in front of his cage and there's the sound of the latch being sprung and the door opening. The scent returns, thankfully fainter now than it was before. He opens his eyes a fraction, just in time to see the soldier's face appearing at the bars. He reaches into the breast pocket of his fatigues, pulls out a container of the medicine and tosses it in.

'Here, take that while I sort her out.'

Johnny 99 shuffles forward and collects the medicine while the soldier manhandles the girl into her cage. After what happened the other day he's taking no chances. He keeps a tight hold on the pole so that her head's pulled back against the bars while he undoes the restraint that loops around her waist. Then he lifts the noose over her head and slides it out and latches the door closed. The girl raises her cuffed hands to her neck and rubs there.

The soldier squats in front of her cage. He reaches into his pocket and takes out another container of the medicine.

'Now before I give you this I think you owe old Truck here an apology for all the trouble you've been causing.'

The girl stares at the container. It reminds Johnny 99 he has to take his own medicine, or the soldier will be mad at him. He unscrews the cap and raises the vial to his lips, bracing himself for the bitter taste.

The girl shakes her head.

'I wonder what's going to happen to you, Corporal, if you have to go back to the doctor and tell her you couldn't get me to take my medicine again? Seems like having someone down here is important to her.' She looks up at the roof of the cage, only inches above her head. 'Would someone like you really fit in one of these?'

But the soldier just returns the container to his pocket. When he speaks again Johnny 99 hears the smile in his voice.

'Oh darlin', I ain't going to tell the Doc any such thing. This time my report'll say you drank it all down.'

He looks at the container the soldier's just given him. That's twice the girl will have missed her medicine. He searches his cage for the plastic cup his water comes in and quickly transfers half the contents of the vial to it, then he pushes the cup into the shadows behind him.

The soldier nods at the cuffs on the girl's wrists and ankles as he gets to his feet.

'And you can stay in those for a while. Might teach you some manners.'

He turns around to face the boy, banging the bars with the toe of his boot.

'You done in there yet?'

He makes a show of draining what remains in the plastic container, then he places it near the front of his cage and backs away. Without water to wash it away the taste is over-powering. He presses his lips tight together and concentrates on not returning what he's just swallowed to the floor of his cage. The soldier doesn't seem to notice. He rummages in his pocket for a Ziploc bag, wraps it around his hand and uses it to pick up the spent vial. He holds it up to the flashlight to check it's empty, then presses the seal closed and stands. The beam recedes as he makes his way back down the aisle. The door opens with a soft groan and then there's a click as the locks engage, followed seconds later by the distant sound of boots on metal as he starts to climb the stairs.

He waits a long time after the last footstep's faded to silence. When he's sure the soldier isn't coming back he picks up the cup and slides it out between the bars, pushing it across the concrete with his fingertips. If he lies down and stretches out he can get it almost halfway across the space between the cages. When he can get it no further he pulls his arm back through the bars and whispers to the girl to let her know what he's done. She lies on the floor of her cage like he did and slips her hands out through the bars. Her arms are longer than his so the cup should be within her grasp, but her wrists are still cuffed together, which limits her reach. And he almost forgets that she can't see either; the first time she manages to get her fingertips to it she almost knocks it over. He shuffles to the front of his cage and whispers directions.

She pulls her hands back through the bars, adjusts her position and tries again. This time her fingers wrap around the plastic and she pulls it back in.

He watches as she lifts the cup to her lips and drinks the medicine. When she's done she bends over to retch and for a moment the boy thinks she will be sick and it will all have been for nothing. But then it passes and she leans back and runs her fingers around the inside of the cup. When she's extracted the last of whatever's there she sets it down and looks out through the bars. She still can't see in the darkness, so she's not looking right at him when she says it, but it doesn't matter. She whispers thank you, that she won't forget it.

And that makes him sad.

Because he knows she probably will. She can't have long now. In a few days she'll get sick and then the gray curtain will come down and everything she knew from before will be gone.

CHAPTER THIRTY-FOUR

THE INTERVALS between flash and thunder grow shorter as outside the storm bears down. The sky's roiling now, tortured. Lightning shudders inside the thunderheads, lighting them up all the way back to the horizon. The wind howls around the giant columns and gusts against the window, shaking the glass in the flaking frame.

I should get some rest for what lies ahead, but instead I sit on the floor in my parka, just staring out into the darkness. All I can see is Mags, forced onto her toes, her feet scrabbling for purchase on the Exhibition Hall's smooth tiles. I bury my face in my hands and breath, trying to banish the image, but it won't leave. My fingers still smell of the gun oil I've been working with all day. Right after I got to see her Hicks took me into the dining room and sat me down at one of the tables. He brought a bunch of weapons up from the bunker and laid them out in front of me. It was rifles mostly, but there were some pistols too, including one I recognized as Marv's Beretta. I already knew how to strip the M4s, but he showed me how to break each of the other guns down too. When that was done I set to work with a toothbrush and a stack of cotton buds, working the solvent up into the breech, swabbing out the chamber and bore, wiping each part down before finally setting it aside to dry. While I worked he told me where we'll go next. There's a big hospital over in Roanoke, apparently. He reckons it'll take us three days to hike it. We'll set off as soon as the storm clears.

I don't plan on being around for that. I'm still not sure what part he has in all of this, but I know now that Gilbey's not to be trusted. As Truck was hauling Mags off her feet Hicks took his eyes off her for a split second to deal with me. I guess that was what she must have been hoping for. And in that instant she turned her hand toward me and I saw what was written there. A single word scratched into her palm, the dried blood spelling out only three letters.

Run.

So that's what I intend to do. My backpack rests against the wall, ready to go. While everyone was at dinner I snuck down to the lobby and went through the soldiers' gear for the items I'll need. I've spent the last hour fashioning boots to replace the ones I surrendered to the bellhop cart when we came in earlier. I've wrapped the slippers Hicks gave me with strips torn from the blanket on my bed. Sections cut from one of Jax's plastic gunny sacks go around the outside, held in place with the last of the duct tape from my scavenging kit. They don't look pretty but they seem warm enough and the plastic seems tough. Hicks had meant for Jax to carry a fury back inside it, so I guess it must be. They'll have to do until I can find better.

From outside there's another flash, followed a few seconds later by a clap of thunder. Out of habit I count the seconds between, but that's not what I'm waiting for now.

The soldiers came up from dinner almost an hour ago; I heard them talking in the corridor outside. One by one they slipped off to bed, and then it got quiet, the only sounds those of the approaching storm. Hicks knocked on my door a little while later with a plate of franks. I didn't feel much like eating, but I took them anyway. I'll need the sustenance. I have a long night ahead of me.

Across the hallway Truck starts to snore. I wait fifteen minutes to make sure he's completely out of it, then I grab my bag. I used a drop of gun oil on the hinges earlier and the door opens without a sound. I cross the hall. The thick carpet muffles my footsteps, but nevertheless I tiptoe down the stairs. The generator gets cut after dinner so the emergency lights are off, but the flashlight stays in my parka. I make my way across the lobby in darkness. Outside the sky flares, briefly bathing the shrouded furniture in harsh white light. The sound of my makeshift boots scuffing the marble seems loud, but I don't think it'll carry far enough for anyone to hear it, and besides, the storm's kicking up enough of a racket now to cover it. The wind pushes against the entrance door as I open it and I have to hold tight with both hands to prevent it slamming behind me.

It's colder than I was expecting; the wind snatches the breath from me almost before I have a chance to exhale it. I slide the thin cotton mask up over my mouth and fasten the throat of my parka. It's too dark for goggles and the icy snow stings my eyes. I zip the hood all the way up, but the wind whips and tugs at it, threatening to dislodge it even before I've left the shelter of the portico.

My snowshoes are where I left them when we got back. The huge columns tower over me as I slide my makeshift boots into the bindings and ratchet them tight. I've already fixed the soldiers' guns; it was a stroke of unexpected luck Hicks fetching them up for me to work on earlier. Now I pull out the leatherman and hack through the straps on their snowshoes, then toss them off into the darkness. They're bound to have spares so it probably won't do me much good, but I figure every minute I can put between us now will be worth it. When I've taken care of the last of them I shift the backpack so it sits high on my shoulders, tighten the straps and set off.

It's slow going. Until I get out of sight of the house I'm relying on the lightning to show me the way, but between the flashes I'm blind. I grope my way around the helicopter, listening for the creak and groan of its rotors as they twist and flex in the wind. It takes me what seems like forever to reach the road, but finally I'm passing between The Greenbrier's gateposts. I dig in my pocket for the flashlight. The dynamo whirs as I crank the stubby handle. The bulb glows orange, then yellow, finally casting a faint pool of watery light that hardly seems worth the effort.

I take a right and follow the road, grateful that at least now the wind's at my back. Breaking trail keeps me warm for a while, but it doesn't take long for the cold to find its way inside my parka and through the extra layer of thermals I'm wearing. My makeshift footwear's not as warm as the boots I surrendered either; I can already feel my toes tingling. But then that was to be expected. I tell myself I can handle a little bit of cold, and at least the sacking seems to be keeping the snow out. I've barely made it past the church before I begin to sense a more serious problem, however. The duct-taped plastic has no structure to it. When I tried them out in the room my improvised footwear seemed comfortable enough, but of course that was before I strapped on snowshoes and started pounding drifts. Now the hard plastic of the bindings cuts into my feet with each step.

There's little I can do about that now. I need to keep moving; the corrugated crash barriers I'm relying on to show me the way are already disappearing under the drifting snow. I stop and dig out each signpost, every mile marker, even where I'm fairly certain I'm on the right track. The storm will get worse before it gets better, and I can't afford to get lost out here.

CHAPTER THIRTY-FIVE

IT TAKES me three hours to reach the river, almost twice as long as when Hicks and I hiked it the other day. The flashlight shows only the icy flakes that swirl past me in the darkness and I end up missing the sign for the bridge. Before I know it the road underneath me has disappeared and there's a sickening jolt as I feel one foot sinking through into empty air. I try to back up but the tails of my snowshoes dig in and I lose my balance. The wind gusts, like it means to send me over, and for a second it seems like it might succeed. I stagger backwards, arms flailing, and land awkwardly in the snow, pushing large chunks of it over the edge as I scramble back to safety.

I lie there for a moment, just staring up into the shuddering sky. I can't stay here. The storm's almost on me, the gap between lightning and thunder already little more than a heartbeat. I pick myself up and inch forward again. When I've gone as far as I dare I point the flashlight down, but I can't see the water. There's just a black chasm into which the driven snow twists and tumbles. I bend down and unsnap my snowshoes. My feet are already numb with the cold, but it's a relief to step out of them nevertheless. I tie them to the outside of my pack and start to climb down the rubble.

At the river the skiff bobs and jerks against its tether. I pull off the tarp, shuck off my pack and take out the rope. The length I keep with my scavenging kit would never have done, but with what I've taken from Jax's and Weasel's packs I should have enough. I tie one end to the mooring point, throw the rest into the boat and climb in after it. I take a moment to steady myself then cast off, using one of the oars to push the small boat off the bank, like I saw Hicks do. I'm not as practiced at this as he was though, and it pitches and dips alarmingly as I struggle with the current. The windup torch sits meekly between my feet, its yellowing beam only sufficient to illuminate the rope that's slowly paying itself out into the dark water behind me.

Stroke by stroke I work my way across the churning waters. The wind kicks up icy spray; waves lap furiously against the prow and crash against the sides. My arms are soon burning, but in the darkness between flashes it's hard to tell how much progress I'm making. At last I hear a creak and a second later the front of the boat rides up as it crunches into something. Above me lightning strobes, for a second illuminating the crumbling remains of the bridge towering over me. One more pull on the oars and the prow nudges concrete and comes to an unsteady halt. I climb out and carry the end of the rope to the piece of bent-back rebar Hicks used as a mooring point on this side. I feed it through and tie it off to the metal eye that's bolted to the prow, then clamber back in and push off again. It takes me a while to turn the boat around, but as soon as I'm pointed in the right direction I ship the oars; I can use the rope to pull me back now. I brace my feet against the sides and start grabbing armfuls of it. The wind that was at my back on the way out is in my face for the return. Even in the lee of the bank I can feel its strength.

There's a blinding flash of light, followed by a crash of thunder and for a second the sky above me reveals itself, a seething maelstrom of grays and blacks, lit from within. Heavy flakes start to tumble and swirl out of the darkness. The visibility drops, like a thick curtain pulling itself around me, and soon I can barely see the front of the little skiff as it pitches through the waves. The wind wants to push me back but I refuse to let it. With each armful of rope I curse it. The thermals I wear are supposed to wick the sweat away but they're already overwhelmed, and soon it's running freely down my back and sides. I look down into the boat. Only half a dozen loose coils remain and I'm beginning to wonder if I'll make it. Then finally just as the last of them starts to unwind I feel the bottom nudge something.

I pick up the torch and wind it. The beam shows me nothing more than swirling snow, but when I point it over the side I see chunks of ice bobbing up and down in the dark, agitated water. I must be close to the bank. I grab an oar and feel for the bottom. Waves are lapping furiously at the sides, but it's no more than a couple of feet deep. The rope's tied to the hook on the prow; if I untie it to give me the extra few yards I need I'll lose the end in the water and then this will have been for nothing. I give one more pull. The boat moves forward and I feel the hull grate over something that might be rubble. The last of the rope slips over the side.

I look down at my makeshift boots. The duct tape's fraying where the snowshoes' bindings have worked against it, but the plastic underneath seems to be holding. I've wrapped several strips of tape around the top where my pants go into the boot, and the material there is waterproof. It should be enough.

I stand up. The boat rocks dangerously as my foot sinks into the icy water. The surface is uneven and I stumble, but in a couple of steps I'm up on the bank. I grab the tarp from where I left it by the water's edge and step back into the shallows to bundle it in, resting the oars on top so the wind can't catch it. I take the bottle of gas I stole from Boots' pack and douse the thick canvas. I cup my hand around the lighter. It takes a dozen or more tries for it to hold flame, but eventually I get the tarp to light.

I step back out of the water, pick up the rope, start to pull the boat across the river. The flames creep up over the sides, like a funeral pyre. For a while I can follow it, but before long the storm has swallowed it whole. I keep grabbing armfuls of rope until eventually I feel resistance. I give one last heave to make sure it's grounded, then I find a loose lump of concrete and wrap the end of the rope around it several times and tie it off. I go down to the water's edge and heft it as far as I can into the river. The wind drowns the splash; I never hear it. The rope sits on the water for a second and then slowly slips beneath the surface as the concrete sinks to the bottom.

I open my pack and grab some of the firewood I brought from my room. I use the last of Boot's gas to light it. The wind harries the fragile flames, threatening to snuff them out, but whatever he adds to the mix makes it tenacious. I huddle close but it's too small for any warmth. I tell myself that was never its purpose, but the truth is I need it now. My makeshift boots seem to have kept the water out, but inside my feet ache with the cold. The exertion that warmed me on the crossing is working against me now, too; inside my parka I can feel my sweat-soaked thermals cooling against my skin. I set an MRE to heat. As soon as it's ready I wolf down the half-mixed contents before they too have a chance to give up their warmth. When I'm done I scatter the packets that came in the carton around, wedging them under crumbling concrete or impaling them on rebar until the area around me is strewn with trash.

The fire's already burning down and I'm starting to shiver, but at least down here I'm mostly sheltered. I look up. Above me the wind howls over the collapsed bridge, sending flurries of powder tumbling over the edge. I'd like to stay a little longer, but that's not possible. I need to get back now.

Hicks told me Gilbey had a code to get them into The Greenbrier, except that when they got there it didn't work. There's no keypad for the vault door in the Exhibition Hall, though; it only opens from the inside. Which means there must be another door somewhere, one that *will* take a code. I don't know where that might be, but my guess is finding it won't be too difficult; it'll be big, way bigger than the one I've already seen. The blast doors at Eden and Mount Weather and Culpeper were all large enough to drive a truck through, and there's no reason The Greenbrier should be different. Places like that needed to be stocked after all.

Once I find it what's on Marv's map should get me in, just like it has everywhere else I've tried. I don't have that map on me of course; it's tucked behind a pipe organ up on the balcony of a little chapel in Covington. But that doesn't matter. I've studied it often enough over the winter that all I have to do is close my eyes and I can see the twelve numbers and letters Marv had written there.

I stand, hoist the backpack onto my shoulders, pull the

straps tight. My makeshift boots feel heavy and when I look down I see they've iced up from when I stepped into the river. I knock the worst of it off and then slowly start to climb back up.

This will be the last night Mags spends in that bunker.

CHAPTER THIRTY-SIX

EXCEPT THAT'S NOT how it works out of course, but I guess that bit you already knew, from how we began.

I don't think it was the plan. That was as good as I could have come up with in the circumstances, and on a different night it might even have seen me through. It was the storm. I just didn't account for how bad it would get on the way back.

Without Marv's map it's hard to be sure, but I reckon it's a little shy of six miles from the spot where the bridge gave out to what remains of The Greenbrier's gates. I don't know how many of those I made in the end, only that it wasn't enough. Not that it matters. One mile or five, the truth is the storm had me beat before I hauled myself back up from the river; it just took me a little while longer to figure that out. I guess Marv was right: the cold really is a vicious bitch; it can seriously mess with your thinking. I only wish I had learned that lesson in time.

I'd like to tell you she was the last thing I thought of, as the drifting snow covered me over and the last of my body's heat leached out into the soft, enveloping flakes. But she wasn't. By the time my head came to rest in that gray powder I couldn't have told you where I was headed or why.

CHAPTER THIRTY-SEVEN

IT IS the footsteps that bring him back, echoing down the stairwell. He doesn't know how many he has missed, but he suspects a lot because they are loud, as though their owners are already right outside the door.

He hears the lock click and he opens his eyes. Although somehow he doesn't think his eyes were actually closed, it is just that now it is his turn to use them again. Weird. He blinks and looks around the cage. He feels like he has been away somewhere, although he knows that is impossible. For as long as he can remember the cage is all that there has been.

Something is wrong.

Down here in the darkness time has little meaning; it is difficult to say where one part of it begins and another ends. But that unrelenting sameness makes it easy to tell when a piece has gone missing, like it just has. He can't have fallen asleep, can he? He doesn't sleep anymore. He hasn't in a very long while.

Something is definitely wrong.

The door is already opening. The girl must have heard it

too because she's sitting up, waiting. He tilts his head to one side and sniffs the air. The scent from her cage is weaker now, but still, infuriatingly, there.

Somewhere at the end of the row a flashlight comes on. The doctor's heels click sharply on the concrete as she approaches, like she's angry; he can tell from the soldier's shuffling gait that he's struggling to keep up. He suddenly realizes his face is still pressed against the bars. He scurries back to his corner. Moments later the hem of a lab coat appears in front of his cage, glaringly bright in the flashlight's beam. The soldier's grubby fatigues arrive seconds after, the bottoms spilling over the tops of his boots.

The doctor bends down to check on him, but it's a cursory examination. She glances at the untouched tray and turns to the soldier.

'No more food for 99, Corporal. And you'd best prepare a cage in the other room.'

'Yes ma'am.' The boy can't see the soldier's face but he thinks he detects a trace of a smile in his voice, like this is a task he might relish.

The doctor takes a couple of plastic containers from her pocket and slides one through the bars and then he is forgotten as she turns around to face the cage opposite. The girl starts to inch forward but the soldier raps the bars with the stick.

'Stay right where you are, missy.'

The doctor bends down.

'Magdalene, show me your hands.'

The girl hesitates for a moment and then raises her cuffed wrists. The doctor leans forward so that she can see what's written there. The boy sees it too and now he understands what the girl has done and where the intoxicating smell has been coming from.

'Very clever, dear.' The doctor turns to the soldier. 'You didn't think to check her hands, Corporal?' The soldier's boots shuffle awkwardly on the concrete but he doesn't say anything.

The doctor slides the container through the bars and takes a step back. The girl reaches forward and grabs it, like she's worried that at any moment she might change her mind. It takes her a moment to unscrew the cap with her wrists still bound together but she manages it. She holds the container to her lips and drains it, gasping with the taste.

'Well, Magdalene, it appears Gabriel has taken your advice. He wasn't in his room this morning when Sergeant Hicks went in to check on him. Every indication is that he has absconded.'

The girl wipes her mouth with the back of her hand and says *Good.*

'Do you really think so, dear? I have to say, it doesn't say much for his devotion to you, does it? And how far do you think he will get? He set off into a blizzard, without footwear. The best we can hope for now is that the storm clears and he can be found before he succumbs to hypothermia. I will have to remove those appendages that he will inevitably lose to frostbite, and then, assuming of course that he recovers, he will join you down here.'

The girl doesn't look up. She stares at the floor of her cage for a long while. When she finally speaks her voice is little more than a whisper.

'Only someone like you might consider that to be the best that could be hoped for.'

The doctor lets out an exasperated sigh.

'And perhaps you would prefer that he die out there in the cold?'

He strains to hear the girl's response, but she has nothing to say to this. She just crawls to the back of her cage and turns her head away.

CHAPTER THIRTY-EIGHT

FROM SOMEWHERE FAR AWAY IN the darkness I hear my name. The voice is familiar, but muffled, like it's coming to me from deep under water. I really don't want to open my eyes. There's an immense coldness lodged inside me, but I'm too tired even to shiver; I just want the voice to go away so I can sleep. For a moment it recedes, once again becoming distant. But then it returns, and this time it's insistent.

I manage to open one eye a fraction. A large wooden crucifix hangs at an angle on the wall in front of me, the loin-clothed figure nailed to it looking only marginally less comfortable than I feel. All around me long wooden pews sit in silent disarray. It takes long seconds to process these clues, but at last I have a conclusion I think I might be willing to stand over: I'm in a church.

I wonder how long I've been out. The windows closest to me are darkened with snow, and at least where the panes remain intact, years of silt and grime, so it's hard to tell. Further up there's a gaping hole in the vaulted roof. The section of sky that shows itself looks bruised, restless, but the storm seems to have mostly blown itself out.

A while then. A day, maybe more.

My breath hangs white and heavy in the air above me. Somebody's covered me with their parka, but it's still bitterly cold. I smell burning and realize there's a fire. I shift my gaze and now I see the smoke, rising upwards in slow, lazy coils from somewhere behind me. I try to sit up so I can move myself closer, but my limbs are stiff, unresponsive, like I haven't used them for years.

'Best stay where you are. Don't want to warm you up too quickly.'

I try to turn my head in the direction of the voice, but even that small act seems beyond me; the muscles in my neck respond to my commands with only the vaguest of twitches.

'When I was stationed up in Fairbanks we had a soldier fall through the ice. By the time we fished him out he'd been in there for almost half an hour. We walked him all the way back to camp and then some idiot thought it'd be a good idea to give him a hot drink. Stopped his heart in a second.'

I'm not sure I could stand right now, let alone walk. The hot drink sounds really good though. I wonder what Hicks keeps in that thermos he always has on him. I reckon if I was offered some I might take my chances.

I hear him getting up and the next thing he steps into view. It must be his coat that's covering me because he's only wearing his thermals. Without the bulk of the parka he looks painfully thin, but if the cold's bothering him he's not showing any sign of it. He squints down at me with his one good eye.

'How're you feeling?'

I manage to croak an okay. The truth is I hurt everywhere. The pain's worst in my hands and feet; it's like some-one's driving hundreds of tiny needles into my skin. He kneels down next to me and reaches for my wrist. I feel his fingers slide inside the cuff of my mittens, underneath the liner, and press lightly there. I don't know what he's doing, but whatever it is I don't have the strength to resist.

'Pulse's almost back to normal.' He withdraws his hand and pulls the parka back over me. His eyes drop to my cheeks. 'Picked yourself up some frostbite too, although I've seen worse. That was a damn fool thing you did, setting off into weather like that.'

Part of me wants to tell him I know; that I was taught better than that; that I only did it because I was desperate and needed the storm to cover my tracks. But this explana-tion seems impossibly long and I'm far too tired to give it, so instead I just ask where I am.

'St. Charles.'

It takes me a moment to remember that's the name of the church just a little ways west of the entrance to The Green-brier. Close then. But I guess that doesn't matter now.

'So what was your plan, son? Clear everybody out of The Greenbrier, then while we're off looking for you, you sneak back in and get the girl?'

I don't know what else to say. It was a bit more compli-cated than that, but what he's just said sounds like a pretty fair summary of it. I nod.

'Well, if it makes you feel any better it was working. Right up until the part where you almost froze to death, that is. You were lucky I found you when I did.'

He stands and steps over to the fire. I hear the hiss from the damp branches as he adds more of them to the flames.

'Were you the only one sent after me?'

'Nope. Doc was pretty riled up when you split. Soon as the storm broke she had everyone out looking for you, even Pops.'

'Are they back yet?'

'I doubt it. They were headed north along the river when I parted company with them. Truck's plan was to pick up 64 and continue on after you. He's probably somewhere south of Lynch by now. Man's as ignorant as the day is long, but he's backwoods raised, so he knows how to follow a trail. I figure when he doesn't find you by tonight he'll cut his losses, come back.'

'How did you know I hadn't headed south?'

Hicks turns back and looks at me.

'You think being a soldier's just about shooting stuff, son?' He shakes his head. 'Our enemies stopped putting on uniforms long before I signed up. Most important part of it's figurin' out who those folks are, and what they might be about to do next. If you can't tell that you've no business being anywhere near a gun.'

'I saw the look on your face when Truck hitched the girl off her feet. I knew it then; no way you were leaving without her, no matter what she might have written on her hand. Having you clean them weapons was just a test. Once I saw you'd removed the firing pins I knew you were fixin' to bolt. Nice touch with the boat though. Even had me doubting you for a moment there. But then I saw the wrappers you left scattered around, down by the river. You left them so they wouldn't blow away; so we'd find them. Somebody taught you different'n that though, didn't they? Because you've been bagging your trash since the first time we met, and habits like that are hard to break. Damn stupid if you ask me, the way the world is now. But you learned it, so it's what you do.'

Hicks is still speaking but I'm only half-listening. Another, more important, thought is coming to me now. Something's wrong; we're right across the road from The Greenbrier, but for some reason I'm not already back there.

'So what do you mean to do with me?'

Hicks returns to one of the pews and sits down.

'Well that depends on you, son. I figure you wouldn't have gone to all this trouble if you didn't have a plan for breaking the girl out of the bunker and getting her to a cure. If you do I'd be mighty interested in hearing it.'

I look up. I'm still not sure whether I can trust him. But right now I'm not sure I'm long on other options.

'In Eden we had a scanner. One of those machines like in the hospital, basically a big magnet. Marv and I had to go in it each time we came back inside. It was supposed to destroy any trace of the virus we might have picked up while we were outside.'

Hicks looks down at me, like he's considering this.

'Did you mention any of that scanner stuff to the Doc?'

I shake my head. He scratches his jaw, like maybe that's not a bad start.

'This Eden place, are you sure you can find it? 'Cause if you don't mind me saying you seemed a little vague on its location when we spoke earlier.'

'I can find it.'

He nods.

'Fair enough. And what makes you think they'll let you in when you get there?'

I can't see Kane ever letting us in, certainly not once he figures out Mags is infected. But I reckon Hicks doesn't need to hear this part yet. Besides, that's not the bit that worries me. I've found a way in before; I'm sure I can do it again. It's getting back out afterwards that'll be the trick, and right now I don't know how I'm going to do that. But I'll worry about it later. If I can't get Mags into the scanner it won't matter anyway.

'I can get us in.'

'Alright then. I might have some questions for you about that, but first things first. What was your plan for getting back into The Greenbrier?'

'The bunker has to have another entrance. Something bigger, like maybe where the supplies would have been brought in. It'll have a keypad.'

He nods.

'There is. It's round back of the West Virginia Wing. We tried it when we first got here but the codes the Doc had didn't work. It hasn't been opened since.'

'I have a code that should work.'

I told Hicks earlier that Marv hadn't given me any codes, but if he remembers this he doesn't call me on it. Instead he squints down at me for a long moment, like maybe I'm being re-evaluated.

'And how about you? How far do you think you can walk?'

Right now I'm not sure I can even stand.

'As far as I have to.'

He shifts his jaw like maybe he doesn't believe it, but he doesn't say anything.

'Alright then, you'd best rest up. I'm going to fetch your boots. We'll see what shape you're in when I get back.'

He stands up and heads for the entrance. Outside the day's already darkening.

'Hicks, wait.'

He turns around.

'Why would you help us?'

'I have my reasons.'

I shake my head.

'You'll have to do better than that. I'm done taking people at their word.'

He doesn't say anything for a long while, just stares down at me like he's making his mind up about something. Eventually he must come to a conclusion because he reaches up with one gloved hand to the patch over his eye. I'm expecting an empty socket, maybe a scar, evidence of whatever it was that took the sight from him there. It won't bother me to look at it; I've seen my share of things like that, and worse. But what I see when he lifts the patch causes the breath to catch in my throat.

He's squinting hard, like he can't bear even the little light the day has left, but there's no mistaking it: the pupil that looks back at me is impossibly dilated. And it's not dark, like his other eye. It flashes silver, like when you shine a flashlight into an animal's eyes at night. When he thinks I've seen enough he pulls the patch back down.

'Turns out Doc didn't get it all. She has me on her meds, to suppress it, but I know it's there, working its way through me, building itself up, just like in the furies that got themselves fried by the burst. It's not a feeling I much care for. So maybe we can do each other a favor. You bring me with you and I'll help you get the girl out of the bunker, buy you the time she needs when we get to Eden.'

He turns back towards the doorway.

'I'll be back with your boots. You can give me your answer then.'

CHAPTER THIRTY-NINE

I LOOK over at the church's arched entrance for a long time after Hicks has left. One of the doors is missing and the other hangs inward on its last studded hinge; beyond the growing darkness beckons. I'm right across the road from The Greenbrier. I wonder if I should take my chances while he's gone.

I sit up slowly. My feet are still wrapped in the scraps of blankets I tore from my bedding, but the plastic sacking and duct tape have been removed. I spot the remnants of my makeshift footwear on the other side of the fire, lying in a puddle of melt water. I guess Hicks must have cut them off while I was out of it. Well, that settles it. Even if I had tape they're beyond repair, and without boots I'm not going anywhere. I have little choice but to wait for him to come back.

I shuffle backwards and lean myself against one of the pews. I'm not sure what to make of what I've just learned. It makes sense, of course, now that I know. It's not just the silver hair, or how gaunt he looks. I've never seen him eat, or sleep. I wonder if it explains how quick he is too. The articles

I collected for my shoebox said the virus hotwired those it infected, that it replaced their internal wiring with its own. Except that the virus's circuits were way faster than ours had ever been designed to be.

Well, infected or not, right now I need his help, and not just to fetch me my boots. He's been inside the bunker, which means he'll know where Mags is being held, so I won't have to search the whole place looking for her. My spirits lift a little at the prospect of seeing her again, and for a moment I put aside what might happen afterwards and allow that thought to sustain me.

I'll need to watch him, though. I still don't even know how Mags came to be infected, only that Gilbey's version of it isn't to be believed. However it happened I tell myself Hicks can't have been part of it; he was with me the whole time. And if all he was planning to do was deliver me back to Gilbey he could have just done that already. There would be no need to bring me here.

But even if he means to help us he has the virus; I'll need to be careful. I look down and suddenly realize it's his parka that's draped over me. The snaps have been cut out, the zipper replaced with plastic, and I suspect every other trace of metal will have been removed from it. Nevertheless I throw it off me like I've just found it crawling with fire ants.

Without the extra layer it's cold and in spite of Hicks' warning I shift myself a little closer to the fire. Even the faint warmth it casts is intoxicating. My entire body aches, but my hands and feet are the worst. I pull off my mittens and liners and examine the damage. Small blisters dot my fingertips and the flesh there feels waxy and hard, like it's been frozen. When I try and curl my fingers into a fist I can manage little more than a claw. I relax my hand again and feel along my cheeks. The skin there's the same.

It's my legs I'm most worried about though; I'll need them soon. Outside dusk's already settling. Hicks said Truck would probably have given up looking for me by now. If that's the case he'll be back in The Greenbrier tomorrow. Which means I'll need to break Mags out of the bunker and get us away from here before then.

I start unraveling the strips of blanket I'd used to wrap my feet. As the last of them falls away I see the slippers underneath are striped with blood. I pull them off as gently as I can and examine the damage. It looks worse than it is. The snowshoes' hard plastic bindings have done some work, but the cuts don't look deep. I clean them as best as I can and then cover them with bandages from the first aid kit I keep in my backpack.

When I'm done I lever myself up onto the pew. Even that small effort exhausts me and I have to rest before I can continue. When I try to stand it's like my legs have gone to sleep; I can't trust them to bear me up. I lower myself back onto the pew and start massaging my thighs with my frozen fingers.

I'll try again in a little while.

———

It's hours before Hicks returns, but suddenly there he is, standing in the doorway with a pair of boots in one hand and an extra set of snowshoes in the other. The last of the light's already left the sky; there's little to see behind him other than darkness.

I ease myself back down onto one of the pews to take a

break. Things are a little better than when he left. I'm able to hobble around now; I can make it almost the length of the aisle before I need to sit down again. Pins and needles still stab up from the balls of my feet with every step, but at least that means feeling's returning.

He drops the boots at my feet and sets the snowshoes on top of his pack.

'Did you have any problems?'

He shakes his head but doesn't elaborate.

I figure I've earned dinner so I reach into my backpack for an MRE. I tear the top off the heater and slide the packet with my meal in it inside. I add a little water from my canteen to start the reaction and then lean it against the side of the seat. It starts hissing, telling me it's getting to work.

Hicks sits down on one of the pews opposite. His gaze shifts to the fire and I catch him eyeing the bloodstained remains of the slippers I left there. When he looks back at me there's an expression on his face that's not hunger but maybe something not too far removed, a memory of what that feeling once was. I point at the MRE in case he wants one, although now that I know what's wrong with him that seems foolish. He just shakes his head and reaches for the thermos, unscrews the cap and raises it to his lips.

My dinner's as warm as it's going to get so I pick up the pouch and start scooping out the contents. Outside the wind gusts, sending a flurry of gray flakes tumbling down through the gaping hole in the rafters.

'So what will you do after?'

What I really want to know is whether I can trust him to help me get Mags out of The Greenbrier and back to Eden. But there's little point asking a question like that flat out, so I figure I'll come at it sideways. *Softly, softly, catchee fury.*

'One problem at a time, kid. I reckon we have our work cut out for us just getting you and the girl back to wherever this Eden place is.'

I take a mouthful of mostly-mixed chili beef.

'Yeah, but you must have thought about it. You'll never be able to come back here. Won't you miss the others?'

Hicks sighs, like he's resigning himself to answering my questions.

'Less than you might think. Truck's got a mean streak in him wider than a four-lane highway; I'm not sure his own mother ever missed that man. Weasel's no better. I told you they were all for shooting me on the roof in Atlanta and tossing Ortiz out the back of the chopper, just in case. You've seen what Jax is like – it's been a long time since all of his dogs were barking – and Pops can't be much more than a quick look down the road behind him.'

'And Boots?'

He takes a sip from his thermos and grimaces at the taste.

'Yeah, Private Kavanagh. Seems harmless enough, right? You know we found him at The Greenbrier, the night we arrived?'

'You said he got locked inside when the order to evacuate came and then couldn't figure a way to let the other soldiers back in.'

He squints at me over the top of the thermos.

'Yep, that's what he told us. The button's right there by the door of course. Big green thing, hard to miss, even with those Coke bottles he wears for glasses.' He takes another sip and holds the thermos up. 'A suspicious mind might wonder whether Private Kavanagh saw the writing on the wall and figured the supplies in the bunker might stretch a lot further if they didn't have to be split quite so many ways. You remember I told you it took us a while to convince him to open up when we arrived.'

I nod. Hicks had said it was only when Boots found out Gilbey was working on a cure that he let them in.

'Well, I might not have told that part exactly how it happened. Boots didn't give a damn about no cure. He only agreed to let us in when Doc threatened to contaminate the bunker if he didn't.'

'And what about Dr. Gilbey? She saved you.'

'She did, and I'll always owe her for that. But something's changed.' He sets the thermos beside him on the pew and looks at me, as if deciding something. 'I'm not sure your girl getting infected was an accident, Gabriel.'

I put the spoon down.

'Doc runs things too tight for something like that to have just happened.' He shakes his head. 'I guess I should have seen it coming. She's been down in that bunker by herself this last ten years, thinking of nothing but finding a cure, and that's a heavy load for one person to bear. Could be you and the girl showing up pushed her over the edge, or maybe she'd already taken that step a while back and I hadn't noticed.'

He raises the thermos to his lips and takes another sip.

'Well, if it's true it can't be excused. And I can't have anything more to do with her.'

CHAPTER FORTY

IT'S STILL a few hours till dawn when we set off.

Away from the fire it's cold. I've zipped the parka all the way up, but it bites at my frostbitten cheeks through the thin cotton mask. I sit on the steps in the shelter of the church's arched doorway and strap on my snowshoes. I've bandaged my feet tight and my legs feel a lot better; I can make half a dozen circuits round the inside of the church now without having to rest. That's not much, I'll grant you, but you've got to look at where I started from just a few hours ago. And as Hicks says, one problem at a time. The first thing is to get Mags out of that bunker. After that we'll see how many miles I have in me.

Hicks takes us west on route 60, away from The Greenbrier's gates. We walk in silence. I'm beginning to wonder where we're going when he cuts off the road and switches back onto what looks like it was once little more than woodland trail. The wind's died and the only sounds are of my breathing and our snowshoes crunching through the ice-slicked powder. Limbless, lifeless trunks push up through the snow on either side, closing around us as we start to climb. I'm keeping to Hicks' tracks but inside my boots my feet are starting to hurt. I'm more worried about my legs though. The slope's not that bad, but already I can feel the muscles there tiring.

The path inclines, skirting around the hill that sits behind The Greenbrier. We've been following it for maybe fifteen minutes when ahead of us a low concrete structure slowly separates itself from the darkness. Snow's banked high against its featureless sides. More sits in heavy layers on its flat roof.

A large funnel-like entrance cuts into the hillside. The drifts have gathered deep between its walls, almost obscuring a huge metal gate at the end; only a series of rectangular vents near the top point to its existence. A rusting sign warns against trespassing. Another carries a faded symbol of a lightning bolt, and underneath the words *Danger High Voltage*.

Hicks hikes up to the gate. I'm wondering how we're going to get it open, but he just starts scooping snow from a spot near the center. I kneel down next to him and join in. My hands have loosened up a little, but it still hurts to work my fingers. Thankfully Hicks is making a better job of it and soon I can make out the outline of a smaller door set into the steel. When he's cleared enough snow he reaches for the handle. The door sticks in its frame, but after a little pushing it gives and then swings inwards with a dull metallic groan. Gray powder tumbles in.

I unsnap my snowshoes and follow him through into darkness. He pulls a flashlight from his parka and flicks it on. A cone of red light illuminates a square concrete-lined tunnel maybe twice as high as I am tall that ends abruptly at a massive blast door. Two huge buttressed hinges bear its weight, the only other ornamentation six circular steel plates bolted to the wall above. I'm not sure what purpose they serve, but the shadows cast by the bolts make them look like giant clocks.

Hicks shines his flashlight at a spot on the wall. A stubby metal cowling stands proud of the concrete.

'You're up kid.'

As I step closer I'm relieved to see the keypad's just like the ones in Eden and Mount Weather. I pull off my mittens and hit reset to clear whatever might still be stored in the circuits from when Gilbey tried this, years ago. The dusty plastic keys slowly illuminate, and a red light at the bottom blinks on. There's a gentle whirring from above my head as a camera focuses. I glance up.

'Don't worry about that. Doc's the only one in there and she'll be sound asleep.'

I tell myself it's just jitters, like I'd get when I was about to step into Eden's tunnels, but somehow in spite of Hicks' words it feels like we're being watched. I close my eyes and the section of Marv's map that showed The Greenbrier, complete with the code he had written next to it, appears before me. I carefully punch in the twelve numbers and letters. There's a pause and then the light underneath the keypad switches to green. From somewhere behind the door I hear a faint whine, rising in pitch as electric motors that have lain dormant for a decade shake off their slumber and get to work. Moments later there's a grating sound, like the teeth of cogs being forced into service. The pitch of the motors increases and then from somewhere inside the door there's a heavy clunk, followed by the muted screech of metal being dragged against metal and finally the familiar sound of bolts sliding back into their recesses. Another set of motors come to life, slowly pushing the dull, cold steel towards me. When it reaches the wall the motors suddenly die and silence returns to the darkness.

I follow Hicks into a long, straight tunnel. Large-bore pressure pipes run along the walls; more hang from the ceiling. Behind me, above the blast door, huge vents have been drilled through the thick concrete. Each one houses a fan, the heavy metal blades protected behind mesh screens. The steel plates I noticed on the other side were covers, allowing the bunker to be sealed off.

We make our way into darkness, our footsteps echoing off the walls. I start the count. Here and there Hicks' flashlight picks out cardboard boxes, their sides stamped with the names of the supplies they once contained. Each is empty now, the contents long since consumed.

It's two hundred paces before the tunnel ends at a door marked *Decontamination*. Another camera bolted to the concrete above blinks down at us as we pass under it. We enter a shower room. Nozzles protrude from the walls on either side, making the space seem narrow. The flashlight's beam paints everything in shades of crimson so it's hard to tell what color the tiles actually are. If I were forced to guess I'd hazard blue.

The decontamination area ends and we step into a long corridor. From somewhere off in the distance there's the low drone of a generator. Safety lights hum gently, bathing the painted walls in shades of gray and green.

Doors lead off to the left and right, each room's purpose stenciled, military fashion, above. We pass a series of numbered dormitories. Some of the doors are open; inside I can see row after row of steel bunk beds. A large but cheerless cafeteria comes next, and then a smaller lounge area, stacks of decade-old magazines still arranged neatly on the coffee tables. After that an infirmary with a dozen or so beds, and then a room with a large mural of the White House, a lectern on a podium in front of it, a television camera standing ready to transmit the news of what's just happened to those who might have survived. A little further along two drab halls filled with chairs that look like the auditorium where Miss Kimble used to bring us for assembly. The sign above one reads *Senate* and the other *House of Representatives*. Dusty pictures of men I recognize from her first grade civics and government class hang from the walls.

The door at the very end says *Power Plant*. The thrum from the generator increases as Hicks pushes it open. I follow him into a cavernous room and up onto a narrow metal gangway. A tangle of pipes snakes above my head; tanks, pumps, generators and other assorted machinery crowd into the space below. At the end of the walkway we step through another door. The noise from the plant recedes as it closes behind us.

Steel stairs spiral down into darkness, the beam from Hicks' flashlight sweeping the concrete as we descend. The steps continue for longer than I was expecting, but at last we reach the bottom. I look around. A single door leads out of the shaft we've just come down. Hicks steps over to it and punches a code into a keypad. There's a muted click as the lock releases and he pushes the door open.

CHAPTER FORTY-ONE

I FOLLOW HIM INTO A LONG, low-ceilinged room. Plastic cages stacked two deep line the walls on either side. Hicks hands me the flashlight.

'Stay right here. I'll be back in a minute.'

He opens a door to what looks like a storage room. I have a second to glimpse rows of empty shelves and then he disappears inside, closing the door behind him.

I shine the flashlight along the rows of cages. They're all empty now, but I wonder what used to be kept in them. Hicks said when they took him off the roof in Atlanta Gilbey had put him in something that had been designed for a chimpanzee. These certainly look like they were built to hold a creature of about that size. I haven't seen an animal since Jackson, Sam and Reuben's dog, on the morning of the Last Day. I assumed whatever survived the strikes froze to death in the months that followed, but maybe the doctor brought some with her when she came here.

I point the flashlight into the darkness, but it doesn't reach very far. I figure there has to be another room at the end of this one. Maybe that's where Mags is. Hicks said to wait, but I want to let her know that I'm here, that she'll soon be free. I start to make my way down the aisle.

The beam slides over the bars, causing the shadows behind to shift and merge, so when I first see it I almost miss it. A small plastic tray, the kind that might once have held a TV dinner. I bend down to examine it through the bars. The compartments are all empty save one; in it there's what looks like a scoop of beans, long cold, the sauce congealed. I'm about to move on when something causes me to shine the light further into the cage. And that's when I see him. A small boy, lost inside dark overalls that are way too big for his tiny frame, pressed into the shadows at the back. His hands cover his face, but I can see his head is shaved; his scalp looks pale, almost gray. He slowly splays his fingers, revealing a pair of solemn eyes that stare back at me, the large silver pupils reflecting the crimson beam from Hick's flashlight.

I take an involuntary step backwards, my mind already measuring the gap between us, trying to work out whether more might be called for. He doesn't appear threatening, though. He makes no move towards me, just continues to watch from the spot he seems to have picked out for himself in the corner. After a moment he raises one impossibly thin arm and points behind me.

I turn around and shine the light into the cage opposite.

She's lying curled up on the floor, asleep. She's wearing the same dark overalls as the boy, but her wrists and ankles have been bound. I bend down as quietly as I can, suddenly afraid to wake her. What if she opens her eyes and I see what I've just seen in the cage opposite? I take a deep breath.

'Mags.'

She looks up and as she blinks back the sleep I feel relief

wash through me. The shadows under her eyes seem a little heavier than they were earlier, but that's probably just the flashlight. The pupils are dark, human. She picks herself up, a little awkwardly because of the restraints. Her hands reach for the bars, but then she remembers, and quickly pulls them back.

'Gabe. What are you doing here?' Her eyes narrow. 'And what happened to your face?'

At first I'm not sure what she means; it takes a second for me to work it out.

'Oh, frostbite. I guess I got careless.'

'Does it hurt?'

It does a little, but I shake my head.

'This is what happens when I'm not there to watch over you. What are you doing here? I thought I...'

There's a noise from behind me and her eyes dart down the aisle between the cages.

'Gabe, you need to get out of here.'

Her voice is low, urgent. I look over my shoulder, but it's just Hicks walking towards us carrying a large plastic crate with the number 100 stenciled on it. I turn back to Mags.

'It's okay. He's helping us.'

He sets the crate down on the floor.

'I thought I told you to stay put.'

He looks at me for a long moment like he's deciding whether he's done taking me to task over wandering off, but then he must figure we have more pressing matters to attend to. He squats down next to me and looks at Mags.

'Now we need to do this my way. Understood?'

She looks at him as if she still doesn't know what to make of this, but in the end she just nods. He turns to me and I realize I'm expected to answer too.

'Yeah, sure.'

He looks into the cage.

'You got a blade on you?'

I nod.

'Well give it to me then.'

I hand him the leatherman; he thumbs out the knife.

'Alright, now move to the front of the cage and slide your hands through.'

I keep the blade sharp; it doesn't take him long to cut through the plastic at her wrists. When he's done he passes it through the bars. While she's working on the cable ties at her ankles he unsnaps the lid on the crate, pulls out a set of thermals and hands them to her. 'Change into those. Go on now, nobody'll look at you.'

She hesitates a moment, then starts unsnapping the fasteners on her overalls. I turn away, but when I hear her wince I glance back over my shoulder. Mags has always been thin, but not like this. Even in the scant light I can see the bones along her side, the play of muscles across her stomach. And before she pulls the thermals down over her head I catch a glimpse of something else: a chain of dark, ugly welts, tracking from one hip up her ribcage to her shoulder.

I turn away, but I feel something, also dark and ugly, welling up inside me. The best we can hope for now is that we get away from this place and never see Truck or any of the other soldiers again. I know there may be no limit to the things I would do to the person that has inflicted those marks on her, however.

When Mags is done changing into her thermals Hicks passes a pair of latex gloves and a roll of duct tape through the bars.

'Put those on and tape the cuffs to your wrists.'

She snaps on the gloves and then uses her teeth to tear a couple of strips from the roll.

'Alright. Now I'm going to let you out. But you need to do exactly as I say until we're outside. Got it?'

Mags looks up from wrapping the tape around her wrists. I can tell she doesn't care much for the instruction, but she agrees. She eyes the leatherman, but Hicks just shakes his head so she leaves it behind her on the floor of the cage. He unlatches the door and swings it open. She crawls out and stands, a little unsteadily at first.

'We ready?'

She nods in the direction of the cage opposite.

'What about him?'

Hicks looks over. The fury presses itself further back into the shadows.

'What about him?'

'We can't leave him here.'

'We can and we will.' He turns to me, like this is something I need to pay particular attention to. 'You think Doc's just going to let this go? Truck's probably already figured out you gave him the slip, which means he'll most likely be back here in a few hours. With a bit of luck it'll be too late for them to set out after us right away, but even so I reckon we'll have a day's head start at most. Boots will slow them down, and that might just be enough if you two can keep the pace. But not if we're hauling that thing along. It's been in there so long it probably can't even stand straight.' He looks into the cage. 'Besides, it's about to turn. I reckon it's got a day or two left at most.'

The fury glances up as he says this, but Hicks doesn't seem to notice. Right now all I care about is getting Mags out of here and back to Eden as quickly as possible, and what he's saying makes sense.

'Mags, you sure?'

She nods. 'I'm not leaving without him Gabe.'

I look down into the cage. Its eyes are still freaking me out, but it doesn't seem like it means us harm. If what Hicks says is true and it's about to turn I really have no interest in bringing it with us, however. But I also recognize the tone in Mags' voice. Once she's set her mind on something there's little can be done to change it.

'Hicks, we have to take the kid.'

'Aw hell Gabriel, it's not a kid. Might have been once but not anymore, and certainly not in a few days from now when it's looking at you like you're a side of prime rib and I have to put a bullet in it.'

The fury shakes its head as it hears this, but Hicks isn't even looking at it now.

'They don't sleep, you know. Which means you won't be able to either. How long do you think you'll be able to keep that up?'

'Gabe, I'll watch him.'

Hicks turns to Mags.

'And who'll watch you, darlin'? Christ. Here, gimme your flashlight.' I dig the windup from the pocket of my parka and hand it to him. He points it into the cage and cranks the handle. The dynamo whirs and the bulb glows orange, then yellow, finally casting a faint pool of almost-white light that barely reaches the back of the cage. The fury instinctively presses itself even further back, raising its arms to block the beam. But then it realizes what Hicks is doing and drops them again. Its eyes narrow to slits, but it holds its head up and forces itself to squint back.

'See that? And that's just something you'd pull from a crackerjack box.' He tosses the flashlight back to me. 'In a couple of days it won't be able to stand the daylight. What do you plan to do then? Cut it loose? Or were you planning on another moonlight stroll, son?'

I look back at Mags, but her expression hasn't changed.

'We're taking it, Hicks. You can come with us or let us go.' I watch him close as I say it, though. Because there's a third choice, of course. He could just stop us, right now, and make his peace with Gilbey. His fingers don't stray any closer to the pistol on his hip, but I can see him working through the options himself. In the end he shakes his head like he's trying to figure out just where this all went wrong.

'Alright, alright.'

He looks at Mags and the cage he's just sprung her from and then back at me, like he's deciding which of us is less likely to cause him trouble.

'Gabriel, you remember that first room we passed as we came in? In there you'll find a crate with 99 on the side of it. Bring it to me. And come straight back y'hear? No exploring this time.'

I hurry off down the aisle, winding the flashlight as I go. I get to the storage room he meant and step inside. The ceiling's low and I have to duck my head to avoid hitting it off the bulkhead lamps bolted to the concrete. Rows of shelves line the walls on either side. For as far as I can see with the flashlight they look empty, but the beam doesn't stretch as far as the wall at the end.

I find a single crate a little further back, the number 99 stenciled on the side of it. It looks like it's been sitting there a while. I drag it down, dislodging a thick layer of dust. Motes drift lazily through the beam, settling on the concrete floor.

I'm about to turn back but something makes me point the flashlight further along the aisle. Up against the back wall I can see stacks of empty crates, just like the one I'm holding. They're nested inside one another, so only the bottom crate in each stack is visible, but it looks like they each have a number stenciled on the side too.

Spidey's been keeping up a low-level grumble ever since the camera by the blast door, but he takes it up a notch at that, and maybe then I should have paid more attention. But something else catches my eye. I set the crate I'm carrying down and make my way towards it.

All the way back in the darkness there's one more crate. It looks just like all the others, but as I get closer I can see it's not. This one doesn't have a number stenciled on it; it has a name instead.

It says Amanda Gilbey.

CHAPTER FORTY-TWO

MAGS HAS ALREADY PULLED on her pants and is lacing up her boots as I return. The fury's moved closer to the front of its cage. It peers out through the bars, its eyes shifting nervously between me and Hicks.

I set the crate down and unsnap the lid. Inside there's everything it might need – jacket, gloves, boots, even a small pair of goggles. Spidey really hasn't been happy since I went back into the storage room and now he grumbles about this too. But I'm still a little distracted by the other crate I saw in there, and mostly just keen to get us out of here, so I hush him.

Hicks unlatches the cage and swings it open. But the fury shuffles toward the back and won't come out. It keeps staring up at him, its eyes filled with mistrust. Mags looks up from unpacking the crate.

'Sergeant, why don't you stand back a little further?'

Hicks squints down at her like he doesn't believe this is where his orders are coming from now, but in the end he just sighs and does as she says. The fury hesitates a moment longer and then crawls out. It looks around uncertainly. Squatting on all fours like that it looks like a miniature version of the thing that attacked Ortiz. For a second the memory of the fear I felt in the hospital twists my insides and I wonder if Hicks is right and we're making a terrible mistake.

Mags bends down next to it.

'Can you stand, Johnny?'

It grips the side of the cage and tries to pull itself upright, but all it manages is a chimp-like crouch. She has to help it into the clothes from the crate. When she's done Hicks tears several strips of duct tape from the roll and hands them to her.

'Seal the cuffs of the mittens to the arms of the jacket. Last strip's for its mouth.'

Mags looks like she might be about to argue, but Hicks just shakes his head.

'We're done discussing this. It's that or I go fetch the catchpole.'

She turns back to the fury.

'It'll be okay Johnny. Just till we get out of here.' She tapes up its mittens. It doesn't object as she stretches the last strip across its lips.

———

We leave The Greenbrier the way we came in.

Mags holds the fury's hand as we climb the stairs back to the upper levels. It manages them without too much difficulty; by the time we reach the top I think it might already be standing a little taller. When we enter the plant room it cranes its neck, swiveling around to take in each detail, like it wants to look everywhere at once. Hicks keeps a close eye on it as it steps up onto the metal gangway, but it just grips Mags' hand and follows her across. We leave the plant room and make our way down the long corridor in silence. We pass through the decontamination showers and then we're back out in the tunnel.

I counted two hundred paces from this point when we were coming in, but somehow it seems longer on the way out. The camera above the entrance door is still blinking as we pass under it; I keep looking back over my shoulder long after the little red light has been swallowed up by the darkness. At last I spot the circular vents and the huge blast door pushed up against the concrete ahead of us. We step through into the chamber between it and the outer gate. The access door where we came in is still open. Hicks stops and reaches into his pocket. He pulls out a small plastic container and hands it to Mags.

'Take this. It'll taste like the worst thing imaginable, but I guess you already know that by now.'

She stares at him for a moment, like she's working something out. Then she unscrews the cap, but instead of raising it to her lips she bends down and hands it to the fury.

'Drink that Johnny. Quickly now.'

'Aw, you can't be serious.' Hicks looks at me for support, but I can't help him. The fury hesitates, like it's unsure what it should do.

'Don't worry; the sergeant has another one for me.'

After only a moment's pause it knocks it back. Mags holds her hand out for another of the vials. Hicks looks at her like he's wondering whether any promise of a cure might be worth this, but in the end he digs into his pocket and hands one over. She unscrews the cap and lifts it to her lips. I watch as her face contorts and she bends over and clutches her stomach like she might have to throw up but after a moment it passes. She wipes her mouth with the back of her glove and reaches for the fury's mitten.

'Come on, let's get you into some snowshoes.'

As soon as she's gone Hicks grabs my arm and pulls me back into the tunnel. He reaches into his pocket and hands me four more containers like the ones he just gave to Mags.

'She needs to take one of these a day. Try and give them to her at the same time each morning.'

I slip the vials into the pocket of my parka.

'Aren't you coming with us?'

He shakes his head.

'That's all of the Doc's medicine I could lay my hands on. If she insists on sharing it there's only enough for another two days. I'm guessing that's not near enough time to get you where you're going?'

It took us more than six days to get here from Mount Weather and Eden's further north again. I shake my head.

'Alright. I'm going to stay here, see if I can't pick up some more. You plan on going back the way you came down, right?'

I nod.

'If there's anything more you remember about the location of this Eden place Gabriel, now'd be a really good time to tell me. Make it a helluva lot easier for me to find you if I knew where you were headed.'

He looks at me hard for a while, but I just shake my head.

'Fair enough. Well, stick to the interstate for as long as you can. If you have to get off it for any reason leave me a sign. I'll catch up to you soon as I can.'

He steps back over to the wall and hits the switch to start

the close sequence. A second later the electric motors kick in, whining under the load as they slowly start to pull the huge blast door back from the wall.

He looks over my shoulder again. Mags is still over by the access door strapping the fury into a pair of snowshoes, so she's got her back to us. His hand slips into the pocket of his parka. He hesitates for a moment and then passes me something cold and heavy wrapped in a Ziploc bag. I don't need to look down to know what it is.

'There's a round in the magazine; all you need to do is pull the slide back to chamber it. You remember how to do that, right?'

I nod.

'Good. Now when they turn it's quick, like someone's just flicked a switch inside them. If you so much as think that might be about to happen you don't hesitate, no matter what the girl says. Y'hear me?'

I nod again.

'Alright. Best be on your way then. I'll see you on the road.'

I have to step out of the way of the blast door as it inches its way across the concrete. When I turn around to look back into the tunnel he's already gone.

CHAPTER FORTY-THREE

DAWN'S still some time off as we leave the bunker and outside it's bitterly cold. I can see Mags' breath smoking with it; she hugs her arms to her sides and stamps her boots to warm up. The fury doesn't seem to notice. It just stares at the blackened stumps poking through the ashen snow, like they're the most wondrous things it's ever seen.

My feet got a break from the snowshoes while we were inside, but as soon as I snap them back on I can feel the bindings pressing into the cuts I have there. Right now I'm more worried about the shape my legs are in however. They were tiring badly on the way up here; I wonder how far I'll be able to make it. But as I look over at the fury I realize that's going to be the least of our problems.

Marv wasn't ever big on actual explanations for stuff; I picked up pretty much everything I needed just from watching him. Even so, it didn't take me long to work out snowshoes. There's really not a lot to it. You have to raise your legs a little higher than usual, because the powder gives. And the shoes are bigger than your regular boots so you need to widen your stride to keep from tripping over yourself. But that's pretty much it. The Juvies certainly didn't set any snowshoeing records on our way from Eden to Mount Weather, but even they got the hang of it before too long.

That's not how it's going to be with the fury, though. As I watch it taking its first tentative steps I begin to realize the trouble we're in. The recent storm's brought fresh snow, but even without it the drifts up here'd be too deep for its short legs. And to make matters worse the snowshoes are too big; every time it lifts one of them it almost can't help but bring it down on the other. Neither of those things are the real problem, however. It's just like Hicks said; whatever time it's spent in the cage is preventing it from standing upright, and if it can't do that it'll never keep its balance in snow like this.

I think about it for a moment and then I take the handsaw from my pack and trudge up the hill. My recently thawed fingers are still clumsy and I struggle with the blade, but I return a few minutes later with a couple of the straightest looking branches I can find. I hand them to Mags and she shows it how to plant the makeshift poles. When it looks like it's got the hang of it we set off through the trees, following the path Hicks and I took coming up.

———

It takes us a long time to make it back to the road.

Once we get there I keep us to the tracks Hicks and I made on the way here, but after the church there's no choice but to start breaking trail. My snowshoes sink into the deeper powder. With each step now I can feel the bindings digging into the cuts across my feet.

We continue on, stopping regularly to dig the fury out of

the drifts. It seems to take forever, but eventually I see The Greenbrier's crumbling gates up ahead. We cross the road. The station house stares back at us from behind its candy cane pillars. We make our way past it and down onto the railway line.

The sides close up around us, and with nowhere to go the snow deepens again. Our pace slows further. By the time we reach the siding where the corroded railcar rests against the buffers the sky's already getting brighter. It's still barely light at all, yet whenever I turn around now I catch the fury trying to raise its arms to shield its eyes. Every time it tries it loses its balance and pitches over and we have to stop and haul it upright.

The I-64 overpass appears around a bend. Beyond I can just see the crown of the tunnel as the track continues on through the hill. We've been traveling an hour and I doubt we've covered a half-mile. I can already feel the muscles in my legs burning, and inside my boots my feet are killing me. Even Mags seems to be struggling. In the heavier drifts she favors her side, like drawing breath is causing her pain.

The first of the day's light slowly seeps over the top of the shallow ravine as somewhere behind the gray clouds the sun finally rises. I walk us under the overpass. The fury collapses in the snow, relieved to be back in shadow. I ask Mags for the roll of duct tape Hicks gave her to bind it, back in the bunker. She hesitates a moment, like she's not sure what I'm planning, but then she digs it out and tosses it over. I pull off my gloves. I work as quickly as I can but my fingers are still numb from their recent freezing and thawing and it takes me longer than it should to tear several short strips from the roll and stick them to my sleeve of my parka.

When I have enough I step closer and tell the fury to

hold its head up. It looks at me uncertainly, then at Mags. She says it'll be okay. It hesitates a moment and then tilts its face up to me. I pull a piece of tape from my sleeve, trying to ignore the silver eyes that stare back at me through the goggles. I work as quickly as I can, masking the lens so that only the narrowest slit remains through which light can enter. As I'm stretching the last piece into place the surgical mask Mags gave it slips down. Its skin is gray, the color of the snow, but the tape that Hicks insisted Mags place over its mouth in the bunker is missing. She must have removed it before we set off.

I yank my hand back like I've just burned it, but it just continues to stare back at me through the slit in its goggles. I glance over at Mags, hoping she hasn't noticed. I fumble my fingers back into the mittens, trying to pretend nothing was wrong.

We make our way up the slope and onto the highway.

CHAPTER FORTY-FOUR

ALL MORNING we track east on I-64. It's early yet but I keep looking around, hoping to see Hicks cresting a hill or rounding a corner behind us, but there's no sign of him. I tell myself it's early yet.

I stop us every hour for frostbite checks. Mags doesn't let me stand too close and she keeps her eyes open. When she looks up at me I try not to stare at the darkening circles there, but I can't help it. It's only been a few hours but already they seem worse than when we were back in The Greenbrier. I tell myself that's just being outside, in what passes for daylight. As long as she keeps taking Gilbey's medicine she'll be fine.

We take our lunch an hour after we cross into Virginia. There's no shelter on this stretch of the highway so we sit in the snow in the lee of a road sign and set our MREs to warm. I'm just grateful to have some time out of the snowshoes. Something inside my boot feels slick, like I might be bleeding again.

The fury picks a spot for itself a few feet away and

slumps down into a drift. Mags asks it if it wants anything, but it just looks up at her like it's figuring out if it needs to worry about its answer and then shakes its head. She unwraps a HOOAH! and hands it over anyway. It sniffs at the candy bar, then lets it fall into its lap.

I catch her wincing as she sits back down. I ask her what happened to her ribs but she just goes quiet and says it's something best forgotten about. We finish our MREs in silence. As soon as she's done she gets up. She walks over to the fury and pulls it to its feet and I watch as they set off down the highway. I gather our trash, step back into my snowshoes and hobble after them.

Hicks said Truck would probably wait until morning to come after us. I pray he does. But even so I don't know how we can hope to stay ahead of him, limping through the snow like three broken things.

———

Darkness is threatening to overtake us as we take the exit for Covington, the town where we stopped with the soldiers on the way out to The Greenbrier. I'll need to go back to the church to retrieve Marv's map, but we won't be sleeping there. If the soldiers are on the road they could be here later tonight, and it's the first place Truck would check.

I spot a low brown-brick building with a sign that says US Army Reserve Center right off the interstate. We make for it as the last of the light leaves the sky. Mags gets a fire going and we sit on the floor under a poster of a soldier that says *Does Your Future Look As Exciting As Ours?* while our MREs heat. The fury picks a spot on the other side of the room. It's still working on the HOOAH! Mags gave it for lunch. Each time I look over it raises it to its lips but by the time we're finished with our MREs the candy bar remains largely untouched.

I roll out the sleeping bag Mags and I used to share. There's an awkward moment while we both stare at it, then she says I should take it. She says she'll sleep in her parka; it's not that cold. It's freezing in here; the thought that she may already not be able to feel it scares me, so I announce in a voice that's supposed to be authoritative but I suspect just sounds a little hysterical that she has to have it. I tell her I need to go back out to get Marv's map anyway. There's a Walmart right on the other side of the highway. I'll pick up another while I'm gone.

I head for the door before she has a chance to argue.

————

It's long after dark when I limp back to the center. Mags is propped up against the wall in her sleeping bag, *Owen Meany* open in her lap. The fury sits in the corner, where it was when I went out. She looks up at me as I step inside.

'How'd you do?'

I tell her I did pretty well, which isn't so far from the truth. I've recovered Marv's map from the church; it's back where it belongs in the pocket of my parka. And I've managed to find us a bunch of things in the Walmart that we could use.

She smiles, but she looks tired.

'Want to get some sleep while I take the first shift?'

I shake my head. We've agreed we'll take it in turns to watch the fury. I'm pretty beat, but there's a few things I need to do first.

'Wake me in a couple of hours, okay?'

I nod. Within seconds she's curled up inside the sleeping bag, fast asleep.

The fire's burned down, so I set to work coaxing it back to life. From across the room the fury watches me. The branches hiss and steam as I feed them to the flames, but eventually they catch.

I lay the sleeping bag I found down close to the spot Mags has chosen and dig into my pack for the first aid kit. I take off my boots and socks. Blood's soaked through the bandages so I remove them and clean the cuts with water from my canteen, then smear them with some Neosporin I found in the Walmart and tape fresh dressings in place. When I'm done I toss the bloodied bandages in the fire, climb into the sleeping bag and lean back against the wall. My eyelids feel heavy, but I need to stay awake. I take Marv's map from the pocket of my parka and spread it across my lap.

Hicks said to stay on the interstate, but we've been on the road since before dawn and I reckon we've barely covered fifteen miles. In a few short hours Truck and the other soldiers will set off from The Greenbrier, assuming they're not on the road already. If they hike sunup to sundown they should be able to cover thirty miles in a day, even dragging Boots with them. At that rate they'll be on us before we even reach I-81. I take the flashlight from the pocket of my parka and wind the stubby handle. The dynamo whirs and the bulb glows, finally casting a faint pool of yellow light across the familiar folds and creases. I turn the map over to find Covington and for a moment I forget where I'm pointing the beam. It slides across the wall and for a second is reflected back by a pair of silvered eyes. The fury turns its head away and buries its face in its hands.

My heart jumps and a cold flush of fear snaps me upright. Somehow outside, in the daytime, it's just a kid, no bigger than we were when Kane brought us to Eden. But now, here in the darkness, it's something much more than that. Or less.

I extinguish the beam and refold the map. As I'm returning it to the pocket of my parka my fingers brush the object Hicks handed me earlier. I take it out. The sweet smell of the gun oil drifts up as I remove Marv's pistol from the Ziploc bag. The magazine slides out easily when I press the switch. I feel along the top for the bullet and lever it out with my fingertips. Nothing pops up to take its place. Just one then. I push the round back in with my thumb and slide the magazine back up into the handle. The fury looks at me as it clicks into place, and for a moment the light from the fire catches its eyes. It holds my gaze for a moment, like it knows what that sound means.

I slip the gun inside my sleeping bag and settle back against the wall to wait.

CHAPTER FORTY-FIVE

I WAKE with a start and the feeling that I've just cried out in my sleep. The dream's already fading, but I remember a tunnel, and a shrill voice I haven't heard in a long time, urging me to run faster. I blink sleep from my eyes, worried I might still be there. But I'm not. I'm sitting upright, my back to the wall, the frigid air pressing against my sweat-soaked thermals. I must have drifted off while I was supposed to be watching the fury. I quickly look over but it's where it was earlier, huddled in the corner on the far side of the room. Mags is curled up in her sleeping bag next to me.

The fire's dead and black on the ground and it's cold. It's still sometime before dawn, but I know I won't sleep again so I get up and head outside for more firewood. Mags is awake when I get back. I set a couple of MREs to heat and then get to work on a fire. She asks the fury if it wants anything, but it just holds up the HOOAH! it's been working on since yesterday and says it's fine.

When we're done with breakfast I hand her one of the little plastic vials Hicks gave me. She takes it, unscrews the

cap and finishes it with a grimace, then holds her hand out
for another. I hesitate. I know the path she means to commit
us to; I've known it since she demanded the second container
from Hicks on the way out of the bunker yesterday. But what
if he can't get us more medicine? There's only three of the
vials left. With the pace we're setting that's not even enough
to get her to Eden, and that's as much as I care about. I glance
over to the other side of the fire. The fury's got its knees
hugged to its chest, but I can see it watching to see what I'll
do. I don't intend it harm, but Hicks said it's only a day or
two from turning, which means anything we're giving it now
is just a waste. I guess that's not the way Mags sees it though.
She reaches out to touch my arm, but then thinks better of it
and pulls back.

'Gabe?'

I look back at her.

'Listen, you either give me another container or the next
one I get I'm just going to give to him anyway. But it's not
going to come to that, is it?'

In the end I relent and she takes the medicine and hands
it to the fury. I pack up our gear while she gets it ready. The
Walmart had a big outdoors section and I picked up a pair of
hiking poles to replace the branches I cut for it. I also found
ski goggles with a darker lens and a kid's jacket with a hood
like a snorkel. The goggles are for an adult so they're a little
big, but Mags adjusts the strap and they seem to stay on. I've
taped the lens like before, leaving only a small slit through
which light can enter. Mags hands it the jacket and it tries it
on. It fits okay and she gets to work taping its gloves. It can't
grasp the zipper pull with its mittens on so she has to help it.
Its face disappears inside the hood as she slides it all the
way up.

Dawn's just starting to creep into the sky as we set off. The fury hangs back inside the shadow of the doorway and Mags has to coax it out. It still doesn't want to look directly at the light, but it manages to hold its head at a more hopeful angle than anything it could muster yesterday.

I had another look at Marv's map over breakfast. Route 220 out of Covington stays parallel to I-81 for most of its length. We can follow it almost as far as we need to north and then rejoin the interstate for the last couple of days and it doesn't look like we'll have added much to our journey. I discuss it with Mags as we head down to the highway and she reckons we should take it. I stick a patch of duct tape to the exit sign so Hicks knows which way we've gone.

We follow I-64 east for a third of a mile or so. The road crosses a wide river the map says is the Jackson and then a little further on we come to an embankment that drops down onto railway lines. According to the map they'll take us north out of town as quickly as 220 and I figure if Truck's looking for places we might have gotten off he'll check the roads before anything else.

I hang back while Mags takes the fury on ahead. I watch as they make their way down the slope. It seems to be doing better with the snowshoes this morning. I don't know if it's the poles I got it or the darker goggles, but it's managing to stand almost upright now; it only fell once on our way out here. Just as I'm thinking this it snags an edge and goes head over heels down the embankment. Mags catches up to it and digs it out, then they set off again.

I shuck off my backpack and set off after them, dragging it behind me to smooth out our tracks until we get to the first bend.

———

The railway line follows the river for a ways and then it continues north while the dark, brooding waters wind out west. About a mile from the interstate we come to a set of signals; the hooded lights hanging from the rusting gantry arm stare down at us as we pass underneath. After that the track opens up. Endless rows of rusting tank cars sit silent in their sidings, hauled to their final resting place by huge locomotives. They tower over us from under a blanket of gray snow as we walk between them.

We leave the tracks at a railroad crossing. The barriers are down and an arrow points to a sign that says a train is coming, but we don't wait for it. The Jackson curves back around to greet us as we rejoin 220 and leave Covington behind. The road hugs the eastern edge of the valley, rising and falling as it winds its way north into the Appalachians. I keep looking over my shoulder, hoping for Hicks' lean, rangy form to appear around a bend behind us. But that morning there's nothing.

Sometime around noon we come to a pickup that's slid off the road. There's been no other shelter for miles so I break the window and we climb inside to eat our lunch. There's a narrow bench seat in the back and Mags holds the door open to let the fury in. It looks up like it might join us but I guess it's not feeling sociable because it turns around and slips into the back under the tarp. We eat quickly and set off again as soon as we're done.

The wind drops and the same gray clouds that were scudding across the mountain tops this morning now just hang there like they've no place better to be. We come to a narrow bridge; a ribbon of ash-choked water flows sluggishly south underneath us as we cross. If we're where we're supposed to be on the map this should be the Jackson again, but this river seems much smaller than the one that accompanied us out of Covington. I spend some time looking for a sign, but there's none.

The road runs true for the next few miles and then it veers west through a break in the ridge at a place called Gulley Run. I can't see any mention of it on Marv's map, and that's not the direction I think we should be headed. I spend some time looking for mile markers to make sure we're still following the right path, but the snow's drifted deep here and I can't find any.

I look back over my shoulder. Behind us the valley's straight enough to see for miles, but there's nothing. Hicks should have caught us by now; I'm beginning to worry he missed the tape I left on the exit sign. He told us to stay on the interstate as long as we could, but I reckon he meant I-81, and we never made it that far. I wonder if he would even have been looking for directions that soon.

In front the valley stretches out for miles, barren and lifeless, without even a barn or a stand of trees to break the emptiness. Have I made a mistake, bringing us this way? With the pace we're setting we can't hope to outrun the soldiers, and there's no shelter here; nowhere to hide; no way out but on or back. If Truck manages to pick up our trail at Covington and they follow us in there we'll be trapped.

I stop and pull out the map again, pretending to examine it while I consider our options. It doesn't take me long to realize we don't have many. If we turn around now we could march right into them, but that's not even my main concern. As I reached into my pocket my fingers brushed the last two containers of Gilbey's medicine. Enough for just one more day if Mags keeps sharing. Eden's still maybe five days ahead of us, at our best pace. Without Hicks I don't know how I'm going to get us there in time to save her; I only know we don't have time to backtrack. I fold the map and point ahead, like I know where we're going. The truth is the road I've put us on is looking like a bad call, but there's nothing to do now but keep following it.

———

All afternoon we continue north. I look for mile markers but find none. I'm still stopping us every hour for frostbite checks, although I'm not sure why, other than for the break it provides. I don't think Mags can get frostbite anymore, and I already have it. I dread it now, the moment she lifts her goggles on to her forehead. I find myself staring at the darkening shadows under her eyes, trying to convince myself they're not getting worse, but struggling to find the evidence of it.

As dusk settles we pass a row of mailboxes, only their rusting tops visible above the snow. We'll need shelter soon, but there's no sign of the homes to which they once belonged. I stop to search them. I tell Mags I'm looking for kindling but in reality I'm desperate for anything that might tell us where we are. But there's nothing.

Darkness falls around us. The temperature's dropping fast and I'm starting to panic. We haven't passed shelter since the pickup where we ate lunch, and that's too far behind us now to contemplate. At last we come to a widening in the road that somebody has bothered to name Mustoe. It doesn't show on Marv's map, but that doesn't matter; as we round a bend I spot a small farmhouse, set back a ways from the road.

We trudge up to it as the last of the light leaves the sky. I haven't managed to replace the pry bar I lost at the hospital, but as we get closer I can see I'm not going to need it; the door's already busted open. It looks in a sorry state. If we had alternatives I'd walk us on by, but we are beggars now not choosers. I unsnap my snowshoes and bring us inside.

CHAPTER FORTY-SIX

HE SITS IN THE CORNER, one wrist held up to his mouth. His small teeth probe for the edge of the tape binding the mitten to the cuff of his jacket, unaware that that is what he is doing. The candy bar the girl gave him sits untouched in his lap; there is nothing there that holds his interest. He knows what he wants now, but he doesn't dare admit it, even to himself, because that might make it real.

Across the room the fire has died down and it is dark, but he can see perfectly well. The girl lies curled up in her sleeping bag. She mumbles in her sleep, like something is troubling her. She watched him earlier, while the boy slept. He asked her where they were going. She said they were going to bring him somewhere and fix him. He hopes it isn't far. He heard what the soldier with one eye said, when he pulled the boy back into the tunnel and gave him the thing that smells of oil and metal. He does not want that to happen. But it is there, all the time now, gnawing at him, twisting his insides. If it would just stay out of his head he thinks he might be able to brace himself against it. It doesn't, though. It slips between his thoughts, wrapping itself around them, until he can no longer be sure which are his own and which belong to it.

The days are a little better. As long as they are outside the wind carries their scent away, and he has other things to focus on, like planting his poles, and placing his snowshoes in the tracks the boy has made for him, and shielding his eyes from the light. The light is cruel, but he sees it has a purpose: its terrible brightness helps to keep the other thing, the thing inside him, at bay. Now it is dark, and there is nothing to do but sit and wait. His thoughts – *its* thoughts – are free to roam where they will.

His gaze shifts to the boy. He sits on the other side of the small kitchen, his back against the wall. He is still awake, but it will not be long now; his head has already fallen to his chest once. Even as he watches it slumps forward again.

He shifts his head to one side and tastes the air. He remembers the way the girl used to smell, when they were back in the cages and she cut her hand. But her scent is becoming less interesting to him now.

Not the boy, though; that it is getting worse. It was over-powering earlier, when he was changing the bandages on his feet. The thought of it makes the hunger rise up inside him now, so sudden and strong it surprises him.

He could sit closer. Just a little. There would be no harm in that.

He stops working on the cuff of his jacket with his teeth and places one hand on the floor, preparing to shuffle himself forward. For a moment it seems like he will succumb to the blackness, but instead he shakes his head to clear it and pushes himself back into the corner. He brings his wrist to his mouth again.

He likes the boy. He made him poles so he could manage the snow, and he tried to fix his goggles so the light wouldn't hurt his eyes so badly, even though he was scared.

His teeth find the edge of the tape, start to work it free.

He wishes the boy wasn't frightened of him.

But maybe it is good that he is.

CHAPTER FORTY-SEVEN

IN THE DREAM I'm back in the tunnel. It is strange but familiar, a mix of Eden and Mount Weather and maybe other tunnels as well, ones that will lead to places on Marv's map I have not yet visited.

I'm in the darkest part. The blackness wraps itself around me, threatening to smother me. There's a flashlight in my hand, but it's so big I'm struggling to get my fingers around it. I look down and see why; it's the one Jack got me for when I had to go up in the attic. I hold it in both hands and flick the switch to turn it on, but of course it doesn't work. I press it to my cheek, because that used to calm me down, but something's wrong. The metal that used to be smooth now feels rough against my skin. I hold it out in front of me, and then I see why: large, scaly patches where the virus has taken hold. Even as I watch it eats through the metal, revealing the fat batteries nestled together inside.

I toss the flashlight away, horrified that I had held it to my face. And that's when I hear it: its scuffling approach echoes up through the darkness behind me. Ahead in the distance I think I can just make out the faintest sliver of light. I start running for it but somehow I don't seem to be making any progress. It's like the darkness has a substance, a heft, that pushes against me, holding me back. The sound is getting louder; any second now I'll feel its weight across my shoulders. I try to turn around, but something prevents me. I keep running, but the end of the tunnel's not getting any closer. And then I feel it: long, bony fingers, closing around my leg, and that's when I scream.

I wake with a start. The fire's gone out and the sweat's already cooling on my skin. I scan the room, peering into the blackness for angles, shapes, anything to prove I'm no longer in the tunnel. But without the fire I can't make out a thing.

I reach for the flashlight I left beside the sleeping bag. The dynamo whirs as I crank the handle. The fury's still sitting in its corner. It raises its hands to ward off the beam, but for an instant I catch the reflection from its eyes as it squints back at me. I keep the flashlight trained on it a second longer, then lay it on the ground.

I don't care much for sleep after that. I just sit there, staring into the darkness, trying to figure out what we're going to do. It's been two days since we left The Greenbrier, more than enough time for Hicks to have caught up with us. Something's gone wrong and I have to face it now: we can't rely on him to bring us more of Gilbey's medicine. My hand reaches inside the pocket of my parka for the two containers that remain. I tell myself it'll be okay; she's been taking whatever's inside those vials ever since she got infected. Some of it will still be in her system, and that has to count for something. If we ration what's left maybe I can still get her there before it's too late.

That thought does little to soothe me, however, and in

the end I can't sit there any longer with my thoughts. It's still early but I get up and start rebuilding the fire. Mags must have been awake too, because as soon as I start moving around she sits up in her sleeping bag.

I set a couple of MREs on to heat and we eat them in silence. She doesn't seem much interested in what's there, though; she picks at it for a while, then pushes it aside in favor of her coffee. I take one of the little plastic containers from my pocket. She holds her hand out, but I don't pass it to her right away. I know what I have to do now. Hicks was right. I've already waited too long for this.

'Gabe.'

'No, you need to listen to me now, Mags. I've thought about this. You can only take half of it. The rest we'll save for tomorrow. That'll give us enough for four days. In that time I can get us there.'

'And what about Johnny?'

I shake my head.

'I'm not giving you any more to give to it.'

Her eyes flick to the container. For a moment she looks like she's considering wrestling it from me. I'm much bigger than she is, but I doubt that would stop her from trying; I suspect the only thing that does is the knowledge that she'd probably infect me in the process.

She looks back at me.

'You have to promise me, just half, then you'll give it back?'

She doesn't say anything. Eventually she nods once, like she understands.

I hand her the vial and she unscrews the cap. She raises it to her lips and tilts her head back. When she's swallowed half of it she stops and replaces the cap. I hold my hand out for it, but instead of giving it back she tosses it across the room. The fury hesitates for a moment and then picks the container up. It looks at me like it's wondering what it should do, but before I have a chance to say anything she turns to it.

'Drink it Johnny.'

It casts one last glance in my direction then unscrews the cap and drains the remainder of the liquid.

We pack up our things and leave the farmhouse without speaking.

———

For the next two days we hike north. Soon after we set off on the first morning a ridge rises up in front of us and the valley forks left and right. I take out Marv's map but it isn't clear which way we should go so I take us east, figuring that's the general direction we need to be headed. But after a couple of miles of heavy drifts the road runs out and we have to turn back.

We eat lunch by the side of the road, not much further on than where we started. I want to say something about what happened earlier but I'm not sure what so we sit apart and spoon the cooling mix from the MRE pouches in awkward silence and then pack up our things and continue on. We pick up a river that Marv's map says is the south branch of the Potomac and at some point after we must cross into West Virginia, but there's no sign to welcome us. As night bears down we stop at a small chapel sitting at a crook in the road just outside a place called Durgon. Its cinder block sides are crumbling and the corrugated roof looks like it may not have many more seasons left in it, but Mags has been slowing all afternoon and I'm not sure how many more miles she has in her.

I get a fire going and start fixing dinner, but she says she isn't hungry. She just climbs into her sleeping bag and tells me to wake her when it's her turn to stand watch. The fury waits until she's asleep and then asks for something to bind itself with. I toss it one of the cable ties I stole from Jax's backpack. I guess it already has somewhere in mind because it picks it up and slopes off into the darkness, and later when I check it's tethered itself to a radiator. In the night I hear it struggling and the following morning its restraints look like a dog's been chewing on them, but the plastic's held. Mags frees it as soon as she wakes up. As she's sipping her coffee I hand her the last of Gilbey's medicine and ask her not to share it but she does anyway and there's nothing I can do to stop it.

We set off shortly after. I check the road, but it's empty. I don't know what's happened to Hicks, only that he isn't coming. Today we'll get off 220 and finally start heading east. If we can keep up this pace I figure another four days' hike to Eden. There's no more of Dr. Gilbey's medicine left, and Mags has been on half rations since yesterday. All I have left to cling to now is that she won't change as quickly as Marv did.

The valley bends east. A grainy, reluctant dawn's seeping into the sky, and for the first hour we find ourselves hiking into it. The light troubles the fury, but there's little I can do about it, even if I cared. The road eventually curves north again into Morose, the biggest town we've seen since Covington. As we reach the outskirts it inclines slowly to a bridge. Underneath us the gray water burbles, but I don't bother unsnapping the throat of my parka to listen.

I'm just desperate to get us off this goddam road I've put us on.

———

We take our lunch in a *Shop 'n' Save* right next to the on-ramp for the highway. We eat quickly and set off as soon as we're done. We're finally heading in the right direction, but now the Appalachians stand in our way; we'll have to hike through them to get back on I-81.

After we quit the town the road runs flat through a long narrow valley that looks like it was once woodland, then starts to climb. A sign sticking out of a drift says the place is called Culkin, but it's another place too small to show on Marv's map. There's little in the way of shelter and we lose the light and have to backtrack a mile to a farmhouse we passed at a bend where the road crosses water. The door's shut but the lock's weak in rotten wood and it doesn't stand to my boot. I get a fire going and break out our MREs, but Mags says not to make her one; she's just going to go right to bed. She asks for a couple of Tylenol and I give them to her with a cup of coffee. She swallows them and then disappears inside her sleeping bag. The fury's found a spot for itself by a downpipe in the far corner. I hand it a cable tie and check to make sure it binds itself securely, then I turn in.

I lay awake for a long time, just listening to the sound of the house creaking in the cold. From time to time there's a scuffling from the far corner as the fury struggles against its restraints, but then long stretches of silence. Sometime in the early hours I drift off, but the sleep that finally comes is filled with dreams of dark, endless tunnels and faceless things, long and bent and spider-thin, that stalk me through them.

CHAPTER FORTY-EIGHT

I'M up before dawn next morning. Mags is still curled up in the sleeping bag next to me. We have another long day ahead of us so I figure I'll let her rest. I build up the fire with the last of the wood I cut the night before, but the branches are damp and in the end I have to use a little of the gas to get it going.

While our MREs are heating I dig the tin mug I carry from my pack, fill it from my canteen and stick it among the coals. When the water's bubbling I tear open a packet of coffee and dump it in. The bitter aroma fills the room. I put on my gloves and fish the mug out of the fire then take it over to where she's sleeping.

She's pulled the sleeping bag up over her head and is balled up inside it. I set the mug down and gently shake her shoulder through the material. Her bones feel thin, sharp, and that frightens me, but I leave my hand where it is while she slowly wakes up. I miss even this contact. At last she sits up, drawing the sleeping bag around her.

'You okay?'

'Yeah.' She winces as she hugs her knees to her chest. 'Sore. Must have pulled a muscle yesterday.'

The fire's not casting much light. Even so I can't help but notice how dark the shadows around her eyes have become. I look away quickly.

'What is it?'

'Nothing.' I look back at her and force a smile back on to my lips. 'Here.'

I reach for the steaming cup. She searches for her own mug so I can transfer the contents. As she holds it up the surface catches what little light the fire's offering; the tin's pitted and pocked, like something's been eating away at it. I pour the coffee in and stand up quickly, muttering something about needing to get more water. I grab our canteens and head for the door.

The first of the day's light's just beginning to creep over the horizon as I step outside. I stumble into the snow, pulling my parka on as I go. A wire fence runs from the back of the farmhouse and I follow it, only stopping when I feel the snow giving way to shingle under my boots. I squat down and dip our canteens. The gray water bubbles over the stones. I can feel the cold coming off it, yet I leave them there long after they've filled.

My eyes are burning, but I refuse to let the tears come. That's for children and there's no place in the world for those anymore. So instead I scream. A long, throat-rending howl, wordless and incoherent; nothing but anguish and rage. I yank the canteens out of the water and pummel the wet river gravel with my fists. I keep it up until my arms ache, until my lungs burn with the effort.

But there's no one listening. No one to bargain with, no one to curse, no one to whom she even matters other than me, and I gave up whatever power I had in this when I handed her the last of the containers. I stand up and wipe my eyes with the back of my hand. Behind me the wind gusts. The fence wire's cold and it creaks in the staples. If there's a more godforsaken sound I'm not sure what it is.

When I get back to the farmhouse Mags has already packed her sleeping bag and is lacing up her boots. She's freed the fury and taped its mittens. I hand her one of the plastic canteens.

'Thanks. Hey, I thought I heard something outside. Everything okay?'

I nod and then busy myself with my backpack, not trusting myself to speak. Her MRE lies untouched next to the remains of the fire.

———

The Appalachians rise up in front of us. At first the gradient's not that bad, but then it steepens and even though the snow's settled since whenever it last fell the going's heavy. The road sweeps one way then the other as it winds ever upwards, but always it seems the wind is in our faces.

The morning's no brighter than the ones that have gone before, but the light seems to be troubling Mags now. After an hour we stop for a break. I tell her it's time for frostbite checks, but she just shakes her head and asks for the tape. She tears a couple of strips from the roll and starts masking her goggles, just like I did with the fury's. We set off again as soon as she's done.

Sometime around noon we come to a deep ravine. A single crumbling column is all that remains of the bridge that once spanned it, its rust-streaked concrete sides jutting from the snow at the bottom.

The slope's steep and the fury struggles from the get-go. It reverts to the crouch it had when we first stepped out of The Greenbrier, nervously inching its way down. I watch as once again it stumbles, miring itself in a bank of deeper powder. Mags starts to turn herself around to help it, but she's exhausted, barely able to lift her own snowshoes clear of the snow.

Inside my mittens my hands tighten into fists. We don't have time for this. I tell her to keep making her way down; I'll go dig it out. I start to climb back up, but with each step I feel the frustration that overcame me down by the river returning, and now it has a focus. When I reach it I grab the throat of its jacket and yank it out of the snow. It weighs next to nothing; I lift it clean off its feet as I haul it upright. And for a second I hold it there, as another thought slips darkly into place. This thing has no future; in a day or two it'll change and then we'll leave it tethered somewhere or maybe it'll surprise us and I'll need to pray I'm quick enough to put the bullet Hicks gave me in it. But meanwhile I'm letting it destroy what little chance I have left of saving her.

I glance down the slope. It's still a long way to the bottom. Beneath me the bridge's one remaining support rises up from the ravine floor. Long, twisted spines of rusting rebar poke through its crumbling concrete sides.

'Gabe.'

Mags has stopped and is looking up at me.

'Everything okay?'

I nod, slowly setting it down. I pick up its poles from where they've lodged themselves in the snow and hand them over.

It takes us an hour to make our way to the bottom, another two to climb back up the other side.

———

After that the road narrows. It continues to ascend, more sharply now, and for hours we hike ever upwards, towards a ridge that never seems to get any closer. The wind strengthens, whipping the snow into eddies, sending it dancing in gray flurries around us, filling in our tracks almost as soon as we make them. Finally, just as dusk's slipping into the sky, the way flattens a little and crests. A large rig lies on its side, the timber it was carrying scattered across both lanes. We sit with our backs to the logs for shelter, our breath escaping in frosted plumes as we sip water from our canteens. The fury picks a spot on the far side of the road and hunkers down, watching me suspiciously from inside its hood. I could care less. I'm well beyond worrying about its feelings now.

I gaze out into the failing light as the wind swirls snow around me. The jagged peaks that rise up on the other side of the valley are the Blue Ridge Mountains. I reckon we're no more than a day's hike from Mount Weather.

Except that's not where we're headed; our destination's still several days' hard hiking to the north. I look beside me at Mags. Her head's resting on her knees, her arms hugged tight across her chest. An emptiness colder than the coming darkness settles inside me as I realize we're never going to make it.

———

Night's already drawing down as we set off again. I've checked the map and the first place we'll come to is called

Devil's Backbone, but we still have a way to go to get to it and I can already feel the temperature dropping.

The road snakes along the spine of the ridge for a while and then we begin our slow descent into Virginia. I spot our shelter miles before we reach it: a long, low building with a tall spire that juts up into the darkening sky like a needle. An enormous storage tank sits on the other side of the road, a narrow staircase spiraling up around its ribbed metal sides.

By the time we finally hike down off the mountain the day's long gone and what's left is iron cold, kettle black. Mags is stumbling through the drifts now, and for the last hour she's been coughing inside her respirator, just like Marv was doing, right before he quit. I try and put that thought from my mind. Getting us to our next destination; that's all I need to focus on now. Anything else is for after. And then as we turn off the highway I hear a voice, from somewhere just beyond the reach of the flashlight's beam.

'Turn that damn thing off.'

I point the beam at the source of the growled greeting and look up. A lone figure sits next to a large sermon sign. Some of the plastic letters are missing, but enough remain to make out what it used to read: *The Devil's Backbone Church of Christ*. His one good eye squints back at me as he stands.

I don't think I've ever been happier to see a person.

CHAPTER FORTY-NINE

HE RAISES the thermos to his lips and takes a sip.

'Yep, I saw your sign.'

It's just Hicks and me, sitting on either side of the fire. Mags is curled up inside her sleeping bag, already fast asleep. I made her eat some of an MRE after she took the medicine Hicks brought with him, just so she'd be able to keep it down. The fury's in a room behind the altar, cable-tied to a radiator.

'Gilbey had herself kittens when she found out you'd busted the girl out of the bunker. Truck was none too happy you'd fooled him either. It didn't take no orders from the Doc; I've never seen him so keen to head back out. He tracked you as far as Covington, but lost your scent soon after. I wanted to follow you up 220 but he was headed back that way to try and pick up your tracks and I figured that was my chance to cut free. I told them I'd continue on to I-81 in case you'd gone that way while they doubled back to see if they could pick up where you'd gotten off.'

'How'd you know to wait for us here?'

He takes another sip from the thermos.

'I didn't. I took a chance that your Eden was a place called Mount Weather and that's where you were headed. Round about here's where you'd be thinking of getting off if that were so.'

I shake my head, perhaps a little too quickly.

'I don't know about any Mount Weather. We're going further north.'

He squints at me over the thermos.

'Well, I guess I called it wrong then. Not that it matters, seeing as I found you.'

'Where are Truck and the others?'

Hicks shrugs.

'Can't say for certain. My guess is he picked up your trail out of Covington, followed you up the mountain road. Boots will be slowing them down some, but I'd say they're half a day behind us at most.'

'You had no problems getting more medicine?'

Hicks shakes his head.

'Doc wants you both real bad. She doesn't want the girl turning before she can get her back in a cage.'

He looks over at Mags.

'She doesn't look good. How long was she without meds?'

'She had none today until you got here. A half dose yesterday and the day before.'

He whistles softly through his teeth.

'Doc said Truck might have been holding back on her too.'

I look up at this.

'She'll be alright, though, now that she's got more of Gilbey's medicine.'

I say it as certainly as I can, but there's a pitiful tone to my voice; I can hear it. I'm not asking a question; I'm a child seeking reassurance.

He takes a sip and puts the thermos back down.

'Doc's medicine don't work like that, son. It holds back the virus, slows it down. It can't undo the damage it's done. We'd best get her to this Eden place soon as we can. How much further is it?'

'Ninety miles. Mostly interstate.'

'And you're sure you can find it? Without a map or nothing?'

I do have a map; it's in the inside pocket of my parka. But I don't need it now.

'I scavenged that area for five years. North of Hager I know like the back of my hand.'

'We're going to Maryland?' He says it *Merlin*, just like Marv used to.

I shake my head.

'Pennsylvania. Just over the state line.'

He rubs his jaw, like he's working something out.

'What kind of time you been making?'

'Maybe thirty miles a day.' In reality it's been more like twenty. On a good day, twenty-five. Only we haven't had so many of those lately.

'Three days. She ain't got that long. Can't you go any faster?'

'I can.' My feet are mostly healed now; Marv and I could do forty miles in a stretch if we had to.

'And the girl?'

I nod, but only because I need it to be so. This last couple of days Mags has been struggling, and I know it won't get better until I get her to Eden. I think of Marv on that last hike out to the Blue Ridge Mountain Road. I tell myself it doesn't matter. She never weighed much, even before, and I'm used to hiking with a full backpack. If I have to I'll carry her.

'So what's been slowing you down?'

I don't say anything but my eyes flick in the direction of the altar.

Hicks takes another sip from his thermos. He stares back at me for a long moment.

'Alright then. Well if we push I reckon we can be at this Eden place night after tomorrow. It'll involve a couple of long days and we'll have to hike through the night some, but I'm guessing you'll not object to that.'

He screws the lid back on the thermos and stands up.

'What are you going to do?'

But he doesn't answer. He just nods at my sleeping bag.

'Best get some rest, kid. Early start tomorrow.'

CHAPTER FIFTY

THE DOOR OPENS and the boy watches as the soldier enters. Light from the fire seeps into the room, for a moment bringing with it traces of color. The soldier closes the door softly behind him and everything is gray again.

The soldier is carrying a flask. He sets it down on the ground. The boy wonders whether he means to just sit and watch him, like he used to when he was in the cage. But then the soldier reaches into his pocket. When he pulls his hand out he's holding something between his fingers. He draws his thumb over it and a short cruel-looking blade folds out of the handle, clicks into place.

The boy tugs at the plastic binding his wrists, but the soldier has ratcheted the ties tight and they don't budge. He shuffles backwards, pushing himself further up against the radiator.

The soldier crouches down in front of him.

'Don't worry. I ain't here to hurt you.'

The soldier doesn't smell like the boy, or how the girl used to, but there's the trace of something on his breath. The boy feels dizzy for a moment. Something unwelcome wakes and stirs inside him.

'Hold still now.'

The soldier slides the point of the blade between his wrists. The blade must be sharp because it slices through the plastic without the soldier having to work it. The cable tie drops to the floor. The boy places his hands in his lap and rubs his wrists.

The soldier examines the knife for a moment, then tosses it away like it is no more use to him. It skitters across the floor, bounces off the baseboard and comes to rest in the corner. He steps back and sits down opposite, next to the door. As he leans back against the wall his parka falls open. The shadows are dark but the boy can smell the oiled metal that hangs there.

'I figured it was time we had ourselves a chat.'

The soldier reaches up and flips his eye patch and the boy sees now why he smells different. The soldier is like him. Or at least part of him is.

The soldier reaches for the thermos.

'You like the girl don't you?'

The boy nods his head warily. He does like the girl. She got him out of the cage. She's going to bring him somewhere and fix him. He only hopes it won't be much farther.

The soldier picks up the thermos. The fingers of one hand close around the lid while the other steady the base. He starts to unscrew it.

'You know she's not well don't you?'

The boy nods his head again. He's sorry about what's happening to the girl now. He remembers what it was like. The headaches. The pain. Like the blood in his veins had been drained and replaced with something else, something cold and hot at the same time.

The lid completes its final revolution and the soldier places the thermos carefully to one side. He pulls back the parka and now the boy can see the gun nestling in its holster. The soldier removes the lid and places it on the ground.

It takes a second for the smell to reach him but then the boy's jaw clamps shut and the muscles there clench in a long, shuddering spasm. He feels something flare and writhe inside him, a compulsion so fierce, so complete that it threatens to bend his very bones if he does not obey. The fingers that were resting in his lap a moment ago curl into claws. He places them on the ground and tilts his head, scenting the air. The smell hangs so heavy that he can taste it; it feels slick in his throat. The thermos is only a few feet away. He leans toward it, the way a ravenous dog might approach its wounded prey.

He is almost lost to it now, but the part of him that is still the boy is vaguely aware that the soldier's hand has reached inside his parka. With an almighty effort he pushes himself back. His fingers will not unbend so he places them in his lap and pulls his knees up so they cannot be seen. The soldier's hand lingers over the pistol a moment longer, then he slowly withdraws it.

'Not as far gone as I thought you'd be by now.' He picks up the lid, places it back on the thermos and begins to screw it shut. 'All the same, you ain't got it in you to make it where we're headed.'

The smell recedes but still it lingers. The soldier is talking, but the boy can barely pay attention to what he is saying now. He continues to stare at the thermos. The muscles along his jaw ache, but he does not seem able to relax them.

'Hey, stay with me now.'

The soldier holds his hand in front of his face and clicks his fingers. The boy finally tears his eyes off the thermos and looks up.

'Thing is, the girl ain't got much time. If we hustle I reckon I can get her there before she turns. But not if we have to haul you with us. Only she's not going to leave you behind. And the boy won't go against her. So the way I see it...'

The soldier leaves the sentence for him to finish.

'You want me to leave.'

The soldier nods.

'I do. Find somewhere dark. Hunker down. It'll be over soon enough.'

'What will it be like?'

The soldier doesn't say anything for a long time, just stares at the child sitting opposite him in the darkness.

'I've thought about that a lot. Can't say I have an answer for you, though. Don't plan to find out myself.' He pulls back the parka so the handle of the gun is once again visible. 'Maybe it'll be like going to sleep. Do you remember that?'

The boy nods.

The soldier pulls the patch down over his eye. He picks up the thermos and stands.

'I'll leave the door open for you.'

'Are they going to fix you?'

The soldier stops at the door. For a long moment he just stands there with one hand on the handle. The boy thinks he's going to turn around but he doesn't. At last he just shakes his head.

'There's no fixing me, kid.'

CHAPTER FIFTY-ONE

IN THE DREAM I'm back in the tunnel. The scuffling echoes towards me along the curved granite walls. I know it's somewhere behind me in the darkness, but always when I try and see it something stops me; an invisible restraint that prevents me from turning my head. I reach down to wind the flashlight, but when my fingers turn the stubby plastic handle nothing happens.

I look up. I think I can just see the faintest glimmer of light, somewhere ahead of me in the distance. I try to run, but it's like I'm wading through deep snow. I hear it again, much closer now. The tunnel's definitely growing lighter, but I know I'm never going to make it.

I feel a sudden weight across my shoulders as it lands on the back, and a second later I hear the snapping of jaws inches from my neck. I'm pitched forward; I feel my shoulder bounce off brace wire, but somehow I manage to stay on my feet. I know it can't last. It's lunging forward again and again, straining to get inside the parka, but my hood and the backpack are getting in its way. I'm trying to free myself from the straps, but when I reach down I realize they're not straps but its arms.

And then finally I lose my balance and I'm pitched forward, and suddenly I'm no longer in the tunnel but tumbling out into gray morning light between two crumbling gateposts. I don't need to read the sign on the flaking paintwork to know where this place is. My boots sink into the drifted snow and I fall forward, flailing in the deep powder.

Behind me the fury's keening and howling like an animal caught in a trap. Its emaciated arms are wrapped around its head and its face is pushed into the gray snow, like it's trying to burrow its way out of whatever torment it's suddenly found itself in.

I look down and realize I'm holding Marv's gun. There's only one bullet; I can't afford to miss like I did in the tunnel at Mount Weather. I take a step closer, using my other hand to steady my aim. My finger slips through the trigger guard and I take a deep breath. There's a sharp crack as I squeeze. The grip whacks itself against my palm and the pistol rears up. A neat black circle appears in the back of the fury's head and it stops moving.

The thick, sulfurous smell of gunpowder fills my nostrils and for the first time I begin to realize something's very wrong. I let the gun fall from my fingers.

I look down again. The fury's head is shaved on both sides. But in the center there's a familiar strip of hair, once so dark it was almost black, now shot through with white. Blood, thick with the cold, wells up from the hole the bullet has made. It trickles down her neck and drops into the gray snow.

———

I wake with a start. Hicks is standing over me shaking my shoulder.

'Time to get up. Lot of ground to cover today.'

I blink sleep from my eyes. The dream's evaporating, but not quickly enough. I look around. It's still at least an hour till dawn and cold. I banked the fire but it's died overnight. There's no wood left so I pull on my boots and parka and head outside to find some more. When I get back Mags is awake, sitting up with the sleeping bag pulled tight around her.

I dump the meager collection of branches I've gathered on the ground and busy myself with the fire. The wood's damp and won't light, but for once I'm glad of it. The fury's gone, and soon I will have to tell her. I don't know what Hicks said to make it leave, but I can guess. When he came back from behind the altar I closed my eyes and pretended to be asleep. I heard it, though, soon after, making its way to the back of the church. I didn't stir from my sleeping bag as the door opened and it stepped out into the wind.

I fiddle with the branches for longer than I need to and then finally I use some of the gas and they catch. The withered limbs hiss as I feed them to the flames, sending up coils of dense gray smoke that smell of decay. I fill the mug with water from my canteen and place it among the smoldering branches.

What little heat the fire's offering draws Mags closer. She sits next to me, cowled up inside the sleeping bag, the faint light playing across her features. I don't want to look at her, but I can't help it. The circles under her eyes are almost black now, and underneath her cheeks have sunken in, sharpening the angles of the bones there. The water's starting to bubble so I mix in a packet of coffee and fish out the charred mug. She reaches for the cup she uses. As she holds it up so I can transfer the contents I see the virus's scabrous advance; I doubt it'll hold liquid much longer. The cup disappears inside the sleeping bag and she huddles around it, like she needs to extract every last ounce of the warmth that's there.

'How're you feeling?'

She takes a sip of the coffee.

'So-so.'

'Just a couple more days. Hicks reckons we can be there tomorrow night.'

I take a couple of MREs from my backpack and start unwrapping them. She shakes her head.

'Not for me.'

'Mags.'

'It's too early, Gabe. I'll eat later, when we've been on the road a while. Promise.'

I hand her one of the plastic containers. She picks it up, unscrews the cap and raises it to her lips. She hesitates a moment and then knocks it back with a grimace.

'Have you given Johnny his yet?'

I don't know what to say, so I stare down at the MRE that's hissing away at my feet.

'Gabe?'

Hicks voices carries over to us from somewhere behind me in the darkness.

'It's gone. Left in the middle of the night.'

'Gone where?'

Hicks steps out of the shadows. He's holding the thermos in one hand.

'Can't say that I know.'

Mags throws back the sleeping bag and gets to her feet. She has to steady herself on one of the pews.

'Didn't you try and stop him?'

She doesn't wait for a response; she's already pulling on her boots.

'Mags. Maybe it's for the best.'

She stops what she's doing. And what scares me then isn't the dark circles under her eyes, or the way there are hollow shadows where her cheeks used to be. It's the way she's looking at me, like I've said something that has surprised her, and now I'm being re-evaluated.

'He's not a bird with a broken wing, Gabriel. He's a child, just like we were, when Kane took us.' She points at Hicks. 'And when I was in that cage and one of *his* soldiers wouldn't let me have Gilbey's medicine that child gave me his.'

She reaches for her parka and then turns around to look at me again.

'Don't you see? We can't allow ourselves to think like them, like there might be some reason that makes it okay to do bad things to people.'

She goes back to gathering up her things. I stare down at the floor. I doubt I could feel any worse than I do right now. Hicks looks at her like he's just starting to figure out what he's gotten himself into.

'Alright, calm down now. It can't have gone far. I'll go find it.'

'No.'

'I thought you wanted it back.'

'I do want *him* back. I just don't trust *you* to do it.'

She looks back at me.

'Are you coming with me?'

I don't know how I've let it come to this, but there's only one thing now that might save us. I look up at her and slowly shake my head.

'No, Mags, I'm not.'

CHAPTER FIFTY-TWO

I SAY goodbye to them by a faded red *Do Not Enter* sign at the top of the off-ramp, just as dawn's taking shape over the mountains to the east. Hicks passes me a handful of the plastic containers with Gilbey's medicine. I ask him how many he has left for Mags and he says plenty but I make him take them out and show me anyway. He says they're going to try and make it to a place called Falling Waters by nightfall. It's a little town just off the interstate a mile or so shy of the Maryland state line. There's a small church that sits at a bend in the Potomac; they'll wait for me there till sunup. He sets off down the ramp. Mags hangs back.

'Thank you for doing this.'

I look down at the snow.

'I knew-' I realize I'm about to say *it* but at the last minute I stop myself '-he was going to go. I didn't stop him either.'

'Yeah, I figured. Thanks anyway.'

She reaches out one mitten like she means to take hold of

my hand, then thinks better of it. She's about to pull it back when I grab it. She looks up at me.

'Take care, Gabe. Find him quickly then catch us up.'

She turns around and sets off after Hicks. I watch her making her way down to the interstate as I hike across the overpass. The wind's picked up. It swirls the snow around her. The highway curves around to the east not long after the off-ramp joins it and within minutes she's gone.

I turn my attention back to finding the kid. I told Mags I'd know where to look for him, that I'd find him faster on my own. But that was just to get her to leave with Hicks. The truth is I'm no Marv, or Truck. And whatever tracks the kid might have laid down earlier, the wind's long covered them.

I tell myself it won't be difficult. All I have to do is put myself in his shoes and try and figure out where he would have gone. Truck's hot on our heels so I doubt he'll have gone back the way we've come. He knows we were headed north on I-81, so it's unlikely he'd choose that way either. Taking the interstate south would certainly get him out of everyone's way, but as I look at it stretching out for miles behind me I figure he'll have passed on that too. He'll only have had a few hours to find somewhere to hole up before it got light, and there's nothing that might pass for shelter that way as far as the eye can see. That only leaves east. The map says there's a town on the other side of the highway. I tighten the straps on my backpack and make my way down towards it.

I start checking houses as soon as I leave the interstate. He struggles with the snow so he won't have gone far, and out here by the highway it's sparsely populated, just the occasional dwelling set back from the road. I don't even have to check all of them. He's too small to go clambering through windows and he doesn't have the means to force a lock, so he'll have been looking for somewhere that's already been broken into. I allow my hopes to rise a little. It won't be long until I find him.

But as I get closer to town roads start branching off to the left and right, each one lined with squat little boxes, and a lot of them have busted front doors. I begin to realize the enormity of the task that lies ahead. It might have taken Marv and me all day to work a single street like this when we were back in Eden; I have to find him in the next couple of hours if I'm to have any hope of catching Mags and Hicks.

I make my way up to the next house along, a single story brick and shingle with a sagging snow-laden roof, trying to figure out how else to narrow my search. Darkened windows stare back at me as I trudge up to the screen door and unsnap my bindings. And that's when it hits me: he'll have taken his snowshoes off outside. That should speed things up considerably. I'll still have to hike up to each stoop or porch to check, but at least I won't have to venture inside.

An hour and three streets later and I still haven't found him, though. I cross the road and start up the next one along. The house on the corner is burned to the ground, just a charred chimneybreast standing alone in what I guess used to be the yard. The next one's not much better; the walls have been stripped to the studs and when I look up there's little left of the roof between the gables. But the third house looks more promising. The boards have been pried off, exposing the insulation underneath, but otherwise it looks in decent shape, and I can see the front door's open. An old Bronco, long since sunken onto its tires, sits at a haphazard angle on the scrub of ground that might once have passed for lawn. There's no tracks to tell anyone's been here, but when I walk around to check the porch I find what I'm looking for: a pair of red snowshoes, already almost covered with snow. Another hour and I might have walked on by.

I climb the steps. The front door's ajar; I push it back and look in. There's no mistaking which way he's gone; the prints left by his small boots stop at a door near the end. The pair of hiking poles I got him lie abandoned next to it.

I unsnap my snowshoes and step inside. There's little to distinguish this place from the countless others like it I've scavenged over the years. The wallpaper's peeling from the walls and the ceiling's stained and cracked, in places the wood behind showing through. I call out but there's no answer, so I make my way down the hall and open the door. A narrow staircase winds down into darkness. I pull the flashlight from my pocket and turn the handle, but the beam doesn't extend much beyond the first few steps.

It was Marv's job to scavenge the dark places, that was the deal. Claus may not live inside my head anymore but I'd be grateful for that arrangement now, just the same. I call out again. Still there's no answer, and now that's beginning to worry me, too. He has to be down there. I wonder if he's already turned. Hicks said it could happen at any moment, and when it did there'd be no warning; it'd be like a switch had been flipped. I look behind me at the busted door. Spidey's offering all sorts of helpful suggestions, most of them variations on a single theme: let's get out of here and catch up with Mags and Hicks, tell her we couldn't find him. I'd be lying if I said I wasn't tempted.

I pull off my mittens and slip my hand into the pocket of my parka, feeling for Marv's pistol. I take it out and pull the slide back to chamber the only round it holds.

I take a deep breath and start down the stairs.

CHAPTER FIFTY-THREE

I HAVEN'T MADE MORE than a couple of steps when the toe of my boot catches on something and I stumble. I grab for the railing to steady myself and almost drop the gun. The beam from the flashlight briefly shows a pair of ski goggles, the lenses taped, before they skitter off down the stairs and are lost to darkness.

I stand there for a long moment, my heart pounding, my breath white and heavy in the air in front of me. Once I've calmed myself a little I continue my descent. When I reach the bottom stair I stop and look around. In the corner nearest to me there's a small furnace, the flue pipe snaking up to a rough hole cut into the low plasterboard ceiling. A washing machine and dryer sit side by side next to it, a pile of moldering clothes heaped in a laundry basket on top. Cardboard boxes have been stacked against the wall opposite. Snowmelt's got to them, turning the card to mulch, spilling their contents across the concrete floor.

My pulse is still racing but the fading beam refuses to show me any further so I inch forward, the flashlight in one hand, the gun in the other. My finger's already slipped through the slit Hicks cut in my liners and now it curls around the trigger. I slide the safety, feeling it click under my thumb.

I advance slowly, sweeping the darkness in front of me with the flashlight. It slowly illuminates a small boy, his knees pulled to his chest. He looks asleep, just like the little girl I found, in the closet in Shreve, all those years ago. She hadn't been able to move, but still Marv had grabbed the straps of my backpack and hauled me away, like he'd found me with my hand out to a maddening dog.

Johnny's not like that girl, though. He may not have gotten the hang of snowshoeing yet, but he can move just fine. My eyes flick to the floor. His mittens lie discarded, the frayed remnants of the duct tape still clinging to the cuffs.

The flashlight's starting to dim. I raise the gun and level it at his head. My hand's shaking a little and I only have one bullet, but I reckon from this distance not even I could miss. My finger tightens around the trigger. I feel the last of the slack come out of it.

'Johnny.'

I hold the pistol on him, waiting for his reaction. For a long time there's nothing and then his eyes fly open, flashing silver as they catch the beam. The muscles in his jaw are working now, clenching and unclenching, as though he's grinding his teeth. Just like the little girl in the closet was doing, after Marv held the knife with the blood on it under her nose.

I call his name again, louder. At last his face softens. He raises one hand to ward off the weakening beam and squints back at me.

'Didn't you hear me calling you?'

He nods.

'It was the other one's turn. I had to push him out of the way.'

I don't care to dwell on what that might mean. I reach into the pocket of my parka and toss him one of the plastic vials. It bounces across the dusty concrete floor and comes to rest at his feet.

'Take that then put your mittens back on. We've got to get going.'

He looks at the container but makes no move to pick it up.

'The girl sent you back for me.'

He doesn't say it like it's a question, but I nod anyway.

'The soldier said I was holding you up. Maybe it'd be better if you went back and told her you couldn't find me.'

The truth is it might. I don't say that, though. Instead I tell him Mags has gone on ahead; before we start worrying about slowing her down first we'll need to catch up. A look of concern crosses his small face as he hears this.

'The girl isn't with you?'

I shake my head.

'She and Hicks set off up I-81 this morning. We'll meet them on the road.'

His brow furrows and he reaches for the container. He unscrews the cap and downs the liquid inside, grimacing with the taste. He reaches for his mittens. As I'm taping them up he looks at me.

'The soldier's like me you know. You shouldn't trust him.'

————

We head back out to the porch. The kid hangs back in the

shadow of the doorway, looking up at the darkening sky. The wind's picked up since I went inside; there's definitely more weather coming. I tell myself Hicks will know to find shelter before it hits, and besides, there's nothing I can do about that right now; I just need to focus on keeping us ahead of it. Storms this late in the season normally blow themselves out after a day or two. But right now that's time I can't afford.

I coax the kid out and we snap on our snowshoes and make our way back up to the interstate. I can see he's trying, but we're moving far too slowly. It's already well past noon. At this rate it'll take us most of the night to reach Falling Waters.

I'm waiting at the top of the on-ramp for him to catch up when I happen to look back in the direction we came that morning. The snow's drifting across the road; I can barely make out the church where we spent the night. But then the wind drops and in the instant before it picks up again I spot movement. I tell myself it could be anything: the weakening light playing tricks with my eyes; some random piece of debris blowing across the highway. Part of me already knows better than that, however.

I motion to the kid to stay where he is, then I crouch down and edge up onto the overpass, staring at the spot where I thought I saw something. For what seems like an eternity there's nothing and then I see it again, closer now. Four figures walking line abreast towards us. Even at this distance Jax's bulk is unmistakable.

I glance behind me at the small figure waiting in the middle of the road. By the time I get him down the on-ramp they'll be at the interstate. We'd never make it around the bend in time, and even if we did they'd spot us on the next straight. My feet are mostly healed; if it was just me there's a chance I could outrun them. But not with the kid. I cross to the guardrail on the other side. It's a near vertical drop to the road below.

I tell him we're going over. He shuffles forward and looks down suspiciously then turns back to me.

'Go on. The snow's deep. It'll be fine.'

He takes one more look and then clambers up onto the guardrail. He stops on the top like he's about to change his mind so I grab his parka and push him over. A second later I hear a soft *whumpf* as he disappears into a drift in a cloud of snow. I glance around. There's no time to do anything about the tracks we made getting up here. They shouldn't be visible from the other side, so as long as Truck doesn't take it on himself to cross the interstate he shouldn't see them. I unsnap my snowshoes, throw my leg over and the next thing I know I'm falling into soft powder.

It takes me a moment to dig myself out, then I find the kid and drag him under the overpass. We scooch behind one of the concrete pillars and wait. A few minutes later four figures appear at the top of the off-ramp on the other side of the highway, right by the *Do Not Enter* sign where I stood and said goodbye to Mags a few hours ago. They stop for a long moment as if in discussion and then the one who might be Truck bends down. He stays like that for a while, like he's looking for something in the snow. Hicks said Truck was backwoods raised, but I don't care if he was suckled by bluetick coonhounds, there's no way the tracks we made this morning will still be visible. At last he stands up again and they start down onto the interstate.

We watch them until they disappear around the first bend.

CHAPTER FIFTY-FOUR

ALL AFTERNOON we follow the soldiers up I-81. Mostly we keep to the median, always making sure there's a turn in the road between us. On the long straight stretches we have no choice but to wait them out and then hustle to catch up. In the low ground between north- and southbound lanes the snow's drifted deep and it's heavy work. The kid's making a real effort to keep up, but our progress is painfully slow.

The sky darkens; it has a mean look to it now. A churning mass of thunderheads crowds along the western ridge and then moves down into the valley behind us. The wind picks up. It blows off the mountains, driving the snow across the highway, filling in the soldiers' tracks until only the deeper indentations made by Jax's snowshoes remain. There's little shelter from it, even in the gulley.

We pass a succession of exits but Truck shows no sign of quitting the interstate. Just as dusk's settling we come to a long, straight section that inclines steadily. I break a HOOAH! from one of the MRE cartons and watch as they slowly trudge away from us in the failing light. The kid's happy for the rest, but I'm worried we'll lose their tracks and stumble into them waiting for us, so I climb out onto the road and lay prone in the powder to watch. Just as I think they're about to disappear over the next crest I see them heading for the off-ramp.

It takes us the best part of an hour to catch up to where they got off. Night's almost on us and I'm having trouble picking out Jax's prints now; if I hadn't seen them take this exit I reckon I'd have walked us on by. Deep inside the clouds lightning shudders and for the first time I hear the low rumble of thunder, still some ways off, but doubtless headed our way. We make our way up to the interchange. A familiar Exxon sits at the top of the off-ramp, its forecourt canopy collapsed onto the pumps under a blanket of snow. I realize this is where Mags and I first got on I-81, almost three weeks ago now. I take us up to the Waffle House where we spent the night. It's just as we left it, the door leaning inward on its one remaining hinge. I tell the kid to wait inside, I'll be back soon. He stares at the busted door, but makes no attempt to comply.

'Where are you going?'

'To find where the soldiers are sleeping, see if I can't figure a way to hold them up.'

I spotted a sign for a Holiday Inn as we were leaving the highway. I reckon Truck will have seen it too. There's a good bet that's where they'll be.

'I want to come with you.'

'Well you can't.'

This comes out a little harsher than I intend. But it's already full dark, the temperature's dropping and I don't need to look at the map to know we've not made it a dozen miles today. Falling Waters is still the best part of a day's hike

ahead of us, and there's a storm coming. And on top of that I
have to think of something to stop the soldiers from catching
up with Mags and Hicks. So right now I don't have time to
spit, much less worry about whether the kid might get lonely
if I leave him by himself for twenty minutes.

'Are you going to use your flashlight?'

I'm tempted to tell him to quit acting bixicated, but
instead I just shake my head.

''Course not. They might see it.'

He stares at me as I start back towards the road. I've gone
barely half a dozen paces when I hear him behind me again.

'You're going the wrong way.'

I turn around. He's pushed the goggles up onto his forehead. One arm is extended and a small duct-taped mitten is
pointing at right angles to the direction I was taking.

'I can see the big soldier's prints. They went that way.'

I don't know how he can make anything out in this darkness, but he seems pretty certain and I have nothing to go on
other than the Holiday Inn sign so I beckon him forward and
tell him to lead on. We follow what's left of Jax's prints across
the interchange and down an access road on the other side.
Lightning flares and the kid drops his poles and scrambles to
pull his goggles back down, but I've seen what I need. Ahead
there's a sign that says *Welcome To The Rest Easy Motel* and
underneath *Low Extended Stay Rates!* Behind it a flat-roofed
building two stories tall overlooks a small parking lot. From a
window on the ground floor the soft glow of firelight seeps
out onto the snow outside.

We hike up to a door on the corner that says *Reception*. I
tell the kid to wait. He hunkers down against the wall and I
make my way across the parking lot. An old Taurus sits
under a blanket of snow in front of the room the soldiers have

taken. Next to it there's a pickup, parked at a hasty angle, its tailgate still down. I snap off my snowshoes and creep between them, painfully aware of the sound my boots are making as they crunch the powder. When I draw level with the pickup's fender I stop and look out. The faint orange light from a fire escapes from behind a set of grubby curtains. For a long moment I just listen, but I can't hear anything above the sound of the approaching storm. I take a deep breath and break cover, crossing the walkway to crouch underneath their window. I stop again, straining to hear. But there's nothing. I start brushing snow aside with my mittens.

I had hoped to find four pairs of snowshoes, but I guess the soldiers have learned their lesson from when I took my leave of The Greenbrier. Well, it was worth a try. I have no other plan for stopping them, so the only thing to do now is cut out of here and try and put as much distance as possible between us overnight. I'm about to head back to where my snowshoes are waiting when lightning flares again, followed closely by the heavy rumble of thunder. I hear a voice from inside.

'Sure is getting nasty out there, Truck.'

On the other side of the window the curtain twitches. I have half a second to press myself under the sill before it gets pulled back and Weasel's face appears at the grimy pane above me.

I hold my breath. I don't dare move. If he looks down now he's bound to see me.

'You sure they ain't gotten off here?'

'Weez, I told you. They ain't left the interstate.' *Innuh-stay.* There's no mistaking Truck's drawl.

'I dunno. Maybe we missed somethin'. Doc was sure they was headed for Mount Weather.'

'We didn't miss nuthin'. Why don't you make y'self useful. Go out and cut us some more firewood.'

'Aw, Truck. It's nasty out there. Why can't Jax do it?'

'Because I told you to. Go on now. I ain't goin' to tell you again.'

The curtain closes and from behind the door I hear footsteps and then the sound of something being moved out of the way. I crawl towards the adjacent room, but when I reach up for the handle the door's locked and won't budge.

There's no time to find another hiding place, so I throw myself into the gap between the Taurus and the pickup. I figure I might be able to squeeze under one or other of them, but their tires have long since given out and there's no way I'll fit, so instead I shuffle forward and press my face into the snow. Through the gap between the pickup's front wheels I see the door opening. Light from the fire inside spills out, followed a moment later by the aroma of cooking frankfurters. I haven't eaten since the HOOAH! out on the interstate and my stomach betrays me with a growl so loud I'm sure Weasel will hear it and come to investigate. But just then from inside I hear Truck barking another order.

'Dammit Weez, shut the door. You're letting all the heat out.'

A pair of black boots fills my vision as Weasel steps out of the room, then the light from inside disappears as he closes the door behind him. I hear him mutter a curse and then he bangs something with his hand and finally a cone of pale yellow light blinks into existence, illuminating the stretch of walkway visible to me through the pickup's wheels. A large rubber flashlight appears on the ground a couple of feet from the fender. The beam shines right under the truck, showing me its perished tires, its rusted springs. A pair of snowshoes drop to the snow and a second later Weasel bends down and starts fiddling with the straps. I'm close enough to see the repairs he's had to make to them from my last hatchet job. I hold my breath. If he lowers himself just a little further he can't help but see me. But if I try and move he'll hear me for sure, so I just lay there, holding my breath, and wait.

He's almost done with the second snowshoe when the beam from the flashlight suddenly goes out. He curses again and then picks it up and shakes it. It flickers back to life for a second and then dies.

'Piece of shit.'

He bangs it against the wall, hard. The beam returns and he goes back to work. When he's done he stands and picks it up, returning the underside of the pickup to darkness. The yellow cone moves to a spot somewhere further along the walkway, mercifully in a direction away from where the kid's hiding. A second later Weasel's boots disappear from view as he sets off after it. When I'm sure he's gone I pick myself up and peer over the hood. He stops at the end of the walkway in front of a soft drinks machine and bends down to check the dispensing tray. When he finds nothing he hits the front of the machine with the flashlight and moves on.

I wait to make sure he's not coming back and then retrieve my snowshoes. My hands are shaking a little so it takes me a second or two longer than it should to strap myself in and then I set off for where I left the kid. His head pokes out from around the corner as I approach and I wave at him to follow me.

Moments later we're making our way out of the parking lot, back towards the interstate.

CHAPTER FIFTY-FIVE

THE NEXT BIT'S my fault.

In my defense, after my near miss with Weasel I suspect there's little more than adrenaline pumping through my veins. But instead of taking a couple of deep breaths to calm myself I slide over and let it climb up into the driving seat. It doesn't take it long to find the fast pedal, and soon it's goosing it like it doesn't particularly care for the gas miles we'll have to show for it later.

I set off at a pace the kid'll never be able to match. He doesn't say anything of course, just lets me push on ahead, with every step putting more and more space between us. Maybe he figures I'll slow down soon enough. Or perhaps he reckons he's being ditched again, because that's just how things seem to be working out for him lately.

I tear across the parking lot, still hell-bent on setting a new Shenandoah County snowshoeing record. Lightning flares, briefly illuminating the sign we passed on the way in, and beyond it I see the access road that'll bring us back up to the interchange. I tuck my head down and make for it. I don't look behind me to see if the kid's keeping up, because, like I said, right then there's a wide-eyed lunatic with his hair on fire behind the wheel of the Gabemobile.

Just as I'm coming up to the sign a dark shape steps out from behind. It takes me a moment to work out it's Weasel. I guess he must have struck out behind the motel and doubled back to try his luck finding firewood out here. His flashlight's given out on him again and he's just standing there shaking it to try and get it to come back on. There's a second where he still hasn't seen me and I have time to wonder whether I might yet be able to duck back into the parking lot. Then the sky lights up again, bathing us both in stark white light.

The only consolation I have is that he seems every bit as startled as I am. He steps backwards and would probably have ended up on his ass in the snow if there wasn't a station wagon parked up behind him. He stumbles against the wing and drops the flashlight he's been screwing with; it lands in the snow on the hood and suddenly blinks back to life. There's a moment where we both just stare at each other, then he's scrabbling in the pocket of his parka while I ditch my mittens and reach for Marv's Beretta. He gets there first and pulls out the handsaw he's brought with him, but the thick gloves he's wearing prevents him levering the blade out of the handle. He fumbles with it for a while and then in his frustration he throws it, but from his aim it's unclear whether he meant to hit me or just be rid of it. It sails off into the darkness. I hear it plop in the snow somewhere behind me as I pull out the gun.

'Damn. I knew it. I jes *knew* it. You did get off the highway. What you up to Huckleberry, sneakin' around here? Trying to mess with our snowshoes again?'

I raise the pistol a fraction, like this isn't his hour for having questions answered.

'You got a bullet in there this time? Bet you ain't. I'll *bet* you ain't.'

He pushes himself off the station wagon and takes a step towards me.

I pull the slide back and tilt the Beretta forward. The flashlight half-buried in the snow on the station wagon's hood must be throwing off just enough light for him to see into the chamber because he takes a hurried step backwards and raises his hands.

'Alright, alright. Take it easy now.'

I risk a quick look behind me. The kid's disappeared, probably run off into the darkness at the sight of one of the soldiers. I'll worry about finding him later. I return my gaze to Weasel. A thin smile's spreading across his face.

'You ain't gonna pull the trigger.'

I haven't actually figured out what I mean to do yet, but that option's definitely not been cleared from the table. I raise the gun and point it at his chest.

'I worry you're putting too much stock in our friendship, Weasel.' I emphasize the last word on purpose. The smile flickers for a second and I see his features harden. He shakes his head.

'Nope. I'm countin' on you not wanting more company than you already got right now. Gunshot's a pretty distinctive sound, Huckleberry. Loud, too.' He nods in the direction of the motel. 'Truck'll hear it. What, you think he's in there right now watching TV with the volume turned all the way up?'

I realize he has a point. Even if there was more than just one bullet in Marv's gun there's no way I want Truck and the other soldiers out here hunting for me with their automatic rifles. But I can't take him with me. And I can't let him go back to the motel. They'd be on me just as quick.

There's another flash and for an instant the parking lot lights up again. A crash of thunder follows moments after and out of habit I log the gap. Storm's close now. It occurs to me that the thunder would probably mask the sound of the gunshot, if I timed it right. I curl my finger around the trigger, feeling the cold metal through the slit in the liner. All that's left is to figure out if I have it in me to pull it.

Turns out that's a question that'll need answering before the night's out, but not right now. Lightning crashes again and this time, on the roof of the station wagon, where a moment ago there was nothing, something crouches. I have just enough time before it goes dark again to recognize the kid. He's pulled his hood back and his over-sized goggles hang around his neck. He looks just like a smaller version of the thing that attacked Ortiz in the hospital. Something must show on my face because Weasel turns around and looks behind him, just as the kid slides down the windshield onto the hood.

A strangled cry escapes his lips. He tries to step away from the car but his feet get all tangled up in his snowshoes and this time there's no saving him. He stumbles sideways, his arms pinwheeling, and ends up on his back in the snow. The kid jumps off the hood and lands on all fours next to him. Weasel's got a hand to the fender and is already trying to haul himself upright, but the kid just narrows his eyes to slits and moves his face close. He lets go of the fender with a whimper and quits.

I slide the pistol back into my pocket and reach for a cable tie.

'Alright Johnny, let him up now. We got to get going.'

But he ignores me, continuing to hold his face inches from the soldier's, tilting his head from side to side like he's tasting the air. I'm beginning to wonder if I've been hasty putting the gun away. Suddenly the sky strobes again and he starts. He fumbles for his goggles, pushing them back up.

'You okay?'

He fiddles with the strap for a while, making sure they're on right, then he nods. It's hard to tell what's going on behind the taped up lens, but I'm beginning to suspect there's more than one person inside that little head of his now. And the kid who just answered my question may not have been whatever was crouched on the roof of the station wagon just a moment ago.

CHAPTER FIFTY-SIX

WEASEL DOESN'T GIVE us much trouble after that, at least not for a while. He holds his hands meekly out in front of him while I cable tie them together. When I'm done I collect his flashlight from the hood. It's temperamental but the beam's way stronger than the little wind-up I keep in my pocket so I figure I'll have use for it later, at least while the batteries hold. I motion forward with it and he starts walking ahead of us up towards the interchange. I keep the gun on him the whole time, but I doubt he even notices. Every few steps he looks over his shoulder to check if the kid's still behind us.

There's a KFC next to the on-ramp and I head for it. I don't have to worry about breaking in; all that's left of the door is a mostly empty frame, all buckled and bent around the lock where a long time ago somebody took a pry bar to it. There's a little drift, but the snow only reaches in a couple of feet. A sign over the entrance just says *Hungry?*

I'd prefer somewhere a little harder to find, but right now the kid and I need to be gone. I tell him to wait in the restaurant and he climbs up into one of the booths. Weasel starts to perk up a little now it's just me and him and I have to push him through a set of swing doors into the kitchens. I set his flashlight down on one of the counters. The light flickers for a second but then steadies.

'Truck'll find me.'

'Yeah, I know.' I'm kinda counting on it actually. The jury's still out on whether I might have been able to put a bullet in him back in the parking lot, but I'm pretty sure I don't have it in me to tie him up somewhere and just leave him to starve.

'Then we'll come get you, Huckleberry. Just you wait. You're goin' in a cage. I'm going to come visit you every day. You and...'

He stops.

'The girl. Where's the girl? She ain't with you, is she? Where's she at, Huckleberry?'

I push him forward again, but he turns around to face me, and now there's a triumphant look on his face.

'Did she turn already, is that it? She did, didn't she?' He lets out a whoop. 'God-*damn*! How was that? You didn't have to shoot her did you?'

Probably wasn't Weasel's smartest move. I'm tired and cold and hungry, and given where my dreams have been going lately that was just way too close to the bone.

So I punch him.

I've never actually hit someone before. Afterwards, when I think back on it, I'm pretty sure I don't do it right. In *Thirty Days of Night* Eben rams his fist right through the back of Marlow's skull and it doesn't seem to bother him at all. But later my hand will hurt, a surprising amount. I guess Eben had already turned into a vampire by that point. And *Thirty Days* was a film, of course, and not real.

I guess if I'd been smart I would have swung at him with the flashlight. But right then there's just a satisfying crunch as my knuckles connect with his nose and for the second time that evening Weasel ends up on his ass. By the time I step over him and grab the hood of his parka, blood's already running freely down his face. He's holding his cuffed hands to his nose to try and stanch the flow but it drips between his fingers as I drag him into the storeroom, falling in heavy red drops that spatter on the tiled floor.

———

It doesn't take me long to bind him. Once I'm happy he won't be able to free himself I tear off a strip of duct tape and go to place it over his mouth. He fusses a little at that so I pinch his busted nose. He howls, spraying blood and mucus all over my liners and the cuffs of my parka, but this time when I approach him with the tape he holds still. He has two final words for me as I stretch it over his lips, and as you've probably guessed those words are not *Happy* and *Birthday*. For good measure I tear off an extra-long strip and wrap it all the way round the back of his head and spend a few more seconds tamping it down. I doubt it'll hush him any better, but it'll be fun when Truck eventually finds him and has to pull it off. When I'm done I search him for anything we might use. There's a pocketknife that looks like it's seen better days but I've been looking for a blade since the leatherman got left behind in The Greenbrier so I take it. The only other thing I find is a radio. Weasel's no longer in a position to call for help, but I figure better safe than sorry. I transfer it to my parka and step back out into the kitchen.

The flashlight's on the counter where I left it, but when I pick it up the beam finds the kid, crouched on the floor next to the spot where Weasel fell when I hit him. I guess he must have heard the ruckus and followed me in. His eyes narrow and I point it away quickly.

'Come on, we need to get going.'

He gives no sign that he's heard me. The beam flickers again and threatens to go out but then steadies.

'Johnny, come on.'

He looks up at me slowly, like he's coming back from a far away place. Eventually he picks himself up and slouches off in the direction of the door.

———

Outside the weather's worsening. I watch it through the broken door as we strap on our snowshoes. The kid seems a little distant, but right then I'm mostly focused on getting us back on the road. It won't be long before Truck starts to wonder what's happened to Weasel. I reckon he'll send Jax or Boots looking for him first, and if they don't find him he'll come himself, and sooner or later – I'm hoping later – he'll be found. I need to put some distance between us before that happens. The wind's already covering the tracks we made getting up here, but I bend down to sweep the snow that's drifted in clean of our prints too. When I'm done I grab Weasel's snowshoes and we set off towards the interchange.

The world reveals itself frequently now, out of a darkness rent by lightning. The sky's restless with it. Towering thunderheads crowd into the valley behind us and hang low along the ridges on either side. The storm lights them from within, occasionally sending blue-white forks to stab down at the mountains below.

We pass the on-ramp but don't take it. The interstate's too exposed; the storm'll be on us before the night's out and I don't want to get caught without shelter. According to the map route 11's less than a quarter mile west and it runs pretty much parallel all the way up as far as Falling Waters, where by now Mags and Hicks will be waiting.

We make our way up on to the overpass. The wind's merciless. It blows straight up the valley, drifting the snow across the road in front of us, forcing us to lean into it. I stop in the middle and dump Weasel's snowshoes over the guardrail. I wait until we're on the other side before I allow us his flashlight. It flickers and starts but the beam's much brighter than the wind-up I carry and I'm glad of it.

We head into town and turn north onto 11, but even with the wind at our backs it's still bitterly cold. The night's sharp with it now. My hood's zipped all the way up but it finds its way in regardless, biting at any inch of exposed skin like a thousand tiny needles. I have to keep us out in it if we're to have any chance of catching Mags and Hicks, but I don't plan to make the same mistake I did when I quit The Greenbrier. I reckon I'll walk us for a couple of hours then rest for a while, get a fire going and warm up before we set out again.

CHAPTER FIFTY-SEVEN

WE MAKE it as far as a place called Winchester before the cold finally drives me off the road. We haven't come as far as I'd hoped. The kid's slowed down a lot. He seemed to be coping better with the drifts earlier, when we were coming up the interstate. Since we left Weasel in the KFC it's like he's regressed to that chimp-like crouch he had when we first left the bunker.

We head through the center of town on what looks like the main drag. I spot what we need, right on the corner: a First Citizens Bank with an ATM lobby. There'll be nothing in there worth having - the banks mostly got passed over for anywhere that might have had food or fuel - but I'm not here to scavenge. All I'm looking for now is somewhere to shelter.

I make my way in, drop the armful of dead branches I hacked from a stand on the way into town and shuck off my backpack. The kid pushes his way through the door behind me and skulks off into darkness on the other side of the lobby. I don't see anywhere to bind him so I don't bother. We won't be here long.

There's a trashcan in the corner, overflowing with ATM receipts. I scoop out a handful for kindling and then dig out the squeeze bottle of gas I carry and douse the sorry-looking pile of firewood. Marv said I had to keep the gas for emergencies, but I figure this qualifies; one look at the blizzard that's building outside tells me it's no time to be walking the streets looking for fuel tanks that might have been missed. I pull off my mittens, fish in my pocket for the lighter and fumble with cold-numbed fingers to spin the wheel. After a few attempts the gas catches and I lean in and hold my hands as close as I dare.

The wood's damp and once the gas has burned off the flames die down quickly. I shuffle myself closer, but the sad excuse for a fire's doing little to ward off the cold so I unzip my parka and jam my hands up into my armpits instead. I flex my fingers a few times to get the blood flowing. My knuckles are starting to hurt where I hit Weasel, but at least that means feeling's returning. I turn my attention to dinner. While my MRE's hissing away I fill the mug I carry with water from my canteen and nestle it among the flames. I upend the carton and go searching among the various items that tip out for a packet of coffee. I really don't care for the taste, but it's warm and Mags says it keeps you awake, and right now those are both things I need.

A few minutes later I've wolfed down something the packet said was meatballs in pasta and I'm staring out the grimy window, letting the mug warm my fingers, when something inside my parka squawks. It takes me a moment to work out it's the radio I took from Weasel. I dig in my pocket and hold it up. For a while there's just static, but then I hear Truck's voice, rendered tinny and distant by the small speaker. It's clear they haven't found him yet. Good. I leave the radio on the ground beside me while I finish the coffee. I hear Truck a few more times and then for a long time there's nothing.

Outside lightning bathes the intersection in its harsh white glare, briefly illuminating a sign on the gantry arm that points east along route 7. A half-day hike in that direction would bring me to the turnoff for the Blue Ridge Mountain Road, to the spot where I left Marv and made my way on to Mount Weather, the place that over the winter became our home. For a moment I allow myself to wonder if I'll ever see it again, but then I stop. It doesn't matter. The only thing I care about in what's left of this world is somewhere ahead of me, hopefully already most of the way through West Virginia, waiting to cross into Maryland. I reckon another three hikes like the one we've just done and we'll catch up to them.

The radio's still hissing static. I pick it up, slip it back in my pocket and drain the last of the coffee. I call over at the kid to let him know we're heading out again.

————

We meet up with I-81 a mile or so outside town. We pass underneath it and continue north on route 11.

I keep looking behind me, worried about what's coming our way. I no longer need to count the gap between flash and crack to know how close the storm is now. The wind shrieks down the valley with seemingly little to get in its way. It drives the snow in long, shifting ridges that span the width of the road. The kid's really struggling with the drifts. He can barely make it a hundred yards without falling, and each time I have to go back and haul him upright.

Sometime after the underpass Weasel's flashlight blinks out for the last time and I toss it into the darkness. The cold's relentless. Whatever warmth had managed to seep into my fingers from the fire evaporated within minutes of stepping outside again. I switch the little windup between my hands so I can keep one of them jammed up into my armpit at all times. I'm not sure it's doing any good. Inside my mittens my fingers tighten; I have to keep opening and closing them to make sure they'll wind the stubby handle.

We pass a collection of buildings huddled tight around a junction. A CITGO gas station sits opposite a diner, a faded red Coca Cola sign still clinging bravely to the wall. Up ahead there's something big, lying on its side across the road. The snow's drifted high around it, disguising its shape. I stop and stare at it while I wait for the kid to catch up. Back in Eden I used to know every car, pickup and rig on the turnpike just from the shape it made under the powder, but the best I can muster now is fallen dinosaur. I wonder if it's the cold, starting to affect my thinking. Maybe we should stop here, find a place to warm up. But we haven't even made it to West Virginia yet, and Mags and Hicks will be all the way through it now, getting ready to cross the Potomac into Maryland come first light. We'll never catch them if we keep stopping. Lightning flashes somewhere close by, and I catch a glimpse of a set of huge double tires, poking up into the sky at the end of a thick axle. From there I finally figure it out: it's a cement truck.

I look around. Behind me the kid's gone down in a drift. I pick up my snowshoes and start making my way back towards him. The wind's definitely getting stronger; it fights me with every step. I grab hold of his arm and pull him to his feet. We set off again but we don't make it far before he's mired once more. I turn around to dig him out then grab his parka and drag him behind the truck. We sit in the snow, our backs to the underside of our temporary shelter. The wind howls around it, sending snow up into the sky in furious flurries.

'This isn't working. We'll never catch Mags like this.'

I say it mostly to myself, so I'm surprised he hears; even in the lee of the fallen monster it's surprisingly loud. He looks at me for a long time then just nods, like he understands.

'It's okay.'

And then I realize that he expects me to leave him here. I shake my head.

'No, I mean I'll need to carry you. Just till the drifts get a little better.'

He shakes his head, but I'm not paying attention. I'm already shucking off my backpack, making a list of the things I'll need.

———

Now I know what you're thinking: chalk another one up to the bitch, right? But I don't reckon it's that. It's cold, for sure, almost more than I can stand now, but as far as I can tell I'm still thinking straight.

I certainly know what Hicks would say, and I'm not sure Marv's views on the subject would be much different. But the truth is neither of them are here. I told Mags I'd bring him back, and that's certainly a part of it, but perhaps not the main part. If he's as close to turning as Hicks reckons it's probably not going to end well for him, whatever I do. But if that's how it's to be maybe I want it to be somebody's doing other than mine.

The wind gusts shrill through a gap in the cement truck's chassis and I have to shout to make myself heard.

'Are you feeling okay?'

He hesitates for a second and then I think I see him nod inside his hood.

I slip off my mittens and dig in my pocket for the roll of duct tape. It takes a while for my fingers to find an edge, but eventually I manage to tear off a strip. I stick it to the sleeve of my parka and then pull the zipper on his jacket down. But when I go to stick the tape over his mouth he shakes his head and pulls away. I guess right there is where I should have thought it through some more, but I just figure he doesn't care for being gagged any more than Weasel did. I'm about to explain this bit's not up for discussion when he holds out his hand. I pass him the tape. The mittens he's wearing make it difficult and the wind's certainly not helping, but in the end he manages it. I zip his hood back up then start transferring the things I'll need from my backpack to the parka's large side pockets.

He squirms a little as I pick him up and hoist him onto my back, but then the lightning flashes and he grips tight and buries his head in my parka. The arms around my neck feel no thicker than the branches I cut for firewood, but they're surprisingly strong. I stand. He weighs less than my pack would after a day's scavenging. We'll make much better time now; I don't know why I didn't think of this earlier.

Okay, a little bixicated there, maybe. But in my defense, it wasn't an altogether terrible idea.

There was just one kinda important thing I forgot.

CHAPTER FIFTY-EIGHT

WE CROSS BACK into West Virginia at a place called Ridgeway. It's somewhere approaching the middle of the night and the cold has turned cruel now. With each step I curse it through chattering teeth.

I stop us at the first place we come to, no more than a hundred yards over the state line. A sign above the door with a grinning pig's head says *The Hogtied* and underneath it *Cold Beer To Go!* A single pickup, buried deep under a decade of snow, waits patiently in the parking lot. I stagger up to the entrance. The outer door hangs askance in its frame, but the inner one seems to have held. I guess the cold's finally getting to the kid because he continues to cling tight even after I bend down to let him off; I have to pry his arms from around my neck and slide him to the ground. He crouches there for a second and then scurries off inside, the door swinging shut after him.

A single withered tree still pokes through the snow on the other side of the road. I dig the handsaw from the pocket of my parka and cross over to cut a few limbs but I'm having trouble gripping the handle and it's slow work. When I think I've finally collected enough wood for a fire I head inside.

The Hogtied's not a big place. To one side there's a bar. The shelves are empty, anything that could have been drunk or been used to start a fire long since removed. The wall behind was once mirror but the few shards that still cling there now just throw back crazed reflections as the beam from the flashlight slides over them. Across the room a dozen or so booths crowd around a small pool table, the balls arranged haphazardly as if a game had been interrupted.

There's no sign of the kid. Maybe I should have given some thought to that, but I figure his mouth and mittens are taped and right then I'm too cold and too tired to go looking for him. I make my way over to the nearest booth. Snowmelt must have found its way in through the ceiling, because the floorboards are buckled; they flex and groan under my boots. I dump the firewood on the ground and sit next to it, already fumbling in my overladen pockets for the squeeze bottle of gas. I know I should really check behind the bar before using it; there could be a bottle of liquor back there that's been missed. But the shelves look empty and now I'm down I'm too tired to get up again. I fumble off the cap and squirt a measure Private Kavanagh would have been proud of over the blackened branches. Within minutes there's a small fire going, steam rising lazily from the hesitant flames.

I dig out Weasel's radio to see if there's any news on the search, but all I get is static. As I set it down I spot a corner of a newspaper that's been missed, tucked underneath the table behind me. In different times that would have been treasure, but now I just twist the pages into tight twirls and feed them to the fire. I hold my hands as close as I dare, desperate to catch whatever heat's thrown off before it's lost to the cold.

The soft hiss from the radio is somehow soothing and I feel my eyelids growing heavy. I can't afford to nap; if I do I may not wake for hours. I dig the mug from the pocket of my parka, fill it with water from my canteen and set it among the flames. We're making better progress now I'm carrying the kid. If I can keep it up there's still a chance I might catch up to Mags and Hicks before morning.

When I reckon the water's as hot as it's going to get I tear the top off a packet of coffee and dump it in. The dark, sour aroma mixes with the smoke from the fire and the damp, moldering smell of The Hogtied. I put on my gloves and fish the mug out of the already dwindling flames. I need to drink the coffee to wake me up, but right now the warmth soaking into my frozen fingers feels good. I lean back against the booth.

I'll just close my eyes for a moment.

CHAPTER FIFTY-NINE

HE SITS in the corner in darkness. The restroom is small, windowless, a single stall occupying most of the available space. Its door is missing, or maybe there never was one. A steel urinal runs the length of the wall opposite; holes dot the space above where a vending machine once hung. Graffiti spreads across the crumbling plaster, competing with the sprays of mildew that climb from the tiled floor.

The air is musty, stale, freighted with a decade of enclosed decay, but he doesn't notice. His hood is pulled back and his goggles lie discarded among the garbage strewn across the floor. He purses his lips and drags the back of one mitten across the tape at his mouth, trying to lift an edge.

A door opens in the next room and he looks up. The boy has come back inside. The door closes again, the sound of the storm abating. There's the creak of boots on floorboards and a few moments later the sweet cloying smell of gasoline and then the damp smokiness of fire.

None of these things are important.

He resumes his work on the tape.

There was something on the boy's jacket. He smelled it earlier, in the restaurant, and afterwards, when they stopped in the bank. Outside the wind was strong and it carried the scent of it away into the swirling darkness. But now they are back inside the heavy, coppery aroma sings to him.

The blood, on the tiled floor of the kitchen where they left the soldier; somehow some of it must have gotten on the boy's jacket. Just thinking about it now causes the hunger to well up in him, so sudden and strong the muscles in his stomach twist and coil with it.

He drags the mitten across his mouth again and this time a corner of the tape lifts. He feels for it with his fingers, but it is too small yet for them to find purchase. Soon. He goes back to work.

It is stronger now, the thing inside him; it will not allow itself to be confined much longer. It is a large animal, straining on a fraying leash, a tether that cannot hope to hold. He has felt its claws, raking his insides, desperate to tear its way out. He is ashamed of what he will do when that time comes, and yet giddy with the anticipation of it.

More of the tape lifts and this time when he reaches for it with his mittens his fingertips grasp it. He rips it off, letting the spent tape fall among the litter scattered at his feet. His small teeth set to work on his mittens. Soon they too lie discarded.

He shuffles over to the door and opens it a crack. Over by one of the booths the boy is sleeping. He will do it now. But as he steps through lightning flares, for a moment bathing the inside of The Hogtied in stark white light. He raises his hands to his eyes to block the light, but he is too late, and for a second the blinding glare pushes the thing inside him back.

He blinks and looks around, unsure of how he came to be here, but certain of what he had been about to do.

Outside the storm is getting worse. The wind is shrill; the door shudders in its frame with the strength of it.

The soldier with one eye was right.

He must go now, quickly, before it is too late.

CHAPTER SIXTY

THERE'S A CRASH OF THUNDER, loud enough to rattle the Hogtied's remaining windows in their frames. I wake with a start.

This time when I pulled the trigger I saw her face. It takes me a moment to figure out it was just a dream and there's an instant where relief washes through me. But then the lightning flashes again and I see him, crouched on the other side of the fire, his small shoulders hunched up like whatever carrion bird is etched into the handle of Hicks' pistol. He shrinks back at the flare and his eyes close to slits, but they never leave me. As soon as it darkens again he inches forward, taking a cautious step around the dying fire. The tape on his mouth's gone and as I look down at the small hands splayed out in front of him I can see that so too are his mittens. His palms rest flat on the water-buckled boards, but the fingers are curled into claws.

I fumble in the pocket of my parka. The forgotten mug of coffee slips from my lap, spilling its now-cold contents across the floor. His eyes flick to it for a second, then return. My fingers close around the grip; I feel the compact heft of the metal as I pull it out. The round's already chambered from earlier. I level it at him and flick the safety forward.

He tilts his head to one side, regarding the gun with animal interest. I slip my finger inside the trigger guard, feeling it curl around the metal there. I shout his name and he pauses, like some part of him remembers. But then he sniffs the air and takes another step forward. I can see the muscles along his jaw working, clenching and unclenching, like he's grinding his teeth.

Hicks told me this moment would come, and that when it did I shouldn't hesitate. I push myself back against the booth and take aim at his head. I squeeze gently, feeling the last of the slack go out of the mechanism. But at the last second I shift the barrel to the left. There's a sharp crack and the muzzle flares.

I drop the gun and hold my hands up, ready to hold him off. But his face has softened. He blinks uncertainly, looks at me and then at the door.

———

After that the kid and I have a chat. I tell him I'm not going to shoot at him anymore and he promises in turn to warn me if he's feeling he might get like that again, although if Hicks is right and it's like a switch being flipped I'm not sure how much stock I can put in that. The bottom line is I need to start being a lot more careful than I've been so far tonight.

I fetch his mittens from the restroom and he puts them back on and then I tape them to the cuffs of his jacket and hand him an extra strip for his mouth. I use a little of the water from my canteen to scrub the front of my parka and then I mix up a paste with coffee powder and the contents of one of the little bottles of Tabasco that comes in the MREs. I work it into the material everywhere I think Weasel's blood might have gotten on it. It smells really bad, but then that's the point.

When I'm done I hold out the parka and ask him if it's any better. He sniffs it and nods his head warily. I'm not so sure, though. I suspect the kid may not have long now till whatever's inside him takes over for good. I feel his tiny body stiffen as I haul him onto my back, just like the girl in the closet did when Marv held the knife with his blood on it under her nose.

The wind's strengthened while we were inside. It shrieks around The Hogtied and I have to lean my weight into the door to open it. As I step outside I look up into the skies. I'm not sure how long I was asleep, but the storm's used the time well. It's almost on us now.

I point us north and we set off. Lightning strikes all around, the intervals between flash and clap so short as to defy the counting. At least when it flares I can see though, and for the next hour I search those half-seconds of light for road signs, telephone poles, abandoned cars; anything to mark our place in the world.

The cold is raw, an onslaught. It claws my fingers inside my mittens, threatening to crack the bones there with the sharpness of it. I pull the zipper up as far as it will go and tuck my chin to my chest but I have no defense against it; it slips inside the parka with absurd ease. The muscles across my shoulders and back tighten; soon they ache and grind like the cogs of a long-neglected machine.

There's another strike, so close that for an instant it smells like the air has been charred, and the road in front of us is briefly bathed in stark white light. The heavens crash, like they're being torn asunder. The kid starts, but then he grips my shoulder and I know this is something different. I set him down and he crouches there, wrestling with whatever other thing is locked inside his head. He's like that for a while and I'm beginning to wonder if he's ever coming back. But then he looks up and nods inside his hood and I bend down and let him clamber back up again.

———

We don't make much more than a handful of miles before the storm finally catches us. Soon heavy flakes are tumbling and twisting out of the tortured sky. The wind picks them up and drives them, swirling them around us in furious flurries.

I can't see worth a damn now and the cold's so bad I'm struggling to wind the flashlight's stubby handle. We're nowhere near as far as I'd like us to be, but we'll have to take shelter. There's a town up ahead. I figure we'll stop, get another fire going, maybe let the storm blow itself out for an hour or so.

I feel the kid squeeze my shoulder. I reckon he needs some more alone time so I start to bend down to let him off, but instead he lifts one mitten from around my neck and points. A flash of lightning illuminates a sign close to road that says *Pikeside Bowl*. I ask why he wants to go that way, but even if he can hear me over the wind I realize he can't answer through the duct tape. He just keeps pointing in the same direction.

We need to get inside and I guess this place will do as well as any, so I turn off the road. I pick my way between the cars in the parking lot, heading for where I assume I'll find the bowling alley. Another flash illuminates a low flat-roofed building straight ahead of us, the only feature along its squat length a covered entranceway. In the instant before it goes dark again I spot a familiar figure, sitting in a chair behind the glass.

I stagger up to the entrance and push the door open; a flurry of flakes follows me in. As I bend down to let the kid off he raises an eyebrow but doesn't pass further comment on it.

'Been watching for you. Figured you'd get off the interstate once you saw the storm coming.'

'Where is she?'

He motions behind him and I look over his shoulder. There's a fire going by the counter where you rent shoes. Mags is curled up tight inside her sleeping bag next to it. I go to step around him but he holds one gloved hand out to stop me.

'Best let her rest. She's had a long day.'

He looks down at the kid.

'You had any problems with it?'

I shake my head.

'Alright. Let's get it tethered then.' He reaches down, but the kid takes a step back and moves behind my leg. All I want now is to sit as close as possible to Mags and the fire and sleep, but instead I find myself saying I'll take care of it.

'Suit yourself. There's places at the back you can tie it.'

The glow from the fire doesn't stretch much beyond where Mags is sleeping. I wind the flashlight and head down the way Hicks said. Screens hang from the ceiling, their gray surfaces thick with dust. Behind them rows of wooden lanes stretch off into darkness. I take the kid to the nearest one.

'Alright here?'

He nods and sits on the floor next to one of the machines that returns the bowling balls.

I take out Weasel's knife and make an incision in the tape around one cuff so it can be lifted then I rip it off. Once he has a hand free he removes the tape from his other wrist and finally his mouth and then he feeds his arms through the rack. I pass him a cable tie that's already looped and he slips his hands through and ratchets it tight with his teeth. When he's done he holds them up to let me see.

I walk back to the lobby. I just want to sleep now, but there's something I need to know first. Hicks is still sitting in the chair by the entrance, where I left him.

'How's she doing?'

He holds the thermos up to his lips and takes a sip, like he's considering the question.

'This is as far as we could make it.'

I'm not sure what that's supposed to mean. I'm deciding whether I want to know more when he speaks again.

'Virus has gotten a good hold of her, son. I'm not sure how much longer she can hold out, even on Doc's meds. Only hope now is we get her to that scanner of yours quickly.'

I look back at where Mags is lying by the fire. We haven't come as far as I'd hoped, but if the storm clears overnight and we start out early I reckon we can still make it to Eden by tomorrow night. I just need one more day.

Hicks gestures in the direction of the bowling lanes where I've left the kid.

'Any problems finding it?'

I look back at him and shake my head.

'I ran into Truck and the others as we were coming back on to the interstate.'

He raises an eyebrow.

'And how'd that work out? I guess not so bad seeing as you're here and they're not.'

I tell him about following the soldiers off I-81 at the Fairfax turnpike and how I accidentally bumped into Weasel while trying to steal their snowshoes.

He takes another sip from the thermos.

'So what happened to him? There still a round in that weapon I gave you?'

I shake my head.

'There isn't, but Weasel's still alive if that's what you're asking. Or at least he was when I left him tied him up in a KFC out by the interchange. I figure Truck'll find him eventually; might just take him a while though. I dumped his snowshoes off the overpass. Unless they're carrying spares that should slow them down a bit too.'

Hicks just nods.

'You did good. Mind if I take that pistol from you now, though? Firearms make me nervous.'

I dip my hand into my parka and fish Marv's gun out. He pulls the slide back and tilts the Beretta forward so he can see the chamber's empty, then he thumbs the switch and ejects the magazine. When he's satisfied he slips it into his pocket.

'Alright, best you get some rest. It's only a few hours till dawn and we've got a long hike ahead of us tomorrow.'

I head back to where Mags is sleeping, unfurl my sleeping bag and climb into it. The fire's dying down and I don't have it in me to go out for more wood to build it up again. I pull the parka over the top and close my eyes.

I'm already drifting down in to that place where thoughts no longer cohere when something in my pocket squawks. It occurs to me I never told Hicks about the radio, but when I look up he's no longer in his seat and I'm too tired to go searching for him now. The last thing I think I hear before the weight of exhaustion pulls me under is a staticky voice that can't possibly be right and then I'm gone, dragged into a deep and mercifully dreamless sleep.

CHAPTER SIXTY-ONE

IT'S STILL SNOWING when I wake, large ashen flakes drifting down out of a sullen sky, but the storm seems to have mostly played itself out. Hicks is back in his seat by the entrance, keeping watch over the humped gray shapes in the parking lot.

I've slept longer than I intended to. I sit up and look around. Beside me Mags is still curled up in her sleeping bag. I'm desperate to wake her but I figure Hicks is right; it's best if she rests as much as she can. We have a long day ahead of us if we're to make it to Eden tonight.

A few lumps of charcoal are all that's left of the fire so I pull on my boots and parka and make for the door. I mutter a good morning at Hicks, but he just looks back at me from behind those blinkered shades and goes back to staring out at the lot. When I get back Mags is sitting up, the sleeping bag wrapped around her. She's got her back to me but I can see she's rubbing her temple.

I sit down next to her and start building a fire.

'How're you feeling?'

She lets her hand fall back inside the sleeping bag and turns to offer me a wan smile.

'Okay, I guess.'

It's barely light out but she's squinting. The circles under her eyes are black now. I force myself to smile back. She pulls the sleeping bag tighter around her.

'Is it colder this morning?'

It's not but I nod anyway.

'Yeah, but I'll soon have a fire going.'

'Did you find Johnny?'

'He's in the back. I'll go get him as soon as I'm done here.'

'Is he okay?'

The news that I'd found him seemed to cheer her up a little, so I don't mention what happened in *The Hogtied*. I set to work on the fire. As soon as it's lit I put water on to boil and hand her one of Gilbey's containers. She washes it down with the coffee and then asks me for a couple of Tylenol but shakes her head at breakfast.

As soon as I'm done with my MRE I head down to the lanes to cut the kid loose. The scant light that filters in through the entrance doesn't make it much beyond the fire and I find myself dragging my heels as I make my way back into the darkness. Tell the truth I'm worried what I'll find. But as my eyes adjust to the gloom I can see he's right there where I left him, sitting on the ground hugging the thick metal rails of the ball return machine. I don't want to give up Weasel's knife so I go looking for anything else that might do to free him. I find a box cutter in one of the drawers behind the refreshments counter; the blade's rusty, but it'll do the trick. I ask him if he's okay and he hesitates for a moment but then gives me a thumbs-up. As I lean in to cut the plastic ties I can see he's been working on them and it doesn't take much for me to finish the job. I throw the 'cutter away and hand him his medicine. When he's taken it he asks for a strip of tape for his mouth then he puts his mittens back on and I tape them too, making sure to add a couple of extra turns for good measure. I start to make my way up to where Mags is sitting by the fire but he holds back.

'What's wrong?'

He points up towards the entrance and I understand. He's already wearing his goggles, but I guess they're no longer enough. I tear another strip of tape and cover the remaining slit then zip his hood all the way up. I bend down and hoist him onto my back and we make our way up to join Mags. She looks up when she sees us and her eyes widen.

'It's okay, he's taped pretty good. This is how we got here last night.'

I set him down next to her. She looks over at Hicks, but he just shakes his head like he wants no part of it and goes back to eyeballing the parking lot.

We pack up our things and get ready to leave. Outside the storm's moved on, but the powder's soft and deep from the fall overnight. I hoist the kid onto my shoulders. He wraps his arms around my neck and buries his head in my parka and we set off.

———

All morning we trek steadily north. Hicks takes us out to the interstate at the first opportunity. We can't be that far from Hager and I think sticking on 11 might have been faster, but I don't reckon there's much in it so I don't argue the point. The road curves this way and that but at least it stays pretty flat. I keep checking behind me to see how Mags is doing.

Hicks is breaking trail and I'm following in his footsteps, so the snow she's treading's as packed as it's going to get, but before we've gone much more than a mile she's struggling.

We pass an exit sign for Falling Waters and shortly after there's a succession of overpasses. The last of them has collapsed and we have to take off our snowshoes and pick our way down through the rubble. Hicks clambers up the other side. I let Mags go ahead of me; I can hear her breathing hard inside her respirator as I follow her up. When we reach the top I ask if she wants to take a break, but she just shakes her head and waves Hicks on.

The road swings east for a couple of miles and then starts a long, slow descent. We come to a faded yellow sign that says *Maryland Welcomes You* and a little ways further on we reach the Potomac. There are separate bridges for east- and westbound traffic; the westbound crossing's given way but thankfully ours has held. I stop in the middle and wait by the guardrail for Mags to catch up. Beneath us the river flows sluggishly south.

We reach Hager soon after. Hicks stops at a large stone church on the far side of town. A bell tower with a tall steeple looms over us as we trudge up to the entrance and unsnap our snowshoes. Two heavy oak doors bar our way, but they're not locked and we step through into a darkened foyer, our boots shedding snow on the cold stone. Stained-glass windows sit high on the walls on both sides but they're silted with grime and admit little light.

Hicks chooses a spot near the door and sits with his back to the wall. I set the kid down and ask how he's doing. He hesitates for a moment then nods tentatively so I unzip his hood.

'It's pretty dark in here.'

He lifts the goggles onto his forehead and squints around. But then he catches Hicks pulling the thermos from his backpack and scurries off into the shadows.

There's a stack of hymnals that have been missed that'll do for a fire; I gather them up and use the last of the gas to get it going. Mags wraps herself around the coffee I make but shakes her head when I offer her an MRE and just asks for a couple more Tylenol. While she's taking them I go through her pack and throw out whatever she won't need to lighten the load. She looks like she might object when I find *Owen Meany* so I jam it into the inside pocket of my parka instead. When I'm done Hicks raises the thermos to his lips and looks over at me.

'How much further we got, kid?'

'We're close. I reckon we can be there tonight.'

'So what's the plan?'

'We go in as soon as we get there.'

'Sure you're up to that? You won't need to rest up or nothing?'

I don't need to look over at Mags to see how she's doing. She started coughing again as we were coming into Hager, and that worries me. The kid's no better; he's barely holding it together now. He's been squeezing my shoulder for the last hour, asking to be set down, but we don't have time to wait while he sorts himself out. I shake my head.

'Fair enough. You have the code for the blast door?'

I don't, but I nod anyway.

'Alright. And what'll we face when we get in there?'

I hesitate. The truth is I don't know. Up until now my main concern's been that Kane would send Peck to Mount Weather for us at the earliest opportunity. Now if I'm going to get Mags to the scanner I'd much rather he and the

Guardians weren't in there waiting for us. But they could well be, and I guess Hicks deserves to know what he's up against.

'Kane's secret service agent, Randall Peck.'

'He any good?'

'Yeah.'

'Anybody else?'

He already knows about Kane. Quartermaster used to be the Defense Secretary but I suspect it's been a while since his fingers fitted a trigger guard. I tell him about Scudder. He was a soldier too, even though he was mostly Eden's maintenance guy.

'That it?'

'And maybe six Guardians.'

'Guardians?'

'Kids like us that Peck has trained. He used to keep two of them at the portal. Another two patrolling inside.'

'Armed?'

'They could be.'

Hicks shifts his jaw, like he's considering this.

'Alright, then. Well, it's your show from here.'

CHAPTER SIXTY-TWO

WE TAKE I-64 east out of Hager. For a long while the highway runs straight. Giant billboards clutter the fields on either side. Most have collapsed, the metal supports weakened by rust or virus, the wind and the storms doing the rest. Those that still stand look down on us as we pass, their tattered hoardings showing weather-faded images from a world that no longer exists.

The road finally starts to curve north and we pass a Food Lion, and then a little further on I spot the farm store, its familiar parapet walls towering over the adjacent lots. Next to it's the veterinary clinic where I found Benjamin, what now seems like a lifetime ago. We come to a junction. A collapsed traffic light gantry lies across the intersection, almost drifted out of sight. I take us out around it but we keep to the road. Less than a mile further on I find what I'm looking for: a sign, mostly buried under a blanket of snow, that says US491 above an arrow that points right. On the other side of the road there's another, its message hidden under a thick crust of snow and ice. Hicks stops in front of it and scrapes it off while Mags catches up. He stares at it for a moment and then turns to me.

'Raven Rock. Is that it kid? Is that where Kane's been holed up all these years?'

I shrug my shoulders like I don't know, but I do. Marv told me Eden's real name just before he died. Hicks looks at the sign some more and then shakes his head.

'Well I'll be damned. You have to hand it to him. I'd forgotten that place even existed. Suspect most folks had; must be fifty years since they mothballed it. No-one would have thought to look for him there.'

———

We turn off the highway. The road narrows until there can't be more than two lanes of blacktop under the snow, and at times it's hard to know if we're still on it. I follow the telephone poles, but there are stretches where they've fallen or been cut and then I'm down to picking my way through the bare and blackened remains of the trees, searching for anything that might look familiar.

The light's already slipping out of the sky. I reckon we've only got maybe ten more miles to go, but from here most of it's uphill. Mags is coughing behind her respirator now, pretty much all the time. The kid's been squeezing my shoulder for a while to let me know he needs time to de-fury himself so I bend down and let him slide off while she catches up. He stumbles off to the other side of the road and crouches down in the snow.

Hicks stops beside me and points back down into the valley. I follow his finger. It takes me a while but then I spot them: four figures side by side, about a mile into that long straight stretch of road out of Hager. They can't be more than seven or eight miles behind us. There's little wind, nothing to cover our tracks. Truck'll have no problem spotting where we've gotten off.

Mags stops beside me and unsnaps her respirator. She bends over, the palms of her hands on her knees, trying to catch her breath. I want to ask her if she's okay but that's a question without any meaning to it now so I don't.

'I'm sorry. We have to keep going.'

She stays like that for a while, like maybe she hasn't heard me. But then she nods once and hauls herself upright.

———

One by one I tick off the landmarks I remember. An old house with lap siding and a wraparound porch where Marv and I stopped for lunch. The fire truck whose final journey somehow ended out here in the middle of nowhere. The white sign by the crossroads at a dip in the road, its once-neat black letters spelling out *The Zion Lutheran Church*, and underneath, *Little Is Much If God Is In It*.

We come to a junction, the red of a stop sign just visible above the snow and I stop to dig out a mile marker. I'm pretty sure I know the way from here, but night's falling and it would be easy to get lost. I can't afford to lead us wrong now.

As we set off again Mags stumbles. She kneels in the snow and unsnaps the respirator, trying to catch her breath. Hicks stares back down the road into the gathering darkness then looks over at me.

'How much farther?'

I figure a mile, maybe a shade less, to the state line and

another beyond that to the turnpike. From there three more to Eden.

He whistles softly through his teeth but doesn't say anything. He doesn't need to. The soldiers are running us down. Sometimes on the switchbacks I can see their lights now, always closer.

I bend down to Mags.

'We need to go.'

She nods and gets to her feet. As she clips the respirator back in place the filter on one side detaches and falls silently into the snow; when I look at it I can see the steel retaining ring on that side has given out. I dig in my backpack for one of the spare cotton masks I carry while she unfastens it. As soon as she's tied it on we set off again.

We continue on past Fort Narrows. From the road I can just make out the barracks, row after row of low brick buildings, the snow drifted almost up to the eaves of their roofs. I'm pretty sure this was where Marv was getting the things he'd stashed under the floorboards up at the farmhouse. There are things in there I could use, but I can't stop now to go looking for them. Hicks has promised to buy us the time we need when we get to Eden. I'll have to rely on him for that.

The road curves around and we come to a railroad crossing, the top of the dead lights just visible above the snow. I don't know exactly when it happens because there's no sign, but shortly after that we return to Pennsylvania.

CHAPTER SIXTY-THREE

IT'S WELL after dark when we leave the turnpike and start making our way up the mountain. We're close now but I'm not sure how much more Mags has left in her. The 'pike was mostly flat, but even there she was struggling to put one snowshoe in front of another. And she's coughing continuously, just like Marv was in the end. We don't do frostbite checks anymore, but I've seen the blood that flecks the cotton mask I gave her to replace the respirator. The kid's in bad shape too. He doesn't squeeze my shoulder now; he just grips tight and butts my neck with his head, like he's trying to find a way in. I'm not sure setting him down would do any good, even if we had time for it. There may not be much left of him in there anymore.

We pick our way between the withered trunks that poke through the gray snow. As we pass the farmhouse where Marv and I used to store our scavenging gear Mags stumbles again. She tries to push herself back up, but it's like she's used the last of whatever strength she's been saving to get this far. I turn around and start back down the slope to help her up but Hicks gets there before me and extends a gloved hand. She looks at it as if she means to wave it away, but then she reaches up and allows him to pull her to her feet.

We stop at what used to be the tree line and I scan the darkness. I know the portal's somewhere up there ahead of us. It's little more than a hole in the side of the mountain, though, barely wide enough for a man to squeeze through. Even in daylight it's hard to spot. I guess that's what Kane must have been hoping for when he had Peck collapse the tunnel entrance.

Hicks points down the slope.

'Don't mean to rush you kid.'

On the turnpike four lights have appeared around the curve of the mountain. I look back up, desperately searching for our way in. I used to find it by lining myself up on the transmitter tower, but it's way too dark to see those bristling antennae now. I'm beginning to wonder whether Kane's re-opened it. Maybe the Juvies were right all along; maybe he never meant to come after us and all this was for nothing. But then I see something: the faintest glimmer coming from a spot not more than a hundred yards further up. Hicks has spotted it too.

'Is that it?'

I nod. He looks down the mountain at the lights making their way along the turnpike. He studies them for a moment and then turns to face me.

'The tunnel. How long?'

'One thousand and fifty-three paces.'

He raises an eyebrow, like it's high time for me to start providing useful information.

'How long will it take you to get through?'

Flat out, with fresh legs, I reckon I could clear the tunnel in a couple of minutes. I look at Mags. She's exhausted; she won't be running any part of it. And first I'll need to deal with whoever's waiting for us at the portal.

'Fifteen, maybe twenty minutes.'

He looks down the mountain at the approaching soldiers.

'Yeah, I doubt we've got that. If Truck catches us in there it'll be like shootin' fish in a barrel.'

He unzips his parka and reaches inside for the pistol.

'Best you get going then. I'll hold them off here long as I can. Let me have the code for the blast door so I can follow you in.'

'I don't have it.'

'What?'

He raises the gun like suddenly he might have a different target in mind, one much closer. I hold my hands up.

'It's okay, I know how to get us in. Peck always keeps a couple of Guardians posted at the portal.' I point up at the spot where light's escaping through the snow. 'That'll be their fire. Give me Marv's pistol. I'll make them open it.'

'You and I need to put some serious work into our communication, kid.' He says it without a trace of humor, like he's come too far for such a threadbare plan, but he digs in his pocket and tosses me Marv's Beretta. There's no clip and when I pull back the slide the chamber's empty.

'Yeah, there ain't no bullets. If you'd thought to tell me this was what you were planning maybe I could have brought some.' He slides his pistol back in its holster. 'And don't think I'm sending you in there with an empty gun either. We'll have to take our chances with Truck.'

I slip the Beretta into my pocket and we continue up the hill. The glow from whatever fire the Guardians have got going grows stronger as we approach. Another coughing fit grips Mags and she drops to her knees in the snow. I have to pry the kid's arms from around my neck, but once he's off my back he calms down a little and just crouches down in the snow. Hicks stands over him while I unsnap his snowshoes and then I help Mags with hers. When I'm done I slide Marv's gun from my pocket.

'Wait here okay? I'll call for you when I'm ready.'

Another coughing fit hits her. When she's done she just nods.

'Don't worry. This'll all be over soon.'

I take one last look down the mountain. The flashlights have already left the turnpike and are starting up the slope.

Hicks gestures for me to go first, just like Marv used to, so I lower myself through the hole in the snow and start crawling down the rubble, trying to make as little noise as possible. This was when I'd call ahead, so whoever was on duty would know I was coming, but I won't be doing that tonight. I inch forward through the darkness, the empty gun cold and heavy in my hand. I tell myself it'll be okay; the Guardians at the portal didn't used to carry anything more than billy clubs and there'd be no reason for that to have changed in the months since our escape.

Kane can't have imagined we'd ever try and come back.

CHAPTER SIXTY-FOUR

TURNS out I needn't have fretted, at least not on that score. There's only one Guardian waiting for us as we make our way down into the tunnel. It's Angus, and he's fast asleep in one of the plastic chairs, snoring fitfully. There's a sizable fire at his feet. He's got his boots so close to it that I reckon the rubber soles might be in danger of melting.

Something's not right, though. The Guardians didn't ever come out to the portal by themselves. And I don't think I've ever seen Angus and Hamish separated. I look around, checking I haven't missed anything, but everything else seems normal. The step-through scanner waits where it always has. There's an old familiar flashlight sitting on the table next to it, the light from the fire reflecting softly off its scarred metal sides.

Angus sleeps on, oblivious. His ample rump's wedged pretty tight in the chair, but in the firelight his face looks thinner than I remember. Without the farms they'll have been relying on what was left in the stores, and I know better than most how little that was. I guess it's been a lean winter in Eden.

I wait until Mags and the kid have made their way down to wake him. In different circumstances the look on his face might even have been comical. He blinks several times at the gun and then does a double take as he sees Hicks standing next to me. But it's not until he sees Mags and Johnny that his eyes really widen. After that he's like a steer that's just been shown the branding iron; it's hard to get him to focus on much else. In the end I have to get her to take the kid over into the corner just so he'll pay attention to me.

'Where's Hamish?'

His eyes flick over to Mags and Johnny.

'Inside.'

'Why's he not out here with you?'

'We're the only ones left. Peck took all the other Guardians and went looking for you.'

It's the thing I've been worrying about all winter, but right now I can't imagine better news.

'How long have they been gone?'

Angus's gaze returns to the kid.

'Hey, focus. You want me to bring him back over here?'

His eyes snap back to me.

'No, no. Don't do that. This morning. They left this morning.'

'Why aren't you and Hamish with them?'

He looks down at his boots.

'Peck said we was too outta shape.'

'So who's in there? Just Kane, Quartermaster and Scudder?'

He cuts another glance in the direction of Mags and Johnny and then shakes his head again.

'Sergeant Scudder's gone with them too.'

We're so close now; the scanner's right at the other end of the tunnel, only minutes away. All that's left is to get us inside.

'So how do you get back in? Did Kane give you the code for the blast door?'

I know even before I'm done asking that can't be it. Kane would never trust the codes to any of the Guardians, and even if he had, this knucklehead wouldn't be able to remember it. Angus shakes his head again, confirming my suspicions.

'I buzz Hamish on the intercom.'

I point the gun at him.

'Alright, on your feet.'

I lift the old flashlight from the table and stomp out the fire. No point in making it easy for Truck to find us. I still haven't figured out what we're going to do about the soldiers, but I'll worry about that once we're inside. Only Hamish and the blast door stand in our way now, and for the first time in days I allow myself to hope. Suddenly getting Mags her scanner time seems like it might just be possible.

Turns out I couldn't have been more wrong.

CHAPTER SIXTY-FIVE

HAMISH SHOWS LITTLE MORE resistance than Angus did. His eyes narrow when I step through the blast door and then widen again at the sight of the gun. He reaches for the club on his hip and for a moment it looks like he might try something, but then he sees Hicks. When Mags and the kid step out from behind me his mouth drops open and he stumbles backwards against the wall and slides to the ground.

The spot Hamish has picked out for himself's as good as any, so I tell Angus to take a seat next to him. I start digging in my pocket for cable ties to bind them both, but Hicks just says to get Mags to the scanner; he'll take care of it. Behind me the electric motors continue to whine, still winding the four tons of carbon steel out into the darkness. I point him to the large button on the wall that starts the close sequence but he just nods.

'Go on now. I got it.'

I follow Mags and the kid through the locker room and the showers to the scanner. She's already killed the lights and it waits in the darkness, the faint glow that follows me in reflecting dully off its polished metal skin. From its hollow center a narrow platform extends, like it's spent the long winter months just sitting there hoping for my return. I look up at the camera mounted high on the wall. The red light's blinking but if what Angus has told me is true there shouldn't be anyone in the control room looking at the screen.

She sits on the platform and beckons the kid over. He looks at her dubiously and then sniffs the air around the machine, but eventually he takes a seat next to her. She unzips his parka then wraps an arm around his narrow shoulders and lays back down, pulling him close. He struggles a little at first and I step forward, ready to pry him off her if I need to, but she holds a hand out and shakes her head. He seems to calm down after that. She gives him a moment to settle and then nods at me to begin.

There's a big red button on the wall that will stop the scan in an emergency, but to start it you have to go next door, to the control room. I've never actually been in there, but I figure operating the machine can't be that difficult; Kurt managed it for years after all. I step through into a small, windowless room. A desk with a bank of screens and a keyboard built into it sits in the center, a microphone on a long angled stalk jutting from its surface. I flick the switch on the side and all three screens come to life. The one on the right shows a grainy black and white feed from the camera next door, but with the lights off it's hard to tell what's going on in there. On one side of the keyboard there's a row of switches and on the other a large green button with the word 'Start' written on a piece of tape above it. The plastic around it looks grubby, like it's the only part of the apparatus that ever got touched. I press it and the switches light up all at once and then start flickering in seemingly random order. Lines of information scroll up the center screen, too quickly for me to read. A digital counter next to the button I've just pressed blinks to life and displays nineteen minutes and thirty seconds.

On the screen showing the feed from the camera I can just make out the platform retracting, drawing Mags and the kid into the machine's interior. She's holding him tightly to her, keeping his arms pinned to his sides inside hers. He doesn't struggle, almost like he finds the close darkness soothing. The platform slides in the last few inches and another light on the panel comes on. The digits on the counter flash several times and then it starts counting down.

There's a long pause and then from the next room I hear it, like someone's started up with a jackhammer on an oil drum. It's loud, even in here, and I wonder how the kid's taking it. As he sat next to her on the vinyl I heard Mags explaining there was nothing to worry about; that this was the machine that would fix him. He seemed calm, but the child that got that explanation only a few moments ago may not be the one who's in there with her now.

I watch as the display slowly counts its way down. After a minute of nothing happening I figure the scanner's on its version of autopilot and doesn't need my help anymore. I get up from the console and step back into the corridor. The banging sounds even louder out here. I was going to head out to the tunnel, but now I look towards the cavern. There shouldn't be anyone in there. Kane and Quartermaster are the only ones left, and they'll be asleep. But it'll only take a second to check, and I figure better safe than sorry. As I walk along the corridor the sounds from the scanner recede. When I get to the end I stop and strain for anything that might suggest our presence has been detected, but there's nothing. I step out onto Front Street. It's long after curfew and the arc lights are off, but the dim glow cast by the handful of bulk-head lamps that remain on is enough to see by. The window-less metal boxes; the narrow concrete streets, the domed, brace-wired roof; it all seems familiar and yet somehow strange. We've only been gone a few months, but after a winter in Mount Weather this place seems small, cramped. I wonder how we ever spent ten years here.

I take one last look then turn around and walk back to the scanner room. I don't need to check the control panel to tell me how many minutes are left on the scan; the timer inside my head's done that count often enough, and it's been running since I pushed the button to start it. The volume builds as I approach, once again becoming deafening. I shout in to Mags to check she's okay. There's no answer, but I know what it's like in there; I doubt she can even hear me. I peer into the machine's dark interior. It's no use, though; with the lights off I can barely make out the soles of her boots. It doesn't seem like she's having any difficulties with the kid, however; there's no sign of him struggling.

I take one last look and then make my way back out towards the tunnel to check on Hicks. As I step into the shower room I suddenly realize how exhausted I am.

But that doesn't matter. We've done it. The scan's already almost halfway through; in a few minutes Mags and the kid will be free of the virus. I have no plan for getting us out, after, but I'm not sure I need one. With Eden locked down we're safe. Truck won't be able to pull the same trick

Gilbey did to get into The Greenbrier. The blast door's electrified, and even if it weren't it'd take a long time for the virus to eat through that much metal.

We can sit it out if we have to.

He can't wait out there forever.

CHAPTER SIXTY-SIX

IN MOUNT WEATHER'S main cavern, nestled between the infirmary and the gym, there's a building that stands head and shoulders above those around it. The plaque on the outside says 'Command, Control, & Communications'. I checked it out when I first arrived, but I don't think it got much in the way of visitors after that. In Eden that building was off limits to anyone but Kane, Peck and Quartermaster, and even though we were miles away and they were storm-bound I guess to most of the Juvies it still felt wrong to go inside.

We were all pretty busy those first few weeks anyway. When Mags started the generators up it got crazy for a while. I guess when the order had come the facility had been evacu-ated in a real hurry, because a lot of stuff got left on. For a while after the power came back we did nothing but run around switching everything off. We ended up getting most of it, but Mount Weather's not small and inevitably things got missed. If it was a hair dryer or something with an electric motor it'd run for a few days before it'd burn itself out, and then maybe a smoke alarm would sound. But that was the worst of it. We were lucky.

I guess nobody thought to check Command though.

Once things settled down I brought Mags over there. I remembered a staircase from the top floor landing that led to the roof. I figured we'd take a blanket and look up at the mesh of brace wire and rock bolts spread across the cavern's huge dome, and maybe it'd be like when we'd sneak up on the roof of the mess in Eden.

But as we stepped inside we were met by a pulsing red glow, coming from behind the door to the Situation Room. When we went to investigate we found a large glass and metal sign, the kind that lights up from within, mounted high on the wall. It blinked slowly, flashing a single word: DEFCON1. Neither of us knew what that meant so we started trawling through the user manuals that had been left behind in case it might be warning of a problem with our new home. Turns out it wasn't that at all.

DEFCON stands for Defense Readiness Condition, apparently. DEFCON1 means maximum readiness; that sign was only meant to light up when nuclear war was imminent. I climbed up on one of the desks and tried to disconnect it but the box was sealed and so we just closed the door behind us and left. I didn't go back, afterwards, but I used to think about that sign from time to time. At some point the bulb will give out, but as far as I know it's still blinking away in there, letting us know things have gotten pretty much as bad as they can and we're probably all screwed.

———

As I make my way through the showers a draft of cold air hits my face and spidey dials it up to DEFCON1, so suddenly that it stops me in my tracks. This isn't a faint twinge, that vague walking-through-cobwebs scratchiness I sometimes get inside my head when something's not right. It's like somebody's just poured ice water down my spine.

I've done the walk out to the tunnel often enough to know what's wrong, but I don't want to believe it. So instead I just stand there, straining to hear. It's no use, though; the racket from the scanner drowns out everything else. I take a deep breath and creep forward, slowly making my way into the next room. Narrow metal lockers stand in tired rows around me, their surfaces dented and scarred. But it's no good; I still can't hear a thing.

Ahead there's the door that leads to the chamber where I left Hicks with Angus and Hamish. It's still ajar from when I came through earlier, but from here I can't see past it. I inch towards it, hoping to catch a glimpse of what's waiting behind. As I get closer a sliver of the tunnel's darkness finally shows itself, enough to confirm what the draft I felt in the shower room had already told me: the blast door's still open. I'm about to stick my head around to get a better look when something impossibly large, clad in the gray-green of a camouflage parka, steps into view on the other side, then disappears again.

Cold fear floods through me and I take a step backwards.

Jax.

The soldiers are inside.

Behind me the scanner's still banging away. I need to turn it off, immediately; the sound will draw them. I seize that idea, mostly because it involves fleeing, and before I know it I'm running back towards the showers.

But then I stop.

I have to be smarter than that. I need to think this through.

There's no way they haven't already heard. And there's only one way into Eden anyway. They'll be there soon enough, whether or not I let the scanner run.

Besides, I can't shut it off. The scan needs twenty minutes. Mags has been in there for less than half of that.

I need to buy her some time.

But how? There's only one door between the blast door and the scanner room: the one right in front of me. I don't need to check the handle to know it doesn't lock.

I turn around, looking for anything I might use to brace it. But there's nothing. The lockers are empty and the only other thing in here's a stack of plastic crates our clothes used to go in when we came back from the outside.

From the next room I hear the sound of boots and I duck behind the door, pressing myself up against the wall. Through the gap between door and frame I see Truck step into the doorway, only feet from where I'm hiding. He pokes at the wad of tobacco he's got tucked behind his lip for a while before he speaks. He has to shout to make himself heard above the din from the scanner room.

'Hey Huckleberry, what's with all that bangin'? You back there? If you are Weez here wants a word with you. He's mighty pissed at you for bustin' his nose like that.'

I don't give myself time to think, I just take a deep breath and slam the door in his face. There's a startled curse from the other side, but before he has a chance to open it again I grab the nearest locker and tip it over. It pitches sideways and crashes to the floor. I send the one next to it the same way; I'm already reaching for the one after before it's even got itself settled. There's not much in the way of method to it; I'm just trying to put as much metal in front of that door as I can. One by one they topple, bouncing off each other, occasionally popping their locks, until the last of them comes to rest. When I'm done my heart's pounding, threatening to drown out the racket behind me. I step back and examine my handiwork. It's as good as I could have hoped for: the door's mostly hidden under a haphazard heap of metal. Lockers pile on top of each other all around it, three and four deep.

From behind the carnage I think I hear the handle dip. The door shifts a fraction as someone on the other side tests it, but then it stops. Whoever's there tries again but when it moves no further they let go.

The next thing I hear is Truck's voice.

'Is that it? You done in there, Huckleberry? You'd better have something more than that. Because we're coming for you now, boy.'

There's another pause. And then without warning something crashes into the other side of the door. There's the groan of hinges about to part company from frame and then the screech of metal on metal and I stare in disbelief as my entire barricade shifts back a couple of inches.

I bend down to brace the locker nearest me just as Jax slams into the door again. This time I feel the impact in my arms. There's another shriek and I'm pushed backwards, my boots scrabbling for purchase on the tiles.

He hits the door again and this time I stand up and back away from it. I can't hope to hold them here. The gap's already almost wide enough for someone to squeeze through.

I run back to the scanner room. The noise is deafening, louder even than the sounds of Jax's assault on the barricade behind me. My hand hovers over the emergency stop button.

Mags has barely had half the time she needs in there, but I can't wait any longer. They'll be through in moments.

I hit the button and the banging from the machine stops immediately. There's a pause and then a loud click as the locks disengage. My ears are ringing but behind me I hear the Viking slam into the door once more.

The electric motors start up and the platform slowly starts to slide back out. I bend down and call to Mags that we have to go; the soldiers are coming. But there's no response. I grab her leg and squeeze, calling her name again, louder this time.

Beneath me the platform continues to slide out, finally revealing her face. Her eyes are open but they stare up sightlessly. She doesn't respond when I shake her shoulder. Her lips part and a single, bloodstained stream of saliva drips from the corner of her mouth and begins to pool on the vinyl beneath her cheek.

The platform reaches the end of its travel and stops. The arm she has draped around the kid falls away and he slips out from underneath it and slides to the floor.

CHAPTER SIXTY-SEVEN

WHAT HAVE I DONE?

The scanner was supposed to rid Mags of the virus but instead it's fried her circuits, just like the girl in the closet in Shreve.

From behind me there's another crash and now a sustained shriek as Jax pushes the lockers back the final few inches.

The soldiers will be here in seconds. We have to go. I look down at the kid, lying on the floor. I can't carry both of them.

I bend down and pick up Mags, surprised at how little she weighs. She doesn't resist as I lift her off the platform. Her head falls back and her cheek comes to rest against my neck. The skin there feels impossibly cold.

I take one last look at the kid and then I set off down the corridor towards the cavern. I step out into the dim glow from the emergency lights. Eden's narrow concrete streets are still deserted.

I glance along Front Street, my mind racing. I need to

put her somewhere safe from the soldiers until I can figure out what to do. In front of me there's the mess. Its bulkhead door is stout, the buttressed hinges thick; I doubt even Jax could breach them. But the door doesn't lock and there are few places in there to hide other than up on the roof. I consider it for a second and then discount it. I can't count on that way being open to me.

I make for the old pedestrian tunnels, leaving the main cavern behind. The darkness slips around me, and for once I am glad of it. I pass the stores, the power plant cavern and the reservoir, finally coming to a halt in front of the door to the armory. Scudder must have fixed it because the red light at the bottom of the keypad is blinking. I only pray he didn't think to change the code.

I enter 011016, the verse from the Book of Matthew that was Kane's favorite. The light flickers rapidly for a second and then switches to continuous green. From somewhere behind the door I hear an electric motor, and then the sound of bolts being drawn back. Finally there's a click and the door recesses a fraction.

I step inside and lay her on the ground. The light switch is where I remember it. The air's still heavy with the smell of gun oil, but when the bulkhead lamps flicker to life they illuminate mostly empty racks. Only a couple of assault rifles still stand to attention near the back, the dark metal gleaming dully in the pale yellow glow.

I close the door and kneel down beside her. Her breath comes in short, irregular gasps. Occasionally her throat convulses weakly, as if she's having trouble swallowing. I turn her onto her side because that's what the first aid book I used to keep under my bed in the farmhouse said you had to do. Her lips are tinged with blue. I touch my hand to her cheek, no longer caring whether she might still be infected. The skin there feels frozen. I shuck off my parka and cover her with it. It seems futile, but I don't know what else to do.

I close my eyes, trying to remember anything else I read in the first aid book that might be useful right now. But there's nothing. The only thing I can think of is Hicks. He's been living with the virus for ten years. If anyone knows what to do for her it'll be him.

Spidey doesn't think this is much of an idea, even by my standards. He reminds me that I left Hicks to close the blast door and now the soldiers are inside. It had to have been him who let them in.

I look back down at Mags, lying on the floor under my parka.

He might still be willing to help her. He told me Gilbey wanted us both back, real bad. And there's something else I might be able to trade. I bend down and take the map from my parka and slip it into my pants pocket. I grab one of the guns from the rack and a magazine from a crate on the shelf. It slides up into the slot and clicks home.

I take one last look at Mags and then step out of the armory. I re-enter the code and wait while the motors slide the bolts back into place. Then I shoulder the rifle and run back to the main cavern.

CHAPTER SIXTY-EIGHT

THE SOFT GLOW from the curfew lights appears around the curve of the tunnel. As I draw level with the stores I slow down and inch along the granite, trying to be as quiet as possible. I'm straining for any sound but all I can hear is the thumping of my heart, the pulsing of blood in my ears. When I get to the end I stop. From here I can see all the way down Front Street. Eden still looks deserted.

I step out of the darkness and dart around the side of the mess, pressing myself into the shadows. I take a couple of deep breaths and follow the building's riveted steel down as far as Juvie Row.

I halt at the corner and look down the street. The second dorm along's where I used to bunk. I make my way towards it, stopping at the end of the mess building to check the way's still clear before scooting across. When I reach the door I place my hand on the latch and gently press down, feeling for the mechanism's biting point. There's a soft clunk as it engages and then a gentle groan as the door swings out on its hinges. I step inside. The main lights are out but the safeties are on. The air is musty, stale, like no-one's been in here in months.

I make my way past the showers and head straight for the stairs, taking the steps two at a time. The metal amplifies the slightest sound but I know how to tread softly and I pad silently up, the rifle bouncing on my shoulder as I ascend. When I get to the third floor I stop and reach up for the access hatch above my head, feeling for the bolts with my fingertips. Thankfully they're still loose and within moments I've removed the last one. Out of habit I check there's no one on the stairs or the landing below and then I slide the panel out of the way. The metal protests a little as it shifts, but then it's done.

I unsling the rifle, slide it into the crawl space and pull myself up after it. Moments later I'm climbing out onto the roof. The cavern's granite dome is right above me. I keep as low as I can until I reach the front of the building and then lie down on the cold metal.

The mess blocks my view of the corridor that leads to the tunnel. Its roof would have offered a better vantage point, but as I look over I can see I was right not to try it. The pee bottle I left there after my descent through the vent shaft is gone. If Peck found that it's a good bet he would have locked down the hatch too.

I turn my attention back to the narrow strip of Front Street I can see. There's still no sign of the soldiers. They should be in here by now; I wonder what's keeping them. Just as I'm thinking this I hear a shouted warning and a second later there's a loud bang followed by a muffled crump and plumes of dust belch from the corridor that leads to the blast door.

A few moments later the arc lights flick on, instantly

bathing the cavern in their harsh white glare. I wait, trying to work out what's happening. Soon I hear footsteps from somewhere behind me, near the back of the cavern. I crawl over to the side of the roof just in time to see Kane marching up from Back Street.

He's not the President I remember. The mane of white hair, normally so carefully combed back, is wild, unruly, and the heavily stubbled face underneath looks gaunt, stretched. His suit is crumpled, and there's no tie; I think it's the first time I've seen him without one. His back's as straight as ever though, and in spite of the unkempt air he cuts an imposing figure as he strides up towards Front Street.

There's another sound from the back of the cavern and as I look around again I see Quartermaster, struggling to catch up. He's still a large man, but a shadow of his former self. I guess no belt's gone untightened over the winter months.

I turn my attention back to Kane. He's already reached Front Street. He must see something I can't because he stops mid-stride and raises himself up to his full height.

'What's going on here? Who are you men?'

There's a pause and then I hear a familiar voice. The accent's Southern, just like Kane's, but it has none of the charm or polish.

'Well look who we got here.'

From around the side of the mess Truck steps into view. He's still wearing his parka but now it's unzipped. In one hand there's a dark shape that can only be a pistol.

'I'm your commander-in-chief, soldier. You will address me as Mr. President or sir. And holster that sidearm.'

Truck makes a show of hitching up his pants, then he turns his head and spits a stream of something brown onto the dusty concrete to let Kane know what he thinks of that.

Just as he does this Quartermaster rounds the corner, huffing and puffing.

'And if it isn't the *De*-fense Secretary.' Truck turns back to Kane and points the gun at his chest. If Kane flinches from up here I can't see it. 'It's your lucky day, Mr. President; Doc said we was to bring you back alive.' He holds the pistol there a moment longer and then swings it in Quartermaster's direction. 'Doc never said nuthin' about you.'

There's a loud bang. Quartermaster's mouth opens even wider and he staggers backwards, clutching his chest. His legs give out and he collapses in the middle of the street. Kane watches but makes no move to help. For a few seconds Quartermaster continues to stare up at the cavern, his chest rising and falling beneath his hands. Then he draws one final gasp, lets it out, hitches in a smaller one and just quits. His chest stops mid-heave and settles slowly.

Truck slides the pistol back into its holster and adjusts his pants again.

'Boots, bring the President here out into the tunnel and put him with the others, willya?'

Private Kavanagh appears and takes the President by the elbow. Kane shows no sign of resisting as he's led away. I tear my eyes off Quartermaster. Down on Front Street Truck's issuing more orders. He turns around and points a finger at somebody behind him.

'Jax, you go find the girl now. Well, I don't know. Try behind you for a start.' A second later I catch a glimpse of the Viking as he appears briefly on the other side of the mess before he lumbers off into the pedestrian tunnel.

I haven't seen Weasel yet, but I'm guessing he won't have strayed too far from Truck's side. I don't know where Hicks is, but with Jax off looking for Mags and Boots out by the blast door I figure the soldiers are about as split up as they're going to be. I'm not sure when I'll get a better chance. I don't have much in the way of a plan, other than to get Hicks to Mags before she gets any worse. For now that will have to do.

Seconds later I'm lowering myself down onto the landing. I head down the stairs as quietly as possible and make for the door. I push it open a crack and peer out. Main Street's still deserted. I step out and cross quickly to the other side. The arc lights have banished the shadows and there are few places to hide so I press myself up against the side of the building anyway and inch forward towards Front Street. When I get to the corner I stop. Quartermaster's lying right there, still staring up at the cavern's granite dome, his blood already darkening the dusty concrete beneath him. I slide the rifle off my shoulder. I pull the handle back to chamber the first round and raise it. My thumb slides up and flicks the switch that takes it off safe.

I take a deep breath and step out onto the street.

Truck's got his back turned, so at first he doesn't notice me. On the other side of him I see Weasel. He's holding one of the electric batons in one hand; his other's gripping the end of the catchpole. The noose is around Johnny's neck, but the kid's as he was when I found him and Mags. It looks like they've had to drag him out here.

Weasel's eyes narrow as he spots me. A dark purple bruise has spread itself across the bridge of his nose and there's a neat rectangle of angry-looking skin around his lips where the duct tape's been pulled off. It looks like a chunk of hair's missing from above his ear too. He raises the baton and points it at me. The arc lights catch the two ugly metal prongs that protrude from the end.

'Hey Truck, behind you.'

Truck turns around to face me. He pokes the wad of tobacco around with his tongue then rests his hands on his hips and squirts another stream of brown juice onto the ground.

'Well what have we got here? Looks like Huckleberry's found his-self a weapon.'

I keep the rifle pointed at him and take a step forward.

'Where's Hicks?'

A half-smile creases Truck's lumpen features; his dark eyes twinkle with amusement.

'Well wouldn't you like to know?'

If staring into the business end of the rifle's bothering Truck he's not letting on. Maybe he reckons I don't have it in me to do this. I think of how I found Mags in the cage, the marks I saw across her ribs. I doubt he could be more wrong.

'I would.'

Trucks stares at me for a long moment and then fishes in his pocket. My finger tightens on the trigger, in case he's about to try something, but when the hand re-emerges it's holding a radio. There's a squawk of static as he presses a button on the side of it and just like that I realize how stupid I've been.

'Hey Sarge, come on out willya? Huckleberry's here lookin' for ya.'

CHAPTER SIXTY-NINE

THERE'S a long pause and then Hicks appears at the end of the corridor that leads to the blast door. He squints up at the arc lights then takes a moment to look around the cavern, like I'm not even there.

'So this is Eden. Yep, I can see why you left.'

He turns his gaze to me.

'You let them in.'

I don't need him to answer. A half-memory's already floating to the surface, something that even now I might dismiss as little more than a fragment of a mostly-forgotten dream. The last thing I heard on Weasel's radio as I fell asleep by the fire in the *Pikeside Bowl*. It was Hicks' voice, not Truck's. He must have had a radio too. There was never any need for Truck to track us. As long as we were with Hicks they knew where we were all along.

'You've been playing us, getting us to lead you here.'

He takes a step out onto Front Street. His hands are held clear of the pistol on his hip but his parka's unzipped and his gloves are off. I suddenly realize I've got the rifle pointed in the wrong direction; he's far more dangerous than either Truck or Weasel. I swing the barrel around so it's leveled at his chest. He doesn't seem to care.

'Now, son, you might want to take a moment to consider where'd you'd be if it weren't for me. Doc was all for sticking you in a cage right away, with the girl. She's a smart woman, the Doc, but she's never been much for the bigger picture. Maybe if she were she wouldn't have been so quick to come up with something like the virus. Only one use for an abomination like that.'

He shakes his head ruefully and takes another step towards me.

'But what's done is done. All that matters now is cleaning up the mess as best we can. And for that Doc needs warm bodies, and lots of them. And I needed you to bring me to them.'

Warm bodies, and lots of them.

And that's when it hits me, the thing that was bothering me when he first took me into the bunker to find Mags. All the empty cages. The crates stacked against the back wall in the storage room. With all that's happened since I haven't thought on it, but now I see. There were never enough live infected. Hicks flat out told me when I asked him how many they'd managed to capture.

'It wasn't just Mags. All the other survivors that found their way to The Greenbrier. Gilbey used them for her experiments too.'

Hicks shakes his head, like he's disappointed in me.

'Survivors? Son, the state most of them were in when we found them they wouldn't have lasted the month. It's like Doc says: it's all just a question of timing. But you're right on one score: this place was always the prize.'

He looks around the cavern again.

'Except there's no one else here is there? Wasn't just you and the girl who fled; you got them all out, didn't you? Probably stashed them someplace nearby and then went looking for somewhere with a little more distance from that fella.' He inclines his head in the direction of the tunnel, where Boots has just taken Kane.

'It's Mount Weather isn't it?' He raises a hand as if to dismiss the question. 'S'alright, you don't need to say. Has to be. That story you fed me out in Lynch needs a little more work by the way. I've been to Culpeper. It doesn't even have a tunnel.'

He takes another step in my direction. There's not much more than twenty feet between us now.

'There's still a way out of this for you, though. You and the girl. Where is she by the way?'

I guess he must see the look on my face as he mentions Mags.

'Aw hell, you've already put her through haven't you? I thought you'd have the sense to test it first.' He nods in the direction of Johnny. 'I mean son, what'd you think would happen?'

I shake my head, like I don't want to hear it.

'She just didn't get enough time in there. We're going to put her through again.'

'Wouldn't do no good. Besides, what'd you think that explosion was?'

I stare at him in disbelief.

'Why would you do that?'

But he just sighs, like he's weary of explaining how stuff works to me.

'Haven't you been listening to a thing I've been telling

you? There weren't enough bullets in the world to stop those things, back when we still had people to shoot them. There certainly aren't enough scanners. What're you going to do, son? Drag every last one of them in here and wait while they go through individually?'

I hadn't given it any thought; there was only ever one person I cared about curing. But that's still no reason to destroy it. And then I remember the storage room in the bunker. There was only one crate on the shelves other than the kid's. It had said Amanda Gilbey on the side.

'Dr. Gilbey has a daughter that's infected. She's doing all this to try and save her.'

He smiles at me.

'Well, you're finally getting it. If the scanner had've saved your girl there's a chance it might have worked on Amanda, and I couldn't risk that. I told you: the Doc's our only hope now. I can't have her losing focus.'

'But you didn't even wait to see if it would work. You could have put yourself through first.'

He shakes his head again and when he looks back at me the smile's gone.

'Son, the things I've done I don't deserve a cure. I'll get what's coming to me, and that pretty soon. But there are things that need taking care of first.' He looks around the cavern one more time then returns his gaze to me.

'So this is how it's going to be: Jax is going to find the girl, then you and she and those two we found in the tunnel and Kane and whoever else is still hiding out in here are coming back with us. But first we'll take a visit to Mount Weather. I have a deal for you, though. You give me whatever codes you might have and when we get there, if they work, I'll let you go. You have my word on that. You can head on down south. Do whatever you want with what little time we've all got left. I swear I won't say a word. Your friends'll never even know it was you who sold 'em out.'

'But you'll infect them with the virus, put them in cages like you did to Mags?'

'Aw hell, kid, pay attention. If Doc doesn't find a cure for the virus they're done for anyway. We all are. You just gotta think about yourself now. Do you want to wind up in one of those cages? And that's not even the worst of it. You haven't seen what Doc does to them in that other room.'

But I'm not even listening to him anymore. I raise the rifle. The cold metal presses against my cheek.

'You're going to help me with Mags and Johnny and then you're going to let us walk right out of here. And you're going to forget you ever even heard of Mount Weather.'

Hicks shakes his head. He shifts his reaching arm a fraction. The parka falls back, exposing the pistol.

'You're overplaying your hand here kid. None of that's going to happen. You think maybe because you got lucky with that MRE you can hit me? You'll get maybe one shot, assuming you don't freeze up of course. Took you three to hit that carton, remember? And it wasn't shooting back at you.'

I reach up with my thumb. The rifle's already off safe, but I snick it forward one more notch, to its final position.

'You're a lot closer than that carton, Hicks. And I've got thirty shots actually. All I have to do is hold the trigger down, right? Like that rookie down on the line in Atlanta? I may not hit you with the first few. But I doubt I'll miss with all of them.'

Hicks' expression doesn't change, but for the first time I think Truck looks a little nervous. The smile disappears from his face. His eyes shift to Hicks and then back to me again. He takes a step back towards the pedestrian tunnel.

Hicks squints at me for a long moment, like he's reassessing the situation.

'Fair enough, if that's the way you want it. Corporal, the kid'll empty that clip in a little over a second. If I don't get him first you take him down. Understand?'

Out of the corner of my eye I see Truck draw his sidearm.

'And then you find the girl and bring her back to the Doc. She might still have use for her. Kane will tell you how to get into Mount Weather. I don't care much for how you get that information from him.'

'Sure thing, Sarge.'

My heart sinks. He's right of course. Kane has the same codes Marv gave me, and I've no doubt he'll hand them over once Truck goes to work on him. He'll take the Juvies back to The Greenbrier, whether or not I shoot Hicks. Mags will either die in the armory or she'll end up in that other room he was talking about. I'm not sure which would be worse.

And then from the depths of the pedestrian tunnel I hear a sound like something very large pounding metal. Hicks must hear it too.

'Looks like Jax has found your girl. Last chance, kid.'

The pounding continues, echoing up from the darkness. Hicks turns his head a fraction, but his one good eye never leaves me.

'Private, go down there and see what that idiot's up to.'

Weasel drops the catchpole and starts off into the tunnel.

For long seconds there's nothing but the sound of Jax pounding on the armory door. And then without warning something bursts out of the darkness. It's moving too quickly and at first all I see is a blur as whatever it is hits the light. Then I catch a single snapshot of Mags, barefoot, suspended in the air as she swings whatever it is she's holding. And in that moment I'm back on the bus we took to the White House on the Last Day. But instead of an old hardback copy of *Black Beauty* it's the gray metal stock of a rifle that arcs downwards towards its target. There's a dense crunch as it connects and a large wad of tobacco sails out of Truck's mouth along with something that might be a tooth. She doesn't wait for him to land; by the time he hits the concrete she's already closed the distance to Hicks. She comes to a stop with the barrel inches from the back of his head.

'What was that switch you were talking about, Gabe?'

I don't answer her. I suspect I'm wearing the same slack-jawed expression Truck is right now. She glances over at me.

'Never mind. I don't think I'm going to need all of my bullets.'

CHAPTER SEVENTY

I KEEP the gun trained on the soldiers while Mags binds their wrists. She works her way quickly along the pew. None of them resist. Hicks just looks bored; the only time he shows interest is when I take his pistol. I earn a look that tells me the cable ties probably won't be holding him for long.

Truck's still out of it. A long strand of something brown drips from the corner of his mouth, searching for a place to settle on his fatigues. Even in the chapel's gloomy interior I can see his cheek's swelling up nicely, and there's a nasty bruise spreading along his jaw. When he finally comes to I suspect it's going to hurt something mean. It'll be a while before he thinks of tucking a wad of Grizzly there.

Weasel's already back with us. He's got a bruise just like Truck's to go with the one across his nose, but he's traded his front teeth for it. I think it makes him look better, although I doubt he agrees. He stares at me with barely concealed contempt while Mags slips a cable tie around his wrists. He cusses at her as she ratchets it tight. The general gist is that it's cutting off the circulation, but there's a lot of extra words in there it'd be easy to take offense to. When she's done she picks up the baton and zaps him in the neck with it. He yelps but after that he stays quiet and goes back to glowering at me while she moves on to Boots.

The Viking's the only one not present and accounted for, but he'll do just fine where he is. Mags came around just in time; she was headed back to the cavern when she heard him making his way along the tunnel towards her. She retraced her steps and hid in the darkness beyond the armory. Even for someone with Jax's limited faculties the open door was too much of a temptation. She waited for him to wander in and then locked it behind him. Once Hicks gets free he'll get the code out of Kane, but by then I mean us to be gone.

Mags finishes up with Boots and crosses the aisle to tend to the President. He's been quiet since we dragged him in from the tunnel, but now as he sees her approaching he raises his hands and backs himself up along the pew. I suspect it's not so much what's in her hand as the dark shadows under her eyes and the way her cheeks are sunken in. She holds the baton up and flicks the switch on the grip. Blue light arcs between the prongs; he stares at it for a second then lowers his arms and slides them behind his back. When she's done I see her reach inside his jacket and slip something into her pocket. Whatever she's taken, he doesn't fuss over it. He just looks up at the single piece of framed needlework that hangs, yellowing, from the wall. I don't need to read it to know what it says. *Ora et Labora*. I'm not sure about *labora* but I suspect his days of praying may be just about to start.

Mags comes over to stand next to me.

'All done?'

'Almost.' She reaches over and pulls the dog tags from

Boot's, Truck's and Weasel's necks and slips them into her pocket next to whatever she took from Kane.

'Let's get out of here.'

As we reach the door I hear Hicks' drawl from behind me.

'Be seein' you real soon, kid.'

I stop.

I told Mags we should shoot them, every last one. I said it'd be the smart thing. We wouldn't have to worry about Dr. Gilbey and without Kane I wonder if Peck would be so interested in finding us. But Mags said that wasn't how we were going to go about things, and she has more cause to want it than I do, so I agreed.

But now as I hear Hicks's words I know he's one more thing we'll never be rid of. I slide his pistol out of the gun belt I took from him. The cylinder clicks around as I thumb the hammer back. Mags reaches out and puts a hand over it.

'I got this.'

She walks back down the aisle and stands in front of him.

'No, you won't, not if you're smart. But I worry you're not, Sergeant, so pay attention now. You needn't bother with Mount Weather; by the time you get there we'll be long gone. And there's something else you might want to consider before you set off looking elsewhere for us. Gilbey's not the only one with the virus. We have trays and trays of it. Ask him if you don't believe us.' She points across the aisle at Kane. 'If I so much as suspect you're taking an interest in us we'll pay The Greenbrier another visit, and this time we won't come empty-handed. We have the code for the bunker. Remember that.'

———

364   R. A. HAKOK

We close the door to the chapel behind us and head back up to Front Street. The sound of Jax pounding on the armory door echoes up from the depths of the pedestrian tunnel.

The kid's sitting by the corridor to the blast door, where we left him. He rubs his eyes, like he's just been woken from a deep slumber, and squints up at the arc lights, like maybe they're too bright. For a second I think I catch a flash of silver, but when he looks at me I see the pupils there are dark, human.

I tell Mags I have one more thing to attend to, so she takes him by the hand and leads him out to the tunnel. I head over to the command building and make my way inside. It doesn't take me long to find what I'm looking for and then I'm back out on Eden's narrow streets. Quartermaster's still lying on the dusty concrete where Truck shot him. I look down at him for a moment, then I step around him and leave the cavern for the last time.

The scanner room's in ruins. Hicks was as good as his word; there's little left of the machine that's recognizable. Its polished metal skin is twisted and charred, like a giant can that someone's stuck in the fire without remembering to stick a hole in first.

I walk through the showers and into the locker room. I have to pick my way over the remains of the barricade to get out. Mags is already kneeling by the open blast door, going through the soldiers' backpacks for what we'll need. I figure she's got that covered so I head out into the tunnel.

Angus and Hamish are propped up against the wall outside, their arms cable-tied to the brace wire above their heads. I pull out the knife I took from Weasel. Their eyes widen and as I kneel down I detect a sharp odor. During the course of the evening's entertainment I think one or other of them has had an accident in their overalls. I sigh. To think I used to let these clowns intimidate me.

I hold my hands up.

'Alright, settle down; I don't mean to hurt either of you. I'm just going to use this to cut your restraints. But before I do I need you to listen.'

I remind myself to take it slow. The message I have for them isn't complicated, but I'm dealing with a pair of intellects rivaled only by the plastic that's currently binding their wrists.

'Those soldiers you saw earlier, they've killed Quartermaster. You can go back inside and have a look if you don't believe me. Kane's in the chapel with them right now. We've tied them up, but I doubt it'll take them long to get free. Before that happens Mags and I intend to be on the other side of the portal, and we mean to blow it behind us, like we did last time.'

I pause to let this sink in.

'Now it seems to me that you've got a couple of choices. You can go back in there and rescue Kane and afterwards take your chances with the soldiers. Or you can leave now with us.'

They look at each other. It seems like Angus is custodian of the family brain cell today. He turns back to me and his face gets as close to thoughtful as I suspect it ever does.

'Where are you going?'

'Mount Weather.' I get a blank expression for that. 'The bunker where the rest of the Juvies are.'

'And we can go there with you?'

I shake my head.

''Fraid not. I'm going to draw you a map of the route Peck

and the other Guardians have taken. If you stick to it you should be able to find them.'

Hamish looks at me.

'You want us to go get Peck?'

I nod.

'I do. And when you find him you need to give him a message. You need to tell him the soldiers you met earlier have Kane and they mean to bring him to a place called The Greenbrier.' I see the worried look on Angus's face. 'Don't worry I'll write it all down; all you have to do is show it to him. But you need to tell Peck if he wants to save Kane he'll have to hurry. I don't think the person they're bringing him to see is a fan of the President's work.'

Angus comes to a decision quicker than I gave him credit for. He looks up to his wrists and I cut him free. While I'm working on Hamish Mags appears at the blast door. She holds up an olive colored metal orb, just like the ones from the crate I found under the floorboards in the hallway outside Marv's room when we first escaped from Eden.

'They brought loads of them. Should be plenty.'

I stand up and put the knife away.

'Alright, let's get out of here.'

EPILOGUE

HEAVY CLOUDS HANG low on the horizon, threatening the dawn that's reluctantly taking shape to the east.

Behind us the farmhouse burns. The flames have already made their way up into the roof; thick black smoke coils up from the rafters, smudging the morning sky. Whatever Marv had stashed under the floorboards went up like the Fourth of July, but we don't stay to watch. Peck has a day's start on us.

We make our way down to the turnpike, picking our way between the gnarled trunks. There hasn't been a fresh fall and the snow's settled. Good tracking skiff, Marv would have called it. We've barely made it a hundred yards before Hamish has his first yard sale, all the same. Angus is faring a little better, but I can already hear him breathing hard behind me.

I stop when we get down to the road and wait while Mags and the kid continue on. Angus trudges up to me a few minutes later, his face beet red. He bends down, his hands on his knees, gasping for breath. Hamish is still coming down the slope. He's covered head to toe in powder, but from the way he's driving his snowshoes I suspect he has at least one more tumble in him before he joins us on the 'pike.

When Angus gets his wind back I hand him a piece of paper. On one side there's the message I want them to give to Peck, on the other a simple map. We didn't meet anyone on the way up, which means he must have taken the Catoctin Mountain Highway, the route Marv and I followed when we first went to Mount Weather. Angus looks at the paper and then back up at me.

'It's not hard. You just stick on this road till you hit a town called Shiloah. A little ways beyond it there's a big highway. Turn right when you get to it. If you hike sunup to sundown you should be on it maybe a couple of days before you need to start looking for the first sign. Don't worry too much about the names. I've written down all the numbers you need to look for.'

Angus looks dubiously at the map and then the road.

'Can't we come with you?'

I shake my head. Benjamin's way through Ely's shorter, but it's a harder hike. And we need to travel fast now if we have any chance of getting to Mount Weather ahead of Peck and the Guardians.

Angus looks crestfallen. His brow furrows; I can see him searching for something to say that might convince me. Eventually he raises one arm and points down the road at the kid.

'We won't hold you up no more than that.'

I look at Johnny. The snowshoes are way too big for him; I'll definitely have to find him another pair. There's no getting around how short his legs are, either. Whatever way you cut it he's going to struggle when the drifts get deep. I turn back to Angus.

'Yeah, but him I can carry.'

Angus stares forlornly down the 'pike.

'You'll be okay. Just keep an eye on the skies and remember to get off the road before it turns dark.'

There's nothing else to say so I shift the straps on my backpack and set off after Mags and the kid. When I reach the first bend I look over my shoulder. Hamish has joined Angus now. They're both standing in the middle of the road where I left them, staring down at the map.

I catch up with Mags. The going's not bad along this stretch and we can walk side by side. The kid marches on ahead. The snow might have settled, but I suspect it'll not be long before he tires of breaking trail.

'You think they'll be alright?'

I turn to look at her.

'Yeah. The way's easy and they have most of the soldiers' supplies. There shouldn't be any more storms. I can't see them catching Peck and the others, though.'

'Guess that's up to us then.'

I nod.

'You think it'll work?'

'Without weapons Hicks'll have no choice but to return to The Greenbrier. And all Peck cares about is Kane. I reckon as soon as he finds out the soldiers have him he'll forget about Mount Weather and strike out after them with the Guardians. While they're working things out between them we can be gone.' I pause. 'As long as Peck believes us.'

'He will. We have something of Kane's, and the soldiers' dog tags.'

I look over at her.

'That was clever, taking his glasses. I wish I'd thought of it.'

'Don't feel bad. I thought we'd got that straight. You're the tall one. I'm the smart one. Remember?'

She stops and lifts the goggles onto her forehead. I've given her a fresh cotton mask to replace the one she was wearing on the way up. She pulls it down and smiles at me.

'Frostbite check?'

We've barely come a quarter of a mile so there's really no need. But I reckon if I ever turn that invitation down you can take Hicks' pistol and shoot me where I stand.

She tilts her head back and closes her eyes. Her skin looks like it's lost some of its gray pallor overnight and the shadows under her eyes are fading; I can already see the faint smattering of freckles that run along her cheekbones underneath those long, dark eyelashes. I pull down my mask so that I can kiss her and a moment later I feel her arms slip around my waist. The rifle slides off her shoulder but she ignores it and for the next few moments at least the cold is forgotten. Eventually she pushes me away and slings the rifle back onto her shoulder. She pulls the mask up and sets off again.

I stand in the middle of the road for a moment, watching her walk away. Sometimes I worry that the feelings I have for her will be our undoing. That the world we live in now is too dark and gray and cold to abide them. That it will keep trying until it finds a way to do us harm.

I pull my mask back up. Underneath my thermals the dog tags shift against my skin. I told her we should each wear a set because that's what Marv and I used to do, when we went out, with the crucifixes. She said she wanted Truck's and the kid asked for Weasel's so I ended up with Private Kavanagh's. I already checked hers this morning, while she slept. Now I reach for the chain and pull out the ones I'm wearing, holding them up to the scant morning light. They're as they were when I slid them in last night, but I reckon it's still too soon to show.

Mags said Gilbey told her that the virus was far more resilient than Kane had ever given it credit for; that it would do anything to ensure its survival. Not even what Kane did to the skies could stop it.

I watch as she marches off towards the kid who's waiting for us further up the turnpike. She says she feels better than ever. She's still way too thin, but her appetite's back, or at least part of it. She didn't seem to care much for the MRE I made her for breakfast, but she wolfed down the HOOAH! that came with it, and then went looking for mine.

I tell myself the field the scanner created had to be stronger than whatever Kane's missiles did, way up in the skies, and even though she didn't get the time in there she was supposed to, what she did get was enough.

But the truth is I don't know. I don't understand how any of it works. I can't tell you why the scanner brought Mags and the kid back, when all the others out there in the dark places just got their circuits fried. Perhaps it has something to do with the medicine she was taking. Or maybe once you're gone so far there's just no coming back and they hadn't yet crossed that line.

I hope that's it.

I'm not so sure, though.

The newspaper reports I used to collect said it was like the virus meant to hotwire the person it had infected, that it wanted to replace their internal wiring with its own. Except that the virus's circuits were way faster, and our bodies had never been designed for that kind of speed. All I can think of is how high she jumped in that moment when she appeared out of the pedestrian tunnel; how quickly she closed the gap to Hicks after she had dealt with Truck. I've seen how fast Hicks is and she got the drop on him, like she wasn't even trying.

And that's what worries me.

I take one last look at the dog tags and drop them back inside my thermals. The wind's already chilled the metal. It feels cold as it comes to rest against my skin.

I hope you enjoyed the latest *Children of the Mountain* adventure.

If you'd like to read the newspaper clippings Gabriel collects to try and figure out what happened to the world, or follow his progress on the map Marv gave him, you can get each for free by signing up to my reader list (again, www.rahakok.com, or an email to contact@rahakok.com with 'Reader List' in the subject).

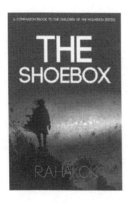

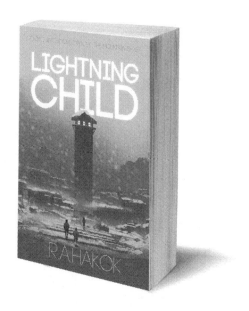

Gabriel and Mags return to the Juvies after escaping The Greenbrier. But something is happening to Mags now, changes that Gabriel can't explain. And to save her he must make a decision that will affect them all.

Lightning Child is available on Amazon. You can read the first chapter at the end of this book.

So we've come to the end of another book. I hope to see you again soon, but before you go...

It's hard to overstate how important reviews are to an indie author, so if you enjoyed *The Devil You Know* and you have a moment to spare could I ask you to post one? If you flip to the last page you should automatically be prompted to give a rating. I think Amazon wants twenty words or more, but if you click either of the links below you should be able to make it even shorter. A sentence or even a couple of words will do just fine!

———

Amazon (US)
Amazon (UK)

———

Thank you!

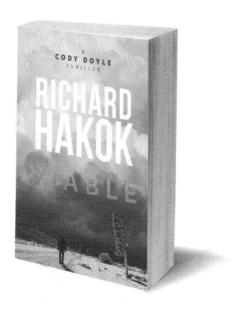

A brilliant young geneticist, desperately seeking a cure for the disease that took her father. A Nevada sheriff, charged with solving a crime that threatens the very existence of his small desert town. But when an unmarked van crashes in sleepy Hawthorne, Alison Stone and Lars Henrikssen find themselves looking for the same man.

Only Carl Gant is not what he seems. And they are not the only ones looking for him.

———

Download it on Amazon

EXCERPT FROM LIGHTNING CHILD

We take Benjamin's route, south through the mountains. We have just the one pack between us and I've lightened it for the hike, but there's the rifles, and where the drifts run deep the kid needs carrying.

I count off the landmarks we pass. The barracks at Fort Narrows. The veterinarian's outside Ely, where I found Benjamin's body. The Susquehanna Bank in Boonsboro that sheltered us from the storms after we fled Eden. We don't stop at any of them. We have to make time now. Peck has a start on us.

The first day we make it almost to the state line before darkness and cold run us off the road. We crest a shallow rise and I spot a small church in the valley below, sitting right on the banks of the Potomac. It has little to recommend it, but we've passed nothing else for miles, and I can't see anything better on the stretch beyond the river. I catch Mags eyeing it, weighing the shelter it'll provide against the shrinking sliver of gray to the west that still separates earth from sky. She turns back to the road, like she means go on, but I pull the mask I wear down and call to her through chattering teeth. It'll do for the few hours we mean to be here. I wait while she considers what I've said, hoping she doesn't call me on the rest of it. Truth is we've pushed hard to get this far; I'm not sure how much more I have in me now. Eventually she nods, points her snowshoes in the direction of the chapel.

There's no need for the pry bar; the door's already hanging back on its one remaining hinge. She heads off with the kid in search of wood for a fire while I make my way inside. I shuck off my pack and start tending to our dinner. My fingers are numb from the cold; it takes longer than it ought to get the cartons open and our rations assembled. I'm still working on the last of them when she returns, dumps what she's gathered on the floor and sets to work, stacking firewood and kindling with practiced ease. I add water from my canteen to the MREs, spilling as much as I manage to get into the cartons, then I shuffle myself as close as I can to the smoldering branches and listen as the chemical heaters do their work, hissing away as they slowly thaw our food. As soon it's passable warm I tear the top off one of them and start wolfing down what's inside. Mags waits a little longer before she opens hers, then starts poking around half-heartedly at the contents. When I've had the last of mine I throw the empty pouch on the fire. The foil shrivels and for a second the flames flicker brighter as it's consumed. I hold my hands close for whatever heat they'll allow, but already they're dying down again.

The wind howls around the gable, rattling the door against its frame. I pull the parka tighter around me. I'm exhausted, bone weary, but it's been worth it. We've come farther than I thought possible when we first set out this morning; farther than I ever hiked in a day with Marv. At first light we'll cross the river and then we'll be back in Virginia, with no more than twenty miles between us and the Blue Ridge Mountain Road.

I wonder where Peck is tonight. Angus said he'd set out with Kurt and the other Guardians yesterday morning. We didn't run into him on the way up with Hicks, so he must have taken the Cacoctin Mountain Highway. That road is easier, but it's longer, and he's no reason to push hard. If we can maintain the pace we managed today there's a chance we might yet overhaul him, make it back to Mount Weather before he arrives. I glance over at the rifles, propped against the wall. If we can do that maybe we can hold the tunnel, keep him out. For a moment I allow myself that hope. Truth is I have no other plan.

I take a final swig from the canteen and announce I'm turning in. But when I go to stand the muscles in my legs have stiffened; I have to reach for one of the pews to haul myself upright. I glance over at Mags while I steady myself, but she's busy fixing herself a coffee and hasn't noticed. On the other side of the fire the kid's focused on a HOOAH! he's liberated from one of the MRE cartons. I watch as he pushes the candy bar up inside its wrapper, then takes to gnawing away at the end of it with those little teeth of his. I'd gotten into the habit of tethering him while we slept; it feels a little strange to have him roaming free now. He looks up at me for a moment, like maybe his thoughts have run that way too, then he turns his attention back to his meal.

I undress quick as I can and climb inside the sleeping bag, pulling the quilted material tight around me. Mags is still sitting by the fire, swirling her coffee as she stares into the flames. When we set off this morning I thought she looked better; that the shadows under her eyes had faded a little, that maybe the angles of her cheekbones were a little softer. But now I'm not so sure.

I tell myself it's just the firelight. Besides, it's early yet; barely a day since she came through the scanner. She didn't get the time inside it it'd been set for, but there's no way she's still sick. I've seen firsthand what the virus does to a person. Marv had been strong, and by the end he hadn't been able to lift a boot from the snow. When she took her turns breaking trail earlier it was all I could do to keep up.

I hold on to that thought for a while. It should bring me comfort, but somehow it doesn't. My mind keeps returning to the image I have of her, bursting out of the pedestrian tunnel. The way she had moved had been...unnatural. She had dealt with the soldiers, each in turn, without so much as a break in her stride. Even Hicks; she'd been on him before he'd barely had time to twitch.

I lie there for a while, trying to work out what it might mean. But it's no use; sleep's already plucking at my thoughts, unraveling them before they have a chance to form. I feel my eyelids growing heavy. I reach up for the dog tags I lifted from Boots. It's too early to tell yet, I know. I run my fingers over them anyway, testing for imperfections that weren't there this morning. Other than the letters pressed into the metal the thin slivers of steel are still smooth.

I close my eyes.

I'll check hers later, when she's sleeping.

———

We're on the road again before dawn. Mags takes the pack and rifles while I follow behind, carrying the kid on my shoulders. If breaking trail tires her she doesn't show it; her pace doesn't slacken, not even on the inclines. My legs are longer, and I have years of pounding the snow to my name, but I feel like it's me who's holding us up now.

We make good time, but it's already stretching into the afternoon before we catch our first glimpse of the Harry Byrd Highway. I set the kid down at the top of the on-ramp and search the snow for signs anyone's passed while I get my breath back. But there's nothing, far as the eye can see. The wind's been squalling all morning, however; if they came by more than an hour ago it'd already have wiped their tracks clean.

Mags adjusts the straps on her pack and sets off again. I hoist the kid back onto my shoulders and follow. From here it's a long steady climb and for the next hour I focus on her boots as they rise and fall ahead of me, following a tireless, mechanical rhythm, like she could do this all day. At last the road levels and off in the distance I see it: a faded blue sign announcing the turnoff to the Blue Ridge Mountain Road.

I catch up to her by a stand of spruce-fir that still clings stubbornly to the embankment and pull the mask I wear down to gulp in air. The thin cotton's iced up where I've been breathing through it, and for some reason that sets spidey off. Mags asks if I'm ready. I don't have my wind back yet so I just nod and she takes off again.

I'm about to follow when I spot something out of the corner of my eye: a length of chain, tangled up in one of the branches that poke through the snow. The old steel crucifix I used to wear, the one I placed on Marv's grave. Mags is already halfway to the first crest, but I just stand there, staring at it. I don't know what waits for us ahead, but I get the strong sense that whatever it might be, I won't be passing this way again.

I hesitate a moment longer then reach down, pull it free. I shake the chain to clear the powder from it, then I slip it into my pocket and take off after her.

———

The mountain road climbs sharply from the highway and soon my thighs are burning. When we reach the ridgeline it flattens enough that I consider setting Johnny down, but ahead Mags has picked up the pace so I just tell him to hang on. We follow the road along the spine of the mountain range, picking our way through the lifeless trunks that push up through the snow on either side.

Somewhere far behind clouds the color of gunmetal the sun's already dipping towards the horizon, but we're close now. We round a bend and I see a familiar sign, its dead lights hooded under black metal cowls, announcing we're entering a restricted area. We continue upwards for another half-mile and then finally the road straightens and levels. The trees fall away and we find ourselves in a large clearing that straddles both sides of the ridge.

Ahead there's the chain-link fence, the coils of razor wire above held outwards on rust-streaked concrete pylons. I stop and search its length for signs of a breach, but there's nothing. Spidey doesn't care for it, all the same. He starts pinging a warning, but like earlier it's vague, non-directional. Mags has already found the section I opened with bolt cutters the day I arrived. She slips through, holding the wire back for the kid. I set him down and he follows her in. While he's putting his snowshoes back on I unsnap the throat of my parka and lower the hood to listen. But the only sound's the wind, rattling a faded *No Trespassing* sign against the bars of the gate.

Mags unslings one of the rifles and hands it to me. We leave the guardhouse behind us and make our way into the compound. I scan the perimeter, counting off the concrete cowls of the airshaft vents as we pass. The snow on top of each is undisturbed, but that means even less than the absence of tracks out on the highway. Kane had the codes to the blast door for each facility in the Federal Relocation Arc; Peck wouldn't have planned on making his entrance the way I got back into Eden.

The control tower rises from the highest point of the ridge, its roof bristling with antennae. Dark windows slant outwards from the observation deck, staring down at our approach. The Juvies were supposed to post a watch while we were gone; if anyone's up there they're bound to have spotted us by now. I keep my eyes on the doorway, waiting for it to open. But no one comes out to greet us.

On the far side the helicopter landing pad, the tattered windsock snapping and fluttering on its tether. Spidey dials it up a notch as we hurry past. The temperature's dropping fast now, but that's not what's quickening my stride. We're almost at the portal.

The path curves around then straightens and at last I see it.

In the lee of the tunnel where the wind hasn't yet had chance to smooth it the snow's all churned up, a wide confusion of snowshoe tracks. Beyond I can see the guillotine gate. It's been lowered, a last desperate attempt to keep them out.

It hasn't worked.

The gate hangs inward at a defeated angle. The metal's

twisted, charred; on one side it's jumped its runners. The bars that remain grin back at me, spare steel teeth in a gaping maw.

Behind the tunnel stretches off into inky blackness.

———

Continue reading on Amazon.

AMONG WOLVES RECAP

The world lies in ruin. Outside a thick layer of ash-filled snow shrouds the frozen ground and through the long winters violent storms rage. A nanovirus that devours metal has wreaked havoc. Bridges and interstate exchanges lie collapsed in rubble; buildings list and crumble under their own weight. The virus attacked people too, leaching the metal from their bodies, turning them into bloodthirsty furies. Nobody knows where it came from.

Only a handful survived. When Washington was attacked, the President, Kane, and a Secret Service agent, Peck, fled with a visiting class of first graders to a mothballed mountain bunker they now know as Eden. Kane tells the children they are the Chosen Ones. Soon the last of them will turn sixteen and he will reveal their matches. Then it will be their job to repopulate the planet.

But after so long inside the mountain supplies are running low. One of the children, Gabriel, and the troubled soldier, Marv, are sent outside to scavenge for things they need. They carry steel crucifixes that allow Peck, and the handful of children he has appointed Guardians, to check whether they've been contaminated when they return.

Gabriel searches the places he scavenges for books. Most of the children can't read, but he and the rebellious Mags remember how. Books aren't allowed in Eden, so Gabriel relays the stories he finds on the outside to Mags when he returns.

One day while Gabriel's outside scavenging he comes across the body of Benjamin, a soldier who was in Eden when they first arrived, together with a bloodstained map that shows the way to a place called Mount Weather. When Kane learns of the map he sends Gabriel and Marv out to find Mount Weather, even though winter is close and the storms are coming. On the way Marv becomes infected with the virus and starts to change into a fury. Before he kills himself he explains to Gabriel everything that's wrong with Eden. Benjamin had been trying to get the children out, but Kane uncovered his plan and sent Peck to kill him.

Gabriel continues to Mount Weather where he finds another bunker, stocked with supplies. He returns to Eden, only to discover that Kane had never intended either he or Marv to return. He sneaks back in through one of the vent shafts, intending to free the Juvies without Kane knowing. But Kane has brought forward the ceremony where the children will be matched, forcing Gabriel to rethink his plans.

While searching for a way to get the children out of the mountain Gabriel discovers stockpiles of the virus, proving that it was Kane who was responsible for releasing it in the first place. Gabriel interrupts the ceremony and confronts Kane, threatening to contaminate Eden if he won't let them leave. The children are scared to go outside but Gabriel convinces them. He holds Peck and the Guardians at bay while Mags and the others escape into the tunnel that leads to the outside. As he's running after them Gabriel is shot but Mags and one of the others, Jake, come back for him and drag him out. Together they seal the tunnel and Gabriel leads the children to Mount Weather.

Made in the USA
Columbia, SC
27 January 2020

87184006R00238